Lynnette,
thanks so me
your friendship:
a blessing in my very
Dawn Kinzer

BY ALL
APPEARANCES

DAWN KINZER

Cover design by Lynnette Bonner of Indie Cover Design – http://www.indiecoverdesign.com

Images©
https://www.istockphoto.com/Photo ID 507294292/Seattle
https://www.bigstockphoto.com/Photo ID 101074652/model
https://www.istockphoto.com/Photo ID 956451426/guitar

By All Appearances/ Dawn Kinzer.1st ed.
ISBN: 978-0-9978154-7-4

To my beloved grandchildren ...
Rohan, Lennon, Ava, and Harrison
You've captured my heart.
Remember that you are *more* than enough,
and I will always be proud of you.

*Now we see things imperfectly,
like puzzling reflections in a mirror, but
then we will see everything with perfect clarity.
All that I know now is partial and incomplete,
but then I will know everything completely, just
as God now knows me completely.*

~ 1 Corinthians 13:12

One

If Liana Tate's instincts proved right, fantasy could change her reality.

She dropped her purse and car keys on the oak desk covered with stuffed binders, fabric swatches, and catering menus. The antique furniture looked out of place, considering its contemporary surroundings in her home. But her grandfather had penned stories at that desk—Liana couldn't part with it.

Six months. She blew out a stream of air and rubbed her temples. What was she thinking? Stubborn pride had taken the place of common sense. Earlier that evening, while meeting with the hospital gala committee, she'd jumped in over her head and now needed a lifeboat to save her. The commitment involved rescuing one of the most anticipated yearly events in Seattle from sinking. With her reputation as an event planner on the line, if the revised plan failed, she'd be tempted to hide out deep in the Cascades.

If successful, she'd have all the clients she could handle. Then maybe she could finally afford an office in the city and an assistant to go with it. She slumped against the desk. In her heart's secret and deep-rooted insecurities, she knew everything—including one day having a fancy office—came down to proving she was worthy of belonging to her high-profile family.

Even more important than a personal career boost, funds

raised during the event would provide care to thousands of patients, regardless of their ability to pay. Liana couldn't fail those needing treatment at the adult and pediatric trauma center. She could only imagine the stress and heartbreak of sitting by a child's hospital bedside, fearing your family might be turned away when all resources were drained.

This was one of those moments when she yearned to have someone who would hold her and tell her everything would be okay. Of course, he'd be attractive—successful—someone approved and loved by her family. After all, her grandfather had encouraged her to dream big. But that vision was often like watching clouds drifting off in the sky until they became barely wisps of vapor.

The corners of her lips slid into a slight smile as Kevin Carter's image filled her thoughts. Now, there was a man she'd like to come home to! It wasn't that she couldn't handle being alone. It would just be nice to know someone cared.

She may not have a husband to dump her woes on, but her father tried to be available, and he often served as a great listener and sounding board. Massaging her aching neck muscles, she slipped into her bedroom, where it took only a few minutes to change from a skirt and heels into jeans and tennis shoes.

Anxious to bounce ideas off him, Liana closed her cottage door and sauntered down the path to the stable, built on the family property by her grandfather while he was still alive. Since her dad ritualistically visited his beloved horses before retiring for the evening, she'd look for him there before trying the main house.

Several nights had passed since she'd checked on the animals herself, and she missed them. They deserved more attention, and her father had assured her the new caretaker he'd hired would also tend to the horses' needs. Liana didn't know anything about the guy, except that he was due to arrive in a few days.

The ground, damp from an earlier rain, gave off an earthy aroma. Tree branches waltzed with the wind, and the cool, May breeze raised goose bumps on her arms. As Liana neared the stable, she inhaled mixed scents of hay, feed, and animals.

An unfamiliar black Labrador stepped into the dimly lit, open doorway, wagging his tail. He barked once, pranced across the ground separating them, and nuzzled his wet nose into the palm of her hand.

"Aren't you a pretty boy?" Liana leaned over and scratched behind the dog's ear. "Where did you come from?"

The Lab trotted next to her until they crossed the stable's threshold. Then he continued ahead and plopped down on the floor near an open stall where a man, almost hidden, spoke softly in a deep, rich tone to the Arabian, Lexus. Liana, mesmerized by the melodic quality, didn't want the soothing words to end.

Inquisitive, she crept closer. The stranger must be the new hire. An experienced thief wouldn't risk bringing a friendly dog on the property. So, the man had arrived earlier than expected. He must have a good reason. She should announce herself and stop acting like a spy.

Mitzi, the three-legged cat, rubbed against Liana's leg. She picked up and cuddled the gray ball of soft, warm fur against her chest.

"Poor thing. Haven't been getting enough attention?"

The stranger in the stall stepped out from the shadows, and Liana's breath caught in her throat. His right eye drooped at the corner, and a patch of naked scalp enveloped the remnants of his right ear. Scars from his forehead continued down in a webbed pattern across his cheek and along the side of his neck.

Adrenaline surged through her body, and without intention, Liana squeezed the animal in her arms. Mitzi meowed and struggled for freedom, her one back leg kicking against Liana's stomach until she loosened her grip. The cat jumped to the floor and scooted into the night.

The man shielded the ugliness with a gloved right hand and turned slightly away. "Sorry—didn't mean to scare you."

"You're the new caretaker?" She struggled to sound calm, but she hadn't been prepared to see—*that*. What happened to the poor guy? Dad should have prepared her. Liana's heart thudded in her chest.

He slowly lowered his hand and extended it, keeping his unaffected profile tilted toward her. "Bryan Langley."

After hesitating, she lightly grasped the gloved hand, the leather feeling cool to her touch. "Liana."

Bryan's firm grip lasted only a moment, but her willingness to touch him may have given him enough confidence to believe she could handle seeing him, because he faced her.

Like a voyeur driving past a gruesome accident, Liana couldn't help staring. Listening to this man's calm, strong voice she'd envisioned quite a different picture. The way he spoke to them—it was understandable that the animals sensed he was safe.

"I live in the cottage up the path," Liana said, almost choking on her words. She tried to repress it, but curiosity mixed with the heartfelt compassion stirring within.

"Your dad mentioned it."

Liana moved her gaze from the scars to his eyes, afraid of what she might see. But despite the disfigured face, Bryan's eyes were warm and kind, like an innocent child's hello, and for a moment—just a moment, they drew her in. Too quickly, he tilted his head away.

Did she make him uncomfortable? Liana averted her eyes from his face. "The Lab must be yours. What's his name?"

"Rainey."

"Friendly dog."

"He likes people." Bryan backed into the stall and closed the lower half of the wooden door. The metal latch clanked into place.

Was he trying to shield himself or make her feel more at ease? She could sympathize with the first, but sensing it was the latter, his sensitivity to her feelings touched a vulnerable spot in her heart.

He switched the brush back to his right hand and focused on grooming the horse. "Your dad didn't tell you I was here?"

Now only viewing his undamaged profile, Liana almost imagined two separate people living in the same body. "I knew he'd hired someone, but work has been crazy for both of us. We haven't had much chance to talk." Still, couldn't Dad have mentioned something this important?

The brushing halted. Still not looking at her, he sighed. "And you didn't expect to come home to ..."

"I didn't—I don't know what I expected." Liana shifted her feet. With the gala foremost in her mind, she hadn't given much thought to anything besides that event. Regardless, if she'd been preoccupied or not, there was no way she could have anticipated this surprise.

"If you're looking for him, friends invited your dad over for dinner." Bryan matched her quiet voice. Still, there was something almost mesmerizing about his tone. He soothed animals, and somehow, he soothed her too. She'd been ruffled by his appearance at first, but the way he almost guarded her now by turning his face, and the way he spoke calmly, helped her feel calm. Like occupying her favorite beach chair at the lake, she wanted to linger in this peaceful place.

Her father's horse hung his head over the stall door. Liana stroked the area between the Arabian's eyes, trying to think of something—*anything*—she could say to relieve the tension in the air.

Liana chewed the corner of her lower lip. Part of her wanted to stay, but standing around while Bryan worked in silence was probably making him feel edgy. She'd give him some space. "I should get back to the cottage. There's a pile of work waiting for me." She attempted to lighten her tone. "It's hard to get away from the job when you literally live in the office."

Not that she intended to do any more. At that late hour and feeling exhausted, she couldn't do much more for her clients at the moment. She only wanted an excuse to leave.

Accustomed to handling awkward situations in her line of work—like when a neurotic bride heaved at the altar—Liana still didn't feel equipped to handle this one. She patted Lexus and turned to leave.

"Liana?"

She veered back around and regarded the man with two

faces.

"I hope my working here isn't—or won't be—too disruptive for you," he said, sounding genuinely concerned.

"No, of course not," she blurted, sounding insincere to her own ears, while in her heart, desiring to emit warmth and acceptance. Her family's social and professional circles believed a person's physical attractiveness was the winning lottery ticket to happiness. Ironically, too often she didn't feel especially happy with her own appearance, so she couldn't imagine how someone with scars like Bryan could either.

"Liana, you're home." Her father strode into the stable. The dog leapt from the floor and flanked his thigh. "I'm glad you and Bryan have met."

Despite the poor lighting in the stable, Bryan didn't miss the relief in Liana's face and her shoulders relaxing. "I scared her *and* the cat, but your daughter was still willing to talk to me."

Dr. Tate smiled. "I guess we both need to be more careful. I've startled her a few times out here myself."

Bryan sent a silent prayer of thanks for the discerning doctor. More than a physician to him in past years, Dr. Tate had been a friend and spiritual mentor. Leave it to him to say the right thing to make the encounter with Liana sound normal.

"How did the meeting go?" The doc adjusted a rope hung on a hook next to the stable door and tucked in the loose end.

Bryan didn't know which gathering the older gentleman referred to, but the question was meant for Liana. It gave Bryan the opportunity to observe the interaction between the distinguished, graying father and the daughter with long chestnut hair. The way he beamed while the two talked made it obvious the man adored his girl.

Mitzi wandered back into the stable, and as the cat passed by, Liana scooped the feline into her arms and nestled the animal under her chin. If she could be so tender with a three-legged hyper cat with a mangled ear, maybe there was hope Liana could learn to be at ease with him. He didn't have many friends left, and it would be nice to have someone to talk to now and then.

While they were near enough to touch, Bryan had been pleasantly surprised by her unusual fragrance. Unlike heavy, sweet perfumes, the scent was similar to the aroma of fresh oranges—or lemons.

Liana's father leaned over the stall door. "We're heading up to the house. Why don't you call it a day and get some rest?"

Even though he wasn't feeling it, Bryan gave a shot at flashing a smile. "I'll finish up here in a few minutes." Without looking at Liana, who had remained some feet away, he resumed grooming.

"Bryan ..."

He halted, his hands resting on Lexus's smooth, black coat. "Yes, Doc?"

"I'm glad you're here."

"Thanks. Me too." Bryan glanced behind the surgeon to see Liana turn and head toward the stable door after giving a quick wave goodbye. His former physician may have been happy to have him there, but Bryan wasn't convinced Liana felt the same way.

Two

A quiet sigh slipped through Liana's lips. Escape. As she stepped outside the stable, leaving Bryan behind, mountain air filled her lungs. Thin clouds drifted across the full moon suspended above the tree line of the Cascade foothills. Her father joined her, and they took the path leading behind the main house, where the deck's light lit up the night.

"Liana, I apologize." Dad kept his voice low, though they were yards away from the stable before he spoke. "I planned to explain about Bryan before you ran into each other."

Since the caretaker might leave the building soon after them, Liana followed her father's lead and kept her voice low. "Dad, it was such a shock."

Even now, she pictured Bryan appearing from the shadows, patches of darkness half concealing his features, her mind scrambling, and reality striking. She hadn't wanted to feel repulsed—*truly*. But inside, she'd initially recoiled. A warning may have spared Bryan perceiving that from her, at least, she hoped so.

"I can imagine. Meeting like that wasn't fair to either one of you, but I wasn't expecting him for a few more days, and you were so busy over the weekend with work, I didn't want to bother you. Then, he showed up this morning before I left for the hospital, but you'd already headed out for the day. I tried calling your cell phone, but you never answered. A message was my only option."

"You only said something about wanting to talk after I got home, so I thought you wanted an update on the gala."

"I'd forgotten about the dinner thing tonight, but I thought I'd get home before you."

She swatted an insect buzzing near her face, her anxiousness subsiding out here in the open. "What happened to him?"

"It could only be described as a horrific tragedy." Her father hesitated a moment, then he started walking again. "About three years ago, Bryan tried to rescue some animals from a burning barn." Her father's voice became solemn. "Most were saved, but he got trapped in the fire."

"He's your patient?"

"*Former* patient." Her father took a deep breath. "Still can't tell you much."

"I know. Doctor-patient confidentially." Liana stuck her thumbs in her front jean pockets. She understood, but the guy worked for her father, on the very property where she lived. Could her dad blame her for asking questions?

Not far from the house, her father stopped and faced Liana. "I thought long and hard about hiring Bryan. Even sought counsel. But since I've turned any follow-up care over to a colleague, we're not crossing boundaries. I needed to fill the caretaker position, and he needed a job."

Dad's arm wrapped around her shoulders, and he gave a gentle hug. "More important than anything else, I prayed about my decision, and I believe God wants Bryan here."

"To work with horses?" Liana had heard that spending time with animals could be therapeutic for people with some disabilities.

"Bryan needs time to think and pray about direction in his life. He needs time to heal—and I'm not talking about physical healing."

"And you think he can find that here." Liana picked up a small branch across the path and tossed it to the side.

"Sometimes it's easier to hear God's whisper in the mountains, in the midst of his creation, than in the city where we're easily distracted by people or things. I don't know God's plan for the future, but I do believe that for now, this is where Bryan needs to be."

Following a brick path through flower gardens, they reached the house, which felt overly spacious and empty without her mother and sister living there. Two years had passed since her mother had left and moved to Seattle. She'd protested her husband giving up a prestigious and lucrative practice as a cosmetic surgeon so he could focus on recon-structive surgery—and for many patients, *pro bono*.

Liana believed her mother's choice had more to do with not accepting her father's decision several years earlier to make his faith more important than attending occasional Sunday church services. Her mother initially thought he was going through a phase. She was wrong.

Then, Liana's sister moved out because she could afford to live on her own, despite the high cost of living in Seattle. The selling price of a small, two-bedroom rambler here was similar to what someone paid for a two-story house with five bedrooms, four bathrooms, a dream kitchen, and a huge backyard in the Midwest.

It was humbling that at thirty years old, Liana still lived in the small cottage on her father's property. She paid rent each month, but a small amount in comparison to what she'd be charged elsewhere.

They crossed the expansive cedar deck and her father opened the back door, waving Liana into the kitchen. "There's something else. Bryan needs a place to live, so I told him to fix up the apartment above the garage. All I ask is that you try to make him feel welcome and comfortable here."

She cringed at possibly disappointing her father, but she wasn't confident she could fulfill his request. Despite Liana wanting to be friendly, the caretaker didn't seem relaxed around her. But could she blame him with the way she kept shooting glances at his scars? Still, she'd try—for both of them.

It wasn't as if she hadn't spent time with other survivors of tragic accidents. There had been many occasions over the years when she'd visited her father at the hospital and had been encouraged to read to patients—both children and adults. For the most part, she'd spent time with those whose wounds were heavily bandaged or covered by other protective materials, so she hadn't been exposed to some of the devastating damage hidden beneath. Still, glimpsing the courage it took to go through surgeries and various treatments made shared conversations and laughter so precious. Those experiences made the hospital gala personal for her.

Her father cut two slices of apple pie from their favorite bakery and slipped them onto separate plates. He handed her one, along with a fork. "So, what happened at the meeting?"

He climbed onto a stool at the kitchen island, and she followed suit, laying the dessert on the granite slab in front of her.

Liana toyed with her fork. "Good news—the committee is willing to approve my idea for the theme. Bad news—I still have to find a place to hold the event."

She usually worked hard to avoid unwanted calories, but sweets were her downfall when under pressure, and the combined stress of the night's fundraiser meeting and Bryan's surprise arrival drained all willpower. She speared a chunk of baked cinnamon apple with her fork.

"Dad, what am I going to do? I promised them I'd find something, but I haven't come up with even one viable option yet." She laid the fork down without taking a bite. "I have a few more ideas to pursue, but those venues don't even come close to what I'd envisioned."

Liana wanted so much for the event to inspire attendees. Their donations meant more people could be given necessary medical care. She was acutely aware that she'd grown up in a home where money was never an issue. If she became ill, she'd be given the best treatment, without question. The fundraiser had to be successful for those not as fortunate.

"It's not your fault the hotel isn't able to accommodate the gala. We've heard for years that Seattle would experience a large earthquake."

"Well, this one did so much damage to the hotel's structure, the management couldn't commit to when the west wing would be habitable. Yesterday, I looked for myself. When the building shifted, water pipes burst, and water flooded the entire area." Liana groaned. "Why did this have to happen now?"

He reached over and grasped her hand. "Sometimes you need to have faith that God will help you find a way."

She squirmed. "Yeah, his ultimate plan," she muttered sarcastically under her breath.

"I know things haven't always worked out the way you wanted. But look at how good you are at what you do—how you help people celebrate special moments in their lives—"

"Dad, I really don't want to go there." Rehashing medical school wasn't going to help. No need to be reminded of another failure. Not tonight.

He nodded and then seemed to wander down a path of his own thoughts. Not taking even a sip, her father picked up his coffee cup and held it midair. "I wonder ..."

"What?" Liana stopped her fork before it reached her lips.

Seeming to return from wherever he'd journeyed, he set down his mug and rolled up his shirt sleeves, as though preparing for an important task. "Bryan took one of the horses out for a ride this afternoon to get a feel for the area and ended up at the old Jones's place."

What could Dad possibly be thinking? She straightened as realization struck her like the back kick of a thoroughbred. "You don't mean that ugly, empty building down the road? You can't be—"

"Oh, I'm very serious. The new owner was there, but Bryan didn't realize it. He stopped to give the horse a short rest and explore, and the guy introduced himself. Made Bryan feel right at ease."

"Who is he? The owner, I mean."

"Erik Jones. He inherited the building from his grandfather, and he's already begun renovations." Her father's eyes lit up. "And here's where the answer to your prayers comes in."

"Remember, Dad, you're the one with faith in this family."

"Sometimes God answers unspoken prayers, Lee." He winked and grinned. "Right now the structure is empty, but Jones is working on updating the plumbing and getting the electrical up to code. It sounds like he's remodeling for commercial use. It might be worth asking what he plans to do with the property and how soon."

Liana's mind raced like a hydroplane running at top speed during Seafair. "It could almost be a blank slate."

She bit down on her fork. How could she approach Mr. Erik Jones, who now possibly held the gala's future—her future—in his hands? "I need to meet this guy, see if the space will work, and then if it does, convince him to let us use it. And I need to make it happen yesterday."

"Bryan could introduce you."

"Dad, no!"

"They've already met, and Bryan is passionate about what the hospital does to help burn victims. He's been there and experienced it. He might have a better chance of convincing Jones to let you use the building."

After their awkward introduction, would Bryan think she was taking advantage of him if she asked for his assistance? She didn't want him feeling used. "I don't want to bother Bryan. I'm capable of handling this myself."

"You're great at what you do, but don't risk blowing this out of stubbornness. Not only could you use his help, I believe he needs to be a part of this. It's important that he interacts with more people." Her father's caring gaze didn't waver. "The truth is, he's expressed interest in volunteering in the burn unit at the hospital, but even that's a pretty safe environment for him. I'm searching for ways to get him more involved in life again."

"What if he refuses?" Liana had just met the man. Surely he wouldn't want to get involved with securing a site for the hospital fundraiser after just meeting both her and Erik Jones that very day.

"He won't." Her father leaned over and patted her hand. "Right now, Bryan is starving for purpose. But it's up to you, Lee. You're calling the shots here."

How could this one situation make that much difference in his life? Liana opened her mouth to spit out another protest, then closed it. Her cheeks warmed as shame flowed through her body. The gala's success needed to take priority over her pride in wanting to find a new location herself.

"Okay. See if he can arrange a meeting as soon as possible. If Dalisay agrees to help, I'll want her there too." It would be important that Liana's best friend attend the meeting for several reasons, moral support being one of them.

The caretaker was going to live on the estate, so it would be impossible to avoid each other. No use fighting it. They'd have to get used to each other's company, even if only in small doses. But her father had always been a great judge of character. He wouldn't hire someone he didn't trust, and he obviously thought highly of Bryan.

Initially, the man's appearance had made her stomach churn and heart weep at the same time, but from his undamaged profile, he must have been quite handsome. She had to admit that Bryan had been nothing but gentle with the Arabian and kind to her. And then there were those eyes—not plain brown, but the same shade as the smoky quartz in the silver ring she'd inherited from her grandmother. They expressed more than any words spoken that evening. Liana half feared they'd appear in her dreams that night.

Bryan slumped down on the stool outside Lexus's stall. He wasn't quite ready to leave the stable. Rainey propped his head on Bryan's knee.

"God knew what he was doing when he created dogs, eh Rainey?" Bryan scratched the top of the lab's head. "They don't care a bit about whether you're calendar photo material or not. Love them, and they love you right back. People? They're different creatures."

This wasn't the first time Bryan had experienced similar reactions as Liana's to his appearance. Some avoided looking to the point of being obsessive, while others couldn't stop gawking. Before the accident, he'd sought and worked hard for public recognition, but no more. Now he hid from it. He was right to bury his dreams deep where no ray of hope could possibly reach them. And with help, he'd learn to accept and live with the fact that his life would never be the same, and what he'd envisioned for his future was no longer possible.

At least he had his faith. In order to survive recovery, Bryan had returned to his childhood beliefs and leaned on God with a dependence necessary to get him through every day, every hour, every minute of suffering. He'd renewed his relationship with a Savior who understood not only Bryan's physical agony, but also the mental, emotional, and spiritual anguish he experienced because of his burns. Now he needed to figure out what God wanted—what Bryan was supposed to do with his life.

After staying with his sister's family while healing from numerous surgeries, it seemed like an answer to prayer when Doc Tate suggested that Bryan stay and work on the estate. He missed being around horses, and the grounds provided plenty of room for Rainey to run. More importantly, he could earn his keep, and in some small way, repay the doctor for his kindness. Bryan wanted to start living as a survivor, not a victim.

"Rainey ... do you think Liana is like her dad?" She'd inherited her father's golden-brown eyes, but the question was whether similarities continued. Ones that counted.

Bryan promised he'd give this job a good try, at least until he decided it was time to move on, but that might have been a mistake. Liana Tate had been nice—respectful—but her initial reaction had thrown reality back in his face—the face that changed his life in an instant.

Knowing she lived on the property, he'd planned a gentler way to present his appearance, but she'd caught him off guard. Bryan squeezed his eyes shut, but he couldn't block out her horrified expression. It made him feel less than human. He wanted Liana to see and accept him as he was—simply a man. Not a monster.

Three

Dalisay would be enthusiastic about getting involved with the gala. Liana couldn't fathom anything less, because her involvement wasn't only important, it was critical. Liana couldn't possibly pull off the outrageous plan without her best friend's help.

Latin music played on the car radio, and Liana tapped her fingers to the beat on the steering wheel as she drove through Issaquah. Pink, purple, and white petunias overflowed from baskets hung on poles lining quaint Front Street. A sign of spring. Liana spotted an open space and parallel parked her Volvo S60 between two SUVs. Sandwiched in, she'd have to be extra careful pulling back out onto the busy road.

A baby grand piano sat prominently in view through the music store window across the street. Liana sighed with a twinge of regret. As a child, she'd wanted desperately to play well and make her parents proud. Despite how hard she'd tried, that didn't happen. She only frustrated them *and* her teacher. After two years, the lessons were discontinued, and it became another failure for a little girl who wanted so much to please. Liana shook off the memory, climbed out of the car, hit the lock button on the key fob, and strolled toward Village Theater.

She swung open the building's large door and stepped into the high-ceilinged lobby. To the left, a wide stairway led to the balcony. Sunlight streamed through the upper windows. Headshots of actors in the upcoming production filled the wall between two main doors leading into the auditorium where she'd find Dalisay.

She didn't have to look far. "What are you up to?" Liana slipped into a seat in the back row next to her friend.

"Daydreaming." Dalisay, dressed in jeans and a short-sleeved plum-colored top, shifted to an upright position in her chair. Her straight, black hair draped over her shoulders, and a clipboard lay across her lap. "I seem to do a lot of that, but I'm still determined to someday design sets for this theater."

"And the 5th Avenue and Paramount." Liana wrapped her arm around her friend's shoulders and gave her a quick hug. "Then it's all the way to New York, baby."

"Hopefully before I'm old and gray. In the meantime, I'm grateful for a chance to work on sets for First Stage."

The smaller theater, located a block away, was used for testing audience response to newly written productions before hitting any larger stages.

"The team met in one of the rooms upstairs this morning to go over some ideas, which is why I asked you to look for me here. Thought I'd spend a little time soaking up the vibes."

"It's so quiet." Liana felt the urge to whisper. There was almost a sense of sitting on hallowed ground.

Dalisay laughed softly. "Not for long. The actors are in tech rehearsals this week. *Beauty and the Beast* opens in two days, so in a few hours this place will be buzzing. It's pretty entertaining to watch the actors move through their warm-up exercises."

"I'm sure it is ..." Liana gazed at two winding staircases—one on stage left and one on stage right—descending to the floor of an elaborate castle room. The set, bathed in blue light, created an illusion of mystery, fantasy, and romance.

Dalisay sat on the edge of her seat and faced her. "So, what's going on?" she asked, her tone laced with suspicion.

"Nothing." She wasn't quite ready to explain.

"Right ..." Dalisay propped an elbow on the chair ahead of her and laid her head in her hand, then refocused on Liana. "Don't believe it. I've been able to tell when you're pretending since the fourth grade, so you might as well get it over with and tell me now."

"It's nothing." Liana swallowed and tried to sound convincing.

"You know I'll keep you here until you spill."

Liana did know. Maybe she should humor her friend. Besides, Dalisay often helped her see things through a different perspective, and she could use her point of view right now. "My father hired a new caretaker."

"And ..." Dalisay motioned for Liana to continue.

"I met him the other night when I went down to the stable looking for my dad. It was a little dark ... and he scared me."

"Like he jumped out of the shadows as a joke?" Dalisay laid her hand on Liana's shoulder. "Was he mean to you?" she asked, her voice rich with concern.

"No! Nothing like that." How could she explain without sounding judgmental? "One side of his face is scarred. *Badly* scarred. I wasn't expecting to see—it surprised me, that's all."

Dalisay sunk back into her chair. "Oh, *that's* all."

"This theater production is a fairy tale, but the correlation with the cursed creature really being a prince and what I experienced kind of freaks me out."

"Trust me. Your *someday-prince* riding in on a white horse is only a myth." Dalisay repositioned the clipboard on her lap. "So, what does he look like?" That was Daysie—straight to the point.

"I told you. Half of his face is disfigured, but his other profile is normal." Liana hesitated. "Dark hair. Striking brown eyes, except the right one droops slightly."

"Age?"

Liana shrugged. "I don't know. Maybe thirty."

"Hmmm ..." A sly grin slid onto Dalisay's face. "You like him." Her tone was both challenging and teasing.

"That's not true." Liana massaged her temples, then abruptly stopped. "I mean—it's not that I *don't* like him. He seems to be a likeable guy, but how could I know for sure after spending only a few minutes with him?"

She'd wrestled with her reaction ever since that night. How could she have felt both repulsed and attracted to the man? How did that make any sense? It didn't—that was the problem. Liana had denied any pull toward the stable, telling herself the draw was mere fascination. "I feel horrible about my reaction, that's all," she said, toying with strands of her hair and twisting them around her finger. "Finding Bryan at the stable was a shock."

"Your dad didn't tell you about this guy?" Dalisay frowned. "Doesn't sound like him not to give you fair warning."

"He meant to, but Bryan showed up earlier than expected." Liana tossed long strands of hair over her shoulder.

"And regardless of his circumstances, Bryan deserves to be treated like anyone else, so I'll do what I can to make him feel welcome." She winked at her friend. "Besides, you know I'm interested in someone. So, no more teasing about Bryan."

"Kevin Carter. *The most eligible bachelor in Seattle.*" A hint of sarcasm had slipped into Dalisay's tone.

"I know you're not fond of him, but your feelings are based on false assumptions and rumors." Bryan seemed kind and sensitive—both extremely important in Liana's eyes, but Kevin's traits extended beyond the list many women checked off when looking for a serious relationship. Liana held up five fingers and pointed to them one by one. "He's handsome, confident, intelligent, successful ..."

"And far from humble," Dalisay muttered.

"Now who's being *judgy*?"

"Look, I won't deny that sparks flew between you two at Carolyn's wedding." Dalisay sighed. "But as perfect as he seems, I don't trust him. Call me protective—I don't care. He's not right for you."

"How can you say that? Isn't he everything I've ever wanted—waited for?"

"He's everything your *mother* has ever wanted for you. At some point, you need to do what's right for you and stop trying to please everyone else."

"What if being with him is *exactly* what I need?"

"Then I'll be proven wrong."

Liana nudged her friend. "Well, don't worry about it. I'm out of Kevin's league. Several women at that same reception were doing everything and anything to get his attention."

"My opinion—you deserve better." Dalisay stood, grasping her clipboard to her chest. "C'mon. My mother has harassed me for several weeks about when she was going to see you. She even offered to give us a free lunch if I'd drag your behind into the restaurant. And I'm starving, so you can fill me in on whatever it is you wanted to talk about while my mother stuffs us with good Filipino food."

Liana's stomach rumbled with hunger at the thought of Mrs. Ouano's cooking. "I'm in." She jumped from her seat. "Besides, you might be more prone to go along with what I propose if you have a full stomach."

They hiked several blocks to the Mabuhay Restaurant, owned by Dalisay's parents. Years ago, Dalisay explained that "mabuhay" was used as an expression of welcome and jubilation, or literally, "long live." Orchids, Melo shell hanging lamps, candles, rattan furniture, and tall bamboo strategically placed, all added to the comfort and warmth of the dining area. But it was the Ouano family that provided a sense of welcome to the atmosphere.

Tantalizing smells of ginger and garlic teased her senses before they even stepped through the door. Guests filled every table. Perla, Dalisay's younger sister, stood at a table with a notebook and pen in hand, apparently waiting for a customer to make a final decision. She flicked a quick wave, then focused her attention back on the gentleman pointing to the menu.

Nenette, a cousin serving as hostess, greeted them. "Haven't seen you around for awhile, Lee."

"I know. But if I came here too often, your aunt would have me so fattened up, I wouldn't be able to get out the door."

The pretty college student laughed. "You know the solution to that. Work for her. I adore the woman, but she doesn't let a person sit down for a second. I burn off more calories here than I do at the gym."

"Once you finish school, you'll get a job teaching and be on your own." Dalisay's eyes sparkled with humor. "But don't think you can get away from her influence. You know her motto. 'Work before play.' Her words haunt my thoughts during the day and my dreams through the night. A diploma won't help you escape them."

Nenette scrunched her nose. "Gee, thanks." A bell tinkled as an elderly couple shuffled in. "Guess I better get back to work. Auntie is in the kitchen. She'll be happy to see you, Lee."

Dalisay and Liana maneuvered around the tables of people laughing, chatting, and filling their stomachs, until they reached the kitchen.

"Hello, Nanay," Dalisay said, greeting her mother in Tagalog, one of the languages spoken in the Philippines.

Mrs. Ouano stopped stirring the *sinigang* simmering on the stove and wrapped her arms around Liana. "My Lee! Finally you come to see us." She released her grip but wagged her finger at Liana. "You wait too long."

"I'll do better, Mrs. Ouano. I promise." Liana peered into the pot filled with okra, green beans, *daikon*, onions, tomatoes, and soft chunks of pork, and inhaled the aroma. "One of my favorites." She enjoyed the Filipino soup's sour and savory taste.

Dalisay picked up a towel and playfully wacked her brother, Bayani, on the shoulder. "What are you doing here?"

He pulled the towel from her grasp and whacked her back

on the bottom. "Helping out, which is more than you're doing. Dad wouldn't take time off to go in for a physical. I told him I'd come in for the day if he'd go to the doctor."

"He's a good son, that one," Mrs. Ouano said, her voice oozing with pride.

"It looks pretty busy out there." Dalisay removed two Styrofoam containers from a stack nearby. "Maybe we should take lunch back to the theater."

"No, no, no. I've been saving a table for you." Mrs. Ouano grasped both Liana's and Dalisay's wrists. "Come. I show you."

She led them to a table next to the window that overlooked the flower garden. "I have Perla bring your favorites. And when you've had a nice meal, I'm going to send a large piece of mango cake home with Liana for her father. Every time he comes in, he orders that cake."

They'd barely draped napkins over their laps when Perla dropped off a plate of *lumpia*. The appetizers, similar to egg rolls, were crispy and packed with meat. Nenette followed with *tapsilog*—strips of marinated beef cooked somewhat crispy with eggs and garlic fried rice. She also brought *pata*—pork roasted until crunchy on the outside, but still tender on the inside.

"Why is it whenever I show up with you, we're treated like royalty?" Dalisay bit into a lumpia.

"I don't know. Why is it I rarely eat meat, but I seem to devour it when I'm here?"

"Well, if my mother asks what you want for dessert, please tell her you'd like the flan." Dalisay moaned. "I haven't had her flan in ages."

Liana laughed. "You got it, but then you have to return

the favor."

"I'm guessing a favor is why you wanted to talk."

"You know I've been struggling to find a location for the gala."

"I can't help you much there. I've wracked my own brain and haven't come up with a thing."

"My dad may have figured out a solution." Liana wiped her mouth with a napkin and still clutching it, rested her hand on the table.

Dalisay's forehead wrinkled. "Then what's the problem?"

"I may want to expand on my original idea of using a fantasy theme."

"What *aren't* you saying?"

Liana took a deep breath. "What I *am* saying—or what I'm about to say—is that I need your help. I can't do this without you."

Her friend hiked one eyebrow.

"Don't give me that look."

"What look?"

"You know—disapproval."

Dalisay laid her fork down. "You haven't committed me to anything, have you?"

"Of course not." Liana wet her lips. She'd never been nervous around her friend before, why was her heart pounding now? "Do you remember the story my grandfather wrote about woodland fairies?"

"Sure." By Dalisay's tone, Liana had her full attention. "We loved that book. It was called *Manalee*, the name of the fairy village. We took turns reading it to each other one whole summer."

"I want to recreate Manalee on a bigger-than-life scale for

the gala. I want guests to walk in and believe they've actually stepped into a fairy-tale world. Imagine it. Starlit sky, huge trees towering overhead, mushrooms tall enough to stand under, cottages built into tree trunks and branches ..."

Dalisay leaned back, releasing a long sigh. "It sounds incredible, Lee, but how can you possibly pull something like that off?"

"To save on the budget, I'm going to donate my services." Liana cleared her throat. "And I'm going to ask you to donate yours." She wasn't only asking for assistance, she was counting on Dalisay's generosity.

"Honey, I'd like to help you out." She picked up her fork and trailed it through the pile of rice on her plate. "And this is a great cause, but my finances are already tight. I have to teach several classes a semester at my alma mater to break even at the end of the month."

"I know ..." Liana was asking a lot of her friend, but there was so much potential for good to come out of this project, including a spotlight on Dalisay's talent, the rewards were worth the sacrifices they'd both be making. "Look. I got involved because I sincerely want to help patients at the hospital. But I'm also hoping my effort will pay off with bringing in more work down the road. This is also a great opportunity for you to show what you can do. This is one of the biggest yearly events in Seattle. Think what it will do for your reputation as a designer when people are blown away by the world you create."

Dalisay sat quietly for a moment. "Okay, you've hooked and reeled me in." She grinned. "And I have to admit ... my mind started working the second you mentioned Manalee."

Relief rushed through Liana's body. "Thanks, Daysie."

Dalisay chuckled under her breath after hearing the nickname only Liana was allowed to use. "So, tell me. Where do you plan to build this fantasy village?"

"I'm checking out a place not far from where I live. Actually, you've driven by it. The grandson is renovating the building. I've never been inside, but it's huge."

"You know the owner? That could be a win, but what makes you think he'll be up for this?"

"I haven't met him, but Bryan has, and according to my dad, he's going to introduce me. The day after tomorrow." Liana's stomach churned. Why was she uneasy about seeing him again? Why was she concerned about how he might react toward *her*? And what would perceptive Daysie think when she met Bryan? "And I need you to go with us."

Dalisay offered a sly smile. "To look at the building? Help convince the owner? Or protect you from the caretaker?"

"All of the above."

Four

They'd arrived—but to what? Liana took a deep breath, then shot a side glance at her best friend. Did she see potential? Or was the dilapidating sight enough to send them both into cardiac arrest, because Liana's heart thudded in her chest.

Dalisay leaned against the exterior of Liana's car and crossed her arms. "Wow."

The sun's blinding rays glinted off the old building. The enormous white structure loomed ahead with six dormers and several broken windows. A few more displayed cracks. A wide set of stairs led to a massive veranda. The grounds could have been beautiful at one time, but now overgrown weeds filled the flower beds, and the shrubs were out of control.

Several trucks stood dwarfed to the right, and a horse from Liana's stable munched on grass while tethered to a substantial maple. Bryan had arrived early, but he must have gone inside, because there was no sign of him. Her pulse quickened, knowing he was somewhere near.

Liana studied the formation in front of her. "I never realized it was so ..." She searched for the right word and turned to her friend.

Dalisay raised both eyebrows. "Big?"

Liana nodded and smiled. "Immense. I've driven by it for years, but it's set back so far from the road, I had no idea."

"I can't wait to see what's inside, and if it's as promising as the exterior, it could be perfect." Dalisay pushed herself from the car. "And ... I'm also looking forward to meeting this caretaker of yours."

Liana didn't follow. Instead, she pulled out her phone and opened her e-mail.

After taking a few steps, Dalisay reversed direction and stood with hands perched on her hips. "Are you coming?"

"After I check messages."

"Honestly, you're compulsive. Notebooks, binders, a physical calendar, and a phone with more applications than you'll ever use. You're always on that thing. Check it later."

"I run a business, Daysie. I never know when something important could come in."

"I thought *this* was important."

Liana tossed the phone in her bag. "It is, but maybe we should wait a few minutes."

"For what? I thought you'd be itching to explore."

"I just think—"

"You're nervous."

"A little." That was a lie. Liana's stomach had roiled all morning like the undercurrent in a fast-moving river. What if the inside of the building disappointed? What if it was beyond expectations, but Mr. Jones didn't accept their proposal?

"About convincing the owner to hold the gala here?" Dalisay turned in a complete circle, scanning the area. "Or being around Bryan?"

"Both. Regardless, I don't think it's appropriate to barge in unannounced."

"So, we'll announce ourselves. We can't stand out here all

day." Dalisay grasped Liana's hand and pulled her from the car. "You said Bryan left a message that he'd meet you here at 10:00 a.m. It's now ten minutes after. Several trucks are parked over there, not to mention a horse from your stable is tied to a tree." She smirked. "We're expected. And besides, wouldn't it be inappropriate to be later than what we already are?"

"I see your point." Liana slipped the handle to her designer bag over her shoulder and took a deep breath.

With Dalisay as her support, she'd sell the owner on providing the space for the gala. Right now it was important to focus on the meeting and not fret about Bryan's presence. She'd warned Daysie, so hopefully, she wouldn't outwardly react to his appearance, and Dad thought Bryan and Mr. Jones had hit it off, so no problem there.

Bryan had offered to help Liana, and she didn't want anyone—especially him—to feel uncomfortable. No matter what—she wouldn't let him throw her today. *Get in there, girl.*

She and Dalisay skipped up the stairs, pushed open the massive wooden doors, and stepped into the spacious entryway. Liana glanced at the roof. It would probably hold. The floor creaked as they made their way through an archway leading into a quiet, cavernous room with an elevated ceiling. Dust particles floating in the air reflected the sun's rays filtering in through grimy windows. Swallows soared through the rafters.

"This is amazing!" Like a fairy herself, Dalisay slowly spun around, eyeing the room.

Visions of what could be filled Liana's brain like a movie put on fast-forward. Dalisay's eyes almost glowed with excitement. The two friends high-fived.

Muffled men's voices carried into the room a moment before Bryan, wearing jeans and a long-sleeved T-shirt, strode through a side door with a gentleman who wore a trimmed, slightly gray beard, and looked to be in his early forties. Engaged in conversation, and standing a number of feet away, the men didn't seem to realize they weren't alone.

Dalisay moved toward the newcomers, but Liana gestured for her to remain next to her and be quiet.

Her friend raised her shoulders, furrowed her eyebrows, and mouthed, "Huh?"

She'd explain later. Maybe. Liana wanted a moment to observe Bryan, who laughed and appeared at ease with his companion. He was so different from the guy she'd met in the stable a few nights before. That guy was tense and self-conscious around her. Or maybe it was only Liana who had been uptight around him.

Dalisay silently tapped her foot, signaling her impatience.

"Excus—" Liana attempted to clear her throat.

At the sound of her clogged voice, the men simultaneously faced the women, and Bryan's demeanor changed. He tilted his scarred profile away.

Brief disappointment zinged through Liana's body. Bryan's light-hearted laughter had been too brief. "Excuse us." She moved toward them with Dalisay close behind.

Bryan stepped slightly behind his companion. "Erik, this is Liana Tate. Liana, this is Erik Jones, the owner."

Liana extended her hand toward Erik. "Nice to meet you. This is my friend, Dalisay Ouano."

Erik, dressed in jeans and a gray sweatshirt, rubbed his palms on a rag hanging out of his back pocket before grasping Liana's hand with a firm shake and then Dalisay's. "Nice to meet you both."

Bryan hung back, but Liana's creative partner in this project approached him and thrust her hand out. "Dalisay."

He accepted with a nod and slight grin. "Bryan."

His shoulders relaxed. Dalisay had looked him in the eyes without flinching. No outward sign of fear, disgust, or even the heebie-jeebies. Perhaps a reminder from God that some people could see past ugliness.

Although Liana had been polite and kind the night he'd spooked her in the stable, Bryan had a gut feeling that until she got accustomed to his appearance, she might feel squeamish around him. So, he'd fought temptation all morning to call Erik with an excuse for not personally introducing the two. In the end, the conviction to follow through on his commitment had won. He didn't break promises.

Grateful they'd planned to meet on-site, he'd taken a horse out for exercise. While the horse stretched his legs, Bryan prayed. His own painful experience and what he witnessed while in the hospital made the gala's success personal. Too many families not only worried about their loved one surviving, they struggled under enormous financial burdens.

He also wanted the opportunity for Erik to showcase this place once it was fixed up, and the publication recognition that would come with hosting the gala would help generate business for him.

They'd only met a few days before, but Erik was one of few people with whom Bryan felt he could be himself. Dare he hope they might even become friends? Erik had exciting plans for this building—his inheritance—and if Bryan couldn't have his own dream, maybe he could play a small part in Erik obtaining his.

Erik flicked his thumb toward Bryan. "My buddy here has kept me in suspense, except to say that you're an event planner with something big coming up. Now, what exactly can I do for you?"

"It's more about what we can do for each other." Liana's instinct told her this property would be perfect for what she hoped to accomplish, and she attempted to squash any anxiety that the owner would reject her proposal. Somehow, she had to sell the idea. But she needed to focus, because Bryan's unwillingness to meet her eyes felt like a failure. If she'd been less alarmed during their first meeting, perhaps he wouldn't be acting so uncomfortable around her now.

"Interesting." Erik cocked his head. "A win-win. I like that."

Liana moistened her lips. "Would you be willing to share your intentions for the building?"

"My wife and I are going to put in a restaurant, but we also want to set certain nights aside for large events—you know, parties, wedding receptions, concerts—that sort of thing."

As Dalisay returned to Liana' side, the two exchanged glances. Her friend's eyes were lit up like sparklers—because of what she saw in Bryan—or what she'd heard from the property's owner?

"It's stepping out a little from the norm, but I'm hoping it will work." Erik stroked his bearded chin. "I was eight years old when my grandfather built this place. I watched it erect from the ground up. He was a unique character. A dreamer. He was a fan of an old movie called *Holiday Inn*."

"That's my favorite musical." Liana found herself getting caught up in his story. "Bing Crosby retires from showbiz to become a farmer. He converts the farm into an inn open only on holidays and then competes against Fred Astaire for the heroine."

Dalisay shrugged. "Never seen it."

"I have." Bryan, still lingering near Erik, caught Liana's eyes, but his gaze was brief. His attention diverted back to the man next to him.

The connection was fleeting, and it surprised Liana that she felt acute disappointment. "You're familiar with *Holiday Inn*?" Liana couldn't picture Bryan curled up in front of a romantic flick, especially a musical. The image did strange things to her.

Bryan shifted his feet and thrust his hands into his front jean's pockets. "A family thing."

Dalisay pulled out a notebook and pencil from her bag. "Erik, are you saying your grandfather wanted to build an inn like in the movie?"

He chuckled. "I think his real fantasy was to sing and act like Bing Crosby. But his father insisted that he follow a family tradition and become a lawyer. His wife died at an early age, and after he worked for years and raised his kids, he found himself alone but with a substantial amount of money put away." Appearing to be deep in thought, he paused for a moment. "So, you're right, Dalisay. He decided to create something similar to the inn in the movie. Unfortunately, before he could complete it, he died from a heart attack."

Liana's heartstrings tugged. Like her own grandfather, the man had a desire to fashion something beautiful—a gift people could enjoy that also offered a reprieve from whatever heartbreak or challenges they faced. How sad that Erik's grandfather didn't see his dream come to fruition. "So, the building has been sitting empty all this time?"

"My dad didn't want anything to do with what he called folly. Grandpa knew that and left the property to me in his will. But I haven't had the means or know-how to do anything about it until now." Erik scratched his right ear. "My wife Maggie and I never had kids, but we've been able to put away enough funds to warrant thinking about building something together here. It won't be what my grandfather dreamed, but I hope it will become a place where people can come and escape for a few hours, enjoy good food, and relax."

Liana's ears perked up at the word "escape." It fit right into spending time in the fantasy world she wanted to create. "Have you made any decisions on theme or décor?"

"Not yet. Maggie's talked to a few designers, but nothing has struck us yet as being out of the ordinary." Erik frowned. "Sorry. I've been doing all the talking. I get excited when I have a chance to talk about Grandpa."

Liana returned Dalisay's grin. "It's actually been helpful to hear your story." Her friend nodded in agreement. Despite her heart beating so strongly, she feared the force might break a rib, Liana dove into her pitch. "We'd like to use this place to host the annual Northwest Medical Center Gala."

Erik straightened. "The hospital?"

"Yes. Every year the event raises millions of dollars to help patients. But this year, the hotel booked to hold the event was damaged in the earthquake. The management can't commit to a date when the wing we'd planned to use will be reopened."

"And you're asking to hold the gala here?" His voice carried some disbelief. "When?"

"The end of October—almost six months." Liana's confidence in selling the idea waned at the tone of his voice.

Erik whistled a long note. "Closer to five unless you want us pounding nails up to the last minute. By the end of October, we may not be in much better shape than the hotel. We've still got a lot of work to do ourselves, like landscaping and remodeling restrooms. We still need to put in an industrial kitchen."

"Please hear them out, Erik." Bryan spoke in a calm, quiet tone. "It's for a good cause."

The owner locked eyes with him for a moment, then nodded. "Okay. I'm listening."

Grateful for Bryan pleading their case, Liana made eye contact and offered him a smile before continuing, and for the first time that day, he didn't attempt to hide his scarred profile. And by focusing on his mesmerizing eyes, his disfigurement almost blurred in her vision. She felt no shudder at the ugly imperfections.

She pulled her gaze from his and focused on Erik. "The gala draws attention from a lot of influential people. Many rewards come with a successful event. First and foremost, the funds raised will help those who otherwise couldn't afford hospital care."

"I get and support that."

"To help make my proposal for the gala feasible, Dalisay and I are donating our services."

"I'm a set designer," Dalisay said, stepping forward. "I'll be the one to draw up plans and coordinate set construction, which will be on a grander scale than normally found in theaters, but I can handle a project this size."

Before Erik could ask more questions, Liana jumped in. "Of course, much of the gala is funded by sponsors. Various businesses want to support the cause. But that money covers a wide range of things like advertising, programs, centerpieces, implementing a theme, and entertainment."

She grabbed a quick breath. "The ticket price will cover food, but our hope is that you'll provide the building rent free. It would mean more money allocated to those in need. And if you serve food that satisfies and excites the guests, they'll not only return, they'll bring friends." Liana stopped herself from rambling on further. She'd highlighted the most important pieces—now for the final pitch. "You couldn't ask for better publicity."

Erik's face lit up. "I'm intrigued."

Liana's hopes soared with the swallows in the rafters. "We're going with a fantasy theme inspired by a book written by my grandfather."

"We have a few simple sketches." Dalisay removed several pages from her notebook and handed them to Erik. "I can draw them in more detail now that I've seen the space. Once you give us the okay, I'll hit every theater in the area for set pieces we can borrow. What we can't get from theaters, we'll put together ourselves, even if we have to beg for donated lumber and paint." Enthusiasm built in her voice. "I'm confident that actors and various people who have worked on building sets will donate their time and help put everything together. And I promise, when the event is over, we'll have everything down and out of here in forty-eight hours."

"What do you say?" Liana didn't want to push too hard, but under the circumstances, she needed an answer—soon.

"I'll need to talk to my wife and think it over before I can commit." Erik glanced at the sketches in his hand. "Give me a day or two. But knowing her, she'll probably love the idea."

Dalisay threw her pencil into her bag. "Before we leave, let me share some additional ideas for the layout."

Liana followed the two as Dalisay pointed out to Erik locations for trees and fairy cottages. Anticipation of the possibilities continued building within her. Maybe everything would come together after all. But until Erik gave them a definitive answer, she'd minimize her elation.

If it hadn't been for Bryan, Liana wouldn't have known about this building, and she certainly wouldn't have had the opportunity to convince Erik to hold the gala on his property. Assuming Bryan followed close by as Dalisay shared her design ideas for the event, Liana turned to thank him, but he was nowhere in sight.

Perhaps it was cowardly to escape while their attention was focused in the other direction, but Bryan needed air. Although Dalisay and Erik were at ease around him, Liana only glanced his way when it would have been blatantly obvious she was avoiding setting her eyes on him. Well, except for the one smile she rewarded him when he'd stood up for her.

He'd sure take more of those.

Why did it feel so important to have her approval, her acceptance? Liana was beautiful, driven, and strong. He'd detected a sense of humor buried in there—*somewhere*. But more so, he admired all that she was doing for the gala. How could he not when the people within the hospital walls had given him his life back—physically, mentally, emotionally, and even spiritually?

He owed so much to those who had helped him, and there were also those patients he cared about but had left behind. If introducing Liana to Erik helped any of them in even a small way, he was grateful for the opportunity.

Liana ... They'd only met a few days ago, yet he couldn't stop thinking about her. Why? He barely knew anything about her. Besides, she'd never be interested in a caretaker when she could easily have someone who would fit in better with the social circles he assumed she hung out with. Someone she wouldn't be embarrassed to be seen with in public.

Bryan couldn't risk being hurt again. After three years, he'd finally escaped an emotional black hole, and he wasn't eager to return.

So, what was he going to do about Liana Tate? How was he going to live only feet away and keep his heart from being wounded all over again?

The meeting had ended, and after walking Liana and Dalisay out to the car, Erik had gone back inside the building to continue his inspection, and Bryan had followed at Erik's request.

Liana turned the key to the ignition, and the engine started. Then she switched it off and shifted on the car seat to face her friend.

Dalisay slipped the sunglasses from her face. "Something wrong?"

"No. Just the opposite. You didn't react at all to Bryan. You acted like he was any normal guy."

"From what I can tell, he *is* a normal guy. Part of his face is messed up, that's all." Dalisay shrugged. "What did you expect? For me to scream in terror or faint? It's not as if you hadn't told me."

"No. I'd like to understand why his scars scared me at first, but they didn't seem to affect you in the least." Liana didn't think she was judgmental about people's looks, but was she more like her mother and sister than what she believed?

Dalisay gave Liana a sympathetic look. "First of all, I didn't meet him under the same circumstances as you. I didn't unexpectedly run into him on a dark night. It's broad daylight, and I had fair warning."

"True." Liana felt a bit better.

"In your family's world, beauty and perfection are not only coveted, they're the norm. People in the theater community, and generally people in the arts, accept differences. Most of the time, we embrace and celebrate them."

"How I can look at him without seeing—?" Although, she had, if even for a moment.

"He's a human being with feelings and a soul, Lee. Try focusing on what *is* good about him." Dalisay gave a teasing smile. "Seriously, those eyes are amazing."

Liana remembered. Not only striking, they held a warmth

she'd rarely experienced, except through her dad's gaze. What was it about Bryan that intrigued her? Drew her in? It wasn't mere curiosity. Of that, she was certain.

My emotions are as messed up as that hotel shaken by the earthquake.

Liana's phone gave a short ring, announcing a text had come in. She tapped her phone to retrieve the message, then sighed after reading.

"My mother wants me to drop by her office tomorrow for a chat."

"The queen summons." Dalisay tossed her long hair over her right shoulder. "Wonder what she's planning to harass you about this time."

Five

Her mother's personal assistant, Maria Williams, led Liana into the office located on the seventh floor of the professional building in downtown Seattle, explaining that Liana's mother would join her in a few minutes. Pivoting back and forth before the mirror hanging on the wall to the right of the large desk, Liana scrutinized her reflection. No strings clung to the crisp white blouse and black skirt she'd recently purchased at Nordstrom's. Her mother couldn't possibly find anything wrong with the simple, yet sophisticated outfit, could she?

Finished primping, Liana gazed at the spectacular view through floor-length windows. Ferries crossing Puget Sound between Seattle and Bainbridge Island moved at slug speed—or so it seemed from a distance.

She glanced at her watch, and her stomach fluttered. A woman closing in on turning thirty shouldn't feel anxious before seeing her own mother, but Liana had never experienced the endearing relationship that Dalisay shared with her mom.

It wasn't that Liana hadn't yearned for a better connection. As an awkward, shy little girl, she longed for encouragement and praise, but it rarely came. She must have been a constant disappointment in comparison to her adorable, younger sister.

Although she grieved for her father when efforts failed at

keeping his marriage together, Liana felt secretly relieved when her mother moved out of the main house and into the city. It had alleviated some of the ongoing tension between Liana and her mother as well and the feeling of being consistently watched and judged.

"I'm glad you're on time." Her mother—Eva Tate—entered the room, then closed the door behind her and dropped a stack of manila folders on the mahogany desk. "I have a full schedule." She scanned Liana. "You're a little pale. Wearing black and white makes you look like the ghost of a dead waitress." Perching her right hand on her slacked hip, she scowled. "I wish you'd wear that Vera Wang suit I bought you. The greatest asset you have are those pretty eyes you inherited from your father, and that suit would bring out their color."

Liana dug her nails into her right palm as the zingers created fresh wounds. Any compliments Mother offered always seemed paired with insults. Liana mentally recorded and filed her mother's words—a mental exercise used to keep her emotions in check.

Her mother settled into the seat behind the massive desk and waved toward the posh leather chair opposite her as though dismissing Liana as insignificant. "Sit. I need to make a quick call."

Out of stubbornness, Liana almost refused. But what would be the point? She obeyed the command out of pure respect, tuned out her mother's phone conversation, and occupied herself by glancing around the exquisite office. Poster-sized photographs of top models represented by her mother's agency, including Camryn's headshot, graced the walls. Liana admired her sister's willowy, tan body. That, along with her large aquamarine eyes and luminous blond hair, made Camryn a favorite cover girl for magazines like *Vogue* and *Cosmo*.

Camryn resembled their mother, who strove to remain as thin, beautiful, and chic as she was during her own modeling career, decades ago. Botox injections and ongoing surgeries were a part of the routine. Though true, Liana would never mention out loud that her mother had acquired a slightly unnatural appearance. Hence the term, *plastic* surgery.

Her mother scribbled on a notepad, ended the conversation, and hung up the phone. "I drove out to the house several days ago to pick up a box I'd stored in the attic. Should've taken it three years ago when I moved out, but it slipped my mind." She grimaced. "You've met the new caretaker?"

"Of course. I live there." Bryan never mentioned encountering her mother. But then, he and Liana had spoken few words to each other since meeting. Liana braced herself. She could guess where this conversation was going, and compassion rose inside toward Bryan. Someone that disfigured should be surrounded by merciful people who could see past the outside, and that was certainly not Mother. Most of the time, Liana couldn't even rise to that standard.

"What was your father thinking?"

"Excuse me?"

"He's gone off the deep end with this religion malarkey. He gave up a lucrative practice as one of the best plastic surgeons, and now he takes a charity case to work the estate? What next? Is he going to convert the place into a home for lost orphans?"

Her mother had no right to insult her dad. He'd never

been anything but gracious toward her. Liana's stomach clenched. Neither her father nor the caretaker deserved to be treated unkindly. "Bryan isn't a charity case. And he seems— nice."

Perfectly arched eyebrows drew up. "I don't care what he seems. Make sure your doors are locked." Eva closed her eyes tight, without crinkling her forehead, and shuddered. "The man is a freak."

Liana cringed inside. How awful that she'd had similar, cruel thoughts at first glance. She, herself, had experienced heartache rooted in a garden of unacceptance, and the fertilizer hadn't been limited to spoken words. "I admit his appearance made me a little uncomfortable at first, but he may have saved the hospital gala." Perhaps Mother would see his value if she knew he'd contributed to the social event Mother championed this time of year.

"And how is that?" Skepticism dripped from her mother's lips.

"You know I've been searching for a new venue. Bryan introduced Dalisay and me to the owner of that huge building down the road from our estate. We may be holding the event there."

"You can't mean that sorry-looking monstrosity stuck back in the woods." Her mother muttered something under her breath, too quiet to be heard. "That's ridiculous."

Liana's palms dampened. Maybe her mother was right.

"And why did the owner of that eyesore need to meet your friend—that girl?"

"Her name is Dalisay, Mom. You should remember it by now. We've been friends since grade school. I've asked her to help with some design work for the gala. She's very talented.

Which you'd come to realize if you ever spent more than two minutes with her."

Liana preferred not to argue about her dad or her friends, but her mother had the ability to push Liana into the ring with her fists up. "Getting back to Bryan. Is he the reason you asked me here?"

"No, there's something else." Mother folded her hands on the desk and leaned forward. "You and I haven't had any time together since I moved out. So, I was wondering if I could I convince you to get away for a few days—just the two of us."

This was the last thing Liana expected. "Are you serious? Why?" Should she feel excited or worried?

"Can't I spend some time with my daughter?" Her tone almost sounded like she felt insulted by Liana's questions.

"We've never gone anywhere without Camryn or Dad."

"That's silly. Of course we have. I thought with both of us working so hard, a little getaway would be nice."

It was worth a try. Maybe they'd fly to Italy or Spain and visit the best restaurants, museums, art galleries, vineyard ... If they spent more time together, they might learn to like each other.

Liana moistened her lips. "It depends on when you can be away from the office. I'd need to make sure I don't have any jobs scheduled."

Her mother opened a desk drawer and pulled out a small stack of brochures. "I found several places that would be perfect."

One cover displayed a water fountain surrounded by a garden in full bloom. A colonial mansion flanked by mature cherry trees filled the second. Both gave the appearance of quiet resorts where they could retreat from the world. A break in such a place could be nice.

Liana opened the pamphlet showcasing the garden, and her enthusiasm deflated. "Gyms."

Inside, photos of weight rooms full of equipment for cardio training and extensive exercise classes dotted the pages. Saccharin testimonies of weight loss accompanied pictures of blissful, chubby women dining on micro meals beside the lap pool.

"You want to take me to a fat farm?"

"Please don't use that term. It's a spa for health and wellness." Mother leaned back in her chair.

"It's a weight-loss clinic."

"At this *spa*, you're encouraged to eat healthy, exercise, and breathe fresh air. The yoga instructor at Crystal Springs is supposed to be one of the best."

"I hate yoga, and I have all the fresh air I want or need." She couldn't be serious. A walnut-sized lump lodged in Liana's throat. "This is your idea of a mother-daughter getaway?"

"It would be good for both of us." Her mother stiffened. "If you were honest with yourself, you'd admit that you'd look and feel better if you trimmed off a few pounds."

"Size eight is not obese."

"I didn't say it was, but it wouldn't hurt to drop a size or two." Her mother sighed as though weary of dealing with her daughter. "I raised you to be independent, but it would also be nice for you to have some male companionship in your life. And in order to attract gorgeous, successful men, you need to work at making yourself worth noticing." She pointed a pen and waved it like a magic wand at Liana's head.

"For instance, cutting and updating your hairstyle would be a start. Something sassy."

"I'm not cutting my hair, and I'm not going to a fat farm with you." Liana's cheeks burned, and her heart thumped like a bass guitar trying to out-beat the band's drummer, but she couldn't let her mother get away with bullying her. "I'm not going to be pushed into doing anything I don't want to do." Liana mentally put her fighting gloves on. "You need to understand that I'm not—"

A knock sounded on the door, and Maria slipped inside. "I'm sorry to disturb you, Ms. Tate, but Mr. Jackson said it's extremely important that he speak to you."

"Thank you, Maria. I was expecting him." Mother stood and addressed Liana. "I need to take care of Jackson, but we can finish this conversation later." Her eyes glared with displeasure.

Liana shouldn't let it bother her, but that familiar ache of rejection stung. She'd strived her entire life to please her mother—to please everyone—but even Liana had her limits. It was time to start laying some boundaries. She stood, tossed the brochures on the desk, and spoke with all the firmness she could muster. "There's nothing more to talk about."

She spun and stalked out the door, refusing to leave the room crying. After all, she was still her mother's daughter, and that meant there was no room for weakness.

Six

Early that evening, before the sun had fully set, Liana stood alone in her bedroom, her thoughts replaying what had transpired earlier in her mother's office.

She pinched the flesh between her rib cage and hipbone.

True, there wasn't much to grab onto, but her mother was right. Liana worked hard to keep her abs toned and waist slim, but a size eight was still unacceptable—at least in the world her sister and mother traveled.

Liana slumped down on the edge of the bed. Her thighs looked like tree trunks compared to her sister's. She lay back and stared at the ceiling. Hot tears trickled down her cheeks and neck. It didn't matter that she ran three miles every morning and starved herself. And it wouldn't help if she used expensive hair conditioners or bought into her mom's *spa* plans. She'd never fit in with the fast, high-fashioned world her sister and mother inhabited.

But did she really want to?

She'd refused to go on that ridiculous—no, that insulting—trip to the fat farm. It was one thing to satisfy her clients, and Liana pushed herself hard to make them happy, but on a personal level, people-pleasing was wearing her out and making her feel weak and small. Something needed to change inside Liana, and although standing up to her mother earlier that day had been difficult, it was a step toward becoming a stronger person.

A dog barked outside. Liana sat up and wiped the moisture from her face. Wrapping her body in her favorite bathrobe, she followed the barking sounds into the front room without bothering to flip on the lights. She sank into a soft chair near the open window. Hidden in shadows, she viewed the outdoor activity.

As the sun fell below the tree line, rays filtered through pine branches. Bryan played fetch with his Lab on the expansive lawn between the stables and flowerbeds.

Unexpected guilt crept into Liana's conscience like a sneaky spy. Desiring to avoid another awkward encounter, Liana had stayed clear of the stable and any other area where Bryan might be found. Aside from the few words shared at the stable and during the meeting with Erik, she hadn't made any effort to speak to him or make him feel welcome.

Was that because she was protecting *him* from feeling ill at ease—or *herself*?

She'd try harder to know him. Everyone could use another friend.

Liana gasped.

Did Bryan have any friends? Or had they all abandoned him? She hadn't witnessed anyone visiting. Her eyes got misty, and she rubbed the moisture from them. She couldn't imagine her life without Dalisay.

In the twilight, Bryan raced and laughed with his dog. Feeling like a voyeur, Liana averted her gaze from the window, but felt compelled to watch again. How could someone so disfigured be so happy?

Her cell phone rang. She picked it up from the end table, but didn't recognize the number on the caller ID. "Hello?"

"Liana, this is Kevin Carter."

Kevin? Was this really happening? Was he genuinely interested in her? "It's nice to hear from you."

He chuckled. "You didn't give up on me, did you?"

"Was there something to give up on?" That didn't come out sounding like she wanted.

Flirting didn't come naturally for Liana. She chewed on her lower lip. Convinced she'd merely been a brief distraction for the architect while attending a mutual friend's wedding, she didn't believe he'd call. Men like Kevin never showed real or lasting interest. She didn't exude pizzazz or sex appeal. Not like her sister. If Camryn even glanced at a man, she gained another worshiper.

"How have you been?" How lame. Camryn would have said something witty or clever.

"Not so good." He spoke in a low, seductive voice. "You've been on my mind." The sound of his slow breath made her pulse race. "I wanted to call sooner, but I've been working night and day in order to meet a deadline."

"I understand." She glanced at the pile of work on her own desk, only a few feet away. Binders full of vendor information, plans, and layouts for several functions she'd been contracted to coordinate needed attention.

"I know this is short notice, but would you join me for dinner Friday night?"

Disappointment washed over her like a tidal wave. "I'd love to, but I'm working that night. An anniversary party for three hundred people."

"Someone important?"

"A couple celebrating their fiftieth wedding anniversary." Her heart warmed thinking about the cute pair, known for their philanthropy. "I've worked hard to make the event special, and I want to make sure everything goes as planned."

"Saturday?"

"I'm coordinating a wedding."

This couldn't be happening. Drat having to working weekends. She glanced out the window. The dog jumped, and his paws landed on Bryan's shoulders, tumbling them both to the ground. They wrestled on the grass, and Bryan's carefree laughter pierced the still, evening air. She couldn't remember ever playing with such joy.

"Liana?"

She needed to come up with an idea—and fast, or she might never hear from him again. "I was thinking ..."

"Yes ..." He dragged out the word in a low, expectant tone.

Her heart accelerated. "What would you say to a home-cooked meal? My place. Sunday evening around seven?"

"I'd say you have a date."

Liana ran her fingers through her hair as she mentally checked things off her list.

She'd been insane to invite Kevin to dinner after coordinating two large parties the same weekend. Preparing a private dinner at her home for one guest should have required little effort. She always strived to eliminate as much stress as possible for everyone involved with an event, yet for what should have been a simple affair, she'd become frazzled.

A rush of adrenaline shot through her body. The clock displayed a later hour than expected, but in her profession, she regularly dealt with time crunches. A deep cleansing breath and she'd be fine.

She still needed to finish cleaning up the kitchen before changing into fresh clothes. Liana turned on the faucet, flipped the switch for the garbage disposal, and stuffed the vegetable peelings and discarded salad greens down the drain. Discolored water floating with refuse bubbled up, filling the lower half of the sink. Onion and garlic stench made her eyes water and her stomach churn.

"No!" She flipped off the switch to the disposal and swatted the counter hard with a dishrag. "Not now!"

Liana wiped a tear from her cheek and glimpsed the clock. She needed help if she had any hope of getting the mess cleaned up and making herself presentable by the time Kevin arrived.

She picked up her phone and punched in her father's number. He wasn't particularly good with plumbing, but he was the only one she could count on.

Bryan knocked on Liana's cottage door, his hand shaking in anticipation. He'd almost forgotten how immobilizing stage fright could be. He'd last spoken to Liana four days ago at the building down the road, when Erik's presence served as a buffer. Not the case this time. Bryan arrived alone.

He hadn't felt attracted to a woman since Jenny, and she'd broken his heart. Not able to stomach his appearance, she'd walked away from their relationship while he was still hospitalized. So, how could he trust *any* woman to care for him again? Jenny knew him—said she loved him—and yet, when life got challenging, what he had to offer wasn't good enough.

The door swung open, and Liana's eyes widened for a second, but she gave a warm smile. "Bryan, what are you doing here?"

He directed his unscarred profile toward her. "Your father asked me to come."

Liana chuckled softly. "Oh, he did, did he?"

While keeping Liana in his peripheral vision, he held up the toolbox in his left hand. "You have an emergency?"

She wiped her hands on a dish towel, then gestured for him to enter.

Bryan stepped into the cottage and followed her to the sink. It was a mess, all right. He wanted to look at her, but her unexpected smile and welcoming laughter had thrown him off kilter, so he tried to focus on the problem in front of him.

"I'm sorry if I sound a bit abrupt, but I'm expecting a guest soon." She did seem a little on edge, but did that have more to do with his unexpected arrival or her guest?

"I'll hurry."

"Great. While you work on that, I need to change. There's a bucket underneath the sink for the water to drain into. If you need anything else, please yell."

"Sure."

"Thanks, you're a lifesaver," she said, sounding sincere.

Bryan, hearing the bedroom door close, relaxed. She hadn't recoiled or turned him away. A spark of hope shot renewed energy through his body, and he smiled. Progress. Maybe she was getting used to the idea of him being around. If so, he could be more comfortable with working for the doc. Aside from situations out of his control, Bryan strived to keep his distance. Hopefully, Liana realized he had no intention of being intrusive.

He pulled the socket wrench from the toolbox and glanced around the cottage. The kitchen, dining area, and office were all laid out in one spacious room, but they were still defined by low shelves, plants, or furniture arrangement. Except for the clogged sink, the place was spotless. Gold fabric couches faced each other in front of the massive rock fireplace. A round glass-top table had been set for two. The aroma of whatever was cooking in the oven aroused his hunger, and his stomach growled. Her dinner guest was in for a treat.

Liana closed the bedroom door and yanked open a dresser drawer. Placing her palms on top of the dresser, she leaned against it, and blew out a shot of air. There wasn't much time to pull herself together. Before slipping on a sleeveless lavender silk blouse and black slacks, she applied her favorite citrus-scented perfume on her wrists and behind her ears. The new silver necklace worked well with the neckline. She picked out a light pink lip gloss for her lips and stared into the mirror.

Her father was developing a terrible habit of surprising her.

Why was she so pleased at seeing Bryan at the door? Maybe because it was an opportunity to convince him that she wanted him around—on the estate—to help her father, of course. Unfortunately, he kept turning away, looking everywhere but at her.

Liana knew what it felt like to be an outsider—looked down upon because you didn't look or dress a certain way. Every time she was introduced to someone as Eva Tate's daughter, they acted surprised. Just because she didn't have shiny blond hair, a runway model's legs, and make her living in front of the camera like her mother and sister.

Bryan was a regular guy, not a monster, no matter what Mother said. Plus, Liana could be nice to him without becoming his best buddy. Couldn't she?

Bryan heard Liana close the door behind her as she returned from the bedroom but continued to rinse out the sink. He'd worked fast, despite the pain it caused his hands to wrench on the pipe. If she'd taken a few more minutes, he could have escaped.

"It's already fixed?" Liana approached him from behind. "Are you a plumber? Or a miracle worker?"

He lifted a gloved hand in the air and gave a short wave of acknowledgment. "I'm merely a guy who wants to do a good job."

She peered into the sink. "You didn't need to scrub everything clean. That's going above and beyond." Liana sounded both surprised and pleased.

"Happy to." Bryan discreetly inhaled the scent of her perfume. "You shouldn't be doing it all dressed up." He rinsed the dishrag under the running faucet, rung the water out, and draped the rag over the sink divider. "Cleaning products are hard on my hands because of the burns, so I hope you don't mind that I used your rubber gloves."

He pulled them off, bent over, and hung them on a rack under the sink. Then he picked up the toolbox next to him and turned to leave.

"Are your hands okay?" She sounded concerned and stepped closer, as if needing confirmation. "Hmmm?"

He surveyed his hands, pretending to inspect them. "Yeah, they're fine."

"Good." Her voice softened. "Thank you. I really appreciate your help."

"You're welcome."

Risking her repulsion, Bryan raised his head and took in her eyes. She didn't return the look but a moment, yet it was long enough to cause an erratic heartbeat in his chest.

"I better get out of here before your guest arrives. From how it smells in here, he'd be missing out on a great meal, not to mention the company." He worked to give her a smile, then moved toward the exit. "Have a good night."

"Bryan, wait."

He hesitated with his hand on the doorknob.

"I didn't get a chance to thank you the other day—for introducing me and Dalisay to Erik and encouraging him to listen to our ideas. He's going to give us an answer tomorrow about using the building for the gala. He might not have even considered hearing us out if you hadn't been there."

"I was glad to help, Liana." He shifted around, captured her gaze, and this time held it. "But I think it would be difficult for anyone to turn you down." Then he stepped outside, closed the door, took a deep breath, and released it. Whew! Where did that come from? He hadn't meant to be so bold.

She'd surprised him with her kindness, but before he

could offer a prayer of thanks, a car approached. Rainey jumped up from where he lay, waiting for his master. With the dog at his heels, Bryan turned the corner of the cottage and leaned against the wall as the car came to a halt. He felt like a criminal hiding, but he didn't want to ruin Liana's evening by shocking the visitor with his appearance.

A guy about Bryan's age stepped out of the Mercedes and strode to the cottage door with a bottle of wine and a bakery box in hand. He knocked and was admitted, but not before Bryan heard the warm timbre of Liana's greeting. He stiffened, debating his next move. It was wrong for him to window peep, but he'd take one quick look.

Bryan stationed himself close to the window's edge and peered through to get a better view. Most women would think the man, blond and fit, quite attractive. And a great catch, if the vehicle he drove represented financial success. The way her face lit up, Liana must be enthralled with the guy.

Envy dropped an invisible weight on Bryan's shoulders, and he switched the toolbox from his right hand to his left. He was right to believe that a woman like Liana—or any woman—could love him as a man. That was his past, and he needed to focus on his future, wherever God would take him. In the meantime, while he figured that out, perhaps there was a slight chance that he and Liana could be friends, and if so, he'd count that as a blessing.

Rainey licked the empty hand with a wet tongue, then nuzzled his nose into his owner's palm. Bryan scratched the top of the Lab's head. "Let's go, boy."

He glanced back through the window, and his chest tightened. God spared him when he should have died, and he'd learned to be thankful for all he'd gained. But would he ever stop grieving for all he'd lost?

Seven

The soft flame from the tapers created an intimate glow within the cottage walls. Kevin smiled at Liana across the table, and her mouth felt as though liquids hadn't passed her lips in days. A sip of ice water didn't help.

She was painfully aware that she didn't measure up to the type of woman he usually dated. Flattered by his interest, if she wasn't careful, her attraction to this man, along with her desire to please him, could carry her away faster than white water rapids.

Toying with a morsel of glazed salmon, Liana shoved it around the plate with her fork. *Play with your food, take small bites, and chew slowly. Then discretely cover the plate with a napkin. By the time your dinner companions have ravished their meal, you'll have eaten a fourth of what's on your plate, but they won't notice.* A lesson in weight management learned from her sister.

Kevin swirled the wine in his glass and then sipped. "What do you do for fun, Liana?"

When was the last time she did anything for pure enjoyment? She dabbed her mouth with the white linen napkin and casually dropped it over her dinner. "To be honest, I love what I do, so I spend the majority of my time working."

"Me too. We're fortunate. Most people only tolerate their jobs." He passed his right hand over one of the candles on the table, playing with the burning flame. "I never wanted to be anything but an architect."

"Your work must be fascinating. Buildings can be both beautiful and inspiring."

Another helpful tactic learned by observing Camryn— *focus on the man and his hungry ego. It not only makes him feel good about being with you, it's possible to maneuver the conversation away from you.*

"They can be." He chuckled. "I'd like to leave my mark on the world. A legacy—something that says I've been here."

No one could say he lacked ambition. "Like a building with your name on it?"

"I'd like to think my motives are a bit more noble." He leaned forward on the table. "Aspiring to have your name on a building doesn't make you a bad person. Philanthropists give their names to hospitals, libraries, and schools all the time."

"You're right." There wasn't anything wrong with having big dreams and going after them. Wasn't she doing the same thing by taking on the hospital gala?

Her date gave her a charismatic smile that turned her into pudding. Hopefully, she wouldn't easily be consumed by the charmer.

Kevin reached across the table, and gently squeezed her hand. "Dinner was great."

"Thank you." She hoped his fingers wouldn't move to her wrist where he'd feel her quickened pulse. "It was nice of you to bring wine and dessert."

"Women can't resist chocolate."

"This woman can." The words escaped before she could stop them. Bad habit. Speaking before thinking. Would he view her response as flirtatious or obstinate? Not wanting to offend, she smiled.

"Is that so?" Kevin's voice teased. He toyed with her fingers. "You can't be concerned about your figure."

Heat rushed into her cheeks. Her face had to be the same shade of red as that new lipstick Camryn was pushing in her latest cosmetic ad. Hating that she could do nothing to stop blushing, Liana avoided the question. "It does look too tempting to pass up."

He'd been thoughtful to bring the cake. It would be impolite to refuse, and she had been craving chocolate for several days. A few bites wouldn't hurt. She stood and picked up her plate, but Kevin leapt from his chair.

"You sit." He guided her back to her seat. "It's my turn to wait on you."

"Oh ... thanks."

Men fell at Camryn's feet, hoping for even a crumb of attention. But aside from her dad, no man had served Liana. Was it wrong to enjoy it just this once? Sure, Bryan had fixed the disposal a few hours earlier, but that was part of his job, so did it count the same? Or more because of the sacrifice— the effort put forth—despite the possible physical pain. He'd also completed the task with an attitude that humbled Liana.

She relaxed back into her chair. "The plates are on the counter, and you'll find a large knife in the woodblock. A small piece for me, please."

"As you wish."

Kevin brought a generous serving, an additional plate, and two forks. With effort, he kept the fudge layer cake from toppling to its side. He handed her a fork and a plate. "Please take as much as you'd like."

"Thanks." Liana slid her fork through the cake, cutting a

thin slice, which she transferred to her own plate.

A large bite of the dessert was consumed by Kevin, and he gave an impish grin. He used his fork to point to her cake. "Give it a try. It's amazing."

The sweet, creamy frosting melted in her mouth. She'd gone way too long without any yummy sweetness. "The coffee is ready if you'd like some." Her voice caught in her throat.

"I'll take a little more of this." He poured his second glass of wine and held up the bottle. "Care for some now?"

"Just a taste. Thank you."

Kevin filled her glass a fourth of the way and handed it to her before sauntering to the stereo where classical guitar music played. He turned the dial on the radio to a jazz station. "Do you mind?"

She liked jazz about as much as she liked finding enormous slugs on her front step. As a matter of fact, she liked jazz about as much as she liked the smell of cooked brussels sprouts, her cell phone cutting out, or technical problems with her laptop. He was a guest, and normally she'd fear sounding rude. But hadn't she decided to not be the same people pleaser she'd been for far too long? Wouldn't it be better to try honesty?

Her cell phone rang, and she caught Kevin's eye. "I can let it go to voice mail."

"Go ahead and answer. You never know. It might be important."

She stood, picked up the phone, and stepped into the kitchen area. "Hello?"

"I'm glad you're home." Her mother's tone sent warning signals through Liana, and she inwardly groaned. "There has to be a more suitable venue to hold the gala than the old Jones's place. I've been unsettled about your decision ever since you mentioned wanting to hold the event there."

Liana turned her back to Kevin and clung to the cupboards next to the kitchen sink. "Mom, this isn't a good time. Can we talk tomorrow?"

"This is important, Liana. It'll only take a minute."

"Mom, I appreciate your concern, but I can't talk right now. I have a guest."

"A man?"

"Yes." Liana cringed inside. She shouldn't have admitted anything.

"Real-ly." Her mother drew out the word as though the idea of Liana entertaining a male in her home was incredulous.

"Bye, Mom. I'll call you in the morning."

She'd diverted questions about her visitor for now. It wasn't that her mother would disapprove of Kevin. Quite the contrary. Her mother would highly approve. But Liana would block any interference tonight. With the cell phone turned off, Liana's mother would have to simmer her inquisitive juices overnight.

Bryan sat at the kitchen table in his apartment, downloading photos from his Nikon D750 onto his laptop. Photography had been a hobby at a younger age, and after his release from the hospital, he'd renewed his love affair. He'd almost depleted his savings on the professional camera and accessories, but he didn't regret the decision. He wanted to capture all he could through a photographic lens. God had provided vast beauty in the world for his enjoyment, and it reminded him every day that he should be thankful for his life and for sight.

He clicked through the new pictures, each one telling a different story and filling the screen with vivid colors. Satisfaction filled his chest over a shot of Lexus and Rainey playing together in the field. The two had become buddies, as much as any horse and dog could be friends.

Bryan shifted his leg and nudged the sleeping dog lying across his numb foot. Rainey staggered to his feet.

"Come here, boy." He hefted the large dog's front legs over his lap so Rainey could see the computer screen. The dog barked and wagged his tail. "I thought you'd like it."

He rubbed the top of the Rainey's head. "You'd probably enjoy a slide show, but I've got to get my circulation going." He gently removed the animal's paws and stood.

"Raining again."

Bryan limped on his tingling foot to the window facing Liana's cottage. Light shown from within, and the visitor's car sat in the driveway.

"He's still there."

Bryan leaned against the wall. He'd been nervous about going to the cottage earlier to work on the messed-up disposal, but he didn't want to say no to the doc. The reward was seeing Liana more relaxed. She looked directly at him with those beautiful eyes without showing any discomfort.

"Maybe it's going to work out here, after all."

Liana seemed to accept his presence on the estate. He'd prayed that the two could co-exist on the property, and God had answered.

Bryan gazed down at the cottage. What would it feel like to sit across the table from Liana? Share dinner—stories—their future?

Closing his eyes, he quietly prayed for God's help. If Bryan was going to not only survive, but thrive in his new surroundings, he needed to let go of impossibilities. He needed to set free his desire for a woman's love. He needed to forget the scent of Liana's perfume ... and how it felt to be near her.

Liana lounged next to Kevin on the couch. He'd been wonderful the entire evening, respecting her decisions on how much wine and cake she was willing to consume—even switching the music back after she explained she had trouble enjoying jazz.

The physical attraction to Kevin scared her. It was stronger than what she'd ever felt for another man. Even her mother would be impressed by his athletic physique. His upper body, V-shaped from his shoulders to his waist, along with biceps, couldn't be possible without frequent trips to the gym unless he'd been blessed with crazy genetics. Liana wouldn't have been surprised to discover the man had a six-pack beneath the navy polo shirt. Not that she was about to look. Blond hair with bleached highlights and a tan that came from a salon gave him the appearance of a Californian, as opposed to someone who spent winters in Seattle.

Kevin played with a loose strand of her hair and continued his story about an unreasonable client. "She went into a tirade when I told her the ideas she wanted to use for the back of the house wouldn't structurally work or meet code. I finally convinced her to do what was necessary."

"Persistence paid off."

"More like patience." He cocked his head and smiled. "If you're smart and wait things out, you can get pretty much anything you want."

Something in the way he said it didn't feel right in her gut. Maybe it was the confidence ringing in his voice. There wasn't anything wrong in believing in yourself, was there? Didn't most successful people need a level of self-assurance or ego?

Liana gave an almost silent laugh. "I suppose no matter what a person does for a living, he or she is bound to run into difficult people. I have my share of them. Brides who think I can control the weather, CEOs who believe they should be able to get crab or lobster for half the market price. Shall I go on?"

"I get your point." He leaned in and tucked Liana's hair behind her ear. With the tip of his finger, he made a trail from the back of her ear, down her neck, to the top of her collar, sending sensual waves through her body.

"As soon I met you at Carolyn and Jack's wedding, I wanted to spend more time with you. You're beautiful ... interesting ... intelligent ..."

She'd welcome more time with him too.

"And I'd like to"—he lightly followed her jaw line with the pad of his thumb—"get to know you better."

His warm breath graced her cheek, and his lips drew closer to hers. Her heart tried to escape her chest as his other hand moved across her thigh. She turned her head the other direction, and he backed away.

Liana closed her eyes. She wanted his kiss—wanted it

since they'd first met—wanted it from the moment he'd walked through her door. But she wasn't willing to give what he sought in the heat of the moment.

"I'm serious, Liana." He reached over and gently rubbed her shoulder.

"I'd like that too." More than he would ever guess, especially after she refused his advance. "But I won't settle for a quick physical adventure," she said, forcing the words past the clog in her throat. "I want a relationship, not something that's going to be hot one night, then turn cold the next day. If we're going to spend time together, I want to learn more about you and give you a chance to know the real me."

"Okay." Kevin leaned back against the couch and nodded. "I understand."

"But ... do you agree?" Her breathing was shallow and labored. If he viewed things differently, she wouldn't see him again. She couldn't. That path would certainly lead to heartbreak, and she'd already had enough of that disgusting medicine.

"I do." He grasped her hand and massaged the top with his thumb. "It is important to take it slow and focus more on getting to know each other better—our likes—our dislikes."

"Thanks, Kevin." Liana sighed with relief. "I realize that may mean compromises on both sides."

Kevin raised his eyebrow. "So, you're willing to try new things?"

"Of course ..."

"Okay. You mentioned you're not a fan of jazz.

"That's true." Liana had a good idea of where this was heading.

"There's a popular jazz band playing at my favorite club

in Seattle on Friday night. Go with me." He grinned. "Maybe you don't like the genre because you don't understand it. This would be a great opportunity for me to teach you."

It was only fair that she give it a chance, especially if she wanted him to take her request seriously. She could handle one evening of clashing notes. "I have a wedding rehearsal at five o'clock that evening, but I'll be free after that. I could meet you at eight."

"It's a date." Kevin glanced at his watch. "I better hit the road. Important meeting first thing in the morning." He stood and still holding her hand, gently pulled her to her feet.

They walked hand in hand, and Liana relished the intimacy.

He opened the front door, and they stepped out onto the covered porch. "It's raining again."

"I have extra umbrellas."

"I'll be fine. But before I leave ... a goodnight kiss?" Kevin's steel-blue eyes held hers.

She smiled and nodded.

He tipped her chin up and brought his lips close to hers.

She closed her eyes to welcome the kiss. Warm lips gently caressed hers, but all too soon, it was over.

He drew away, and the cool night air filled the gap between them and chilled her body. Wanting to savor the moment, Liana was in no hurry to break the spell. She slowly revealed her eyes and found herself looking directly into his. His mouth turned up in a playful grin.

"I'm warning you. I'm coming back for more of that in the future." His lips briefly touched her cheek before he ran to his car for cover.

Liana leaned against the doorframe and watched Kevin drive away. Water dripped from the edge of the roof, plopping onto the wooden porch steps. She breathed in air, freshened from the rain, cleansing her lungs.

Light shone from a window in the garage apartment, exposing the shower descending from the heavens. Bryan must still be awake. She'd do something nice to thank him for coming to the rescue and fixing the clog in the drain. Bryan had saved the night from potential disaster.

But now, she had Kevin to think about. Being near him made her feel good about herself. Made her feel desirable.

Maybe her love life was finally turning around. She hadn't been this attracted to anyone since she'd fallen for Jason. Best friends since kindergarten, their relationship had grown into something more during their teen years. Camryn had destroyed that by flirting with him. But she'd grown tired of him within a few months, and when he came back to Liana, wanting to pick up where they'd left off, she'd refused.

Since then, it had become Liana's nature to find fault with any guy who came along. Less disappointment when the relationship crashed. Because it always did.

Now Kevin had walked into her life, and he was no less than charismatic. Liana wanted to embrace the possibility that he was sincere.

With the sound of rain hitting the porch roof and the light breeze spraying her face with refreshing moisture, she leaned against the railing.

"Are you there, God? Are you listening?" She searched the dark sky, as though she might catch a glimpse of him. "You've let me down so many times," she whispered into the night.

Liana briefly closed her eyes and sighed. "I'm asking you one more time to be on my side. I know this is probably selfish, but please, God, let things work out with Kevin. Please let him be real."

Her cheeks were still warm. Kevin's touch and kiss had evoked emotions Liana hadn't felt in a long time. A walk down to the stable would help clear her head. A smile grew on her face. She was becoming more like her father every day. Not wanting to ruin her silk blouse, she'd take a few minutes to slip into jeans, a light sweater, and boots.

Her hair whipped across her face, shielding her eyes for a moment. The rain had slowed, but the wind had picked up. Before going in to change, she had one more request to make.

"And God ... if it's not too much to ask on top of my other request ... I'd be grateful if you'd help me find a place for the gala. It's probably not a big deal to you, but a lot of people are counting on me."

Eight

Hidden in the shadows beneath the exposed stairway to his apartment, Bryan watched Liana kiss the visitor, and his stomach knotted. He'd reached the bottom of the stairs when the door opened and the couple moved outside. Not wanting to intrude, he scrambled beneath the stairs, knelt down, and wrapped his arms around Rainey to keep him from bounding into the open and disturbing the two lovebirds.

Liana was obviously involved, and whether it was serious or not, it was better for Bryan to know and face the reality that she was out of his reach. A relationship with any woman wasn't in his future. He knew that. Why did he keep forgetting it when Liana was around?

Her boyfriend drove off, and she slipped inside the cottage and closed the door. Bryan sighed with relief. It would damage any trust he'd built if she thought he was slinking around, spying. Not to mention the beating his pride would take if she had the opportunity to compare him to someone who looked like he'd walked off a movie set.

What was he thinking? He barely knew the woman. They'd only spoken a few words. Still, he couldn't believe that Liana was anything like Jenny. He thought she was the love of his life, and he would have done anything for her, but Jenny had walked away when he needed love and support the most.

Time at the stable would relax him. Bryan released his hold on Rainey, stood, and readjusted the camera sheltered beneath his coat. With the extra bulk, it was impossible to zip up the jacket. He'd have to keep it tightly gripped in front so the wind wouldn't expose the equipment to the drizzling rain. There'd been a lull in the blustery weather, but Bryan felt a shift in the temperature. Something was brewing.

With the Lab at his side, Bryan sauntered down the path. The horses would be glad to see him. Dr. Tate had left on a flight to Los Angeles earlier that evening to attend a medical conference and would be gone until Friday evening.

Bryan turned on several small lights, hung his coat on a hook, and greeted each mare individually before checking the lighting and raising his camera to take a shot of Lexus. The Arabian leaned his head over the stall. Rainey jumped up and placed his front paws on the stall door, as if to say hello. Bryan focused the lens and pressed the shutter release.

"You're a photographer?"

The sound of Liana's voice had startled him and revved up his heart. If he hadn't been so focused on the shoot, he'd been more aware of his surroundings.

She'd asked a question, but did she want a detailed answer or was she making small talk? Bryan lowered the camera and twisted his body enough to see her. "It's a hobby."

Maybe she'd seen him lurking in the dark while she made out with Hunky Guy and was there to chew him out. He didn't mean to be a voyeur, but would she understand that he happened to be at the wrong place at the wrong time?

"Do you normally take pictures late at night?" Liana moved close to the Arabian's stall and massaged the area between the horse's eyes and muzzle.

"Couldn't sleep. Thought coming down here might help me unwind."

"Me too. It's peaceful here." Liana slid her hands into the front pockets of her jeans and leaned back against the stall door.

Did Liana want to be alone? There was no indication that she wanted him to leave, so he'd stay.

"You had a nice evening with your boyfriend? The garbage disposal didn't give you any more problems, did it?" Bryan didn't wish anything to go wrong for Liana, but on the other hand, it would have been kind of fun to see how the pretty boy handled a backed-up sink. *Not that I resent the man.* His conscience pricked him. There was a time when Bryan hated being called a pretty boy. It wasn't right to give another guy the label.

"The disposal worked fine, thanks to you." Liana's cheeks turned a slight shade of pink. "And ... he's not my boyfriend."

"Oh." Bryan shifted his stance. "Sorry for the mistake."

"We're getting to know each other. It's nothing official." Liana pushed away from the stall door. "I should get back to the cottage and let you take your pictures."

He felt torn between wanting her to leave and wishing she'd stay and talk. "Hear back from Erik? About the building?" The questions had poured out before he could stop them. Apparently his subconscious wanted her to stay.

"Dalisay and I are meeting with him and his wife tomorrow afternoon. He didn't want to discuss it over the phone. I'm hoping it's not because he wants to let us down easy." Liana chewed on her lower lip. "If I don't get that space, I don't know what I'm going to do."

"Have faith. Everything will work out."

Liana gave a small smile. "You sound like my father."

A strong gust of wind blew the loosely closed stable door wide open. A loud crack echoed, and gazing out the open door, they watched a massive limb from a tree break from the trunk and crash to the ground. Bryan grabbed the latch and pulled the door closed, making sure it was secure.

"Looks like we're in for a big storm." Liana's eyes displayed concern.

"We shouldn't leave until it settles down out there." Bryan's nerves needed calming. The last time he was stuck in a barn because of a storm, it had changed his life. But now he needed to set his own feelings aside and focus on helping Liana feel safe.

The lights in the stable flickered.

"I don't know if Dad warned you, but we tend to lose power during these storms."

"He showed me where the generators are for each building and how to start them." At least they wouldn't be stuck in the dark if the electricity went out.

Liana sank down on a nearby hay bale where Mitzi, the three-legged cat, immediately climbed into her lap, purring and begging for attention. Liana stroked the furry creature and murmured affectionate words.

While she seemed preoccupied with the animal, Bryan made a few quick adjustments on the camera for low lighting, peered through the lens, and focused on Liana.

Her head popped up. "No! Please don't."

He lowered the equipment. "I'm sorry." Bryan felt like a jerk. He should have asked permission. "I didn't mean to cross any lines."

"No, that's not it." She brushed cat hair off her sweater and jeans. "I'm not good in front of a camera. Really."

"I'm not all that great *behind* the camera, so we kind of have something in common." He attempted a grin. "We have some time to kill—it's only practice."

"Okay." She seemed resigned, but scrunched up her face. "What do you want me to do?"

"Just be ... you." Bryan shrugged. "Pretend I'm not here."

Liana smirked. "Sure. Easy."

He stepped back and feigned interest in changing the camera settings until Liana became engaged in playing with Mitzi. Then he slowly raised the instrument and began shooting. After a few minutes, Liana seemed more at ease with having her photo taken, so he decided to take a risk.

"Hold her up and look straight at me."

Liana leaned her cheek against the feline's head, and the cat nuzzled her nose. It must have tickled, because Liana giggled. Bryan clicked the shutter. For a brief moment, she looked directly into the camera and gave a slight smile, her eyes warm and inviting. Light coming from a small wall lamp provided a soft glow. With his heartbeat matching the pounding rain on the roof, Bryan snapped the photo.

Studying her through the lens, he whispered under his breath, "Beautiful."

The smile on her face and the light in her eyes vacated as though a switch had been flipped. Liana jumped up from the hay bale.

"Okay. I think we've done enough." She stroked her palms on her thighs and brushed off stray pieces of hay. "Since this was purely for practice, please delete all the photos."

From the sound of it, something sizeable hit against the window, and they both jumped.

"I'd like to study them so I can do better next time."

"I can tell you what you can do better. A different subject will make a vast improvement." Liana fidgeted with the hem of her sweater. "I—I need to go."

Bryan's heart sank like an anchor thrown overboard. How could she feel that way about herself? If only she'd been willing to look at the photo he'd taken, Liana might have seen herself through his eyes—a lovely woman—an angel in disguise. He didn't want her to leave. "It's still raining." That sounded lame, but what he'd meant was, with flying debris outside, she may not be safe out there until the winds let up.

"Trust me. I won't melt." Her words cut through the air as she flung open the stable door and ran out into the wet night.

He'd done something to make her angry. But what?

Liana closed the cottage door and stood on the rug, allowing it to drink in the water escaping her wet boots and drenched clothes. Tears mixed with sliding raindrops on her cheeks. She shoved wet, matted-down hair from her eyes and glanced at her damp hand, smeared with mascara. She'd made a mess. No—she *was* a mess.

The blinds were drawn. No one could see inside the cottage. Liana tugged her feet free from her boots. She peeled off the cold, clinging clothes, scooped them into her arms, and threw them into the washing machine. Shivering, she scooted to the bathroom, dried off, and enveloped herself in a cozy robe.

After turning off the small lamp on her nightstand, she leaned against a pile of pillows, and still in her robe, snuggled underneath the covers to warm her chilled body.

Rain pelted against the bedroom windows as she stared into the dark. The evening with Kevin had gone so well. That man was attracted to her. *To her!* He made her feel desirable. And then she had to ruin it by going to the stable.

It wasn't Bryan's fault. He had no way of knowing taking photos of her would be like ripping scabs from wounds that wouldn't heal.

She was seven years old, and Camryn was five when it happened. The first time Liana realized that Camryn was the pretty daughter and Liana was not. They'd stopped with their father at a photo shoot to surprise their mother. One of the photographers took one look at Camryn and asked if he could take a few pictures. Liana asked if he would also take some of her, but he brushed her off. From that day forward, Camryn modeled—for catalogs, magazines, even a few commercials before their mother opened her own agency.

After all the attention her sister received, Liana didn't feel worthy of being captured on film. She didn't need people pointing out her flaws or making comparisons to her sister. Family portraits and the necessary school photos were torture, but whenever possible, Liana avoided having her picture taken.

In the stable with Bryan, for the first time that she could remember, she actually enjoyed being in front of the camera. Maybe it was because of his appearance and believing he wouldn't judge her. But when she heard him utter that one word—*beautiful*—she was flung back into reality like a drug addict crashing after being high.

Earlier that evening, Kevin had told her she was beautiful, and she'd soaked it in as though she were a piece of dry bread, lathered with compliments made of melted butter or sweet, clover honey.

She didn't understand why Bryan merely speaking the word deeply affected her.

No—the problem was she *did* understand.

Somehow, Bryan had seen something in her that no one else ever had, including Kevin.

And that both thrilled and scared her.

Nine

"I've talked to management in every theater where I have connections and a few where I pretended to know somebody who knows somebody." Dalisay flung her purse on Liana's sofa and landed next to it. "I can't borrow enough set pieces to even come close to what we'll need to fill the space, even if Mr. Jones tells us the hospital gala can be held at his place."

Liana rubbed her weary eyes. She'd struggled to believe she could stay within budget for the gala and still provide an extraordinary experience for attendees, but this news was strangling the life out of that hope.

"Are you sure you've checked every possibility?"

Dalisay flipped her long black hair over her shoulder, and her eyebrows hiked up. "Are you kidding? I've been to every theater in Seattle and the surrounding area, looking through dusty, spider-filled storage rooms for anything I could borrow, beg, or steal." She leaned forward. "Read my lips. We. Don't. Have. Enough."

"I'm sorry. I shouldn't have questioned you." Liana's neck and shoulders felt like they harbored knots the size of golf balls. "I know you've been doing everything you can. I'm a bit discouraged. And tired. I didn't get much sleep last night."

"Oh, man! I didn't even ask about your dinner date with Kevin. It must have gone well if he stayed—wait a minute—

you didn't—" Dalisay's dark eyes pierced Liana's.

"No!" She threw a decorative pillow at her friend. "We didn't have a sleepover."

"Happy to hear it." Dalisay's lips turned up in a sly grin. "But you had a good time?"

"We had such a great time that he asked me to go with him to hear a jazz band this Friday night." She'd been more *jazzed* about spending another evening with Kevin before the incident in the stable with Bryan. Liana should have known better than to pose for the camera. Having her photo taken brought memories to the surface that made her feel vulnerable, and that frightened her.

"You hate jazz."

Maybe Liana shouldn't have agreed so readily. Could she endure an entire evening of musicians plunking on bases and trumpets blaring? But she'd been the one to suggest they compromise on each other likes and dislikes, so she couldn't back out now.

Liana sighed. "Well, maybe I could learn to like it. Haven't you lectured me to get out more and expand my interests?"

"True." Dalisay hugged the thrown pillow into her chest. "So, you didn't sleep much because the two of you just sat and talked for hours, revealing your souls." There was a hint of sarcasm in her voice.

"Could you make your feelings any clearer?" Liana wished Dalisay would offer even a little support. "C'mon, I like the guy."

"I'll try to be nice, but I can't help it if I'm protective. He's a charmer, and for some reason, I don't trust him."

"Give him a chance, and you'll see that Kevin's not a

player." Liana tucked loose strands of hair behind her ear. Could Dalisay hear the doubt in her voice? "What kept me up last night was that crazy storm." *Mostly.*

She didn't want to talk about her visit to the stable after Kevin left. Dalisay already liked the caretaker, even though they'd only met briefly at Erik's. If she knew he'd talked Liana into having her photo taken, her friend would be even more "Team Bryan." Dalisay was the only person, besides Liana, who knew how she felt about photographs.

Time to change the subject. Liana plopped down next to Dalisay and leaned her head against the back of the sofa. "What are we going to do about the gala?"

"First of all, we won't know if Erik and his wife are even going to allow the event to be held in their building until we talk to them." Dalisay was the practical partner in this duo, and given Liana's recent distractions and emotional state, she appreciated her BFF's opinions. "If they agree, you'll have a place for the gala, but it will solve only one problem."

Liana released a long sigh. "And the other problem?"

"You may need to downscale your grand plan and come up with something else."

"We'll never get another chance like this, Daysie."

"I know." Dalisay dropped the pillow and put her arm around her friend's shoulder. "I want it too. But I think it's easier for me to let go, Lee, than it is for you. I'm not trying to prove anything to my family. If you ask me—which you didn't, but I'm going to tell you anyway—you push yourself too hard when it comes to earning gold stars."

"What was I thinking?" Liana groaned and laid her head on Dalisay's shoulder. "Why can't I be content with planning simple weddings and birthday parties? Why do I have to organize the biggest shindig this side of the Cascades?"

"Because you're a Tate. You come from a family of overa-chievers." She glanced at her watch. "We need to leave. Didn't you tell Erik we'd meet with him and Maggie at two o'clock?" Dalisay stood and flung her purse strap over her shoulder. "C'mon. We can't tackle any problems until we know what they are."

"Hi! I'm Maggie, Erik's wife."

The attractive, slim woman with emerald-green eyes, a smattering of freckles across her nose, and copper-colored hair, stood at the front door. She greeted Liana and Dalisay before they even had a chance to ascend the stairs to the building they hoped would house the hospital fundraiser.

Their hostess grasped their hands in turn. "I've looked forward to meeting you ever since Erik explained what you wanted to do here."

Liana smiled at the woman. So far so good! If Maggie was this enthusiastic about meeting them, perhaps they stood a chance! "We've felt the same about you."

Dalisay nodded in agreement.

Maggie waved them up the stairs. "Come on in. I have a pot of strong coffee and several desserts made by a chef we may hire. It would be great to get your feedback."

Liana shot a questioning glance at Dalisay as they followed Maggie inside, and her friend raised her eyebrows back. All the talk about hiring a chef and wanting their input had to be a positive sign.

But along with hearing Erik and Maggie's decision, Liana

wanted a chance to explain that after all their consideration, the plans would have to change. Dalisay couldn't work miracles from her meager supplies. What if that information changed everything? What would she do?

Erik sat hunched over a laptop, but seeing them, he jumped from his chair at the kitchen table. "Thanks for coming. Excuse me for not greeting you at the door. I was going over several electrical and plumbing bids on work that needs to be done." He stacked and set a pile of papers aside. "Please grab some coffee or tea, as well as whatever else you'd like. Maggie probably explained that we're beginning to look for experienced people to fill our staff, including cooks."

Maggie winked at the other two women. "I think they prefer to be called chefs, honey."

A serving cart nearby held two pots, one with coffee and the other with hot water, and an assortment of teas and mugs. There were enough servings of marble cheesecake, dark chocolate layer cake, fruit tarts, and *crème brûlée* for them to try a small portion of each. Dalisay's eyes doubled in size. Liana tried to conceal a smile. Her slim friend's sweet tooth was about to be satisfied and then some.

"Thank you." Liana poured a cup of coffee and inhaled the aroma.

Dalisay sat down at the table with her sketchpad, a cup of steaming tea, a wedge of cake, and a satisfied grin on her face. One taste of chocolate and her eyes lit up. "This is amazing!"

"That's good to know! I'm anxious to try them all, but I'll start with the *crème brûlée.*" Maggie slid a spoonful of the creamy dessert into her mouth. "Mmm ... fabulous."

To be polite, Liana picked the smallest slice of cheesecake she could find. It wouldn't hurt to eat a few bites. Her nerves would quickly burn through the calories. She grabbed a chair next to Dalisay, and with a shaking hand, opened her notebook. What had the couple decided?

Maggie slid into a chair next to Erik, and they locked hands on the table before he spoke. "We've thought long and hard about this."

"And prayed about it," Maggie interjected.

He held her hand. "And prayed about it. We wanted to tell you in person that we love the ideas you two have come up with, and we want to go ahead and hold the gala here."

Liana's body flooded with relief, then quickly drained. "I can't tell you how happy we are to hear that, but ..."

Erik and Maggie glanced at each other, and then looked at Liana with questions in their eyes. Erik cleared his throat. "But ...?" No doubt he'd been expecting a positive reaction.

The lump in Liana's throat threatened to choke her. Would they now lose all confidence in her? Had all their plans—and the couple's prayers—been a waste of time? "As hard as Dalisay has worked to come up with set pieces that we could borrow, she hasn't been able to find what we need. So, with the budget we have to work with, the only solution we have is to either construct something far less than what we promised, or come up with a much simpler theme and design."

There, she said it. If they backed out, she'd have to accept their decision. But at least she'd been honest with them. And it would be simply one more time when God chose not to throw a little help her way.

Erik winked at Maggie.

Liana didn't expect that reaction. "I'm not joking. I just explained that what you thought you were agreeing to isn't possible."

"I know." Erik grew more serious. "We're not making light of what you stated. It's only that—"

"We feel led by God to go a slightly different route."

"I'm confused." Liana turned to Dalisay to get her reaction, but she shrugged and looked as bewildered as Liana felt.

"It's simple." Erik hit several keys on his laptop. "We'll provide the building at no charge for the gala. But we'd like a receipt for whatever amount you feel the space is worth so we can use it as a tax deduction. It's a win-win for both of us."

"Done." Liana appreciated their encouraging offer, but until she understood Erik's direction, she couldn't embrace victory. What changes had they envisioned?

He swung the laptop around so both Dalisay and Liana could view the website he'd opened. "It was brought to our attention that themed restaurants are popular. Take a look."

Liana never imagined anything existed like what she saw on the website that displayed not several, but one hundred unique themed restaurants in the world. Photos showed airplane diners in Korea, an Alice in Wonderland-themed restaurant in Tokyo, futuristic Parisian bakeries, chalkboard cafés, tree house restaurants, and jungle dining. There was even a toilet-themed dining chain in Taiwan. Liana's stomach stirred. That last option was a bit over the top for her.

"During the last few days, our dreams have been opened to new possibilities." Erik's eyes shone. "As a new venue, we want to draw people from all over the area, including visiting tourists, but we're not in the heart of Seattle, so we need to provide something that's one-of-a-kind."

"What he's taking so long to say," Maggie chimed in, "is that if you're willing to let us use Dalisay's designs, we'd like to build something permanent here. We want to offer fantasy for children's parties so they can escape technology for a few hours and tap into their imagination. And with a built-in stage, we can host plays for children. We'd also bring in musicians—solo performers and bands to entertain adults in the evenings."

Dalisay gripped Liana's arm, as though to test whether they were in a dream—or not.

"Adults can use a break from reality too. So, besides being a themed restaurant, we'd have something special and different to offer from any other venue in the area." Erik's voice raised with excitement. "We'd also like to take a look at creative ways we could continue utilizing the space for large events—like fundraisers and wedding receptions.

"Of course, we'll pay Dalisay for her designs and give credit to your grandfather's novel, Liana—if you agree to all of this." Maggie sounded as enthusiastic as a child receiving a birthday wish. "If we could get enough copies, we could even offer the books to our customers."

"We'll cover the cost of materials to create a replica of the Manalee that's in your grandfather's story, but we'll want help finding people who can build what we need. General contractors don't have experience in constructing the kind of setting we're talking about." Erik bounced glances between Liana and Dalisay. "What do you say?"

The grip on Liana's arm tightened, and without looking at Liana, Dalisay spoke up. "I—I would love to design this space! I'll do it for nothing. To see my vision come to life would be an amazing honor. And I'm sure I can rally the theater community to come and help with building various pieces. Maybe we could offer paid hours for the same amount of hours donated."

"I like that idea." Maggie's eyes sparkled. "And of course, along with marketing the book, we can find a way to also give credit to you for artistic skills."

Dalisay gazed at Liana. "You haven't said a word. Aren't you excited?"

Excited? Absolutely! Liana also felt numb. Stunned. Scared. Her eyes blurred, but she blinked them clear. "It sounds too good to be true."

Did she dare trust this good fortune? She'd prayed about the gala the night before, still questioning if God really cared. But Erik and Maggie confessed to also praying, and they felt led to making this huge decision. Was God really in the middle of this?

"We're serious about moving forward." Erik looked at her earnestly. "Partners?"

Liana moistened her lips and smiled with relief. "Partners."

"Then, let's get to work." Erik swung his laptop around to face him.

"May I ask a question?" Liana's curiosity nudged her. "What prompted you to think about using a permanent fantasy theme? I mean—I know you said you prayed about it, but did God actually put the idea in your head?"

"He gave us peace inside and a feeling of confirmation." Erik leaned back in his chair. "But Bryan showed us the website and suggested that we seriously consider it. He came over shortly after your last visit with a list of reasons why it would initially benefit the hospital but also our business in the long run. He presented such a good case, we gave it some thought."

So, Bryan had come to her rescue. Again. "Why would he put so much effort into convincing you?"

Erik gulped down the last of his coffee. "All I know is that he has ties to the hospital, and he wants the fundraiser to be a success. He'll do whatever he can to help."

The caretaker had once again gone out of his way to show unexpected kindness and support for what Liana was trying to accomplish. Surely, he had many other things to tend to—think about—but he'd taken the time to pitch an idea that would serve not only the gala, but also Erik and Maggie in the future. What motivated Bryan? What was underneath the quiet, reserved, gentle man?

She sighed, confused. Why was she so intrigued by Bryan, when by all appearances, Kevin was everything she wanted in a man and more?

Ten

Bryan flopped down on the sagging, navy blue couch that had seen better days. The swirling maroon design had faded to gray, and springs under the surface pushing the thinning fabric up on the seat cushion looked like mole hills. A cigarette burn had created a hole in one arm during a party he'd given years ago. But the couch would have to last a little longer before he was able to purchase something new. The doc had provided a bed with a new mattress, a nightstand, and a dresser, overwhelming Bryan with the man's generosity.

"Sit down, Sis. Make yourself at home."

Beth slowly lowered herself and then readjusted her position several times. "You know, the time does come when being thrifty is overdone. I'm afraid the springs on this thing have sprung. Even missionaries in Africa with nothing but dirt floors would have a hard time appreciating it."

Bryan's laughter came from his belly. "A missionary can't always be choosy and neither can I." The look on Beth's face as she landed on a protruding coil set him howling again. "I'm sorry. Really I am."

She scowled. "Sure you are."

He jumped up and jogged to his bedroom to grab a pillow and comforter from the bed.

"Did you plant this couch here to get back at me for putting rocks in your bed when we were kids?" she yelled after him. "Fine thing. I come for a visit, and I'm tortured. What more could a girl ask for?"

"Quit your grumbling." Bryan carried the items to the couch, pulled his sister up, and then arranged the comforter and pillow so she'd have a soft place to land. "There you go, princess."

"Thank you, kind sir." She fell into the cushy arrangement. "Ahhh ... now that's more like it." A contented smile filled her face. "For that act of chivalry, I'll make dinner."

"I assumed you were going to, with all the grocery bags you hauled in here." He plopped down on his side of the couch.

"You could have assumed wrong. I might have expected you to cook, considering the fact that I provided the means."

"I'll make you a deal. If you take care of dinner, I'll whip up a batch of my famous apple and cinnamon pancakes in the morning."

She thought for a moment. "Deal." A smirk appeared. "I would have made both, but I like this arrangement better."

"Aside from the lumpy couch, what do you really think of the place?"

"I like it." She glanced around the room. "It's cozy, but the earth tones on the wall still keep it masculine. Very you."

"Earth tones, huh? I thought I used brown and beige."

"Regardless, you've done a nice job with the place. You need a few comfy chairs and a more respectable couch, and you'll be all set."

"If Mack and Jenny hadn't made off with the rest of my furniture, I would have had more stuff than this place could hold." His former bandmate and girlfriend had taken more from him than material things. Bryan tried not to grit his teeth.

"They wronged you big time. And I'm not just talking about leaving this dump of a couch for you."

Bryan searched the ceiling for the right words to express what his heart had struggled with, but no words could adequately describe the betrayal he felt after the fire. "I'm working on letting it go." Maybe someday it wouldn't sting quite so much.

"You're a good person, Bryan. A better man than what Jenny will ever deserve. And a better friend than what Mack ever was to you."

"Wherever they are now, I hope they're enjoying my stuff because I've learned to live without it. God has blessed me with a great job. Rainey has a place to run, and the mountains are only a breath away."

"It is beautiful out here."

"This apartment won't ever look anything like the other places on the estate, but it's mine for now." He stretched out and laid his arm along the top of the couch. "You should see the main house. It's amazing. I even like Liana's cottage more. It's nice, but it's ... comfortable."

"Liana?"

"My employer's daughter."

"Hmmm ..." Beth's eyes squinted as she nodded.

"What's the *hmmm* ... all about?"

"She must be pretty."

"What does that have to do with anything?"

"A sister knows." The corners of her lips turned up. "You're attracted to her."

"It wouldn't matter if I was—and I'm not saying I am," he sputtered. "Look at me. I could never fit in with her life—her high-profile family."

"Don't."

"Don't what? Be realistic?" He rubbed the back of his neck. "I know you love me and mean well, but I need to accept what's happened to me."

"Okay, I won't bring it up again." Beth reached over, touched his hand, and looked him in the eye. "I want you to be happy."

"I'm working on it." He winked. "I'm learning to stand on my own again."

"I can see that." She picked up the framed picture sitting on the coffee table in front of them. Rainey, with his head cocked, stared back at her from the photo. "You're using the camera again."

"Getting back into photography has been ... well, I guess you could say ... therapeutic." He scratched his chin. "I've been thinking about pursuing it more seriously. It's okay being a handyman, and I appreciate the job here, but I need something more creative. Maybe with practice and time, I could find a gig for a magazine or work freelance shooting nature and off-the-grid locations."

"You certainly have an eye and natural talent—and several awards to prove it."

Bryan laughed. "Yeah, that was back in high school. I have a lot to learn before going pro."

Beth pushed her body up from the puffy comforter. "I'll be right back." She slipped outside for a moment and then returned with something in hand. "I think it's time you renewed another passion."

Just seeing the case robbed his breath. Bryan hadn't see it since before the fire ... before his career had gone up in smoke, literally. He rested his hands on his hips. "You shouldn't have brought that here."

"I don't agree."

"I can't live on dreams anymore, Beth."

"Wrong, big brother. You can't live without them."

The day up to this point, couldn't have been more perfect.

As the sun rose that morning, Liana had slipped on yoga pants before hitting the path her family had created, with the help of a crew, behind the cottage that trailed through the woods. Over the years, they'd all enjoyed the walking trail. Three miles later and home again, she'd gulped a blueberry smoothie made fresh in the blender. After a shower, she dressed and prepared for the Tuesday morning commute into Seattle.

The brainstorming session later that morning with several clients had been exhilarating. They had taste and class.

Now Liana cranked up the radio and lowered the windows as she cruised down the road toward home. The wind whipped her hair around her face as she sang along to the country song. What if she couldn't carry a tune. It was a stunning spring Tuesday, and the only thing that could have made it better would have been driving a convertible.

Before she'd left the city, Liana had stopped at a favorite bakery. The backseat held a bag of hearty earthen breads, along with an assortment of pastries. She owed Bryan for fixing the disposal so quickly, as well as proposing the permanent fantasy theme to Erik and Maggie. One way to thank a man was to feed him, but she couldn't fathom cooking him dinner. That would feel a bit intimate. However, she could give him specialty foods as an appreciation gift.

A ballad, filled with words of love and passion, blared from the car stereo. Liana chuckled. What would Kevin think of her choice in music? Excited to spend time with him on Friday night, she felt less enthusiastic about listening to jazz for an entire evening. But she'd agreed to give it a try, and she wouldn't bail now.

She turned the car onto the estate's driveway. An unfamiliar station wagon with Oregon plates sat parked in front of the main house garage. It probably belonged to one of her father's friends or colleagues, but it looked fairly old. Her father's peers leaned more toward luxury models, like the four that were at one time housed in his own expansive garage.

Liana entered her living room, which was bright from the late afternoon sun, and dumped binders and pamphlets on her desk. She dug out a large wicker basket from a hall closet. After draping a checkered cloth inside, she loaded the basket with purchases from the bakery and tucked a thank-you note in the corner.

She sauntered up the path, then around to the side of the garage, and climbed the steps to Bryan's apartment. He didn't answer her knock. Part of her wanted him to be anywhere but there. Then she could leave the gift without having to explain. Liana stepped to the railing and peered below, toward the stable. From that vantage point, she could see Bryan leading a horse inside.

"May I help you?" A female voice came from behind.

Startled, Liana almost dropped the basket. She swung around to see a woman who couldn't have been much older than herself, dressed in jeans and a short-sleeved red blouse. She was about Liana's height but carried more weight in the waist and hips.

"I was—uh—looking for Bryan," she pointed toward the stable, "but I see he's down there."

The woman gave a knowing smile. "You must be Liana."

Liana held out the basket in her hands. "I'll leave this for him."

"Housewarming gift?"

"More like a thank-you. Bryan came to my rescue a few days ago."

Her eyes enlarged. "Oh?"

Obviously the newcomer wanted an explanation. "He unclogged a disposal for me before a guest arrived. He saved me a lot of embarrassment."

The lady lifted the cloth, displaying a wedding ring on her left hand, and inhaled the aroma from the fresh-baked goods. "That smells heavenly. I promised him lasagna for dinner, and the bread will go perfectly with it." She stepped back without taking the basket from Liana's hands. "Would you like to come in?"

"I didn't plan on staying. I just wanted to—"

"Please. At least for a few minutes." She held the door open.

Liana hesitated. She never expected to find anyone other than Bryan at the apartment and didn't want to intrude. But on the other hand, she was intrigued and followed her inside. "Are you Bryan's wife?"

Amused laughter trickled from her lips. "Where did you get that idea?"

"The wedding ring on your hand. You being here. Making

him dinner."

"I'm Beth, his sister."

Liana's shoulders relaxed. "Oh!" Why did she feel relieved? "Sorry. I shouldn't have made assumptions."

"He told me about you and your father, but obviously he never mentioned his family to you. Or that I was coming for a visit, the rat." Beth took the basket from Liana and placed it on the kitchen counter separating that area from the living room.

"No, he didn't." Now that she looked closer, Liana saw the resemblance. Beth had Bryan's blues eyes and dark hair, except hers included short and soft-looking natural curls.

"I'm not surprised. He's become quite private the last few years." Beth climbed onto one of the swivel stools sitting near the counter. She motioned for Liana to do the same. "His couch has a few loose springs," she whispered, as though there was even a slight chance of him overhearing the comment.

Beth hesitated, appearing to think through what she might say next. "The opportunity for Bryan to live and work here is an answer to prayer."

"To be honest, I don't know much about your brother. We've actually said few words to each other since he moved here." Liana cringed inside at that acknowledgment. "I had no clue he had a sister."

"Well, here I am. The younger—but not by much—and sometimes bossy sister." Even as she smiled, her eyes became moist. "Bryan lived with my family after being released from the hospital." She rubbed the corner of her eye. "We loved having him with us, but it wasn't the best situation for him long term. He needed to gain his independence again, and he's found it here. I haven't seen him this content in a long time."

"You have a family."

Beth laughed, almost to herself. "My husband, Richard, is a pastor. We live in Portland with our two kids."

"How old?"

"Jacob is four and Leah is two. Richard took a day off from his church responsibilities and gave me a twenty-four-hour reprieve from mom duties. It's back to work for both of us tomorrow." She smiled thoughtfully. "Leah loves her uncle Bryan. That child can't get enough of him. He calls her his little kitten."

"Do you and Bryan have other relatives?" Liana probably sounded way too nosey, but the woman did practically beg her to stay.

"Our grandmother lives in a retirement home. She's the sweetest woman you'd ever meet, but her memory is a bit lacking these days. When I visit I never know if she'll remember who I am or not. My brother hasn't seen her since the fire. He's afraid it will upset her more than his not visiting."

"My father told me Bryan was burned in a barn fire."

"Mm-hmm. We were raised by grandparents who did whatever they could to give us a happy childhood. So, after our grandfather died, Bryan moved back in to help our grandmother adjust. He planned to stay only until they could figure out what she wanted to do with the place."

Liana was drawn into the story, and she began to put the pieces together, her heart aching for Bryan and what she knew was coming.

"And then one night, lightning struck. He saved the animals but got caught in the fire." Beth grabbed a tissue from a box sitting on the counter and wiped her nose. "Sorry, it's been three years, but it's still hard ..."

"It's okay. Take your time." Liana reached for her own tissue and wiped moisture from her eyes. She was caught up in the emotion held in Beth's voice. Clearly, she loved her brother.

Beth cleared her throat. "By the grace of God, he managed to crawl out before the roof collapsed. It was a miracle he survived at all."

Bryan wasn't merely someone who tended the horses. He was a hero—an extraordinary, unselfish man. A person who had a family, relatives who loved and cared about him. People who knew him before his outward appearance drastically changed. Convinced she'd only heard part of Bryan's story in those few minutes with Beth, Liana was fascinated and wanted to learn more.

Liana glanced at her watch. "I better go." She slid off the stool. "I still have some calls to make." She turned toward the door and spotted a classical guitar propped in the corner of the small living room. "Bryan's?"

A shadow crossed Beth's face as she nodded. "Inherited from our grandfather. I brought it for him."

"He must have been thrilled to get it."

"On the contrary. He wasn't happy at all." A sly grin grew on her face. "But it's staying. Whether he likes it or not.

Eleven

"Was I wrong? Isn't this place stellar?" Kevin lifted the bottle of expensive wine from the table. "Would you like more?"

"No, thank you." She'd barely touched what the waiter had initially poured. "You were right. It's very nice."

The jazz venue was far from the dark, hole-in-the-wall place she'd envisioned. A premier dinner club, it had won numerous awards. Many people occupied tables on the main floor, and additional seating was available in the mezzanine above. Each table offered its own intimate space in the dimly lit room, and candles added to the ambience.

Their waiter focused his attention on Liana. "Are you ready to order?"

"I'd like the salad greens with pine nuts, parmesan, and champagne vinaigrette. That will be it for me. Thank you."

"You can't come here and not try the filet mignon." Kevin grinned. "Trust me. You won't regret it."

Remember, Liana, no more people-pleasing. "Thanks for the recommendation, but I couldn't possibly eat that much food."

"It's your decision, but you don't know what you're missing." Kevin winked at her, then handed the waiter their menus. "I'll have the filet mignon, medium rare, with the herb demi-glaze sauce, and the roasted vegetables. He embraced Liana's hand and lightly massaged the top of her hand with his thumb.

It was important to Kevin that she have a nice time, but she didn't need an expensive dinner to enjoy herself, and she certainly didn't want that much food. It was nice—being here with him—on an actual date. Liana smiled, and with her free hand, slid a wandering spaghetti strap back to the top of her shoulder. The black cocktail dress had been a good choice. Kevin had expressed his approval several times that evening, and she felt confident in her appearance.

Music emitting from the stage vibrated against Liana's chest. The drums drove the ten-piece band while the bass guitar laid the foundation. The trumpets, saxes, and key-board filled in the rest. Spontaneous clapping erupted as instrumentalists finished their solos.

Two salads were placed in front of them, but Kevin didn't seem to notice. She tasted hers, and savored the delicious dressing. Next to her, he subtly moved his body to the music, while tapping his fingers on the table to the beat.

He wrapped his other arm around her shoulder and leaned in. "This music does something to me," he whispered into her ear. Her breath caught in her throat, but it only took a second for Kevin to become so engaged in the music again that she was spared giving a response.

The set ended and the band left the stage for a short break as their waiter arrived with his filet mignon.

Kevin pushed his untouched salad to the side and sliced the meat. "You haven't told me what you think of the music."

"It's different—funkier than I expected."

"Funkier?"

"Most jazz I've heard has been so," she debated her confession, "well—annoying."

He gave her a puzzled look.

Liana gently touched his arm. "No offense. I was raised on classical music where notes are organized, and there's a melody. Jazz sounds like a jumbled mess to me." She smiled, hoping her honesty wouldn't turn him off.

"Improvisation takes another type of talent. It's still based on a pattern of chords. Jazz is earthy. Primal." He took a sip of wine, then grinned. "That's why I like it. It's all about passion. Not stuffy like Bach."

She hadn't thought of jazz in those terms before, but they helped her appreciate the music. Funny how perception could change if you were willing to throw away first impressions and then go beyond them. "I'm willing to learn."

"Lesson number one. There's more than one type of jazz. This band combines jazz, funk, rock, and soul." He tilted his head, eyeing her. "Are you enjoying being here at all?"

She nodded. "The food is delicious, and I'm spending time with you." That was truth. And although she wasn't ready for a steady diet of jazz, it wasn't as bad as she thought.

Kevin returned her smile, leaned closer, and brushed a kiss on her temple.

"Maybe another later when we don't have eyes watching?" he whispered, his warm lips tickling her ear.

A flush burned her cheeks. It was intoxicating to feel wanted.

"I'm getting another drink." Kevin motioned to a waiter. "Would you like anything?"

"No thanks, I'm fine."

She glanced around the room while he explained his order to the young gentleman who responded. She caught the eye of a red-haired woman in her twenties who sat several tables behind them. Her companions, two males and a female, were engaged in a lively discussion. The woman seemed oblivious to her friends, and instead, focused on Liana.

Her stomach clenched. Why was the redhead seemingly so interested in her? How could she escape the stare, if only for a moment?

"Excuse me, Kevin." Liana grasped her purse. "I'll be back in a few minutes."

She maneuvered her way around the tables until she found the ladies' room. She stood in front of the mirror, freshening her makeup, when the redhead stepped inside.

At the sink next to Liana, the woman searched her purse and took out a lipstick. She applied it to her mouth, slipped the cover on, and tossed it back into her purse. "You need to stay away from him."

Liana gasped. "What?"

"If you don't want to get hurt."

"Are you threatening me?" Liana tried to sound strong, but her insides felt like mush.

The woman leaned against the vanity and glared at Liana. "No, it's not a threat. It's the truth. You look like a nice person, so I'm doing you a favor. Kevin Carter is bad news. My advice is to walk away." She sashayed toward the door.

Liana felt rammed in the gut by a train going full steam ahead. "Wait a minute. You need to explain."

The woman didn't turn around but extended her hand in a wave before she exited out the door.

Why the warning? Why had she chosen to be so vague? Liana grasped the edge of the counter, took several deep breaths, and gathered herself together before rejoining her date.

Kevin rose from his chair, and she slid as gracefully as she could into hers.

"Just in time. The band is coming back." He moved a little closer.

"Do you know the woman with red hair sitting behind us?"

He glanced in the direction, and his jaw stiffened. "Why?"

A gut feeling cautioned against a full explanation. "She's been staring."

"We dated for a few months, but don't let Melissa bother you. She's only curious. I heard from a mutual friend that she's engaged. Probably the guy who has his arm around her."

Liana took a quick peek. The redhead was snuggled up to the man next to her.

"See?" Kevin shrugged. "Nothing to worry about."

She tried to assign pure jealousy to Melissa's actions and focus on the music. But after the encounter with the woman, Liana couldn't relax. "Would you mind if I left a little early?"

"Are you feeling okay?" He sounded genuinely concerned.

"Yes, of course, and I apologize for not staying longer. But tomorrow is Saturday, which means I have a wedding and reception I need to coordinate tomorrow night, and I'm really tired. I should get some sleep. I still have a lot of last-minute things to take care of first thing in the morning. If they hadn't held their rehearsal early this evening, I wouldn't be here now."

"I wish I'd picked you up instead of agreeing to meet you

here," he said, sounding disappointed. "I'll pay the bill and walk you to your car."

"You don't need to leave because of me."

"I don't want to hang out here without you."

"Thanks, Kevin." Relief flowed through her. He didn't seem upset with her for wanting to go home.

"I'm going to ask for one thing, though."

She tensed. "What's that?"

"That kiss I mentioned." He lifted his eyebrows and gave her a slight smile.

Warm, tinkling sensations flowed through her body. Melissa had advised Liana to stay away from Kevin, but he'd proven to be thoughtful, even to the point of asking her for a kiss instead of taking it. In a time when some men—and women—held a variety of physical expectations while dating, he'd shown her nothing but respect.

Had Liana found the perfect man? Kevin was successful, good-looking, and he'd encouraged her to move out of her comfort zone and try something new. Life could be an ongoing adventure with him. What more could she want?

Twelve

The blare of the televised baseball game greeted Liana as she approached the back steps to the main house. Good. Her father was home from church. Sometimes he joined friends for lunch after worship, but he must have passed on any invitations today.

No interest in attending services, she gave herself permission to sleep in on Sunday. After coordinating an outdoor wedding and reception the evening before, she'd crawled into bed and zonked out around three in the morning. As soon as she awoke, Liana's mind zeroed in on the hospital gala. Since her father had been out of town all week attending a medical conference, he hadn't received the full update on Erik and Maggie's decision to hold the event.

Liana opened the kitchen screen door. "Dad, I'm coming in."

Cheers erupted in another part of the house. He must have company.

She followed the racket into the family room. Her father, perched on the edge of his favorite chair, seemed lost in the baseball game on the flat screen. An unfamiliar man, who looked to be in his thirties, roosted on the russet-colored leather couch. A stack of hotdogs and a bowl of potato chips sat on the coffee table in front of the two exuberant fans.

"Dad?" She tried to speak over the blasting TV without shouting.

"Liana, I didn't hear you come in." He turned down the volume. "Bottom of the fifth. Mariners are ahead of Oakland, three to one."

She shouldn't interrupt the game. "I was going to fill you in on what's happening with the gala, but we can talk later."

"If you're willing to risk my cooking, c'mon over for dinner tonight."

"Sounds good."

He gestured toward the other man in the room. "Before you leave, meet Danny Woods. His family attends my church. He's a single parent this weekend while his wife's at a women's retreat."

Danny wiped off his right hand with a crumpled napkin soaked with mustard and ketchup stains, then stood and extended his hand. "Your dad's a great guy. My daughter, Sophie, is quite attached to him."

"I agree. He is quite a man." Liana returned the genuine smile and clasped his hand in a brief shake. "How old is your daughter?"

"Four." He glanced around the room with a puzzled expression. "She was here a minute ago." Coloring books and crayons were scattered behind the couch. Abandoned blue and red crayons were sprawled on an open page of one book.

"Sophie!" He charged out of the room calling her but soon returned. "She's not here. I was too involved in the game to notice." His face paled. "Her favorite game is hide-and-seek."

Liana's father shut off the TV. "She's probably exploring. I'll take a look upstairs. There are still a few stuffed animals and dolls in Liana's old room. Sophie may have wandered in there."

"I'll check outside. She spotted the flowers and wanted to pick some for her mom." Danny took a few steps and spun around. "She might have gone to find the horses. We promised a trip down to the stable after the game, but maybe she got tired of waiting. You know how impatient kids can get."

"I'll run down there." Liana started for the back door.

"Don't worry. She'll be fine. The horses are out in the pasture this time of day. If she's at the stable, she might have discovered the new kittens."

"Thanks."

Despite Liana's assurance, Danny didn't look any less worried. Her heart went out to him. A lazy afternoon, junk food, and a ball game had been replaced by fear that his daughter could be in danger.

Liana jogged through the gardens and down the path to the stable door, almost expecting to see the little girl sitting inside on the floor with three-legged Mitzi in her lap. If Liana was four, she'd be there instead of stuck inside on a sunny day. Two gray kittens tumbled over each other in the entrance to the stable. No sign of the child.

"Sophie, are you in there?" Liana froze for a moment and listened. Nothing but meowing.

The horses had been let out for the day to run, so she checked the stalls to see if the child was hiding inside. Empty. Liana also searched the tack room, grain room, and the wash rack area. Sophie wasn't anywhere in the stable.

Liana stepped out the back door of the building. The pasture, where horses frolicked and ran free, lay straight ahead. She leaned against the fence and shielded her eyes from the sun. No child had ventured inside.

They must have found her in or near the house. Liana

swung around to go back, but wildflowers blooming along the trail into the woods caught her eye. Danny had mentioned Sophie was attracted to flowers. There, little footprints lined up in the dirt.

The child had wandered into the woods. On the path leading right to the river.

Liana's heart leaped into her throat. She'd left her cell phone on the desk back at the cottage. There was no way to let her father and Danny know where she believed Sophie was heading without wasting precious time running back to the house for help. Liana needed to find Sophie as quickly as possible. Energy surged through her veins as though she'd chugged a latte with four shots of espresso, and she sprinted down the path.

"Sophie!"

A thistle leaning over the path brushed against her leg, and the needles cut into the bare skin exposed beneath her capris. She winced but didn't stop to check for bleeding.

The narrow river had risen after the winter and spring rains. Not high enough to be over Liana's head but deep enough for anyone to drown. Even a good swimmer would have a difficult time with the current farther down the river, but a child wouldn't have any hope of surviving.

Dear God, please keep her safe. Please, God. Please.

Here she was, a non-praying woman, praying for a second time within a week.

Liana's eyes blurred from fear and what she might find once she reached the river's edge. Her sandaled foot tripped on a tree root. She stumbled but caught herself before falling to the ground. Sharp, excruciating pain in her big right toe shot through her body. Liana clenched her fists and pushed on.

A pine tree branched in her way. She shoved it aside. Her eyes darted to the left and right in case the child had wandered off course. *No sign of her.* A short incline and then a straight shot the rest of the way.

She heard the river and inhaled the water's scent. Almost there.

Liana brushed aside prickly evergreens and stepped from beneath nature's canopy. With her heart still racing, she gaped at the scene ahead. Who would have imagined?

Sophie, dark curls tumbling down the back of her lavender T-shirt, sat perched on the riverbank between Bryan and his Lab. She tenderly ran her fingers over Bryan's scarred face. A giggle burst from her lips, and Bryan's boisterous laughter followed, breaking the peaceful moment. Sophie made gestures in the air with her hands as though telling a story, and Bryan appeared completely engaged. Neither seemed aware that Liana had emerged from the woods.

Relief was replaced by slight irritation. He should know better than to sit there, as though it were an everyday occurrence for a child to show up out of nowhere. How could he not realize that someone might be worried about the little girl?

"Hi, Sophie." Liana spoke calmly, but loud enough to get the child's attention. She turned and studied Liana but made no other moves.

Rainey stood, and with his tail wagging, ran to Liana. He nuzzled his nose on her thigh. "I'm Liana. You know my father, Dr. Tate. Your daddy is looking for you, and he's very worried that you got lost. I need to take you back to the house, so he knows you're okay."

"I want to stay with Bryan." She gave him a hug around his neck and giggled.

Liana attempted to give Bryan a warning look without Sophie catching it. "I'm glad you're having fun, but we need to find your dad."

Bryan gently unwrapped the child's arms from his neck and held her hands. "Come on. I'll go with you. We need to get your daddy's okay if you want to ride Cassie."

"I can take Sophie to see the horses. I'm sure you have other things to do."

Bryan shot her a questioning look. "I have time to spend with my new friend." He pointed to a clump of yellow flowers at the edge of the path. "Sophie, would you pick those flowers over there for me? I'll put them in my apartment, and every time I look at them, they'll make me happy."

Sophie skipped in her pink and white blinking tennis shoes to where he pointed and picked several blooms.

Bryan rose and jammed his hands to his hips. "What's wrong?" He kept his voice low.

"A dad is scared that his little girl may be lost, and I find her playing down here with you. Didn't you consider that someone might be anxiously looking for her?"

"I planned to take Sophie back. I didn't want to scare her. So, maybe I took things a little slower than I should have, but I wanted her to be comfortable around me." His gaze shifted to the little girl. "The kid is amazing. She wasn't frightened at all. Of being lost or asking questions about my burns."

"Bryan ..." How could she make him understand? "There's a father freaking out about his child's safety. Letting him know that she's okay is more important than you feeling good about yourself."

"I'm sorry. You're right." He shifted his weight and met Liana's eyes. "Enjoying a few sweet moments with Sophie was selfish, but you need to know that I didn't bring her here. I would never do anything to hurt a child or her family. She saw me hike into the woods with Rainey. She wanted to play with the dog and followed."

Liana swallowed. Of course he wouldn't purposely harm or worry anyone, but the thought of possibly seeing Sophie floating in the water ... "We should get her back."

Bryan leaned over and picked up a book that lay on the ground. He strode to where Sophie, fully engaged, pulled flowers from the ground. He held out a free hand. "Come on, little one. Your daddy is waiting."

Sophie babbled nonstop as she skipped alongside Bryan, one hand in his and the other grasping tight to the flowers she'd gathered. The few moments alone with the child had felt like an angel's visit.

He understood the concern with Sophie missing. He would've worried himself if he had a daughter and she wandered off. He'd messed up by not taking her back to the house right away and relieving her dad's fears.

It was clear Bryan had failed in Liana's eyes, and that bothered him more than he wanted to admit, even to himself. He'd been hurt enough. If he wasn't careful, his heart would end up with more scars.

Sophie looked up with trusting bright blue eyes and smiled. God was full of surprises. Bryan needed that reminder.

❧

Liana followed quietly behind Bryan and Sophie. The lively chatter of the little girl helped cover the tension between the adults and gave Liana a few minutes to think.

It was wrong to be so hard on Bryan. Sophie was safe and happy when the indescribable could have happened had she wandered anywhere else around the estate and not found him.

Liana couldn't miss the hurt in his eyes and felt ashamed for putting it there. Sophie had made him laugh, but Liana had brutally doused his joy. She'd apologize when they had a moment alone.

They reached the end of the woods and stepped into the clearing. Liana's father emerged from the back door of the stable with Danny.

"Sophie!" His eyes lit up as the tension in his face relaxed. He strode toward them.

The little girl tugged Bryan's hand. "C'mon, Bryan. Talk to my daddy about me riding Cassie. C'mon."

Danny scooped his daughter into his arms. "Honey, where have you been? I couldn't find you, and I got so worried."

"Daddy!" She hugged his neck, then pushed back. "Bryan was taking care of me." She pointed to the black Lab, heeled next to Bryan. "Look, Daddy. That's Rainey."

Danny put Sophie down but held tightly to her hand.

"Come here, Rainey. Come here, boy." Sophie coaxed the Lab with her free hand, and he obeyed. She giggled when he licked her extended, delicate fingers with a wet tongue. "It tickles, Rainey."

"Danny Woods." Sophie's father held out his free hand, and Bryan shook it. "Doc mentioned he hired you to help out around here."

"Sorry for not getting her back sooner. She followed me down to the river because she wanted to play with my dog."

"Doesn't surprise me. Sophie's begged for a puppy."

"You have a sweet daughter, Mr. Woods. I'm thankful she didn't wander off the path and get lost, or worse yet, come out by the river where I couldn't see her."

"You didn't meet up by accident. God was watching over her, and in his wisdom, used you to protect her." His voice hitched. "If you hadn't been there, who knows what could've happened."

Sophie tugged on her father's hand. "Can Bryan take me to ride Cassie?"

Danny glanced at Bryan. "Cassie?"

"One of the gentlest horses you'd ever want to meet." Bryan pointed to a chestnut mare poking her head over the fence surrounding the pasture. "See? I think she's hungry for some human companionship. I'd stay with Sophie, hold the reins, and walk the horse. If it's okay with you."

Sophie grasped her father's arm with both hands and pumped it as she jumped up and down. "Please, Daddy, please! I'll be careful."

"Whoa! Take it easy." He put his free hand on the top of Sophie's head, taming her wild jumps. Danny blew out a stream of air and nodded. "Okay."

The child released her father and twirled around. "Bryan, I get to ride Cassie!"

Danny grabbed her arms, bent down, and waited until he had her attention. "For a little while. Then we'll head home. Promise to do everything Bryan tells you?"

Sophie's head bounced up and down in agreement.

Liana's father laid a hand on Danny's shoulder. "Now that we know everything is fine, and she's in good hands, let's catch the end of the game. I think you need a little time to wind down after the excitement."

Danny addressed Bryan. "Doc mentioned that he's invited you to church. Hope you come. We've got a great group of guys there. A few of us meet at my house once a week for a Bible study, but you know how guys are. We have to take a few minutes to shoot the breeze and talk sports, so it's not all serious."

"Thanks. I might show up someday. For now, God and I have our own thing going."

Danny nodded toward the worn Bible in Bryan's hand. "I understand."

Liana hadn't paid attention to the book he carried, and the realization that Bryan had gone to the river to read his Bible filled her with even more remorse for how she'd handled the situation.

Danny leaned down and gave Sophie a quick hug. "Have fun, be careful, and do exactly what Bryan tells you."

"Okay."

Danny chuckled, then turned toward her father. "So, you think the game will calm me down, eh? Not with the way the Mariners have been playing." The two ambled toward the house.

Liana reached a hand out to the little girl. "Sophie, if you give me those beautiful flowers, I'll put them in a vase for

Bryan. You can pick more for your mom before you leave from the garden over there."

Sophie thrust the flowers into Liana's hands, grabbed Bryan, and pulled him toward the stable. "C'mon. I wanna ride Cassie!"

Liana couldn't leave things this way. "Bryan. Wait."

He hesitated. "Go on ahead, Sophie, but stand back from the fence until I get there." The child galloped off as fast as two short legs could move.

"I'd like to walk with you while Sophie rides. If that's okay." With the little girl occupied and focused on Cassie, it would give them a chance to talk.

Bryan's eyes held a hint of sadness. "Thanks for the offer, but since her dad didn't request a chaperone, I think we'll be fine."

Thirteen

"I owe you an apology, Dad." Liana slipped an empty plate between two bottom rungs in the dishwasher.

"None necessary." Her father relaxed against the kitchen island. "I'm glad you found a solution to your problem."

"I scoffed at your suggestion to consider Erik's building, but it was exactly the miracle I needed. I still can hardly believe it. Not only do we have a location for the gala, but Erik is going to foot the bill for the design. Dalisay is so anxious to get all the details sketched out, she's barely slept the past few days."

"God is good." Her father's face beamed satisfaction.

The door to the deck clicked shut. "Hi, Dad."

Liana's sister, Camryn, somehow managed to gracefully perch on a high stool without her tight skirt sliding much farther up her thigh. The shoulderless coral top exposed additional tanned skin.

"Hi, Lee." Camryn dropped a designer purse, too small to hold much of anything, on the island.

"Hey, this is a nice surprise. How was Jamaica?" Their father gave Camryn a hug.

"What are you doing here?" Liana didn't mean to sound cold. Her sister's entrance was unexpected, not unwanted.

Liana had waited all afternoon until Danny and Sophie left before she updated her father on the hospital gala. She also wanted time alone with him before mentioning her earlier encounter with Bryan in the woods. But her dad didn't get many opportunities to see her younger sister, so she'd try to be patient. Camryn never stayed long.

"Thanks for the love." Camryn couldn't have been more sarcastic.

"She didn't mean it the way it sounded." Their father stepped behind Camryn and massaged her shoulders.

"Dad's right." Liana had longed for a closer relationship with Camryn for years, missing the way things were when they were much younger and best friends. But as Camryn's modeling career grew, it felt like she no longer had time for Liana. She was too busy jetting off to exotic places, gracing magazine covers, attending glamorous events, and dating desirable bachelors. "So ... how was the trip?"

"It was a blast." There was that sarcasm again.

Liana picked up an empty bowl lying on the counter. "How can you sound so sour? I'd love a chance to lounge on a Jamaican beach."

"It wasn't exactly a vacation."

"Of course not," Liana muttered under her breath as she found a place for the bowl on the top rack of the dishwasher. "It's grueling to stand still and have your photo taken," she said in a teasing tone, hoping to lighten the mood, but knowing in reality, she might have made things worse. Dalisay's siblings bantered back and forth—always in fun—but Liana's family took everything too seriously.

"You don't have a clue as to what it's like." Camryn tossed her long tresses over her shoulder. "There's no partying or sight-seeing. It's in bed early to look fresh in the morning for the shoot, and I couldn't eat because they didn't want me to gain an ounce."

"If you want my opinion, you look too thin." Their father opened the refrigerator. "Let me throw a steak on the grill for you."

"You know I don't eat meat."

He shifted the contents stored on the shelves. "Well then, how about a salad? Lots of fresh veggies."

"I didn't come to raid your food. I just wanted to hang out for a few hours." She glanced at Liana. "I didn't realize you and Lee were having father-daughter time."

It was like Camryn to lay on the guilt trip so their dad would feel sorry for her. It wasn't like Liana hung out with him every night. "We're going over plans for the hospital gala."

"We can put it off until later." Their dad pulled out mixed greens, a cucumber, and a tomato.

Camryn opened her purse and took out lip gloss. "You don't have to." She rolled the gloss over her lips, then brought them together in a self-kiss.

He dumped the vegetables on the counter. "It's no trouble to chop up a cucumber, honey." He grinned. "After all, I'm a surgeon. I've had plenty of practice with a knife."

"I meant you don't have to put off your discussion because I'm here. Maybe I could help with some ideas."

Liana tossed a handful of silverware into the door of the dishwasher. Camryn had never shown any interest in Liana's work, so why now? She'd been caught off-guard, but maybe she shouldn't question her sister's motives.

"You've attended a lot of big affairs. It would be nice to get your input, but we already have most of our plans in place, so we can't accommodate any major changes. And keep in mind that we're on a budget and depending on a lot of volunteers and donations, so we don't have money to waste on anything frivolous or outlandish." Liana may have gone too far with that last bit of information, but she didn't want her sister throwing out a ton of ideas that would be impossible to implement. She wanted to strengthen their relationship—not damage it more.

The hurt in Camryn's eyes left no doubt the comment had wounded a vulnerable place. "So, you don't think I understand the difference between an important charity event and a bash thrown by some crazy rich people? I shouldn't have bothered." She grabbed hold of her purse and slid off the stool. "Thanks for offering the salad, Dad."

"Camryn, please stay." He shot a reprimanding look at Liana.

She caught the hint, and guilt pushed her to chime in. "C'mon, Camryn." She wiped her hands on the damp dishcloth. "I didn't meant to insult you—or your friends."

"You've never given me any credit for having a brain in my head." She pulled her hair to the side so it draped over the front of her right shoulder. "I gotta go."

"Camryn, this is silly ..." Their father sounded exasperated.

"Bye, Dad. Love you." She kissed his cheek and then glared at Liana. "I might have had some great ideas." The door slammed behind her.

Liana jerked at the sudden noise.

"Why do you girls do that?"

"I'm sorry, Dad." Liana's face burned.

"It's like watching people stick sharp pins into each other." He massaged the back of his neck. "I don't understand why you can't get along."

Liana used her hip to shut the dishwasher's door, then leaned her backside against it. She crossed her arms and hung her head. "It's complicated," she whispered.

Her father winced and rubbed his forehead as though he had a headache. "You're not kids anymore. You're adults." He released a sorrowful breath. "A day will come when you'll need each other." His gaze locked onto hers. "You both might want to give that some thought."

Liana shut the kitchen screen door and crossed the deck. After the episode with her sister, sharing the plans for the gala with her dad wasn't as fun or exhilarating as it could have been. No longer in the mood, they'd called it a night.

She'd allowed her words to first hurt Bryan, then Camryn. Not a good day.

Tension and stress caused by responsibilities for the gala and other events could be used as an excuse for lashing out at innocent people. But her job wasn't the only reason. Liana couldn't get what happened at the jazz club several nights before out of her mind. The red-haired woman's warning to stay away from Kevin kept replaying in her thoughts. Was Melissa dangerous? Was she alluding to him being dangerous? Or was she merely jealous and messing with Liana's head?

The sun, slipping behind the trees, left a glow in the evening sky and a slight chill in the air. Liana glanced up toward Bryan's apartment above the garage. It was the first time she'd noticed the window blinds facing her cottage being tightly closed. The realization made her cringe.

She clomped down the steps of the deck and followed the path toward her place as though wearing twenty-pound ankle weights. An invisible wall stopped her short of venturing farther. It was as if a supernatural force stood in front of her.

Liana gazed at the apartment window. She couldn't return to her cottage and pretend that everything was okay. She took several steps back toward the garage. No. She couldn't face Bryan again after he declined her request to walk with him while Sophie rode Cassie. She'd hoped they could talk about what happened at the river, but he'd made it clear Liana wasn't welcome.

What could she do but return to the cottage, close the door, and shut him out as he had her? She halted a few feet from her refuge and clenched her fists to her sides. There would be no rest. No sleep. Not until she tried again. He'd accepted her apology, but if he refused her friendship, then it was on him. At least she'd be free of the guilt that burdened her body and spirit.

Liana spun around, and with determination strode back up the path with the speed of a cougar set on its prey. Better to get this over with before she changed her mind. She skipped up the steps to the apartment door, and breathing heavily, knocked. Bryan opened the door wearing blue jeans and a black T-shirt. Even in the dim evening light, he looked strikingly fit—the benefits of physical labor.

Rainey slipped between him and the doorframe and placed his paw on Liana's knee.

Glad for the chance to refocus her attention, she greeted the pup. "Hi, boy."

She scratched the top of his head, causing his tail to thump against Bryan's leg. He stood watching but didn't move or say a word, apparently waiting for her to explain her reason for being there.

Liana licked her lips and swallowed her pride. "Could I please come in?"

࿇

"I ..." Bryan, stunned to see her, didn't know what to say. After he'd brushed her off earlier in the day before taking Sophie riding, he thought Liana might avoid him. He wouldn't have blamed her.

"I'd like to talk, if that's okay," she said softly. So, she wasn't angry with him.

Bryan eyed the inside of the apartment, thinking over her request. When she'd knocked on the door, he'd been praying for clarity about Liana. He was confused about his feelings toward her. Would a friendship be a good thing for them? Was it even possible? If this was God's answer, Bryan knew better than to stand in the way. But being vulnerable again? He'd experienced enough hurt and disappointment before arriving at the estate, yet earlier that day, he'd been handed more.

He stepped outside and closed the door to his home, his sanctuary. "We can talk out here."

"Oh—okay." Liana glanced around. "Can we at least sit on the steps?"

She lowered her body onto the landing next to the wall and propped her feet on one of the steps below. He followed her lead, sitting in the empty space to the right, aware that his unscarred profile faced her.

The wood felt cool through his jeans, as did the evening

breeze that brushed his bare arms. Liana shivered but didn't complain. Rainey pushed his way through and lay between the two of them. Bryan appreciated the warmth radiating from the furry body.

"I'm sorry about today," she began, massaging the Lab's back. "I shouldn't have been so harsh when I found Sophie with you at the river."

Bryan leaned his elbows on his knees and stared at his feet. For some reason her words earlier had really pierced him, and now these had a healing effect. Why he cared what she thought, beyond the fact that her father employed him, he was still sorting out.

She released a heavy sigh. "I ... I wasn't trying to insinuate that you couldn't be trusted—or that Sophie needed a chaperone."

He turned his head to face her. "So, if a child came here tomorrow, you'd feel comfortable with her spending time alone with me?"

"Yes." Liana shifted her body and faced him. "You've never been anything but kind. And when I realized you'd only been reading your Bible ..."

She focused her eyes on Rainey's back and combed the dog fur with her fingers. "Bryan, I feel ashamed for acting the way I did."

He needed a moment to process and accept what he'd heard. Except for the dog's panting, there existed no other sounds. No rustling of leaves. No birds calling. Nothing.

"Maybe we both overreacted," he said, breaking the silence. "I'd like to put it behind us."

Liana nodded in agreement. "I'd like that too."

Without thinking of possible consequences, he placed a

scarred hand briefly over hers, but she didn't flinch.

Her cheeks turned a shade of pink, and wisps of chestnut-colored hair floated in the light breeze, making her look innocent and vulnerable. Another time ... another place... But the Bryan of here and now didn't move even an inch closer.

She took a deep breath. "Since we're living on the same property, it might be a good idea if we got to know each other a little better." Her thumbs nervously played war with each other. "Friends?"

"A guy can always use another." *Lord, are you sure about this?*

Bryan wouldn't lie to himself. Attracted to Liana, a friendship might become more painful than keeping his distance.

Fourteen

Liana closed the binder and rubbed her aching temples. She'd spent the entire beautiful June Saturday in the cottage, working at her desk. The only time she'd gotten up from the chair was to visit the bathroom, get another cup of coffee, and make a turkey sandwich. During an hour-long phone discussion, Dalisay had gone over notes regarding progress on Erik and Maggie's fantasy-themed event space. Liana needed to contact Erik on Monday to set up another meeting.

Almost four o'clock. She should check the mailbox before showering and changing for her dinner date with Kevin. She'd promised to take care of the mail while Dad was away at the convention in San Diego, and it would do her good to stretch her legs after sitting for hours.

Liana strolled down the long driveway. Evergreens and deciduous trees lined the driveway on both sides, their limbs growing toward each other and forming a protective tunnel. Lighting her way, the sun's rays filtered through the needles and leaves. Birds chirped from the higher branches, and a squirrel scampered across the path in front of her before scurrying up a tree trunk. Liana inhaled the woods' earthy scent. For that moment, she felt nothing but peace. As much as she loved the city and all it had to offer, nature—the forest and water—made her feel grounded.

Although he thrived on Seattle nightlife, Kevin must have

similar reactions to the outdoors. Or at least, she hoped he did. Instead of going into Seattle for dinner that night, he was taking her to the Salish Lodge and Spa, built at the head of Snoqualmie Falls. It would be a short twenty-minute drive. Kevin didn't seem concerned about expense, and Liana enjoyed its rustic beauty. A nice break from the clubs they'd frequented the past several weeks.

It made Liana feel special when he insisted on introducing her to his friends, explaining that he wanted to show her off. Striving to not disappoint him or his buddies, she also felt anxious around them. He had a reputation for dating women more like her sister—stunning, and sometimes even exotic looking. So, when he asked her to change into a sexier dress the last time they went out, she didn't mind. *Not really.*

But after a hectic week, she looked forward to a quiet evening at a place where she and Kevin would have more time to talk—alone. Dancing, listening to music, and chatting it up with other groups of people were fine, but if they were going to grow closer as a couple, and she hoped that was what they were, they needed to spend more time together—just the two of them—without an entourage.

Liana reached the end of the road and pulled a stack of mail from the box. As she retreated to the cottage, she sifted through the bills, credit card offers, and advertisements. One envelope with a feminine scrawl was addressed to Bryan. The return address gave Mary Samson as the sender. Liana felt a small twinge but shook it off. It wasn't any of her business who'd written the letter. She'd drop it off, and her job would be done.

જી

Bryan downloaded the last of the photos taken during his hike. He'd borrowed the truck that morning and driven up the pass into the mountains past Snoqualmie and the summit.

He'd parked at the trailhead that Doc mentioned was less traveled and where he hoped he wouldn't run into other hikers. Rainey followed him into the forest and up the rocky overgrown path, occasionally distracted by squirrels racing into the trees.

Bryan sweat profusely, but having to be careful of exposure to the sun, he'd worn a long-sleeved shirt and jeans. His hat protected a great portion of his face, but he'd covered his hands and face with 50 SPF sunscreen to make sure he was safe from sunburn.

Regardless of the hike's demands, Bryan loved the sense of freedom. He didn't venture into town unless he had to, and although the estate offered sanctuary, it felt good to have a change of scenery. He received another reward after reaching a clearing—a phenomenal view of the foothills and valleys below.

Now showered and wearing clean clothes, Bryan's body had cooled down, and he felt relaxed. After tending to the horses, he'd have the evening ahead of him.

Rainey trotted over and lay down next to Bryan's chair. He leaned over and massaged the dog's head. "We had fun today, didn't we, boy?"

The Lab leaped from the floor and laid his head on Bryan's lap, begging for more. Bryan accommodated and scratched Rainey behind the ears.

Bryan clicked through an album of photos he'd stored on the computer. He returned, like he often did, to the one he'd shot the stormy night he and Liana were in the stable. He'd taken a close-up of her cuddling Mitzi to her cheek while the cat purred. Bryan had snapped the photo in time to catch the young woman's smile. The soft lighting gave Liana a look of angelic innocence. Lord, help him, but she stirred something in his heart.

"Maybe we should ask Liana to go on a hike with us sometime. Do you think we could do that? Do you think she'd like hanging out in the woods with us?"

Rainey, staring with large brown eyes, answered by licking his master's hand with his wet tongue.

"Ah, I doubt I'll ever have the nerve to ask her." The dog whimpered, and Bryan hugged the Lab around the neck and patted the animal's back. "But we've got each other, don't we boy?"

The sun lowered in the sky enough to beam in through the apartment window, highlighting his guitar. Bryan hadn't moved it from the corner since Beth placed it there weeks before.

He leaned back in the chair, crossed his arms and legs out in front of him, and stared. So far, he'd successfully avoided the instrument. Pretended it wasn't even there.

Maybe he should pick it up. Not that he ever intended to perform again. That was out of the question. Those days were over. Done and buried. But the doc had told him that playing would be good therapy for his hands. The exercise would help with flexibility.

His heart hammered at the mere thought of embracing a guitar again and placing his fingers on the strings. If he failed to play a decent chord, at least he could tell his sister in all honesty he'd tried. Then she'd have to let up on him about getting back to his music. That alone would be worth the attempt.

Bryan cradled the guitar in his arms as he carried it back to his chair and then gently placed the instrument in his lap. He ran his hands over the body and caressed the dark wood. Beth had restrung the classical with nylon strings. These would be easier on his fingers than the steel strings on his electric. The other advantage was that he didn't need an amp. He hugged the simple, beautiful piece to his chest and laid his chin on top.

Memories of his grandfather flooded his mind. "You passed this on and asked me to bless the world with my music. I was supposed to honor God, who had given me a gift. All I did was abuse it, and now the music's been taken away." A lump grew and wedged itself in his throat. "I'm so sorry, Grandpa."

He blew out a stream of air and sat upright. "Here goes nothing."

It was a blessing his left hand wasn't burned as badly as his right. Less damage allowed more flexibility in his fingers, enabling him to reach and press down on the strings in different spots, creating diverse chords. Maybe he could use a pick to strum the strings with his right hand without too much discomfort. He still carried a pick in his wallet—old habit—and dug it out.

Bryan grasped the neck of the guitar with his left hand, placed the pads of his fingers on top of four strings, and pressed down. A drop of sweat trickled from his left temple and down the side of his face. He nervously swiped it away.

"This is even harder than I thought, Rainey," he whispered.

Closing his eyes, Bryan slowly strummed the six strings from the top to the bottom. The sensation brought him home. Moisture dampened his cheek, and it wasn't perspiration.

He took his time and painfully moved three fingers of his left hand into a new position on the neck. His right hand strummed, and although the sound was weak, it still could be distinguished as a C chord. Next an A minor. Then a D minor seventh. Despite Bryan's aching fingers, he kept repeating the three chords over and over.

Emotion he usually held at bay escaped from a place deep within his soul. Overwhelmed, Bryan leaned over the guitar, resting his forehead on his arms.

"Thank you, Lord," he whispered.

He'd never perform in public again, but he could play for himself. If he didn't give up, at least he'd have that much.

Liana stood outside Bryan's apartment, his letter on top of the pile, ready to be handed off to him. She raised her hand to knock but pulled back. Music, though faint and amateurish, filtered through the door. The corners of her mouth tipped up. Bryan was playing the guitar his sister had left behind.

Not wanting to interrupt, she leaned against the wall and listened. Then feeling guilty for eavesdropping, she knocked, and Rainey barked in response.

A moment later, Bryan opened the door. His eyebrows lifted slightly, and he slipped both hands into his front pockets, as though to hide them.

"Liana. Is everything okay?"

"Yeah. Sure. Everything's fine."

"C'mon in." He swung the door fully open and stepped back.

The last time she'd knocked on his door, he hadn't allowed her inside. Progress. Liana followed his lead, and as she walked inside, her eyes scanned the apartment. The guitar had been returned to the corner.

"A letter came for you." She held the envelope toward him.

"Thanks." He took it from her, read the front, and a big grin broke across his face.

"Girlfriend?" Why did she blurt that out? "I'm sorry. It's none of my business."

Bryan put his palm up. "No—no girlfriend. Mary is Kylee's mom. She's one of the kids I visit in the burn unit at the hospital. I don't get in to see her more than once a week, so I told Kylee she could write to me, and I'd write her back. Her mom addressed the envelope for her."

"Oh." This man kept surprising her. From what her father had said, Bryan rarely left the estate because of his appearance. Yet, he was willing to leave his sanctuary to offer encouragement and compassion to others who had gone through similar trauma. "Seeing the way Sophie took to you, the children in the hospital must love you."

He grinned. "Thanks, but they do more for me than I could ever do for them."

Liana understood, because she'd spent time with young patients herself. But that was some time ago. That was before she'd become a disappointment to the family.

"Would you like to ..." Bryan seemed to hesitate.

"Like to what?"

"Go for a short ride. The horses could use some exercise." His voice sounded hopeful.

"I don't think so. I mean—I'd like to, but—maybe another time."

"Yeah. Another time." Bryan shrugged his shoulders, as though Liana turning him down wasn't a big deal, but the light in his eyes dimmed. "I thought it might give us a chance to get to know each other better—as friends. Like you mentioned."

He seemed genuinely disappointed. Was he lonely? Her father probably did the best he could to offer Bryan companionship, but he worked long days or was often away speaking at conferences.

"It's just that—" She wanted to explain. It wasn't because she wanted to avoid spending time with him. "I have a date tonight, and I don't have time to take the horses out right now. That's all."

"With the same guy who's been hanging out around here?" There was an edge to his voice, as though Bryan might have a problem with Kevin.

"Why? Has he said or done anything to offend you?"

"No. I haven't even met him. But I've seen him around."

"I'll introduce you sometime." Liana put her hand on the doorknob but released it and turned back toward Bryan. "I didn't purposely eavesdrop, but I heard you playing the guitar before I knocked on the door."

He turned his head away, giving her his perfect profile.

"It would make your sister happy to know you're trying. It's good that you're getting back to your hobbies."

"Yeah, hobbies are great to have." His voice held a mixture of amusement and sadness.

Liana closed the door behind her and descended the steps. She had a sickening feeling that her last words, for whatever reason, had been painful for Bryan to hear.

Her heart ached. She hadn't meant to hurt him again.

Fifteen

"You're acting mysterious tonight," Liana teased.

"I am?" In the dim room, the candle's flame reflected in Kevin's eyes, like fire on blue ice.

Transfixed by the effect, Liana locked onto his gaze. "Yes—you are."

"No mystery. I want to take the evening slow and enjoy it."

Liana glanced around the room. "It's been a while since I've been here."

It was early enough in the evening that darkness hadn't fully descended. They could still appreciate the view through the window next to their table. Salish Lodge, nestled in the midst of mountain evergreens, reigned quiet and strong over the plummeting water of Snoqualmie Falls. Despite the rustic feel, the lodge exuded elegance and sophistication.

Kevin toyed with his spoon. "You need someone to help you stop being such a workaholic."

"Did you have someone in mind?"

"Maybe." His lips slid into an enticing smile as he leaned across the table. "Are you taking applications?"

"Maybe." Liana eased back into her chair. "But I'd have to disqualify you before I even looked at your résumé. You're a bona fide workaholic yourself."

"Okay. You got me there. I work hard, but I play just as

hard." He gave her a quick wink. "We could both learn how to take it easy."

"I know how to relax." Liana's eyes didn't waver from his.

"You do?"

"Of course." She offered only a hint of a smile. "And unlike *some* people, I just don't flaunt it."

Kevin leaned back as a deep laugh erupted from his chest. "Touché, my love. Touché."

The beat of her heart quickened. *My love.* He couldn't have literally meant it. The words must have slipped past his lips without him noticing the endearment.

"I'm glad I decided to spend the night." He picked up his wine glass and swirled the ruby-colored liquid inside. "Sleeping in a comfortable bed upstairs is more inviting than driving home."

"It'll be good for you to get a good night's sleep after the week you've had." She stared out the window at the forest surrounding the falls and whispered, "It's beautiful here. No one should ever take a view like this for granted."

Kevin slid his hand across the linen tablecloth until his fingertips reached hers, and with little coaxing, entwined them in his. "You're right. No one should ever take this view for granted."

The heat radiating from her cheeks didn't come from the wine she'd had with dinner. He made her feel beautiful and appreciated. For someone like her who wasn't used to being complimented, it felt intoxicating.

No man had ever gone out of his way to make Liana feel special the way he did. Her thumb gently caressed his. "Thank you for a lovely dinner."

"You're welcome." Kevin flashed a smile, lightening his

tone. He drew her fingers toward him, and his warm lips blessed them. "Let's get out of here. Take a walk and check out the observation deck."

"I'd love to." She followed his lead and stood. "We can get an even better view of the falls from there." And the night air would help to cool her down. "I didn't mention it, but I met with the manager of the lodge before dinner. We went over some options for some of my clients, and she gave me a tour of the spa, the meeting rooms, and the wedding venues. Of course, the lodge's website includes great photos, but there's nothing like seeing the spaces in person. She was going to show me several guest rooms, but I didn't want to be late for dinner, so I'll come back another time."

Kevin draped her shawl across her arms, giving both shoulders a gentle squeeze. They walked hand in hand on the path leading to the lookout. The setting sun dropped behind the trees, and small groups of people strolled by, returning to the lodge. As Kevin and Liana reached the lookout, the remaining couple took one last photo and then vacated the spot.

Liana leaned against the railing as torrents of water poured into the canyon below. Refreshing mist from the roaring falls moistened her face. The sun had almost disappeared.

Kevin's arms wrapped around her from behind, and his warm body pressed against her back. Liana eased into his shoulders, desiring to be close. Only a month had passed since their first dinner at the cottage together, but she was falling for him, and if his actions were any indication, he felt the same.

Since the night at the jazz club, they'd shared dinner several times a week. Other days they tried to meet for a quick lunch or a coffee break at the little shop across the street from his office. At the very least, they talked for a few minutes every night and sent texts off and on throughout the day. Liana didn't believe Kevin was the type of man to gift a woman that much attention unless he was seriously interested.

Liana hadn't given in and told her mother who she was seeing. She hadn't even felt ready to share much with her dad. Only Dalisay knew how much time she was spending with Kevin.

Maybe she should be more open about her relationship. Maybe this time she could trust that a man of Kevin's caliber and status could care for her. After all, things had turned around with the gala. She'd found the perfect place to house the event. Maybe her prayers were being answered.

She closed her eyes as Kevin's lips found the curves between her shoulders and cheekbones. His warm breath bathed her.

Kevin slowly stepped away. Released from his embrace, Liana shivered, but not for long. Grasping her shoulders, he gently turned her body to face him. Hot, moist lips covered hers, while his earthy cologne became a memory tucked away to be relived again when she wanted to remember what it felt like to be with him in this place—in this moment.

Not caring if anyone watched, Liana clung to him. Her heart pounding like the water the rocks below, she moaned when Kevin's lips left hers.

He hugged her close. "You're amazing," he whispered in her ear. He clasped her left hand, drew it to his lips, and kissed the palm.

No man had ever been so sweet. Or gentle with her. Liana wanted to fall into his arms all over again. But still holding her hand, Kevin led her toward the path, away from the observation deck and back to the lodge.

Before they entered the building, Liana stopped and faced him. "Thank you." She gave him a hug. "This evening has been perfect."

"You're not leaving already, are you?" He stood with his hand on the door, waiting to go inside. "We could grab another glass of wine."

She laughed. "I'm driving, so I don't think that's a good idea for me, but you're not, so you go ahead." Liana touched his arm. "I'd love to stay. Really. But it's getting late. I should head home."

"I understand." Kevin cocked his head. "Hey, I just got an idea."

"Oh?" Liana stifled a yawn. She didn't want him to think she was bored—she was purely exhausted from working twelve-hour days.

"You can take a quick look at my room and save yourself another trip up here."

"It's no bother. It's not that far from my home, and the scenery on the way is breathtaking." Liana didn't hang out in men's bedrooms alone with them—no matter how much she enjoyed the company. And although spending more time with Kevin was tempting—she was human after all—they'd had the "discussion." She'd been very clear that she didn't "sleep" around.

"It will take ten minutes." Kevin shrugged. "It's up to you, but you were just saying how tight your schedule is going to be in the next few weeks. I'm only trying to help a girl out."

It would save her some time, and she did want to see one of the more luxurious rooms in person. "Ten minutes—no more."

❧

"Kevin, the room is beautiful."

Liana gazed at the king-size feather bed and admired the black and white photograph of Snoqualmie Falls hanging above the fireplace mantel. A soft, brown afghan lay draped over the edge of the bed, and the flames in the gas fireplace added to the cozy atmosphere. She caressed the comforter, which had to be made from goose down. A desk with a chair was provided for those traveling or staying at the lodge for business. Two soft chairs were arranged in a sitting area.

Kevin tried to hand Liana a glass of Cabernet.

"No, thank you." Why would he offer it to her? She'd told him she wasn't drinking any more alcohol that evening. If he thought it rude to have a glass without offering her something as well, water would have been an option.

He swirled the wine in his glass. "Now you can tell your brides and grooms what to expect."

"I appreciate you letting me see it."

Taking her hand, Kevin pulled Liana to the left side of the room. "Come take a look at this." The bathroom included an oversized soaking tub and a large shower. "Just imagine relaxing in a warm bubble bath."

"That sounds heavenly. I'll describe it like that for honeymooners." She smiled, then slipped her hand from his. "I need to get going so we can both get some rest."

"A minute longer." He grasped her hand and pulled it

around his back, drawing her close.

He massaged her neck. As his fingers combed through her hair, she relaxed into a dream-like state against his body and into the curve of his arm.

"Does this feel good?" he whispered.

"Mmmhmm ..." she murmured. It felt like ... Was he trying to seduce her? Wear her down? No—not Kevin.

The taste of wine that lingered on his lips mingled with hers. He gently enticed her mouth to dance with his, and Liana felt herself dangerously close to going where she feared she might not return.

Kevin leaned his forehead against hers. "I want you to stay with me tonight," he said, his voice husky.

He couldn't be serious. "I—I can't."

There'd been a few times in her life when men had been upfront about wanting to go to bed with her. Sickened by the thought of being used after she'd had her heart broken, she'd never given in again. But she believed Kevin was different. He was falling in love with her. She was sure of it.

"You can." Tilting her chin, he gazed into her eyes.

"But—"

His finger covered her lips. "We could spend some lazy hours in bed. Have breakfast together. How does that sound?"

"It sounds ... romantic." He *did* have feelings for her. She'd never imagined a man like Kevin would ever show interest. He did everything he could to make her happy.

"I knew you'd like it." Something changed in the way he looked at her, and she caught a glimpse of darkness.

The fog in Liana's head cleared as quickly as a reception hall when a fire alarm sounded. The smooth confidence in his voice didn't bother her, but what she saw in his eyes did. Arrogance and pride. Pride in what? Convincing her to stay? She hadn't agreed, but he assumed she would.

"I'm not staying." Even as the words passed through her lips, her heart desired to reclaim them. Something else told her otherwise. It could have been intuition. It could have been misplaced guilt. Or it could have just been fear that once she gave in, the intensity of the relationship would wane.

Kevin's expression soured. "It's not like this is a college dorm room or a dumpy hotel in a seedy part of town. I want to spend the night with you. Like two people in a relationship—a real couple."

A real couple. "I know, but—"

"Don't we have a good thing going?" He strode to the table where the bottle of wine sat, poured a glass, and tossed half of it down his throat.

Liana cheeks flamed. "Yes, I think so." She took a deep breath. "But that doesn't change my personal beliefs about sex. Even though I consider myself quite open-minded, I still believe that people should be in love and in a committed relationship. It's not something you do one night and forget about the next morning."

"And you're convinced I'll forget about you?" He sat on the edge of the bed, then finished off his wine. "You think so little of me?" By the tone of his voice, he was more than frustrated, he was angry.

"And you think so little of me that you'll try to convince me to go against what is right for me?" Maybe he wasn't any different than the rest of the men she'd dated.

"Well, it doesn't seem to matter what I think or feel, does

it?" His voice hinted of sarcasm.

"Yes, it matters." Liana sighed. "But I still need to be true to myself." Better to leave now before things got even worse.

Kevin beat her to the door, leaned his back against it, and grasped her hand. "Wait."

Liana looked into eyes that had softened and become vulnerable. He didn't say anything. He merely looked at her and massaged the palm of her hand with his thumb. She'd wanted to believe he could love her.

Her mother and sister would think her crazy for turning him down. Camryn would have jumped at the chance to share his bed.

Panic ceased Liana's heart. If she walked out, she might never hear from him again. But if she stayed, she'd regret it later.

"Kevin, let me go."

"I'm sorry," his voice croaked. "I'm not used to being rejected, but—"

"But what?"

He held her palm to his cheek. "I don't want to lose you. And if that means waiting until you're ready, I'll wait."

Why the sudden turn? Did he mean it? He'd be willing to put her needs ahead of his own? "You care that much?"

Her resolve waned. If she didn't get out of that room now, she'd find herself back in his arms, with possibly not enough strength to say no a second time.

Sixteen

Bryan bolted upright, his breathing labored. Sweat trickled from his temple, followed the curve of his jaw, and mingled with the moisture covering his neck. His chest and back were damp. His heart raced. Another nightmare.

According to the clock next to the bed, it was a few minutes past midnight. He'd been asleep for less than two hours. Grabbing a corner of the sheet, he wiped his face and neck.

Terrifying dreams crept into his sleep less frequently than right after the fire. But just when he thought he was through with them, once again a nightmare trapped him back in the barn, surrounded by flames, with no way to get out. He seemed destined to experience over and over the heat of the fire as it licked, tasted, and then ate his body.

Bryan didn't know which was worse. Dreams that made him relive that experience or dreams of his life before the fire—reminders of all he'd lost.

Please, Lord, give me strength.

That was all he could pray. Tonight there was nothing more.

Swinging his legs around, Bryan sat on the edge of the mattress, arousing Rainey, who slept near the bed. Moonlight, entering his domain through the bedroom window, laid a path across the floor, beckoning Bryan outside.

Sleep would refuse to come until remnants of what disturbed the night faded. It might help to get some fresh air. Dressed in jeans and a T-shirt, he stepped outside. The air smelled like rain, so before closing the door, he grabbed the jacket he'd thrown over the end of the couch.

Clouds drifted in front of the moon, darkening the sky, and upper branches swayed from the breeze blowing through the trees. With thumbs hooked in his front pockets, and Rainey at his side, Bryan sauntered down the path toward the stable.

The Lab veered to the left and scampered toward a dark figure sitting on the bench built around the only maple tree in the estate's massive yard. The dog barked a soft greeting and then lay at the tree sitter's feet. By the animal's actions, whoever hid in the shadows was no stranger.

"Who's there?"

"It's me, Bryan. Liana."

"I should have guessed. Rainey doesn't take to everyone like he's taken to you." He strolled to the bench and sat, leaving distance between them. "Can't sleep, either?"

"No."

Even in the dark he could half see—half sense—her shiver. "How long have you been out here in the cold?"

"I don't know." She tightened the shawl wrapped around her arms. "What time is it?"

"Just after twelve-thirty."

"Then it's been several hours."

"You must have something pretty serious on your mind."

"I didn't notice it'd gotten chilly."

It might be too forward for him to ask what was bothering her, but if he was supposed to be her friend—and Liana did say she wanted to be friends—then he almost had an obligation to find out what was wrong, didn't he? Wasn't that supposed to be how it worked?

Bryan cleared his throat and leaned his elbows on his knees. "Weren't you on a date tonight with that Kevin guy?"

"Yes." Sadness permeated her voice.

Alarm shot through him. What had he done to her? Bryan didn't want to frighten her, so he kept his voice tame. "Everything okay?"

"Sure."

Bryan wasn't *totally* stupid when it came to women. She wasn't telling the truth. Something happened with the rich dude that upset her. That realization made protective instincts rise inside Bryan. As her *friend*, he owed it to her and to his employer, to protect her.

"I don't mean to intrude." He took a deep breath. "Okay. Try pretending that I'm an older brother. Or an older cousin. A cousin you completely trust."

"What?" She sounded irritated.

Maybe he should quit before he did something that would cause him to be fired. Would Doc ask him to leave because of getting too personal with his daughter? Maybe. But something in his gut pushed him further.

"Did your date ... try something?" He sensed her flinch.

"My relationship with Kevin is my business." She didn't sound angry with Bryan for asking—more like sad about whatever had gone down between her and handsome.

"Sorry." He stood. "It felt like you were bothered by something, and I wanted to help, that's all. Friends. Remember?"

"So, why couldn't you sleep?"

Bryan dropped back down on the bench. If he was going to probe with questions, she had a right to do the same. "I have nightmares about what happened."

"The fire."

"Yeah."

"Now *I'm* sorry."

"It's getting better. They're fewer and further between."

"That's good."

Why had it been so easy to confess that to her? Not even his sister knew he still struggled with nightmares. Bryan leaned his back against the tree, and they sat silent.

Raindrops plunked around them, and one landed on Bryan's forehead. He swiped it with his hand and stood up. "You're gonna get soaked. We should go."

Liana clutched her shawl around her, and as they stepped from beneath the willow's protective umbrella, drops pelted them. Bryan shed his jacket and held it over her head, but it didn't do much to shield her from the blowing rain as they ran toward the cottage. By the time they reached shelter under the porch roof, Bryan was soaked to the skin.

Liana stood in the dim light shining through the window. Wet hair—smudged mascara—it didn't matter. She still messed him up inside.

Bryan was careful to keep his face hidden in the shadows. Standing this close to her, he wanted to feel normal, if for only a moment.

Liana reached for the doorknob but halted and turned toward him. "Nothing happened tonight. With Kevin, I mean." She looked away. "I don't know why it feels important to tell you that."

Whatever the reason, Bryan was relieved to hear it.

"He ... he wanted something I wasn't ready to give." She sighed. "But I've been wondering if I made a mistake."

"You were under the tree trying to figure that out?"

"Yeah, I guess I was."

"For what it's worth, you made the right decision."

"You're sure?" The hope in her voice undid him.

"I'm sure."

She opened the door, then before stepping inside, stood on tiptoe and lightly kissed Bryan's non-scarred cheek. He stiffened. If she noticed, she didn't let on. The door closed behind her without another word spoken.

Bryan stepped from the cover of the porch and stared back at the cottage with blurred vision, rain washing over him. He might not be the kind of guy Liana could love, but if that jerk ever hurt her, Bryan would have words with the man, whether he wanted to listen or not.

Seventeen

"You've got to be kidding! Termites?"

Liana's shoulders tightened, and a dull ache filled in the space between her two temples. *Empty space.* There couldn't possibly be a brain in there, because if there had been, she would never have promised the impossible.

"No, I'm sorry to say ... I'm not." Erik Jones massaged the bridge of his nose.

Liana felt like she'd been kicked in the stomach. Nothing ever seemed to go her way. She wasn't a bad person, but it felt like God had it in for her. "How is this going to affect the gala, Erik? Are we even going to be able to hold it here? Do you realize that everything is in motion? Publicity has already been generated for this thing. People are counting on us!"

"Liana, it's not Erik's fault." Bryan was looking at the damage when she arrived for the meeting. "You haven't even given him a chance to explain."

Bryan was right. Maybe she was freaking out a little too much, but the gala was important to all of them—to Erik, Maggie, the hospital, her career—even Bryan.

"I'm sorry, Erik, for blowing up." She took a deep breath. "I'm a little stressed, but it's no excuse. You've got a lot on the line here, too, and this isn't making life any easier for you either."

Erik gave a slight smile. "We're not giving up, Liana. And

I didn't call you over here to add to your heavy load. I just want to make sure we're being honest and are communicating with each other, because you're right, there's a lot at stake."

"So, give it to me—the whole sorry mess." Liana braced herself.

"It means extra work and a delay in getting some things done earlier than later. But it's not going to affect the gala, is it?" Bryan directed his question to Erik.

"I promise you, Liana, that we'll do anything we have to do to get this place in shape before the event. I can't afford not to." Erik motioned for her to follow him. "C'mon. I'll show you what we're dealing with."

Both Bryan and Liana trailed after the building's owner into the kitchen like two chicks staying close to their mother.

"We discovered the problem when the inspector came in. We were more concerned about updating the plumbing and electrical in here, but we can't even begin addressing those issues until we fix all the damage from the termites. And it's not only in here. After sitting for years, without any attention, this side of the building is infested with the little buggers."

Erik pulled a piece of wall board down to show her the mess behind, and with what seemed like no effort, broke off a small chunk from the wood beam. Liana's head spun, imagining what lay behind the rest of the wall.

"The thing is, you can't tell if you have termites without digging into the structure. And it takes specialists to get rid of them." Erik brushed crumbled wood from his hands. "They may need to inject chemicals through the concrete or into the foundation. Once the termites are gone, we want to make sure that whatever needs to be replaced is taken care of before we do anything else. It's important to maintain a strong structure."

"That won't come cheap. Are you going to be okay?" Bryan seemed genuinely concerned for his new friend.

"We'll have to dig down a little further into our pockets, and we may need to do some creative financing, but we'll be fine. This is an investment, and any huge venture like this is a risk, right?" Erik laid his hand on Liana's shoulder. "Don't look so discouraged."

"I don't want the setback to dampen my spirits. But it's one thing after the other." Liana's mild headache had progressed to a throbbing nuisance. She dug into her purse, popped open a bottle, and downed two pain relievers.

"Trust me, Liana. Trust God. Someday down the road, we'll look on this as only an annoyance. Maybe there's a reason, maybe there's something to learn, or maybe it's what happens when a building is left alone for so long."

Maybe. Perhaps Liana could learn to trust God if he didn't keep throwing roadblocks in her path. Why did everything have to be so difficult? Why couldn't she get a break? People thought she had it easy because she grew up in a wealthy family, as though money made everything better. It didn't.

"I shouldn't have been so hard on Erik."

"You apologized, and he understood why you were upset," Bryan said, following Liana to her car.

"I hope so." Reaching the vehicle, she spun around and

crossed her arms. "This event is important to so many people." She kept her voice down. "I'm ashamed to admit that I'm not only worried about possible lost funds for the hospital or business potential for Erik and Maggie. My professional reputation—my family's reputation—will be held up for scrutinizing. It will either be the girl has finally come through, or it'll be she's failed again."

Bryan didn't know what to say, so he stood silent while she answered her phone.

Lord, please show me what to do.

An idea came to him as Liana ended the call and pulled the car keys from her purse. "Do you have any other appointments?"

"No, I'm heading back home to catch up on paperwork." She sounded worn out. "Why?"

"Would you be willing to go for a drive with me? I'd like to show you something. I promise it will take your mind off your worries."

"Bryan, I don't know ... I have a lot of work to do, and I'm tired."

"C'mon. Please." He held out his hand for the keys. "I'll drive, and you can lean your head back and rest."

"I can't be gone long."

"Just long enough."

Liana sighed with what must have been resignation because she dropped the keys in his palm, then moved to the passenger side of the car and got in.

After slipping behind the wheel, Bryan started the car. He felt more comfortable sitting in the driver's seat—his disfigured profile facing the inside of the car. The vehicle's smoked glass also aided in blocking people's view.

Liana leaned her head back. "I'm sorry if I sounded testy. This headache is killing me, but the pills I took should kick in pretty soon."

"Close your eyes and rest. It'll take a little while to get there, so grab a quick nap if you can."

"Thanks." Liana slunk down in her seat and closed her eyes.

Lord, I hope I'm doing the right thing.

He drove the car to Issaquah and then took the I90 exit into Seattle. Twenty-eight minutes later, he pulled into the hospital parking lot and stopped.

Liana opened and rubbed her eyes, then sat straight up. "You brought me here?"

"Yeah, I guess I did."

"Why?"

"There's someone I want you to meet." Kylee always cheered him up. If Liana could see the joy that the kids in the children's ward embraced, despite their circumstances, maybe she'd gain renewed strength to fight for them—for the gala—and not give up hope.

"Let's go home, Bryan."

"If that's what you want, we'll head there right now. But I'm asking you to stay."

Liana slumped down in her seat. "I don't like hospitals." Her voice was barely audible.

What frightened her? He couldn't imagine Liana being scared of anything, especially walking into a hospital where her father worked. How could he encourage her? "If I can handle going in there, looking like I do—and being stared at—don't you think you're brave enough to take it for a few minutes?"

His passenger didn't respond but stared straight ahead.

"Please, Liana," he whispered.

She closed her eyes, then opened them. "Okay. I trust you. It must be important if you brought me here, so I'll give it a try." Liana stepped out of the car.

That's all he could ask. Bryan hopped out and locked the doors before silently leading the way through the front doors. They walked down the hall into another wing and took the elevator to the sixth floor, where they hiked until they arrived at double doors leading into the burn unit.

"Bryan?" Liana's eyes widened.

"It's okay. I promise." *Lord, God, please don't let this be a mistake.* Bryan opened the door and nodded for her to go in ahead of him.

"Hey, Bryan, you're looking good," a gray-haired nurse greeted him. "Don't you usually volunteer on Fridays?"

"Yep, Friday mornings. I brought a friend to meet Kylee."

A grin spread on the nurse's face. "Oh, she'll be so happy to see you. She's had a good couple of days."

"Awesome." He motioned Liana to follow him.

She cleared her throat. "Isn't Kylee the little girl who writes to you?"

"The very one." He stopped in front of a half-closed door and knocked. "Hey, Kylee, my girl. Can I come in?"

A child squeaked from within the room. "Bryan!"

He opened the door, and gestured for Liana to enter first.

The patient's dark eyes lit up at seeing Bryan. Her upper body was completely bandaged, and she was hooked up to various machines and tubes. Only patches of black hair remained on her scalp, and a large bandage covered her left cheek. Burns covered part of her forehead as well as the tip of her nose.

"How's my girl?" Bryan landed a gentle kiss on her head. Nurse Carmen said you've had some good days."

"The doctors are pleased with her progress," said the woman sitting to the side of the hospital bed. Pretty, even without makeup, she looked no older than thirty. She was dressed in faded blue jeans and a pink T-shirt, and her long, straight, black hair was pulled back in a ponytail.

"Liana, this is Kylee, and her mom, Mary. Ladies, this is my friend, Liana. I wanted her to meet both of you." Bryan stepped to the side.

"Hi." A little shaky, Liana wasn't quite sure what Bryan expected of her, but she reached over and shook Mary's hand. Stepping closer to Kylee's bedside, she picked up the child's delicate hand and gave the little girl a big smile. "I'm so glad to meet the young lady who has been writing to my friend. Do you know how happy that makes him when he gets one of your letters in the mail?"

"It does?"

"Oh, my goodness. You should see him." Liana winked at the child. "He practically dances!"

The little girl gave a tiny giggle. "Are you Bryan's girlfriend?"

A rush if warmth invaded her cheeks. "No, I'm not."

"Oh. I think you should be. You're pretty."

Her heart broke at hearing those words. *Pretty?* Kylee had called her pretty without any resentment in her voice or hint of self-pity about her own appearance. Tears nipped at

Liana's eyes, and she blinked them back. "Well, I think you're pretty too."

"Bryan says I'm bea-u-tiful."

"Well, he's is a very smart man."

Kylee's eyes glistened. "Much smarter ... and nicer than my daddy."

Liana shot a look at Bryan, hoping he'd explain.

"Hey, Kylee, we're going to step over there and talk to your mom for a few minutes. Is that okay?"

"Can I watch cartoons?"

Mary turned on the TV suspended above. "Just for a few minutes. Then you need to get some sleep."

Bryan motioned Liana to move with him to a far corner in the room, and Mary joined them.

He rubbed his left eye and took a breath. "Kylee's father was on meth. He dumped cooking oil on her and set fire to her."

"Oh, my goodness!" Liana's stomach flipped. She could only imagine the horror.

"I got sick that day and left work early," Mary added, with pain in her eyes. "Thank God I did. I walked in right when he lit the match." She sniffed.

Liana's heart ached for the mother. "What happened to him—your husband?"

"He's in jail, where he belongs."

"I'm so sorry." Liana had no other words. Their story was tragic and senseless—what was there to say?

A smile broke on the mother's face. "We try to be grateful. God has been good to us. He spared Kylee's life, and she has wonderful doctors and nurses taking care of her." She touch Liana's shoulder. "And we're grateful for you too."

"Me?"

"Bryan told us about the party—the gala—that you're putting on to raise money for the hospital."

"Mary is the sole provider for their family now, but she doesn't work enough hours to get insurance," Bryan said quietly. "There's no way she could afford Kylee's treatment. Because of funds raised last year, Kylee has been able to receive treatment at no cost to the family."

"It's saved her life—my life. I don't know what we would have done without that help. It makes me feel good to know that others like us will also get help."

Kylee began whimpering, but almost immediately, it turned to crying.

Mary rushed to her little girl's side and spoke softly to her. She pushed a button, calling for a nurse. "The pain is getting worse. A nurse should be here any minute." The woman's voice was strained.

Feeling helpless, Liana didn't know if she could bear hearing the sweet child suffer. What was taking the nurse so long? Why didn't someone come and help the poor girl? Liana moved toward the door to find a nurse herself and get Kylee the attention needed.

"Please wait for me out in the hall." Bryan's eyes brimmed with sorrow. "I want to pray over her for a second, but I'll be right there."

Liana slipped out, but instead of staying near the room or taking time to locate an available nurse, she scurried down the hall and out of the burn unit. She spotted glass doors leading to an outside deck. Needing air, she exited the building and practically threw herself into a chair. She dropped her arms on the table and buried her head in them. A delicate breeze graced the back of her neck where her hair had fallen forward, cooling her skin from the hot, glaring sun.

A few minutes later, she heard the clink of an object landing next to her and raised her head to peer directly at a shiny, silver soda can. Bryan sat across from her with his own drink. He seemed at ease. But of course, if he was going to be comfortable anywhere, it would be here—in this hospital—on this floor.

"Thanks." Liana lifted the smooth can to her lips and savored the cool, bubbly liquid sliding down her parched throat. She set the can down, pushed her hair back from her eyes, and stared at Bryan. "Why did you bring me here?"

"You don't know?" he whispered.

"No, I'm not so sure that I do." Why was this visit was so important that Bryan was willing to leave his safe environment on a day he wasn't expected at the hospital? Why did he feel the need to include her?

"I thought you should know what the gala means to patients." Bryan ran his thumb up and down the sweating can. "Do you really understand that for some, those funds become their lifeline?" Bryan leaned forward. "I was lucky enough—no *blessed* enough—to have the financial means because of an inheritance to cover most of my medical expenses. It wiped me out, but at least I had something to work with. I didn't have insurance with my job. I could have been in the same position as Mary and her daughter." He pointed toward the hospital door. "That five-year-old kid deserves the best medical care possible—even if her dad is a scumbag."

"Of course, she does." Frustration burned within Liana. Did Bryan think so little of her? Did he think her involvement was purely selfish and career motivated? Had she appeared that shallow? "Are you questioning my motives for being involved with the gala?"

"No!" He took a swig of his cola and smashed in the can's side with his thumb. "I only meant to remind you of what we're fighting for, and that no matter how many challenges or setbacks we face, we can't give up."

"I would never—" The anger dissipated, leaving only emotional pain. "You don't know me." Her soft voice hitched.

His warm gaze locked on to hers. "Tell me."

A tug of war played out in her head and emotions, but the side desiring to be vulnerable and understood won over stubbornness and pride.

"I care a whole lot more than you know." Liana waited for courage to catch up. "I don't like hospitals because they remind me that I'm a failure."

Bryan looked confused, but instead of bombarding her with questions, he waited for her to continue.

Liana could trust him, couldn't she? It might feel good to admit what she'd been carrying in her heart for years. Keeping it inside had done nothing to free her from the painful weight.

"I'm not aware of how much you know about my family." Her heart pounded. *You can do this.* "My dad, mother, and sister have always been overachievers and have been successful in whatever they attempted. My mother, a model, now runs her own high-profile agency. My sister, Camryn, has followed in her footsteps and models. Even though the two of us seem to push each other's buttons, I have to admit, she can be witty and entertaining—the life of the party. People love being around her." Liana turned her soda can around on the table. "I thought I could use my brains and be like my dad. All I thought about was being a great surgeon and making him proud."

"Then, why aren't you ...?"

"Couldn't cut it. I knew by the time I was a junior in college that I'd never get into medical school. Straight As in everything but chemistry. Didn't matter how many hours I studied for exams, I choked. So, I switched gears." She released a long sigh. "It still hurts that I wasn't good enough—smart enough."

Bryan reached over and gently laid his hand over hers. "You're right. I don't know you. But I want to, Lee."

Liana averted her eyes, but she didn't pull away. His reassuring touch felt—nice—comfortable. "Dalisay confronted me once. She said I didn't have the right motives for becoming a doctor, and that's why things didn't fall into place. She believes my calling is exactly what I'm doing now—creating memorable moments. It's my way of making people happy."

"What could possibly be wrong with that?"

"Well ... if I'm going to be truthful with you and myself, I am using the gala to prove something to myself and my family." She bit her lower lip. "But I don't want that to be my primary motive. I do care about people, and this is my chance to do something good for the patients in this hospital, despite the fact that I don't wear a stethoscope around my neck."

"You will—we all will—together."

"Bryan, I can't fail this time. I just can't."

Eighteen

Liana didn't want to fight with Kevin.

Was he using her job and unavailability for one dinner party to create an argument and give him an excuse to move on? She wasn't the only one with a full calendar, but he seemed to be working hard at making her feel guilty for not having that particular night open.

Twelve days had passed since the dinner at the lodge. They'd both had busy schedules, but was that the only reason he hadn't found even a few minutes to meet for coffee during that time? She still couldn't shake the feeling that her decision to not spend the night with him had caused him to lost interest.

Had she lost interest in him?

Confused, her up and down emotions had almost worn her out. Until Liana could be reassured that Kevin respected her decision, she didn't know if she still wanted to work on a relationship or not.

She'd felt encouraged yesterday morning when he'd agreed to have lunch with her today at one of the waterfront restaurants in Seattle, a few minutes from his office. Now they sat on the deck outside, viewing spectacular mountains on the other side of Puget Sound. The scent of saltwater mingled with a faint aroma of grilled fish. Seagulls flew overhead, filling the air with sounds of their cawing and squawks. Some flew close to the seawater, searching for fish, while others waddled on the deck, seeking crumbs dropped or offered by restaurant patrons.

"It's such a beautiful afternoon." Liana attempted a smile. "Can't we just enjoy it?"

Kevin stabbed salad greens with his fork. "We're both easily consumed in our work, but I don't want that to be an excuse." He tossed the fork down on the plate. "I was hoping you could break free for at least one night."

"I know you're frustrated, and I am too, but we're here together *now*." She didn't want the little time they had ruined by arguing. "It's not often we can both get away in the middle of the work week for a leisurely lunch. Let's make the most of it." She wanted to enjoy the sunshine—not bicker. "Isn't it nice to relax by the water?"

He glanced around. "It doesn't solve my problem. I still need a date for this dinner thing on Saturday, and once again, you're too busy to go with me."

"I'm sorry, but I can't help it." That sounded like a pitiful explanation—even to her. But it was the truth, so why did she feel so guilty at having to turn him down? "This is wedding season, and June is one of my busiest months. It will get better." She'd tried to accommodate his schedule and interests. Why couldn't he understand her needs? "I made commitments months ago, and I have to follow through on them. It's how I make my living. I have two weddings this weekend, not to mention a retirement party. I'm booked solid."

"This isn't going to work, Liana."

Her throat burned, and her stomach soured. So, she was right. He was going to dump her. Right then and there. But she'd make him say it. "What do you mean?"

"This. You and me. I think we need to call it quits."

"Kevin—"

"I need someone who wants to spend time with me. Every time I turn around, you're making excuses not to. Hire someone else to cover for the weekend."

"I can't afford to pay someone else."

"I've seen where you live. Your family must have enough money to pay a staff of ten people."

"My father has money, Kevin. Not me. I work for a living. And I pay rent in order to live in the cottage. My parents don't believe in freebies, and I'm glad they feel that way."

He scowled. "All I'm asking for is one weekend."

Liana had her answer. Kevin was not the man for her. She'd been duped into believing he was a gentleman and kind, but he was selfish and arrogant. "I can't."

Throwing his napkin on the table, Kevin leaned back in his chair. "You know what, Liana? That's all I hear. *You can't.* You can't learn to enjoy my kind of music. You can't manage to drop the ten pounds you keep saying you want to lose. You can't spend the night with me, and you can't be my date for an important dinner." His jaw clenched, and his chilling eyes pierced hers. "Just what *can* you do?"

"I—I—" She blinked, trying to relieve the prickling sensation in her eyes. Gone was the charismatic man who'd wooed her with his soft words and seductive touch, but why did he have to be mean? Part of her felt sad—disappointed—that she'd been fooled by his charm. Part of her felt relieved that she'd finally seen and accepted his true character.

"Liana! What are you doing here?" Camryn, wearing heels and a short dress the color of orange sherbet, appeared looking like she'd come from a shoot for *Cosmo.*

"I'm obviously having lunch. What are *you* doing here?"

Camryn kept her eyes on Kevin. "I was waiting for Mom at a table over there." She waved at a general area behind her. "We were supposed to meet for a quick bite, but she just called. Can't make it. Got tied up in a meeting. So, I was leaving. You know I don't enjoy eating alone."

"Since when?" Liana didn't like where the conversation was going.

Camryn avoided the question. "Don't be rude, Liana. Introduce me to your lunch partner." She shifted her weight into a pose Liana had seen too many times, and her blood chilled, despite the sun's warmth. Her sister had chosen the worst timing to interrupt them.

Liana turned toward him. "Kevin, meet my sister, Camryn."

He stood before Liana could say another word. "Kevin Carter—a friend of Liana's." He shook Camryn's hand and held on to it longer than necessary. Then he grabbed a chair from an empty table nearby. "Sit down and join us."

Camryn played coy. "I don't want to interrupt."

"You're not interrupting a thing. Besides, you said you don't like to eat alone." Kevin flashed his you're-the-most-incredible-women-I've-ever-met-smile, and one glance told Liana that Camryn was buying right into it.

Friends? Just like that. Did he really think they could even be that much after how he'd treated her? Liana sat silent, trying to keep her food down while Kevin and Camryn chatted as though they'd been life-long buddies. Camryn ordered sparkling water and a vegetable salad with no dressing, but she was so engaged in every word that came out of

Kevin's mouth, she barely took a bite.

Liana needed to warn Camryn. Her sister may be the biggest flirt this side of the Cascades, but even she didn't deserve a guy who was disrespectful and phony.

Kevin poured hot water into Camryn's cup to reheat her tea. "Do you have plans for Saturday night?"

"Well, that depends."

"Would you consider being my date for a dinner party?"

Camryn glanced in her direction, and Liana felt the blood drain from her head.

"Aren't you and Liana ...?"

"Like I said—we're *friends*." Kevin briefly placed his hand on Liana's but quickly turned his attention back to Camryn. "And to be honest, I already asked your sister to go with me, and she turned me down."

"You did?" Camryn raised her eyebrows at Liana.

She couldn't speak—she couldn't think—she could only nod.

Camryn gave him one of her saccharin smiles. "All right then. I love parties."

Liana's stomach rolled. This couldn't be happening. But it was—right in front of her. "Camryn—"

How could she explain her relationship to Kevin now? The timing was horrible. He'd already stated not once, but twice, that they were friends. Forget that not only did he want to make love to her less than two weeks ago, he'd hoped she loved him. *Or so he'd said.* She wouldn't humiliate herself in front of them.

It would be best if she made her exit now. Somehow, she'd find a way to talk to Camryn later, away from Kevin's watchful eyes. Liana folded her napkin, laid it on the table, and stood.

"Are you okay, Lee?" Camryn spoke as though concerned, but there was no compassion in her eyes.

"I have an appointment with a client, so I need to take off. I'll catch up with you later." Liana picked up her purse, intending to leave enough on the table to cover her meal, but on second thought, she slung the strap over her shoulder. Kevin could pick up the tab.

Camryn smiled. "Bye, Liana."

Kevin opened his mouth as though he had something more to say before Liana departed, but Camryn diverted him by asking a question about Seattle architecture, as if she really cared.

Liana left them engaged in their own conversation. If she didn't love her sister, she'd believe Camryn and Kevin deserved each other. But she did care, and she didn't want Camryn to get hurt.

Liana closed the office door behind her, leaned against the wall, and took a deep breath. The client had already been married several times before, but what started out as a small, intimate wedding, had grown from a single bloom into a full-bouquet event. Liana had adjusted her changes so many times, it took a color-coded Excel spreadsheet to keep track of them.

After what happened at lunch with Kevin, it had been almost impossible to keep focus and track the client's ideas as she verbally went in one direction and then veered off in another. Hopefully, Liana's notes covered everything.

A blanket of sadness wrapped around her heart, causing her throat to tighten and her eyes to well up. *Camryn and Kevin.* Liana didn't see that coming. It was hard enough to admit that she'd been fooled by the playboy, but now that her sister had possibly been swept up by his magnetism, Liana was in an obscure way still tied to him.

Clutching the handle to her bag filled with lists and samples, Liana wandered out the front door into the sunlight, shielding her eyes from the glare. She needed to talk to Dalisay—which meant swallowing her pride. Her friend would never remind Liana that she'd been warned about Kevin. Dalisay would sit and listen without offering judgement.

After leaving several messages on her cell phone and not finding her at the apartment, Liana stopped at the Mabuhay Restaurant to see if Dalisay was helping her parents. The place bustled with activity inside, but a sign on the door stated the restaurant was closed for a private party.

"Oh, no ..." Liana had forgotten about the Ouano's anniversary dinner. She'd been invited to the family celebration but had totally spaced. Not in the mood to be around a lively bunch of people, she'd sneak away before being seen.

"Liana, what are you doing out here?" Dalisay held the door open. "Aren't you coming in?"

"I'm sorry. I'm not be able to stay." Liana wet her lips. "I've got a million things to do—and you know I hate walking in to things late."

"Are you nuts? The party's just getting started. And my mom made a ton of food. My family was expecting you and will be disappointed if you don't come in for a little while."

She couldn't lie—not to Dalisay—so she might as well spit

it out. "The truth is, I completely forgot the party was to-night, I've had a rough day, and I came here to unload on you. Basically, I'm a terrible friend."

Dalisay stepped outside and closed the door behind her. "I'm always here for you—party or not."

"So, you're not agreeing that I'm terrible?" Liana tried to muster a smile.

Dalisay waved the question away. "You may be a bit." She offered a wink that said she was teasing. "But we'll discuss that later. I want to know what's got you so shook up you're turning down lumpia. You never turn down my mother's cooking."

"I'll fill you in but not now. You've got the party—your family." Liana gave her friend a quick hug. "Tell your parents congratulations, and please give them my apology for not staying. I wish I could, but I'm not in a celebratory mood at the moment."

Dalisay studied Liana. "Are you sure you're okay? 'Cause I can take off if you need me to."

"I'm fine. Really. Go and enjoy the party." Liana whirled around and waved as she headed back to her car. "We'll catch up tomorrow." She cupped her hand to her ear. "Call me!"

A light was on in the cottage, and only Liana's car was parked in front. Bryan hadn't seen much of her around the estate lately. Had she and that guy been spending time to-gether?

Rainey scrambled up the steps of the cottage.

"Rainey!" The dog looked at him. "Rainey, come back here!" The Lab ignored Bryan's command and pawed at the door, obviously bent on visiting Liana.

It wouldn't hurt to stop and check in on her. Liana opening up at the hospital and sharing her struggle with not getting into medical school had made her even more attractive to him. He appreciated her trust in him that day, believing it didn't come easy for her to be vulnerable with anyone. She understood what it felt like to have a dream crushed. They had at least that in common.

And then there was the kiss he couldn't forget. He needed to keep it in perspective. It was only a friendly peck on the cheek.

Bryan sauntered to the door and before he raised his hand to knock, he heard Liana singing at the top of her lungs. At least he assumed it was supposed to be singing. It sounded more like screeching. Shrill high notes pierced his ears. Anybody who killed notes shouldn't be allowed to sing. The song was remotely familiar, but she was hitting every note sharp. He pounded on the door. Bryan chuckled. He either had to stop the singer from murdering the song, or murder the singer.

Liana opened the door. "Bryan! Come in!"

She swayed, and her knees gave out beneath her. Bryan caught her before she hit the floor and carried her to the couch. He spotted an open bottle of gin on the table.

"How nice—of—you—t-to come-by ..." She fell back against the side of the couch and laid her head on the arm-rest. "What-a—nice man you are. Did-ya know that—you're-a nice man?"

He paced the kitchen floor, thumbs in his back pockets.

He'd never seen her like this.

"Come he ... re, Bryy—yan."

Bryan knelt on the floor next to her.

"No." She pushed herself up and clumsily patted the space next to her. "Here."

He hesitated, then moved next to her. Something terrible must have happened for her to get drunk. "What's going on, Liana?"

She wailed, as though deeply wounded and fell against his shoulder. He pushed her up and then wrapped his arm around her. Boundaries didn't seem to be the highest priority at this point. Wanting to comfort her, he held her while she sobbed, soaking his shirt.

Seeming exhausted from crying, and unable to shed another tear, Liana finally choked out the story of what had transpired during lunch with Kevin earlier that day.

"He was so manipulating. I actually thought for a while that he cared about me, but as soon as he didn't get what he wanted, he was done. You were sooo right. What if I'd slept with him? I'd be even more hum—hum-iliated than I am now. You know whatta mean?"

The guy was slime. Thank God she'd figured that out before she got hurt even more. "There's nothing for you to be embarrassed about, Liana. You'll always be a class act."

"You're kind, and I'm drunk. I'm so sorry you're seeing me this way." She sat up and fell in the opposite direction, her head landing on the end of the couch. "I never drink like this. And I haven't eaten since yesterday ... except for two bites of salad. I think I'm going to have one whopping headache in the morning."

"Yep, I think you will."

She groaned. "How am I ever going to tell Cam-ryn? She won't believe me. But she's got to be warned."

Bryan tucked a pillow under Liana's head, and then he covered her with an extra blanket he found in a hall closet.

"Thanks, Bry—an."

"You're welcome." He silently offered a prayer.

"You know the funny thing? Even though Kevin is a jerk, what happened today still hurt. It's not the first time a guy pushed me aside for my sister," she said sadly. "I don't know why God favored her, but she's always been the pretty one."

"Lee, you're beautiful. I wish you could see that." He brushed strands of hair from her eyes. "And for the record, God only cares about the inside and so do I. That's far more important."

She yawned. "If you believed that, you wouldn't hide out here." Liana clutched the blanket, rolled over so her back faced him, and fell asleep.

Bryan sank to the floor and leaned back against the couch. She hadn't touched him, but she'd still slapped him in the face with reality. Maybe she was right. Was he so concerned about his appearance that he was hiding from the world? Was he avoiding potential opportunities? Was he hindering any good that his heavenly Father might accomplish through him?

Nineteen

Dalisay stepped next to Liana at the coffee shop counter. "Girl, you look like a creature of the night sucked the life out of you. Even when the sun refuses to shine, there are ways to add a little healthy glow to those cheeks."

"Thanks. I love you too." After drowning herself in gin the night before, Liana knew she looked like someone who hadn't slept in a week. She wasn't proud of her appearance or the drinking. She pulled a debit card from her wallet and handed it to the barista. "Triple shot grande nonfat sugar-free hazelnut latte, please. What would you like? My treat."

"A grande caramel macchiato." Dalisay threw her wallet back in her purse. "Thanks, Lee."

"I owe you." Liana stepped to the side to make room for customers behind them. "I'm so sorry for bailing on you last night."

"It's okay. I told my parents you weren't feeling well. And that wasn't a lie—you didn't look so good. But not as bad as you look now."

That was Dalisay. Always truthful. One of the many things Liana appreciated about her. With their coffee in hand, they found a corner table and made themselves comfortable.

Dalisay cupped her hot drink between her hands. "So spill. What was so horrible you passed up a party?"

Holding up her palm for Dalisay to give her a minute, Liana pulled a bottle of pain relievers from her purse and used a sip of the latte to wash them down. A headache still lingered.

"Wow." One eyebrow raised, Dalisay leaned back in her chair. "You have a hangover. The girl who rarely drinks even a glass of wine. And, unlike me, you usually avoid food when you're upset." She shook her head. "You must have some story to tell."

Liana rubbed her right temple. "I don't even know where to begin."

"Just start somewhere, and if I get lost, I'll ask you to fill in the gaps."

She toyed with her coffee cup. "Okay. But please ... don't at any time say 'I told you so.'"

"I promise." Dalisay leaned her arms on the table between them and gave Liana her full attention. Her eyes grew larger as Liana explained what had happened during lunch with Kevin the day before.

"So, I've avoided more heartbreak, but now I'm afraid Camryn might be headed there. All my sister needs to do is flash her perfect smile and flip her hair, and men lose their ability to think straight. Kevin seemed totally enthralled, but how long will it take before he starts trying to control her?"

"I'm so sorry, Lee." Dalisay reached over and grabbed her friend's hand. "I should have been there for you last night."

It helped that she understood and offered her support.

"I wasn't available every time Kevin asked me to do something, and I know he was frustrated that I wouldn't sleep with him, but I thought we had a chance." Liana took a deep breath and slowly released it. "I was such an idiot. I should have seen through him."

"You're not an idiot, and you deserve better."

"Said like a true friend." Liana managed a small smile. "You always lift my spirits."

"I feel awful that you were alone last night. Maybe you wouldn't have gotten wasted if you'd had someone to talk to." Dalisay's forehead furrowed. "What's that look on your face? You were alone, weren't you?"

"Not exactly ..." Liana gave her a small smile. "After I stopped at the restaurant, I stopped and bought a large bottle of gin on my way home."

Dalisay scrunched her face. "You never drink hard liqueur."

"I know, but all I wanted to do was block out the horrible day, and I had the brilliant idea that alcohol would do a fast job. And it did. I concentrated on swallowing and not tasting, and I felt a whole lot better in a short amount of time. Different story when I woke up this morning. Sooo not doing that again."

Her friend leaned in closer. "Get to the part about not being alone."

Warm memories filled Liana—at least those she could remember. "Bryan stopped by and kept me company for a while. He was sweet ... and understanding. The last thing I remember before passing out was being covered with a blanket."

"He's a good guy, Lee."

Dalisay searched Liana's eyes, maybe looking for a clue as to how she felt toward Bryan. "I know, Daysie. He's been an amazing friend, and I need to be a better one."

❧

After struggling all day with the comment Liana had made the night before, and searching his heart as to whether he was being truthful with himself or not, Bryan found himself at Erik's front door.

He and Maggie had moved a large trailer next to the building that would house their restaurant and event space. They'd live in the trailer until they could build a small home at the far end of their property—close enough to watch over their business but with enough distance to still maintain some privacy.

"Bryan, come on in!" Erik held the door open for him.

"I was hoping you'd have a few minutes to talk."

Erik gave him a questioning look. "Sure. Is there a problem?"

He glanced around the trailer. "Maggie here?"

"Choir practice." Erik gestured toward a soft chair. "Sit down and make yourself comfortable."

He shouldn't have come. Erik had enough to deal with, he didn't need Bryan dumping on him. "Ahhh, no. Thanks, Erik, I shouldn't bother you. It's nothing." Bryan reached for the door. "I'll catch ya later."

"Bryan, wait." Erik leaned against the back of a chair. "You've got *something* on your mind."

"Sorry. I thought I wanted to talk about it ..." Pride stood in his way. Bryan knew it, but he couldn't get past it. Pride and stubbornness had been roadblocks in his spiritual walk before, and now they were standing in his way of being honest again.

"You can't—or won't—so you hold it inside. You're a guy. That's what we do."

Bryan released his grip on the doorknob. Erik understood. "I don't know what to do."

"Come with me over to a friend's house. I was getting ready to leave when you showed up. A small group of us from church meet once a week for a Bible study. It's just guys. We shoot the breeze and talk sports, but most of the night we dig into the Word and figure out how it applies to us."

"I don't know ..." Men he didn't know talking about personal stuff. Another skin graft would be easier to face.

"You don't have to say anything." Erik clamped his hand on Bryan's shoulder. "C'mon."

Fifteen minutes later, Bryan stood with Erik at the front door to a two-story house with a professionally landscaped yard, wondering why he'd let his friend talk him into coming.

The door swung open, and there stood Danny Woods, Dr. Tate's friend whose daughter, Sophie, had gone on her own little adventure and had found Bryan by the river.

"Erik, c'mon in. And Bryan! How did you know ...?"

"I didn't." This couldn't be a coincidence. God must have brought him here. "I stopped to see Erik, and he invited me. I had no clue we were coming here."

Erik grinned. "You two know each other?"

"Bryan and I met when I was hanging out over at Doc Tate's place. I'm glad you finally showed up, man!" He nudged Bryan. "Hey, Sophie! Come see who's here!"

"Who, Daddy? Who's here?" The little girl, dressed in a purple shirt and pink tutu, skipped around the corner of the entryway and squealed as soon as she saw them. "Bryan!" She bounded straight for him.

He picked her up, and she hugged his neck. "Hi, princess!" He breathed in her sweet strawberry scent and absorbed the innocent and unconditional love she offered. An angel from heaven. *Thank you, God.*

"Bryan, this is my wife, Karla." Danny's wife was an adult version of Sophie with her long dark curly hair and bright blue eyes.

"It's nice to finally meet you, Bryan. Sophie talks about you all the time." She extended her hand and gave him a warm smile. "But now, sweet pea, we need to go upstairs so Daddy and his friends can have their Bible study." Karla reached for her daughter and took her from Bryan's arms.

Sophie giggled. "So they can talk about Jesus."

"Yes, honey, so they can talk about Jesus. We can have our own fun time reading one of your books before you say your prayers and go to sleep." Karla started moving toward the stairs leading to the second level.

"Okay." Sophie stretched her arms toward Danny. "Daddy, kiss!"

Danny leaned in toward his little girl, and she kissed him on the cheek. "Good night, sweetheart."

Bryan felt a bit envious watching Danny with his wife and daughter. He'd probably never have his own family, and there were times he felt that loss. But God seemed to be bringing people into his life who helped fill the voids, and he was becoming increasingly grateful.

"Come meet the guys, Bryan. Everyone else is out on the deck. It's too nice to sit inside tonight." Danny led the two arrivals through the kitchen and outside where the others sat lounging in deck chairs.

His hosts had been gracious when he arrived, but what about the other men? Would they extend the same kindness?

Or would it take a while for them to feel comfortable with his appearance?

"Guys, this is Bryan. He works for Doc Tate." Danny pointed to a chair. "There's a spot waiting for you."

"So, Bryan ... you follow the Mariners? We were just talking about last night's game." The man sitting next to him and wearing a baseball jersey extended his hand out to Bryan.

"I sure do!" They shook, and Bryan sank back into his chair, feeling welcomed ... accepted ... and relaxed. The men in the group exchanged their views on baseball—the win with the Rangers—and the upcoming three-game series with the Astros. It had been a long time since he'd felt camaraderie like this, and his heart welled up with thankfulness.

Mark Berg, around thirty-five, was married with three kids. He taught high school science and coached the football team. He talked about dealing with his son's Asperger's syndrome, a type of autism. Landon Main, a computer programmer, was in his twenties and single but in a serious relationship. The older and married car salesman, Peter Johnson, was worried about his wife who had recently been diagnosed with breast cancer. Bryan felt most comfortable with Andy Sinclaire, a carpenter about his age with friendly green eyes, auburn hair, a trimmed beard, and freckles.

Although he rarely spoke up during the meeting, Bryan soaked in the conversation and prayers. The opportunity was given to share his story, but they didn't apply any pressure. Bryan, understanding their curiosity, offered general information about the fire, and they seemed satisfied.

As he and Erik were leaving that night, Danny extended his hand to Bryan. "Hope you come back next week." The two men shook.

"Thanks. I'll think about it."

"Do more than think—pray about it. See what God wants." Erik, with a twinkle in his eye, grasped Bryan's shoulder and offered a grin that hinted he knew something Bryan didn't.

The guys were pretty cool. Maybe Bryan had found a place where he could be himself. Maybe he could start stepping back into the world. Maybe ...

Twenty

Jeans and a T-shirt. That's what Bryan suggested she wear. Liana stood, knocking at his door, with no idea what he had in store for the afternoon. She only dressed down when she exercised one of the horses, but he'd assured her that riding wasn't part of the itinerary. After a beautiful week of sun-filled August weather, Saturday had brought gray skies and drizzle, so a picnic didn't sound inviting.

Bryan, wearing jeans and a baseball jersey, opened the door to his apartment. Keeping one hand behind his back, he ushered her in. "Right on time."

Liana gave a small smile and gestured at her faded shirt. "You better have a good reason for requesting this—fashion statement."

"You look great." He whipped a baseball cap from behind his back and handed it to her. "But this is even better."

She grabbed the hat with the Mariners logo embroidered across the front and held it up. "I don't wear these things."

"C'mon—just for a few minutes." He retrieved the cap, then plopped it on her head. "Today is Indulge Bryan Day, and the Mariners are playing the Astros. I know your dad has a big flat screen, but my TV works okay. I thought it would be fun to watch the game together.

"*Fun.*" Liana perched her hands on her hips. "Did I mention that besides not wearing the official attire, I know nothing about baseball?"

"You've gotta be kidding. Your dad loves the sport." Bryan grinned. "Didn't he ever take you to a game?"

"He wanted to, but I preferred to stay home and read novels." Now that she thought about it, she should have tried attending a game or two with him.

"Then you're not American."

"What does baseball have to do with being American?"

"Everything."

"You're crazy." She wanted to be a better friend, but she never dreamed baseball would be part of the equation. "I'm hours behind on what needs to get done today, and you want me to sit and watch grown men try to hit a little ball and run around in a circle."

"It's not a circle. It's a diamond."

Liana couldn't hold back a smile. "All right. I'll stay for a few minutes. And then I'm out of here."

"Deal." He nodded toward the sofa. "Try out the new couch." He patted one end. "No springs poking through."

"My body thanks you." She pointed to the table laden with pretzels, popcorn, candy bars, and a large platter of nachos with melted cheese. "You can't be serious. You plan to eat all of that?"

"No."

"Good. Because that junk will kill you, not to mention put on major poundage before you croak."

"*We're* going to eat that stuff. *You're* going to help me."

"Oh, no. I don't even go near food like that. I can't." She eased down on her end of the couch.

Bryan's eyes widened and his jaw dropped.

"What?"

"Ever had a chili dog?"

"Absolutely not. Do you know what's in those disgusting things?"

"Chili dogs coming up." He headed for the kitchen and soon returned with a full plate.

"Watching a game should be proof enough that I love and support the great U.S.A. Making me eat one of those is going too far."

She opened her mouth to continue protesting, but before she could get the next word out, Bryan reached over the couch and plopped the chili dog in her hand. Liana's eyes widened as she gazed up at him.

"Take a bite." He nodded as she brought the end up to her lips. "Good girl. Chew. Next step is to swallow."

Liana narrowed her eyes. Forget the junk food killing him. She'd get to him first. But surprisingly, her taste buds were pleased by the spicy concoction. As a child, she'd rarely eaten even a plain hotdog because her mother was so opposed to eating anything that contained sugar or fat. After wiping off the dripping chili around her mouth with a napkin, she closed her eyes for a moment and then opened them to see him sitting on the other end of the couch.

"Okay. I concede. It's not half bad." She accepted a plate from him. "And don't you dare gloat. This is a once-in-a-lifetime thing. Today and today only."

Bryan laughed, reached for the remote, and turned on the TV. "Now I just have to turn you on to the game."

Two hours, several chili dogs, and a plate of nachos later, Liana leaped up from her seat with an exuberant cheer when one of the Mariners hit the ball into the stands, bringing with him two other runners across home plate.

Embarrassed by her uncontrolled response, her face burned. "Sorry. I got caught up in the moment." Liana slunk down.

Bryan's eyes shone. "Just shows you're having a good time."

"I *am* having a good time." She smiled. "I haven't enjoyed anything since ... well, you know." By his nod, she knew he understood she referred to the night she'd gotten wasted on gin, not that that had ended well.

Kevin had called the following day, and with few words, had officially broken things off between them. She'd expected it after what transpired between him and Camryn on the waterfront. Liana hadn't spoken to either of them since.

The last month had been a struggle as she wavered between her feelings of wanting to save Camryn from Kevin and realizing that her sister might have to find out for herself the hard way that he could be selfish and deceptive. She'd left several messages for Camryn, asking her to meet for coffee, explaining that they needed to talk about Kevin.

Her sister had responded with a text saying that if Liana only wanted to get together so she could ask her to stop seeing Kevin, she wasn't willing to listen. And she suggested that Liana stop being jealous and get a life of her own.

A knock sounded. Bryan jumped up and peered out the narrow window next to the door. "It's your dad."

"I thought he was spending the day at the hospital."

Bryan opened the door. "C'mon in, Doc."

"Thanks. It's sure damp out there today." Her father stepped inside. "Liana?"

"Hi, Dad."

Her father perused Liana from her stocking feet to the baseball cap, now turned backward on her head. "It's been a long time since I've seen you look so ..."

"Casual?"

"No." His eyes twinkled. "Relaxed."

"Bryan has something to do with that."

"Then he deserves to be congratulated." He reached to shake Bryan's hand. "Or at least thanked."

"It's been a fun day for both of us."

"I'm sure it has." He had a sly grin as he looked back and forth between the younger two. "Hey, Bryan, I came up to invite you to my birthday dinner tomorrow evening. It's a family tradition. Liana is a great cook, and she always makes my favorite. Pork loin with garlic mashed potatoes."

"Yes, please join us." It would be nice to have Bryan join them, especially after what he'd done for her that afternoon. Her mind had been free of anything but enjoying the game, food ... and company.

Bryan glanced at Liana and then turned back to her father. "I—I don't know. I don't want to intrude on a family dinner."

"But you are family now. And it would be a gift to me if you would share in my birthday celebration. It will also give you a chance to meet Liana's sister, Camryn."

Liana felt the blood drain to her toes. "Camryn's coming? She hasn't made the effort for several years." How awkward, considering her sibling had been avoiding her.

"Well, she is now, and I appreciate it. She apparently wants to share some news. Maybe it has something to do with the new beau she's bringing. She's never been interested in having me meet the men in her life before, so I particularly want to meet this one." Her father's voice rang with excitement.

Liana's stomach knotted up. "Do you know anything about him?"

"Only that his name is ... let me think ... it's Kevin ..."

The knots tightened, and her breathing labored. "Kevin Carter."

Her dad's face brightened with recognition. "That's it. You know the man?"

"I've met him." And she thought Camryn's appearance was going to feel awkward.

"Liana, you need to tell him." Bryan's compassionate eyes held hers.

Her father smoothed down the hair on the back of his head. "What's he like? Is he not a decent guy?"

Adrenaline rushed through her body as she wrestled with how much to tell him. "I think you should judge for yourself."

"What aren't you saying, Lee?"

Her father was going to find out anyway, it might as well come from her, but she still wasn't up to telling him the whole painful story. Liana didn't want him feeling sorry for her. "I—I, um ... went out with him a few times, that's all. I never mentioned him because it didn't go anywhere. Camryn doesn't know. She was only told that we're friends, and technically, we weren't seeing each other when she went out with him."

"I'll ask her not to bring him." Her dad moved toward the door. "I'll call her right now."

"Dad, wait!" He'd been excited about Camryn coming for

dinner, but if Kevin wasn't welcome, she wouldn't show up either. "It seems important that you meet him, so don't call her. It's fine. I can get dinner ready and give you time alone with them. Bryan and I can grab a plate and hang out at the cottage."

"It would be ridiculous for you to go to all that work and then not sit down and eat with us."

This was getting messy. "Okay, I'll be there. I can handle being around Kevin for an evening."

"Thanks." Her father sighed. "I appreciate you trying to please an old man on his birthday. I think it's also time that Bryan and Camryn meet."

She hadn't thought of that encounter. Liana could over-look his scars—in fact she hadn't thought of them all after-noon. But superficial Camryn? Not a chance. Thank the Lord Mom wasn't coming to dinner.

Liana glanced at the concerned expression on Bryan's face. Hopefully, she wouldn't regret her decision to be pre-sent and also include him in the dinner celebration.

After Doc left, Bryan glanced at Liana's sad face and flipped off the TV. "I don't think either one of us is interested in the game right now."

"Hmmm?" Liana stirred. "What?"

"I said the game isn't important." Bryan repositioned his body on the couch so he could face her. "I don't want to go to this dinner thing either. Is there any way we could get out of it?" Had he sounded like he was joking? He'd meant to. For Doc Tate, he'd go. But meeting more of the family, he wasn't sure he was up for that.

"Not without disappointing my dad."

"You should tell Camryn you dated the guy."

"I've tried to, but I've wanted to talk to her face-to-face, and she hasn't give me a chance. I think she believes I'm envious of the time she's spending with him and that I only want to break them up."

"You can't tell her in an e-mail or a phone message?"

"No." Liana focused on the floor for a moment and then met Bryan's gaze. "It doesn't feel right. I want to explain in person."

He understood her reasoning, but what if her plan backfired? "What if Kevin has told her? Or what if he brings it up during dinner? Then what are you going to do?"

"I'll deal with it then."

"Well, that's quite a plan." Bryan couldn't hold back the sarcasm creeping into his tone.

"What about you, Mr. Know-It-All?" she snapped. "What's your excuse for not wanting to go? At least you don't have to cook and serve dinner to traitors."

"How can Camryn be a traitor when you've never told her about your relationship with Kevin?" he shot back. "If you had, she might have backed off."

"Who are you to defend my sister? You don't even want to meet her!"

"It's not that I don't want to meet her." Bryan held her gaze. "I don't like seeing you in pain." Oh, man ... he didn't mean to open himself up like that.

Liana's eyes shone with tears. "That's what you're worried about? That they'll do or say something that will hurt *me*?" She wiped her eyes with a napkin. "You're not concerned about how Camryn or Kevin will respond to your scars?"

"No. I don't care what they think." He only wanted Lee's approval. "Have you or your father ever mentioned me, or my appearance, to Camryn?"

Liana leaned back against the couch. "No, there was never any reason to. I don't talk to her about anything or anybody."

"And chances are your father didn't either—just because—just because he doesn't think of me as being different." Bryan rubbed the bridge of his nose. "Seems we're going to need each other at this party. I don't enjoy surprising someone and then seeing them repelled by how I look, but I'm willing to be there—for you and your dad. He's my best friend. I can't deny him a birthday party."

The way the guys at the Bible study had accepted him had renewed some of Bryan's confidence, but he remembered that first day with Liana. He could still see the horror in her eyes as he emerged from the shadows in the stable.

All afternoon during the game, he'd sat with her on his good side even though Liana no longer seemed to notice his appearance.

But there was still that initial look. What if Camryn reacted the same way? The whole dinner would be awkward as Bryan tried to turn his smooth profile to everyone all night and Camryn tried to avoid looking at him—to say nothing of what Kevin might do.

"Bryan—I—" Her eyes glistened as she laid a hand on his. "Thank you. You're right. She offered a tentative smile. "Partners for the evening?"

His heart pounded at her confession. If only Bryan could

be honest with her that he wanted more. He nodded. "Partners."

Twenty-One

The cool, damp cloth was small comfort to Liana's hot, aching forehead, but she'd already taken a couple of pain relievers. Agreeing to this birthday dinner was not only an impulsive move, it was insane. If only she could figure out a way to poison Kevin without harming anyone else. She'd chuckle at the absurd idea if it wouldn't hurt her head.

The aroma of roasted pork loin with fresh rosemary and garlic filled the kitchen. She pulled the meat out to check the temperature on the thermometer, slipped the pan back into the oven, and flipped the knob to warm.

A knock sounded, then the back door squeaked as Bryan stepped into the kitchen. His "smile" appeared about as jovial as her headache felt pleasant. Clearly, he didn't want to be there anymore than she did.

"Are you okay?"

"I'm better now that you're here." Liana leaned against the counter.

He shed his jacket and draped it across a kitchen chair. "Well get through the night, and then we'll reward ourselves with ..."

"Not gin." A slight giggle made her head throb.

Bryan chuckled. "No, definitely not."

"Chili dogs?" The corners of her mouth tugged up.

"Shake on it?" He held out his hand, and after wiping hers on a towel, she slipped one into his. "Chili dogs—on me."

"I was actually planning on eating them."

"Ha ha. Very funny."

Though rough, his hand comforted her, and she regretted having to let go.

He seemed as reluctant as she to break the connection, and as he released her, he spoke in a voice barely audible. "I know you're not into God as much as your dad, but I want you to know that I'm praying for you—for tonight."

Gazing into his eyes, Liana caught a glimpse of his heart, and what she thought might be feelings for her. Wrapping her arms around him, she gave him a brief hug. "Thanks, Bryan."

Voices from the other room disrupted further conversation. Kevin and Camryn had arrived.

Bryan's armpits dampened as he followed Liana into the other room. If he didn't know how uncomfortable this dinner was going to be for her, he would have bailed. He'd seen Kevin from a distance when he visited the estate to see Liana, but even viewing their interaction through his apartment window, Bryan knew women could easily be attracted to Kevin. The guy must live at the gym.

What Kevin thought about him didn't matter. Bryan feared that Liana—even knowing that Kevin was self-centered—might subconsciously make comparisons between the two men that would jeopardize everything he'd begun to build with her. He enjoyed their growing friendship and didn't want her seeing him as a freak again.

Dr. Tate stood in the entryway with Kevin and a stunning blonde wearing a light purple dress that barely covered her backside. Bryan diverted his eyes from the long legs that extended below the dress. Speaking of undeniable attraction. *Help me, Lord.*

"Liana, Bryan, there you are." Dr. Tate motioned them to join the three. "Bryan, I wanted you to meet my daughter, Camryn."

"Nice to meet you." Bryan moved forward, intending to extend his hand in greeting, but Camryn's eyes enlarged as she took a subtle step back. He got the hint when she busied herself, tucking strands of hair behind her ears, that she didn't want to touch him.

Camryn cleared her throat. "Nice to meet you too." Her eyes never quite met Bryan's.

"I'm Kevin." The competition, however, did reach to shake Bryan's hand with a subtle smirk on his face and humor in his eyes. He didn't need words to express his thoughts to Bryan. Bryan read them without any problem. Kevin thought Bryan was laughable—a joke.

Lord, don't let him get to me.

Camryn latched on to Kevin's arm and smiled. "And of course, Liana and Kevin know each other."

Bryan caught a glimpse of Liana, who looked as pale and sick as he felt inside.

"If you'd like something to drink, Dad can get it for you. Bryan and I have some things to finish up in the kitchen, and then dinner will be ready in a few minutes."

With relief, Bryan followed Liana back into the kitchen, willing to take on any chore that kept him there.

❧

Camryn passed the bowl of mashed potatoes to her father. "Dad, didn't Liana tell you she introduced me to Kevin?"

Liana caught Bryan's glance. He was probably trying to gauge her response to the insinuation that she purposely brought Camryn and Kevin together. Determined not to ruin her father's birthday, Liana refused to react. Just a few hours, then she'd be free to escape to the cottage.

"No, honey, she didn't." Her father scooped a portion of potatoes onto his plate. "She's busy with her life, just as you are with yours. But it's a pleasure to be given the opportunity to meet Kevin this evening."

"The pleasure is mine." Kevin flashed one of his million-dollar smiles at Liana's father and slipped his arm around her sister's shoulders.

Camryn beamed as she looked from him to her father. "Kevin and I have seen each other almost every day for the past four weeks. And when we couldn't be together, we've called at least ten times a day."

Kevin leaned over and kissed Camryn's temple.

All this gushing—nauseating. Liana bit the inside of her cheek and focused on the one green bean not touching the other beans on her plate. She felt like that piece of insignificant vegetable. Cold and removed. And she would stay that way if it meant she wouldn't get hurt. Conversation droned on around her, but the bean and the white space around the bean became her world.

"Liana!"

"What?" She felt like the latest bizarre addition to the Woodland Park Zoo the way they were all gawking at her.

With a sly smile, Kevin relaxed in his chair, as though he enjoyed a private joke.

"You haven't paid attention to a word I've said." Camryn scrunched up her perfect button nose. "Where were you? You look like you'd mentally left the country. I hope it was at least some place interesting." She flung her loose hair over one shoulder as she gave a little bounce in her chair and faced Kevin. "Exotic is the perfect solution. Don't you think?"

"Jamaica?"

"Tropical, breezy nights. Sandy beaches."

Liana attempted to clear her throat. "You're planning a vacation together?"

The smile that helped make Camryn famous appeared on cue as she cocked her head and posed. At that moment, Liana wanted to display for Kevin the photos of her sister before the orthodontist made enough cash on her mouth to put his son through his first year of college.

"Not merely a vacation." Camryn leaned in to Kevin's shoulders. "Our honeymoon." She turned the ring on her left hand to display a square cut diamond engagement ring set in white gold.

Liana went numb.

"Well, say something." Camryn stared, obviously perturbed that Liana hadn't showered squeals of congratulations over the announcement.

"I—ah—when did this happen? You've only known each other for four weeks." Liana looked to her dad for help.

Her father gently bounced his butter knife on the end of the table. "Liana's right, hon. You're both adults, but marriage is a serious commitment. What's wrong with taking it slow? Four weeks isn't enough time to really know each other or what you want."

"I love your daughter. I know that for sure." Kevin reached for Camryn's hand. "I'd marry her tomorrow, but we understand your concern about rushing into a marriage. That's why we're not planning to have the wedding before spring."

"June, Daddy." Camryn couldn't have beamed any more if she'd been a spotlight for a theater production. "I'd like a large June wedding with bridesmaids, tons of flowers, and you walking me down the aisle."

"Nine months." Their dad nodded. "I guess that's ample time to plan a wedding, but I'm still not convinced it's enough time to build a foundation for a good marriage."

"Daddy, I love you and want your blessing." Camryn's voice, laced with disappointment, rose in volume. "You and Mom got married at a much younger age, and you knew each other for less than a year."

Their father sighed. "True. And look how that turned out. I want better for you."

"This is different." Camryn gazed up at Kevin with love-sick eyes. "I promise. You don't have anything to worry about."

"All right, Camryn." Their dad gave one nod. "Like you said, you're adults. You can make your own decision, but I hope you continue to think it through. To be honest, I'd feel better if you went through some premarital counseling. I could check with my pastor's schedule, if you like."

"Thanks, Daddy, that's sweet. But if we decide to go through any counseling, it probably won't be with a pastor." Camryn offered a slight smile.

"I'm not a religious guy, Dr. Tate." Kevin's voice sounded lighthearted. "I hope you don't hold that against me."

Liana's father frowned.

"Daddy, please ..."

"I love you, Camryn, and if you really want this, I'll do my part to help make your wedding day all that you've dreamed." Their father's words said he was on board, but Liana knew him, and he was not pleased with Camryn's plans.

Her sister twisted around to face Liana. "You're going to help too, aren't you? After all, you're not only a wedding co-ordinator, you're my sister."

"Camryn, I—" Liana's throat closed in. Under the table, Bryan's hand closed around hers, reminding her he was there in support.

Her father, giving Liana a sympathetic glance, interrupted. "Maybe it would be easier to work with someone who isn't family, Camryn. Liana could probably give you a list of other coordinators and resources."

"Please, Lee, I'd really welcome your help." There was that smile again, but something about it wasn't quite genuine. "And of course, as my only sister, you'll be my maid of honor."

She had to be kidding. No, she wouldn't kid about a thing like that. It was the maid of honor's duty to be at the bride's side, making sure her day was perfect. Camryn would like nothing more than for Liana to be catering to her every whim. Liana's heart thumped as the group around the table waited for her response.

A challenging smirk appeared on Kevin's face.

The man was vile. She'd been foolish to fall for someone

so uncaring about people's feelings. Liana couldn't comprehend why he'd want to jump into marriage unless having a super model as a wife would raise his status.

Liana would *not* show him or Camryn how their engagement affected her, so with all the willpower she could muster, she forced out a response. "Camryn, I'll help with whatever you need."

But she'd still hope and pray that Camryn would come to her senses before the wedding and call it off.

Liana would never have left Bryan in the living room with the two men if she hadn't been confident her father would deal with Kevin if he did or said anything to offend Bryan. Actually, Bryan was probably the strongest man she'd ever met—he could take care of himself. She didn't need to feel so protective.

"Delicious dinner." Instead of putting her plate in the dishwasher, Camryn handed it to Liana.

"Thanks." Liana couldn't imagine how her sister knew it tasted any better than cardboard—she only ate a few bites. But then, Liana hadn't eaten much either—for different reasons. She rinsed off the plate and set it on the counter.

"Sorry I didn't have any cake. It sure looked scrumptious, but you know I can't afford the extra calories."

"It's Dad's favorite. So as long as he's happy, that's what counts."

"Liana?" Camryn leaned against the kitchen counter.

She continued to stack plates in the dishwasher. "What?"

"I know you're not thrilled about my engagement, but can

you at least act it for my sake? It's one of the biggest moments in my life."

The last plate dropped into its slot with a clank. Liana wheeled around and propped her body against the edge of the counter. "Every moment in your life is huge, Camryn. It always has been. I wouldn't expect this to be any different."

"What are you talking about?"

"The world revolves around you, and you always get what you want." Only now, Liana was convinced that what her sister desired would only bring her unhappiness in the future.

"That's not true."

"Yes. It is." Camyrn had won their mother's approval, she'd taken Liana's boyfriend when they were teenagers, and she'd been in the spotlight since they were kids. That was the short list. "I've learned to accept it."

"I know what you're really steamed about."

"I'm not steamed about anything, Camryn. I think you're upset because I didn't bring out a stack of *Bride's* magazines the second you flashed that gargantuan rock in my face."

"Well, I think you're angry because I'm marrying the guy you wanted for yourself."

"You're crazy." Liana didn't have a clue how much Kevin had shared with her sister. Did she know they'd dated? Should she grab this opportunity to let Camryn know what kind of man she was engaged to? Or wait until there was no chance of being interrupted?

"He told me you were all over him the night he took you to the Salish Lodge for dinner. He had to make it clear then that you two could never be anything more than friends."

"That's the story he told?" Liana clenched her fist. The

man was unbelievable. When Kevin had immediately decided to date her sister, Liana knew he wasn't what she'd once believed. But this revelation—was Kevin even more manipulating than she thought? "I think you should know—"

"Hey, what's my girl doing out here?" Kevin sauntered into the kitchen, carrying several coffee cups. "Your dad and— what's his name?"

"Bryan." Liana barely breathed out the name.

"Yeah. Bryan. They're talking horses. Something about one not eating well. Since I don't know a thing about animals, I thought I'd see if the two of you were talking about anything interesting."

Anger bubbled low in the pit of Liana's stomach. "Or did you come out here to see if we were talking about you? How I was 'all over you at the lodge'? I can't believe—"

Camryn latched on to Kevin's arm. "Speaking of Bryan … I can't believe you're so desperate for a guy that you settle for hired help. And someone who's as grotesque as he is. I can almost understand Dad feeling sorry for him, but c'mon Liana."

Was Camryn picking up her fiancé's cruel behaviors? "It's none of your business, but it's not like that. Dad invited him to dinner."

"Your father must have a heart for hard cases. No one else probably would want the guy around." Kevin chuckled. "Talk about scary."

Liana glanced past Kevin. Movement at the door caught her eye. "Kevin, be quiet!" But it was too late. Bryan stood in the doorway of the kitchen, holding a bowl of leftover green beans. Those blasted green beans. "Bryan—"

"I thought I'd see if you needed any help." He gently laid

the bowl on the counter. "Thanks for dinner." He made eye contact with the couple. "Nice to meet you, Kevin—Camryn. And congratulations on your engagement." He strode past them through the kitchen and out the back door into the night.

Camryn watched him leave. "At least he has some manners."

"Which is more than I can say for some people," Liana whispered. Their words had deeply hurt Bryan. She knew it. Feeling his pain made her want to go to him, but she had inflicted part of that hurt by not defending him. Why didn't she stand up for him? Shame covered her like a wet and moldy wool blanket. She had no right to comfort him. Not yet.

Liana's dad walked into the kitchen. "Did Bryan leave?"

She bit on her lower lip. "Yeah, he did."

"That's strange. I thought we were going to play chess."

Camryn perked up. "Kevin can play. He's wanted to find someone who could challenge him, and you know I'm no good at the game."

Their father's eyebrows arched. "Is that true, young man?"

"I'd love to take you on."

"Okay, then. I'll get the game set up in the den."

Camryn stood on tiptoe and kissed her fiancé on the lips. "I need to run upstairs for a moment, but I'll be right back down." As she strolled toward the kitchen door, she whirled around as though she realized Kevin wasn't following her. "Don't leave Dad waiting, Kev. It'll only take him a minute to set up the chess pieces."

"I'm on my way." But instead of exiting the kitchen, he

veered toward Liana.

She wouldn't let him intimidate her. "What are you doing, Kevin?"

"Making sure you're okay."

"I'm fine. Why wouldn't I be?" But he might not be feeling so cocky once she had the chance to talk some sense into her sister. His pride would take a big blow if Camryn broke the engagement and that news became public.

He gave her a smug look. "C'mon, Lee."

"Don't call me that. It's reserved for family."

"Well, I'm family. Almost. And since we're going to be related, don't you think we should make peace with each other? For your sister's sake?"

"From my experience, you'll be interested in what Camryn needs until you get what you want—whatever that is—then the rules will change. What exactly *do* you want from her? What's your game plan?" Would he be so proud as to state it?

"What do *you* want?" Kevin's eyes narrowed as he stared at her. "Not for Camryn—for yourself?"

"I don't think that's your business anymore. And as for that lie you told her about us, I remember that night quite differently."

"I didn't do anything you didn't want me to. And from my vantage point, you wanted a whole lot more. You were just afraid to take it."

She gasped. "How dare you!"

"Is that why you're hanging out with the weird dude that was here tonight? You won't have to worry about getting all hot for him? You won't have to fight your natural feelings?"

"Stop it," she hissed and slapped his hand away as he

reached toward her face.

"If you ever change your mind, Camryn doesn't ever have to know."

Anger coursed through her body. "You're immoral and cruel, Kevin Carter. And all that I feel right now is gratitude that I finally realized just how wicked you are. My sister needs to be warned before it's too late."

"I'm not wicked. However, I do have my vices. Your sister knows I'm not perfect, but she loves me despite my flaws. Anything you say won't change that. She'll only take your accusations as a ploy to get me back."

He stood close enough that she could smell his cologne. The same scent he wore the night at the Falls when he'd tried to manipulate her into staying the night with him.

"So, let's play nice and get along. That's what I'm going to do. All I ask is that you do the same." He reached for her again, and she backed away. "Your dad is waiting for me."

Liana stalked out on the deck and pressed her back against the outside wall. Then, she took a deep breath, hoping the evening air would cool her down.

Her eyes stung, and her vision blurred, but not because she felt sorry for herself. She'd been liberated from Kevin. She'd seen the real man inside the pretty package and was freed from any feelings for him. Camryn probably wouldn't listen to Liana's warnings about Kevin, but she'd talk to her anyway—even at the risk of completely alienating her sister. Liana's heart no longer ached for herself, but for a kind friend.

She needed to find Bryan.

Twenty-Two

The door to his apartment swung open with Liana's knock. She'd rehearsed how she'd apologize once she saw him, but maybe he wasn't up here.

"Bryan?"

A small table lamp next to the couch lit the room. She stepped inside. "Bryan are you here?"

No sound came from either the bedroom or bathroom. He must have gone down to the stable. She sighed. She didn't know whether to search for him there or wait. Either way, she refused to end the night without talking to him.

Feeling like an intruder in his space, she didn't venture any farther while debating what to do. If she tracked him down, he could put her off. And not only could it take awhile to locate him—she might not find him. He could be anywhere on the estate. It would be far more comfortable talking here. She'd wait outside on the steps.

An open Bible lay on the table in front of her, and a photograph on top of the well-worn marked-up pages caught her attention. Words printed on the bottom of the picture stated, "Lava is hot enough to light the fire in the coldest of hearts."

Musicians huddled—one toted a bass, another drumsticks, and a third carried an electric guitar. All displayed unsmiling solemn faces, so often seen in band promos. A striking woman posed behind keyboards. Long, dark curly tresses cascaded over her shoulders. Her tight blouse, open halfway to her navel didn't reveal "everything," but enough to be seductive.

Something familiar about the handsome male holding the electric guitar snagged Liana's attention. She peered closer and gasped. *Bryan!* It had to be him. The man in the photo revealed the same compelling eyes.

❧

Eager Rainey raced up the steps to the apartment ahead of Bryan.

"What are you so anxious for, boy?"

As soon as Bryan opened the door, Liana jumped where she stood, her face a mixture of agony and hope. Rainey trotted to greet her, but Bryan didn't move. How could he feel angry at her for barging into his home, yet be so glad to see her?

"What are you doing here?" he croaked. "What gives you the right to barge in here and make yourself at home?"

"I'm sorry. I shouldn't have let myself in." Liana's face scrunched up, as though in pain. "I came to apologize."

Bryan waited to see if words would come from her heart. He thought they'd gone into the night as a team, but when he heard the rich dude make fun of him ... Liana had stood there, staring at him as though he was exactly how they described him—grotesque. He wanted to believe he could trust her—that she'd gotten past his appearance—but she let him down. Just like Jenny.

"I'm so sorry for what happened tonight. What my sister said—Kevin. How they treated you was intolerable."

Bryan shut the door behind him and leaned against it. "I

expected it. I've dealt with reactions before from people who didn't know me." He needed to say it ... "But you acted like you had nothing to do with me being there for dinner. That—that hurt more than anything else." He swallowed the emotion that was rising from his gut. Men weren't supposed to show pain, and he'd been humiliated enough for one night. "I guess I expected more from you."

"*I* expected more from me." A thin glaze of moisture covered her eyes, making them gleam faintly in the dim lamp light. "I should have put them in their place. You're a good friend, Bryan. And for a moment I forgot that. The only person I was concerned about tonight was me." She took a deep breath. "When they announced their engagement ..."

"The guy is a jerk."

"You got that right," she whispered. "He's untrustworthy, Bryan. I'm afraid for my sister."

Of course she was worried about Camyrn, and it had to be awful for Liana to watch rich dude flaunt his engagement to her sister.

Bryan saw the photograph clutched in Liana's hand, and the calmness he was beginning to feel morphed into an explosion. "Where did you get that?" He pointed at her hand.

"I saw it laying on your Bible, and I was curious. I'm sorry if I did something wrong."

"You had no right to go through my personal things." Bryan tore the photo out of her hand—a memento of his past life—one he should be forgetting. He didn't want Liana to know where he'd come from. Didn't want her to know about his destroyed dreams. Didn't want her to feel sorry for him.

"I apologized, and I meant it. I wasn't snooping. I was going to wait outside for you, and I happened to see the photo—I wasn't thinking. I would never intentionally invade your privacy."

Anger burned in Bryan's belly, and it was sparked by hurt that even Liana didn't respect him enough to leave some things alone. He couldn't risk anyone else knowing what he'd lost. It took enough energy resisting his sister's push to return to music.

"I was curious, but I didn't mean any harm. It could have been a picture of anything." She stepped around the end table and toward him, but he backed away. "About the photo ..."

"I don't want to talk about it."

"Bryan—"

"I said I don't want to talk about it!" He closed his eyes, then opened them to see a tear slide down her right cheek.

"Okay," she whispered, then wiped her cheek with back of her hand. Her eyes brimmed with shimmering sadness. "Again, I'm sorry. I didn't want to hurt you—or make you angry. Seems I've messed up several times tonight."

His angered deflated, and he wanted to comfort her, but confused feelings battled inside. Bryan needed space—he needed to think.

"Forgive me?" She sounded desperate.

"Yes. You're forgiven." He sighed and closed his hand around the photo until it was scrunched into a ball. "But you should go."

Liana nodded and shuffled to the door as if carrying a heavy weight on her shoulders. She rested her hand on the doorknob for moment, then opened the door and left without saying goodbye.

Bryan plunked down on the couch. He slowly unfolded

the crunched picture, smoothed out the photo, and stared into his former bandmates' faces. Ted Minor and Bryan had roomed together in college. He and Mack had struck up a friendship in music theory class their sophomore year.

Beautiful Jenny had been friend, confidante, and girlfriend. Someone he could share his life with, or at least he'd thought. What a joke on him. The fire had damaged his body, but she'd burned him in love. She destroyed his trust in women and relationships, yet something about Liana had spurred hope in him again—*false hope.*

His reflection once mirrored the lead guitarist in the photo. But no more. That person was dead and gone. Destroyed in a fire.

After one last look, he tore the photo into tiny pieces.

Why, Lord?

Bryan wanted to take out his pain on a punching bag. Unfortunately, he didn't have one.

So, instead, he opened the New Living Bible and turned to 1 Corinthians 13:12, a verse he'd highlighted and knew well. "Now we see things imperfectly, like puzzling reflections in a mirror, but then we will see everything with perfect clarity. All that I know now is partial and incomplete, but then I will know everything completely, just as God now knows me completely."

He wanted to believe there would be a time when God would explain why he allowed the fire to consume not only Bryan's body, but also the ambitions he'd held since childhood. Even if he had to wait until life in eternity, there would be answers. Until then, he'd try to cling to the belief that God understood him better than he understood himself.

෨

Liana couldn't sleep. She snuggled with a pillow in the chair by her front window—in the dark. She thought back to the day when she'd watched Bryan play with Rainey on the lawn. The same day Kevin called asking for that first date. If only she'd recognized him as a slime ball then.

Aside from her father, Bryan was different from most men, at least the ones she'd been around. He really cared about people, like the little girl, Kylee, at the hospital. Every time Liana needed him, he'd come through. From fixing the garbage disposal to sitting with her the night she made the horrible mistake of overindulging on alcohol. She would never have gotten through her father's birthday dinner without his support.

That first night in the stable when they met, she never imagined Bryan would become so important to her. Until now, she'd taken his friendship for granted. No more. Something needed to change. *She* needed to change.

From his reaction to her looking at that photo, it must represent an important part of his life—a past she knew nothing about. Liana felt a twinge. She understood so little about what Bryan wanted—what he needed—because she'd been too focused on her own problems.

She uncurled her legs from beneath her, stood up, and wandered to her bedroom. As she climbed into bed and pulled the covers over her shoulder, Liana's heart opened and revealed a truth. She was falling for Bryan.

He was intelligent. Kind. Compassionate like her father. And there were those sometimes intense, but warm eyes ...

Twenty-Three

"Tell me what happened at dinner last night before Erik gets here and we have to talk business. I've been dying to hear how you handled eating at the same table as the creep and your sister." Dalisay broke off a piece of her raspberry scone and popped it into her mouth.

Liana waited until the couple sitting at the table behind them in the coffee shop finished picking up their personal things and left. "It turned out to be worse than what I even thought. The whole evening was a nightmare."

Her friend waited quietly while Liana gathered her thoughts.

"Daysie, they're engaged. Can you believe it? My sister wants to marry Kevin."

Dalisay coughed, choking on her food. "Sorry," she gasped then took a sip of her latte. "You're joking, right? They've only been seeing each other for what—five weeks?"

"Four. And no, it's not a joke. She thinks she's in love with him."

"Kevin? Is he in this for real?"

"I don't know what game he's playing. The only thing I can think of is that he's under the impression that marrying into our family will help his career and reputation. He must have decided that between the two available daughters, marrying a model was a better choice." For the first time Liana could remember, she was grateful Camryn was more attractive.

"Wow. What does your dad think? He's one of the smart-est people I know."

"I'm sure he sees right through Kevin, but what can he do? Camryn is an adult. She can make her own decisions. I think Dad wants to make sure he doesn't do anything to al-ienate Camryn so he can be there when things fall apart."

"You're confident it won't work out?"

"Daysie, he hit on me when we were alone." Remember-ing how Kevin had reached for her the night before made Liana shiver. She'd gone from desiring his touch to being sickened by the thought of him putting his hands on her.

Dalisay's eyes enlarged, and what was left of the scone slipped from her hands. "Wow. Are you going to say any-thing?"

A man dressed in a suit dropped into a chair at a table to the left with his iced coffee and opened his laptop. Liana didn't want anyone overhearing the conversation, so they'd have to keep their voices low.

"I've got to warn Camryn about him. But I'm afraid she won't believe me. Kevin lied to her about us, so if I say any-thing, she'll think I'm jealous of the relationship."

"You must have been miserable." Dalisay ate the last bite of her scone.

"Oh, it gets worse. Camryn talked me into helping plan the wedding. Don't even ask how I caved in on that one. I still can't believe it." Liana sipped her Americano. "No, actu-ally I do. Pride. I couldn't let either Camyrn or Kevin think that I was jealous. And, now I hope my involvement will give me a chance to talk Camyrn out of marrying Kevin. She'll be forced to spend some time with me."

Liana's eyes stung from unexpected tears, and she blinked them into retreat. "How did things get so bad between Camryn and me that everything ends up being a fight or a competition?"

"The two of you have always had problems getting along." Dalisay frowned. "I wish I could have been there for you."

Another gentle wave of sadness washed over Liana. "Bryan came for dinner, even though it made him uncomfortable. He didn't want me to feel alone. He was wonderful, and he dealt with Kevin's and Camryn's insensitivity with class." Liana's throat tightened. "He's a great guy, but I did some things that hurt him last night, and I feel terrible."

Dalisay's eyes filled with compassion. "It will work out. Whatever you did, Bryan isn't the type of person to hold a grudge."

Her friend was right, but Liana also believed she'd need to make the first move. Bryan wouldn't be chasing her down.

"Hey guys, how are things going?" Erik dropped a stack of papers on the table and slid onto a third chair. "Maggie's been working so hard, I told her to go get one of those pedicures she's always talking about. So, you only get me today."

Liana tried to focus on the purpose of the meeting—the hospital gala—and took out her notes and pen. "I'm expected to give a full update at the committee meeting tonight. Most of the people in that group are very supportive, but Marian Henderson must have something against me. She questions or challenges my every move. I've been working some fourteen-hour days, and I know both of you have been putting in a lot of time too, but we've really got to pull things together."

"I've updated my design to include the changes we made last week." Dalisay handed them each a folder.

Erik squirmed in his chair. "I'm afraid not everything is going well on our end."

That was not what Liana wanted to hear, and her shoulder muscles tightened, anticipating what new problems had come up. Of all the areas of her life, she'd love for this one to work right now.

"We have a couple of situations we're working on." Erik rapped his pen on the table. "But don't worry about it. We'll get it figured out."

"What situations, Erik?" Liana dug her thumbnail into the side of her paper cup.

"There's an issue with the plumbing, and I already have someone on it. My main concern has been completing the ceiling, but we may have come up with a solution. It's supposed to look like the night sky with twinkling stars, and we found a company that makes fiber-optic star tiles. The light source uses LEDs that are electronically controlled to make the twinkling effect. The tiles are virtually maintenance-free and should last for years, but the issue is whether or not they'll give the effect we want considering the ceiling height. And it's going to be spendy covering that large area, so I need to work on some creative financing."

Liana toyed with the corner of her notebook. "And if the lights don't work?"

"Don't worry, Lee." Dalisay offered a smile. "We'll figure something out. It's not your problem—it's ours. What else do you need from us?"

They spent the next hour cross-checking lists. The committee was taking care of obtaining items for the auction and gift bags, as well as getting volunteers to put the bags together and hand them out the night of the gala. Volunteers would also manage the coat check. Liana's responsibilities included making sure those areas were set up and the volunteers knew how to manage them.

As they were wrapping up, Liana brought one more item into the discussion. "The dance band is contracted for the evening, but I'd also like to book someone who can provide special entertainment. It's not a necessity, since the band can provide background music throughout the event. But it would mean extra points for me if I could find someone well-known and popular, who's not only contemporary, but also able to reach the older generation. If you have any ideas, I'd be happy to hear them."

"If you could get someone like Casey Marks, he'd be perfect. He's touring on the West Coast in October. I love his music, and so do my parents." Dalisay grinned. "So, what do you think? Could we get him to sing?"

Liana chuckled. "Yeah, if only." Casey Marks would make the fundraiser a fantasy event. The guy was amazing, but way out of her reach.

"This is awesome! Thanks for asking me to come, Andy." Bryan surveyed the view from Poo Poo Point on the west side of Tiger Mountain, just outside of Issaquah. His hat helped shield his eyes from the bright sun. "Interesting name for this spot." Bryan chuckled. *Poo Poo Point?*

Andy joined in with a hearty laugh. "I have to agree with you there. It's named for the sound the steam whistles would make when signaling loggers."

They stood back and off to the side of people preparing to

paraglide off the mountain and groups there to observe. People were so focused on the activity, they didn't seem to notice Bryan. That, along with wearing a hat, helped make him feel inconspicuous.

He appreciated Andy's invite. They'd hung out a few times after meeting at the men's Bible study, but it especially felt good to get away from the estate after the rough evening he'd had the night before at the Tate's family dinner.

"Perfect conditions for gliding. It's early evening, so the winds are calmer, and warm air rises, which helps people stay up longer. When temperatures are cool, the flights end up being much shorter. Watch over there." Andy pointed to a man wearing a helmet who faced the edge where the mountain dropped off. "He's getting ready to take flight."

A bright red parachute billowed out behind him. He seemed to wait for the right moment, then ran toward open space. The current carried him up, and there he was, soaring gracefully through the air. Paragliders filled the sky like colorful butterflies.

"What a sight!" Awestruck, Bryan couldn't get enough. He'd driven by the flight school at the base of the mountain on his way to and from Issaquah when he had to go into town on errands. He'd watched the paragliders land in the field next to Issaquah Hobart Road and had been fascinated by their soft approach to the ground. To see them fly from the top of the mountain felt exhilarating.

"It's cool watching from here, but can you imagine the view they have? They should be able to see Mt. Rainier, Seattle, and Mt. Baker." Andy's face lit up with a huge grin. "Would you ever want to try gliding? You can go tandem with an instructor."

Bryan laughed. "Hey, any time you want to go for it, I'll be here for moral support. But I think I'll keep my feet on the ground."

They watched in silence as a woman readied her chute. Next to her, a man was harnessing himself to a teenage boy.

"You coming back to the group any time soon? The guys have been asking about you."

Bryan had anticipated the question. He'd enjoyed meeting the guys, but was he ready to open himself up to talking about his life? Was it fair to listen to their problems and keep silent about his own? "Not sure. Kind of have some things to sort out right now."

"Could be the place to do that. It might help to get input from people who care and know what they're talking about." Andy shielded his eyes and kept looking straight ahead. "Woman trouble?"

"Partly." That and a long list of other things.

"Liana Tate?"

Bryan studied his friend. "How'd you know?"

"Good guess. I know a little bit about the Tates since her father goes to my church. You don't date or hit the social scenes, so ..." Andy shrugged and kicked at a rock near his foot. "She into you?"

Just the kind of question he wanted to avoid. "We're friends."

"Can't have too many friends." Andy pointed to the sky. "There she goes!" The woman with the yellow chute ascended higher, then she veered to the right. "Beautiful!"

Bryan kept his eyes on the paraglider. He needed to talk to someone, and Andy seemed trustworthy. It would be easier to open up to one guy instead of an entire group. "Last night she crossed a boundary, and I got pretty angry."

"What'd she do?"

"Looked at a photo without asking." Bryan shook his head. "Sounds silly when I explain it like that, but it was personal."

"A mug shot? Was that it?" Andy chuckled. "You didn't want her to know you robbed a bank?" He lifted binoculars to his eyes.

"Funny."

"She apologize?"

"Yeah."

"Maybe she was trying to get to know you better."

"Maybe."

"Dude, you're not the easiest person to get to know." Andy handed the binoculars to Bryan. "Words of wisdom from my dad. If you want to find someone to share your life, you gotta be willing to share your life with her."

Andy was right, or at least his dad was right.

Jenny had hurt Bryan more than he thought possible—and the fallout—he struggled with trust. But Liana wasn't Jenny. Liana had poured her heart out to him more than once, and they'd experienced moments of intimate sharing, even if some exchanges were while she was under the influence of alcohol. But he'd held back. He'd trusted her with very little about himself or his life.

If he wanted to grow closer to her—if he wanted a real chance to for what they had to grow beyond friendship—Bryan needed to find the opportunity to tell Liana about his past.

Twenty-Four

Thursday brought beautiful August weather. The sun's rays filtered through Liana's open window as she lay in bed, stretching her arms over her head. Four days had passed since she'd found the photo on Bryan's Bible. The image continued to plague her with questions.

Turning over on her side, she glanced at the alarm clock. Eleven! She'd been more tired than she realized. But then, she hadn't crawled into bed until almost three that morning, working on last-minute wedding details for the daughter of a Microsoft executive. The bride was impatient and difficult, but what her father offered to pay in order to appease his offspring more than paid for the headaches Liana endured.

Tied up with planning that event, she hadn't seen or talked to Bryan since that evening in his apartment, and she missed him. When did his absence start to feel like a void in her life?

His gentleness, his generosity, and the unconditional kindness he offered people, even when they were rude to him, showed his strong character. Liana had never met anyone like him.

She threw back the covers and headed for the shower. Over the last few days she'd formed a plan—a way for her and Bryan to start over. She hoped it would work.

❧

"A picnic? Now?" Bryan stood in the doorway to the apartment and raked his fingers through his hair. "Your dad is expecting me to get a number of things done today."

"I know." Liana leaned against the deck railing, hoping he'd agree to join her. "But you said you've forgiven me for barging into your place the other night. It's a beautiful day, we both need some time off, and ..."

"And?"

She squeezed her eyes shut. "I have a place I want to show you."

"What kind of place?"

Her eyes opened wide. "What is it with guys?" Liana glimpsed the sparkle in his eyes. "You're trying to get me riled up, aren't you?"

"Busted!" He chuckled. "And from what I can tell, it's working pretty well."

"You're so ..." A smile grew on her face. It was nice to hear him laugh again.

"Charming?" He cocked his head.

"More like irritating." She could give it back to him.

He gave that deep laugh that warmed her insides. "You're really not going to tell me anything?"

"I'll explain when we get there. It's—special." One of her favorite places, and she wanted to share it with him. Would he understand the significance of her taking him there? That she wanted to also learn more about him—grow closer?

"Okay, I'm in. But I need to take care of some chores down at the stable first, and I can't be gone long."

It was a start. "Perfect. Will noon work?"

"I'll bring my camera."

"I'll bring lunch."

☙

Bryan thought he'd been over every square foot of the estate, but after they'd saddled up two horses, Liana led him to a path in the woods almost overgrown by vegetation. Following a narrow switchback, they slowly ascended the hill, ducking low tree branches.

There seemed to be no end to the climb up through the forest. Bryan's inner thigh muscles burned from clinging to the sides of his saddle. When they broke into a small clearing, the scenic view pushed all the muscle pain from his mind.

Blue sky stretched before him into infinity, while the white-tipped Cascade Mountains surrounded the green valley below. A small, one-room log cabin, beaten down and gray from age and weather, overlooked the spectacular landscape. Lavender and yellow wildflowers growing next to the cabin swayed in the gentle breeze.

Liana slid off her ride, removed a backpack from the saddle, and tied her horse to a birch tree near the creek that ran behind the cabin. "C'mon, slowpoke." She almost skipped to the broken-down porch.

Bryan hesitated, but only because he wanted to capture the vision on film. He whipped out his camera and released the shutter. It only took a moment before Liana leaped over a broken step and waved to him. He refocused and snapped the photo of her beckoning to him.

That gesture alone set his heart pounding.

He'd tried denying his attraction to her out of respect to his boss, out of fear of being hurt again, and also believing she deserved better than what he could offer. He was a beast—she was a beauty. But Liana's laughter and warm golden-brown eyes had filled his dreams, replacing his nightmares.

He tied his horse and strode to the cabin. "What is this place?"

A bright smile lit Liana's face. "This was my grandfather's hideout. He brought me here on my tenth birthday and shared it with me." She plopped down on the edge of the top step. "When they were still alive, he and my grandmother lived in the cottage. He was a journalist, and when he retired, he continued to write. Instead of focusing on current events, he wrote what came from his imagination."

"He sounds like an interesting man."

"My grandfather was my hero. This is where he'd come when he needed to be alone with his thoughts. Sometimes he'd spend several days up here with his notebooks and pens.

"Creative people can become loners." He'd certainly found that true about himself, even before the accident.

"I guess." She smiled. "I knew there were days when he preferred to spend time with characters in his imaginary world. Some of his short stories were published. He died before he could finish the adventure novel he'd worked on for several years, but he finished a very special story for me and Camryn."

"*Manalee.*" No wonder she loved the book. Her grandfather had written it for her. Bryan's first guitar had been a gift from his own grandfather, so he understood.

A sad smile appeared. "That's why it's especially important to me that what's created in Erik's event space is amazing and true to my grandfather's novel. He never talked about it much, but he traveled all over the world and experienced horrendous things. Writing fiction—even a fairy story—was his way of dealing with the tragedies and pain he saw."

Bryan dropped next to her. "The real world can be pretty harsh."

"Yes, it can ..." Her voice held such sadness that Bryan wondered about the pain she'd experienced in her own life. "I'm sorry you've gone through so much ..." Liana's sincerity touched him. She wasn't tossing him pity—she was offering compassion.

"Thank you." Bryan was touched by how much she cared. This moment, sitting next to her, in this beautiful place—it all felt surreal. He wanted to hold on to it. "You know ... what happened changed my life, but I'm grateful that I have one. I don't want to waste it."

"You won't. You're too stubborn." She smiled at him, then glanced around the area. "I used to come up here all the time." Her voice sounded even softer, almost as if she were being careful what she said now. The fact that she'd acknowledge his suffering without poking around in it showed she was respecting his privacy. "My grandfather and I sat for hours in silence. He'd write. I'd read Nancy Drew mysteries. After he died, I used to come when I needed to be alone." She sighed wistfully. "I haven't been here since college."

They sat silently for several minutes, taking in the view. Then Liana opened her backpack. "I don't know about you, but I'm starved."

Bryan laughed. "My stomach growled, so I guess that says it."

She handed him a bottle of water and a cellophane-wrapped sandwich. "Peanut butter and jelly. Sorry. It's all I had. But I did manage to sneak a package of Oreos and a small bag of chips out of my dad's kitchen."

"Peanut butter is perfect." Bryan bit into the sandwich and soon finished half. "Liana ... why did you bring me here?"

"I told you. I wanted to show you my special place."

"But why? Why share something so personal?"

Liana's cheeks turned a deep shade of pink. "This was my sanctuary when I felt inadequate or grew tired of being compared to my mom or sister. I'm not like them, but I always felt pressured to be like them. I still do." She stared ahead of her toward the mountain range. Bryan had already seen that she was nothing like Camryn. Another tally mark on her side. "I hoped that maybe if I was willing to share something personal about my life, then maybe you'd feel like you could. The other night when I saw the photo of the band—"

"So the whole point of this is to pump me for details? What is so important for you to know?" Adrenaline surged through his body, and Bryan dropped the sandwich into a brown paper bag. He wanted to walk away—think. Andy had convinced him that he needed to open up with Liana if he wanted any kind of relationship with her. He thought he was ready to answer her questions, but she caught him off guard.

Liana didn't move. "I'm not trying to pry into your life for some deviant purpose." Her voice softened. "I just want to understand."

"You *can't* understand!" He wanted her to—he wanted to trust her with his past. But could she leave it alone once she knew?

He watched an eagle soar, and his anger slowly began to wane. He needed to get a grip on his emotions. He shouldn't have blown up at the one person he wanted to get close to.

Bryan closed his eyes and silently prayed for guidance.

Liana's hand covered the healed wound on his shoulder. Bryan's muscles shuddered under her touch, but the tension eased when she didn't move away.

He took a deep breath. It was time for honesty. "What you found in my Bible is—*was*—a photo of my band."

"Lava."

"Yeah, Lava. And we were hot, just like the name." He allowed himself a little grin. Those were his glory days.

"Why aren't you still together?"

"The fire." Horrifying memories flashed in his mind, and he pressed his back teeth together.

Liana waited.

"We were close to signing a recording contract with a big name label. It would have been official after a few small formalities."

"You never signed?"

"No." Bryan wanted Liana to know him in a deeper way, and she'd never understand the man he'd become without learning about the man he'd been. "My grandfather died from a heart attack about that same time, so I went to stay with my grandmother for a few days after the funeral. Get some financial things situated. My sister, Beth, did what she could to help, but she had her own family."

"Your grandmother must have been thankful to have you."

"I guess." He paused before going on. "One night a big thunderstorm hit. Lightning must have struck the old barn because the building caught fire. I woke up when I heard my grandparents' dog—Rainey— barking. Flames leapt so high you'd think they were reaching up from hell and trying to touch heaven."

"That was when you got burned?"

"My grandmother called the fire department. Several horses, including my grandfather's favorite mare, were in that barn. I ran into the building to save the animals. With everything falling into place with the record deal and all the accolades I'd received, part of me believed I was invincible. I freed the horses, but before I got out, part of the roof caved in, trapping me."

"You were a hero."

"A hero?" He'd never thought of himself as one, but it warmed his insides to hear her say the word. "I've never been so scared or endured such physical pain in my life." He shivered. "But before I passed out, God's presence surrounded me. At that moment, I only experienced peace. The next thing I remember is waking up in the hospital."

"I can't even comprehend the kind of feeling you describe. It seems unfathomable. I've heard stories. Read about similar scenarios of people being in car accidents and visited by angels, but I've never talked to anyone who'd actually lived it." She cleared her throat. "What happened to the band? You didn't stick together?"

"They dropped in a few times." For a moment, he relived the loneliness that had consumed him at times during months in the hospital. "But I think it turned their stomachs to see me burned to a crisp. Initially my head was so swollen, no one believed it was me. They stopped coming to the hospital. And with my stay extending month after month, the band went on without me." Grief over that loss resurfaced, and Bryan fought his emotions. He didn't want to be appear weak in front of Liana.

"They took the record deal without you?"

"That might have made things easier. Without me, the contract was dead. The doctors didn't know if my vocal cords would be permanently affected, and the record company said they couldn't—wouldn't—wait to find out. But more than that, as the record execs so bluntly put it, they couldn't market a lead singer who might end up looking like a beast instead of a prince. I guess love songs don't come across the same when they're sung by someone who doesn't look the part."

He didn't want to believe that was reality, because then beautiful love songs were filled with shallow declarations— even lies—instead of truth that came from the depths of one's heart.

"The band should have waited. With all the surgeries you've had—"

Medical procedures helped only to a point. Half of his face looked hideous. People still cringed and gawked, teens still made callous jokes, and children still pointed.

"It wouldn't have mattered. The deal was called off. It wasn't easy for anyone. I was angry. The band felt let down. None of us knew what to say to each other. Eventually, they moved on without me."

Anyway, they never got over it, and we haven't spoken since." He took a deep breath. "Music was everything—the only thing I ever wanted to do. But life goes on, and I'll figure out what I'm going to do next." Enough. He'd gotten this far. He wouldn't pine for the past like some lost teenager.

"What's stopping you from starting over with a new band?"

"Image is everything in the industry. Image sells. Mine has a greater chance of scaring people away than bringing them in." He shook his head. "There's only so much they can do with reconstructive surgery. Besides, it's painful—and costly. After twenty-two operations, I've had enough." He released a sigh. Bryan never wanted to go through that again, and Doc had said there was no medical need to.

"But—"

"Liana, this is as good as it's going to get." He pointed to his face. "And I refuse to become a sideshow."

"I was only going to say ..." She slid down to the step below her and sat to the left of him. "I was going to remind you what you once told me. That God doesn't care about outside appearances and that he looks at our heart. You have a good heart, Bryan. You love God. He must love you. Can't he open some doors?"

"You remember that night? You were stone-cold drunk." Bryan never expected her to hold up a mirror. He'd have to be more careful about what he preached in the future. Some people actually listened and wanted to hold him accountable to his own words.

"We're not talking about me right now. We're talking about you. And your music."

"I appreciate the encouragement, Liana, but that part of my life is over."

Twenty-Five

"**O**kay, Mom, I'm here." Liana eased her body onto the plush baby-blue sofa and regarded her mother's reflection in the boutique's three-way mirror.

Turning to the left, then to the right, her mother surveyed her stylish plum-colored suit jacket and straight knee-length skirt. "What do you think? Maybe take it in here?" She fussed with the jacket, pinching fabric, trying to get a visual of how it would fit with less material at the waist.

"I'm not the best judge." Liana, not having eaten lunch, poured steaming coffee into a white china cup from the silver pot sitting on a tray in front of her. Her stomach growled loud enough that a nearby clerk turned her head in response. Liana shouldn't, but she was so hungry—she devoured a lemon cookie from an assortment of fancy delicacies.

"So, you mentioned a job opportunity?" Another cookie beckoned her. She'd already splurged, so what would it matter? The second was almond flavored.

Her mother scowled. "Well, I didn't bring you here so you could stuff yourself with sweets."

"Sorry. Busy day. This is the only break I have for lunch." Liana sipped the coffee, which tasted expensive.

"I have a contact number for you to call. Debra Ward is an old friend and the editor for a fashion magazine that frequently uses my models."

Liana rubbed her tired eyes. "I appreciate the lead. Really

I do. But couldn't you tell me this over the phone?"

"I'm aware it was probably inconvenient for you to come here. But I wanted you to be conscious of how important this client is to the agency. With recommending you, I'm also putting my word on the line."

"I have a great reputation, Mom." Liana was exhausted from trying to prove herself to the woman in front of her. "I've worked very hard for it."

Her mother smiled. An honest-to-goodness genuine smile. "I know. And that's exactly what I told Debra."

Liana almost bit her tongue instead of the cookie. Her mother had actually spoken on her behalf? "So, what's the gig?"

"Her daughter's eighteenth birthday party. They want a big bash planned for two weeks from this Friday."

"How big?"

"I think the guest list is up to two hundred people."

"Two weeks! Didn't they realize their darling had a birthday coming up?"

"Of course they did. They'd promised her several weeks in Greece and everything was set, but a few days ago, Debra's mother-in-law was diagnosed with cancer, and they canceled the trip. So instead, they'd like to give their daughter a party before she leaves for Berkley. School starts in three weeks."

"Just call me the miracle worker." And it might take a miracle. But if she didn't pull off this event, she would not only disappoint the family, she would fail her mother.

"Good news is that they have a venue, and Debra's husband is a talent agent. He's already booked one of his own bands. They need you to develop a theme, work on decorations, and coordinate with the caterer. And I suppose do whatever else you do. That's for you and Debra to sort out."

She'd have to put in long days, but that wasn't anything new, and if she pleased the Wards, the referrals she might receive would help grow her business. She'd looked at office spaces earlier that week but still couldn't afford the rent—not yet. "I need to get on this right away. Two weeks ..."

"Can you make it happen?"

"Absolutely." Liana couldn't turn down a great opportunity, no matter how busy her calendar looked. "It's going to be really crazy, but I can handle it."

"I have a lunch date with her tomorrow at the Metropolitan Grill at one o'clock. I told her you'd join us. Then, if she likes you, plans for the party can continue after lunch."

"I'll be there." Liana's mind went into overdrive. She'd suggest several themes, but it would also depend on the birthday girl's style and interests.

"Don't let me down." Her mother didn't need to speak the words—her eyes said enough.

Liana better not blow it.

A fresh pot of coffee brewed, and Liana inhaled the rich aroma in anticipation. After a night with little sleep, she needed a strong dose of caffeine.

She perused the notes for the lunch meeting with Debra Ward. With three solid themes to present, it would depend on the venue, budget, and the daughter's taste if any of them would meet expectations. If not, Liana would have to come up with fresh ideas.

After a jog and shower, Liana dressed in a tailored black

suit. At 11:45 a.m., she closed the cottage door behind her. If she left now, she'd get into the city, park the car, and arrive at the restaurant early. Showing up even a few minutes late would distress her mother and make less than a stellar impression on Mrs. Ward.

She threw several binders on the passenger seat and slammed the car door shut.

"Liana!" Bryan called from a grassy patch near the stable.

Shielding her eyes from the glaring sun, she attempted to see why he wanted her attention. Bryan, with knees bent to the ground, frantically waved and continued to yell for help. She ran as fast as she could in heels to his side. Rainey lay on the ground, his coat matted.

Liana dropped to her knees beside him. "What happened?"

Bryan's hands were crimson, and blood smeared his tan shirt. "I don't know." He wiped his eyes with a shirt sleeve. "We were checking on the horses last night. He took off into the woods after a critter prowling around. I called, but I should've followed him. Thought it was a raccoon. Thought he'd come back—looked for him first thing this morning." His voice cracked. "This is my fault."

"It's *not* your fault. You couldn't go chasing after him in the dark." Liana, seeing a rip in the animal's skin and torn, bloody muscles, tasted bile. "It might have been a cougar. There haven't been any around for some time, but that's probably what attacked him." She stifled a sob.

"He needs a vet."

Poor Rainey! The sweet dog was suffering. With several blinks, Liana freed the tear hanging on her lashes, and it left a trail down her face. "Take the truck."

"You start it, and I'll carry him."

Bryan assumed she'd go with him, but Liana didn't move. This was a crossroad where unfortunately, no matter what road she chose, she'd disappoint someone. If she didn't show up at the lunch meeting, she'd lose an important job. Her mother would take it as a personal embarrassment and hold it over Liana's head if she blew off the opportunity. But the loving Lab could die, and Bryan needed that dog. The animal was his grandfather's and an important companion to Bryan. If she didn't help, he'd never trust her friendship again.

She made her decision. "I'll grab towels and bring the truck over. With me driving, you can sit in the back with him."

Liana kicked off her heels and sprinted to the cottage. She slipped on flats and grabbed four large bath towels from a closet. Rummaging through her junk drawer, she found the extra set of keys to the truck.

It felt like time had dropped into slow motion as she raced to where the truck sat parked next to the stable. The tank registered half full, and as soon as she put it in gear, she hit the accelerator and drove to where Bryan waited with Rainey.

Liana flung open the door and hopped out. "How's he doing?"

"His breathing is shallow. His eyes are closed. The poor guy has lost so much blood." Bryan's voice hitched. "I don't know if he's going to make it."

"Of course, he is." Liana's heart ached at the pained expression on Bryan's face. "Wrap these towels around Rainey, and then let's lift him into the back of the truck."

Bryan hesitated at picking up the expensive, fluffy, white

towels.

"They're just pieces of cloth, Bryan."

The scarlet blood flowing from Rainey's wounds seeped into the towels, staining them. They hefted the Lab onto the bed of the truck as gently as they could. Bryan sat next to the dog and spoke encouraging words.

Liana shut the tailgate. "Ready?" She hopped into the front seat, put the truck in gear, and drove down the driveway to the main road, feeling the urge to hurry but still conscious of Bryan's safety in the open-bed truck.

If she received a speeding ticket for driving over the limit, she didn't care. It was more important to save Rainey. She closed in on an older Toyota Corolla, driven by an elderly gentleman who drove five miles below what the speed limit allowed. With curves in the country road and oncoming traffic, there was no safe spot for Liana to pass the car. She resisted laying on the horn and waving the man to the side. Instead, she whispered a short prayer for Bryan's beloved pet.

They arrived at the animal hospital, and almost immediately several assistants took over. They placed the Lab on a gurney and rolled him into an examination room.

"He'll be fine, Bryan." Liana didn't know what else to say to comfort him. "Dr. Jadan is an excellent vet. Rainey's in good hands."

"Thanks, Lee." Bryan gave a small smile. "You mind if I go pray for a few minutes?"

"Of course not." She didn't admit to praying herself only minutes earlier. Liana opened her purse and took out her cell phone, which showed the time as 12:35 a.m. "I have a call to make, so you go ahead and take your time."

Bryan nodded and found an empty chair in the far corner of the waiting room.

Liana stepped outside. Taking a moment to breathe, she realized her once very clean, pressed suit now displayed numerous wrinkles and dark stains.

She punched in her mother's number, and took a deep breath. This was not going to be pleasant. Not pleasant at all.

It only took one ring for her mother to answer. "Liana, are you on your way?"

"I'm not going to make the meeting, Mom."

"You can't be serious." Her mom sounded angry, which was exactly what Liana expected.

"I have her number, and I'll explain everything to Mrs. Ward later this afternoon. I'll meet her anywhere, anytime, at her convenience." Hopefully, she'd give Liana another chance.

"What's going on?"

"There was an emergency."

"Are you okay?" Her mother's previous tone was replaced by one of genuine concern, which surprised and touched Liana.

"I'm fine." Mom wouldn't like her explanation. Liana braced herself. "Our caretaker's dog was injured, and we needed to get him to a vet."

"You stood up an important client because of a dog?" Her mother practically screeched into the phone.

"Mom—"

"I try to help you, and you can't even follow through on this one thing. Get your priorities straight, Liana."

She'd made the right decision. "I have them straight. That's the point."

"What about the gala?"

"What? Why are you bringing that up?" Liana opened the building's main door for a woman with two charcoal-gray poodles to enter. The woman smiled and nodded her thanks.

"Both your father and I stuck our necks out with the committee members when it came to using your help. Are you going to take care of your responsibilities there? Or are you going to decide at a critical time that something else is more important?"

"What are you talking about? I've spent hours organizing details for the gala. I'm doing everything I can to please you, Dad, the committee, and everyone else who will be attending. It's my reputation on the line. Not yours. It will be great."

"It better be." Her mother hung up.

Twenty-Six

If the double oak doors correlated in any way to the size of the owner's prestige and personality, Liana was in trouble.

Leaning back into her driver's seat, she wiped damp hands on a tissue from her purse and checked out her surroundings. Tucked beneath towering pines, the massive two-story home with wood siding and a cedar-shake roof displayed a sophisticated, yet rustic, appearance. Clay pots filled with crimson geraniums and purple petunias brightened the impressive entrance, as did several hanging flower baskets, overflowing with an assortment of blooms befitting an artist's palette.

A gentle breeze brushed back her hair as she stepped from the car. She'd taken the 7:55 a.m. ferry from Seattle to Bainbridge Island, and after thirty-five minutes on the water, docked with more than enough time to arrive at the Ward's home by nine. The salty air hinted that water lay below the hill where she stood. The air remained peaceful and quiet until a Steller's jay called from his evergreen roost.

Taking a deep breath, Liana sauntered up the stone path. A slender woman, probably in her early fifties, dressed in cream-colored slacks and a white sleeveless blouse opened the door before Liana could knock. She guessed her to be Debra Ward. Black glasses perched on the woman's head served as a headband for shoulder-length sandy-colored hair.

"You must be Liana." Mrs. Ward was direct but not harsh. Her voice held a bit of softness.

"Yes." Liana nodded.

"I'm Debra. I happened to glance out the window as you drove in." She swung the door wider. "Come in. I hope you didn't have any trouble finding the house."

Liana followed Debra into the tiled entryway, which led into an airy room with oak floors and high-beamed ceilings. An impressive, curved wood staircase led to the second story. Liana cleared her throat. "This is beautiful."

Her hostess offered a gracious smile. "Thank you. Our family loves it here. The island offers sanctuary, while still giving us quick access to the city and our work." Debra gestured toward a comfortable-looking chair in front of the stone fireplace. "Please relax. I was about to make spiced tea. Would you like some?"

"Yes, please." She barely had time to glance around the lovely room before Debra returned with their drinks and sat in a chair across from her. "Thank you." Liana inhaled the cinnamon aroma and took a quick sip. "Mrs. Ward, I'm truly sorry for not making our lunch appointment the other day. I appreciate your understanding about the emergency and giving me another opportunity."

"First of all, I prefer Debra."

"Okay."

"And second, your persistence in calling my office for two days, and your willingness to come out here at eight o'clock on a Saturday morning, tell me that you take your work seriously. It's obvious you'll do whatever it takes to pull off a great birthday party for my daughter."

Liana's shoulder muscles relaxed. "I will."

"If it's not private, what exactly was the big emergency the other day?"

She swallowed a lump in her throat the size of an avocado pit. Hopefully, Debra wouldn't express similar feelings as Liana's mother. "A friend's Lab was badly hurt. We think a cougar attacked the dog. I needed to help get him to the vet, but it looks like he'll recover fine."

"Hmmm ..." Debra murmured as she leaned back in her chair and crossed her legs.

"Oh, Mother," a female voice above them teased, "don't give her a hard time."

Liana sat at the edge of her chair and swiveled in order to watch a young woman bound down the staircase in khaki shorts, a black T-shirt, and hiking boots. A stuffed backpack rested on her right shoulder.

The redhead with freckles and bright blue eyes dumped her pack at the foot of the staircase, and with an infectious grin held her hand out to Liana. "I'm Ellie. I happen to think saving your friend's dog is far more important than planning my birthday party."

"Ellie, I agree that her decision was admirable." Debra addressed Liana. "I'm glad your friend's pet is doing well. We're also dog lovers. Our two cocker spaniels are downstairs." Debra scanned her daughter. "Where are you going?"

"Remember? I told you a few days ago. I'm catching the ferry into Seattle with Greg and Amanda. Greg is driving us up to Mt. Si for a hike. If it gets late, we'll crash at his grandparents' in North Bend."

"Make sure you call and let me know what you decide."

"Mom, I always call."

Liana coughed nervously. "Do you have a moment to give me a general idea of what type of party you'd like?"

The birthday girl laughed, then winked. "Anything that's not stiff or formal. I'm turning eighteen, not thirty-eight."

"Ellie!" her mother scolded. Then she addressed Liana. "I wanted a nice party at the Westin Hotel."

Ellie plunked down on the arm of her mother's chair, made a silly face, and draped her arm on the older woman's shoulder. "But I disappointed her and said no."

"I thought—" Debra sounded exasperated.

"Mom wanted black tie." Ellie smiled. "But it doesn't fit me. I'm going to be an environmental lawyer. I like the outdoors. I'm happiest when I'm hiking in the mountains or sailing."

"What type of party do you want? And where?" Planning a party for two hundred guests and pulling it off within two weeks—challenging enough. If the mother and daughter couldn't agree ...

"It's going to be here." Ellie popped up from the chair and practically skipped to the sliding doors in the glass wall at one end of the room. She slid the door open and stepped outside. "Come see."

Liana stepped out onto the deck and took in the view of Puget Sound and Seattle's skyline. The prominent Space Needle reared its head in the distance. Two additional decks built alongside the hill were integrated into the steps leading to the beach. "Wow."

"I know. Isn't it great?" Ellie grinned.

Debra joined them. "So, what do you think? Can you pull off a party that will suit both the birthday girl and her parents?"

"I'm sure I can." Liana's head already swam with ideas. "What time do you want the festivities to begin?"

"We've chartered a boat to bring guests from a marina to our dock here. The trip one way takes thirty minutes, so people will be arriving between three and six o'clock. They can also take the ferry and drive up from the docks at the landing."

"That takes care of any parking issues." A plan began to materialize for Liana. "I'm envisioning white lights everywhere, tables on the beach, Tiki torches, bonfires, several buffets with crab, salmon, a few pasta dishes, and an assortment of breads, cheeses, fruits, dessert … I'm also thinking a taco bar and a hamburger stand. I know a caterer who will do an excellent job." Liana rapped her fingers on the deck railing as she surveyed the beach below. "There's plenty of room for volleyball and a large screened-in trampoline. I could also check into renting a climbing wall and a zip line. Having kayaks on hand is also an option. We'd have to hire people to oversee safety—we don't want anyone getting hurt while having fun."

Ellie's eyes lit up. "Sounds perfect!"

"I agree." Debra nodded.

Liana didn't want to deal with noise ordinances and cops showing up at the front door. "How friendly are you with your neighbors? We don't want any complaints."

"I've already handled that." Debra leaned against the deck railing. "The Murphys are out of town that weekend. And the Jacksons have known Ellie since she was five. They'd come to the party if they weren't so elderly and afraid they wouldn't fit in. My husband and I are treating them to a night in Seattle so they can have dinner at their favorite restaurant and a good night's rest at one of the hotels."

Liana was impressed by Debra's thoughtfulness. "Oh, another thing. My mother mentioned you booked a band."

"Yeah, it's a group called Lava." Ellie cocked her head. "Have you heard them?"

Liana's mouth went dry, and her heart skipped a beat. "I've never heard their music." That wasn't a lie.

"They're great. Or I should say they were. Last time I saw them was about three years ago. My friends and I used to hear them play every chance we got—at least wherever we didn't have to be of legal age to get in. The lead singer, Bryan, was gorgeous. All the girls wanted to date him. The guy had an amazing voice."

Liana's heart moved to her stomach. "What happened? Why did you lose touch with the group?"

"The band broke up for a while. I heard Bryan was in an accident, and then he dropped out of sight. But the band is back together, and my dad is actually representing them. I couldn't believe it! I begged him to let them play at my party. For old time's sake, you know. I'm loyal like that."

Bryan's old band was back together, and he didn't know. Or did he? What if the band wanted him back but didn't know where to find him? Of course they didn't. Bryan didn't want to be found.

Liana's head pounded. Lava—the band from Bryan's past—would be playing at a party she'd be working. On one hand she was intrigued, but something nagged at her—possibly fear of what she might discover and maybe even a bit of jealousy. People in the group experienced a normal life with Bryan. A life when he followed his passion and looked forward to a promising future in the music industry.

Ellie glance at her watch. "I've gotta run if I'm going to catch the ferry." She kissed her mom's check. "Love you." She shook Liana's hand. "I wasn't too excited about this party to begin with, but now I'm really looking forward to it."

"Thanks. I'll do my best to make it fun for everyone." Liana, her brain in a fog, sensed the young woman slip through the sliding glass doors back into the house.

"Liana?"

"Yes?" The fog lifted.

"I'm pleased that you'll be handling this event. And if it goes as well as I believe it will, you'll have more work than you can handle. When I like someone, I'm very free in giving out referrals."

"Thank you, Debra. It will be a pleasure." Liana laughed. "You and Ellie seem to have a close and honest relationship. I admire that."

"Liana, for years your mother and I have primarily remained connected through business, but I know ... I know your mother well enough to assume that she came down hard on you for missing our lunch date."

"She was a little upset." Liana squirmed. "But rightly so."

"Regardless, you should know that she's very proud of you. Always has been."

Convinced her mother's acting skills were well honed from presenting to the public whatever she desired the outside world to perceive, Liana didn't take much stock in Debra's words, but her never-ending curiosity surfaced. "How well do you know her?"

Debra seemed to escape into her own thoughts for a moment. "Your mom and I grew up in the same upper-class neighborhood, but life wasn't easy for her. She missed her dad when he was gone for months, reporting on big news events. He earned praise as a journalist, and I think she pushed herself hard to be successful because she wanted to prove something. In many ways, we're very much alike. The difference is that I have God in my life, while she's never been able to accept his love. But underneath her business-like exterior, your mom has a soft heart and really does want the best for you."

Too much clutter jumbled Liana's brain. A prominent woman claimed to not only know God, but asked Liana to believe that her mother was human with emotions like everyone else.

Liana needed to set that aside for now and ponder that possibility later. There was a lot on the line with Ellie's party, and there were only two weeks to prepare. That, along with worrying about Rainey and a long list of details for the hospital gala that still needed to be covered was enough for Liana at the moment.

And then there was the sticky situation of whether or not to tell Bryan that Lava was performing at the party. He might welcome an opportunity to connect with them again ... or the reminder that they'd moved on might only reopen old wounds.

Twenty-Seven

The sun's rays, reflecting off the river's surface, created bursts of bright light, like a Fourth of July sparkler. A gentle breeze cooled the warm September evening. Soon the leaves would turn. Fall was Bryan's favorite time of year—the smells and change in temperatures invigorated him.

He lowered his body to a spot beneath an old birch tree near the water's edge, leaned against the wide papery trunk, and propped his grandfather's guitar on his thigh. Rainey, wearing a cone around his head, and with several of his wounds from the cougar attack still bandaged, rested as close to his master as he could without landing on top of him. With the horses watered and fed—Bryan's last chore for the day—he could sit under that tree all night if desired.

The smooth curve of the guitar under his trembling hand comforted him but also stirred up painful memories. His grandfather had taught him to play after Bryan's parents died in a freak car accident. His sister Beth, eight years old at the time, clung to their grandmother, following her around the house, not wanting to leave her side even to go to school.

Only ten years old, Bryan had closed himself off, often wandering the farm alone. Until the day his grandfather brought out the guitar and insisted he learn. Bryan hadn't a clue the older man knew how to play, but sharing a love for music brought a new dimension to their relationship and a way for Bryan to heal. He found passion in song, and it became a driving force in his life.

It wasn't until Bryan was consumed in what success could offer in the music business, that his grandfather expressed concern that Bryan might be abusing his God-given gift. A talented musician, his grandfather had put music aside for years after realizing he was headed down a path away from God. He'd come to a crossroads and made a choice. He feared his grandson was headed down the same road, but Bryan disregarded the warning. After all, he was close to reaching his dream, and he'd do whatever it took to get there, regardless that the record label wanted him to write songs that included lyrics he didn't believe in.

At first he thought the barn fire was God's way of punishing him. Everything he lived for was taken away. His music, the success, the way adoring female fans fawned over him. He lost everything, including friends and the woman he thought he'd marry.

But lying in that hospital bed for months, and seeing the courage of kids like Kylee, fighting for their lives, caused his heart to change. The anger morphed into acceptance and then appreciation for still being alive. And in his gratitude, he began reading the Bible and talking to God again.

Bryan watched the sparkling river move on its course. "Lord, I don't know why I had to lose everything, but I do know you want the best for me. And if that's what it took for me to turn back to you, then I want to accept it. But I still need help in that department. I still have times when I'm angry. And I still have moments when I want to wallow in self-pity. Help me to keep moving forward, like that river."

Aching hands cradled the instrument against his body. With practice, maneuvering his fingers along the strings had become easier, but to Bryan, his playing sounded like he'd returned to being that ten-year-old boy. After undergoing several surgeries on his hands, Bryan wondered if he'd ever touch a guitar again, but the doctor insisted that playing the instrument would be beneficial exercise.

His vocal cords survived the fire unharmed, so with a little work, he could regain the tone he'd once had. "I may not be able to stand in front of an audience, but I can still sing for you, Lord. For as long as I live here on earth *and* when I join you in eternity."

Weak sounding chords rose from the strings as Bryan strummed the guitar. But his voice, with clear, melodic tones was carried by the breeze toward heaven in an offering.

Peace filled his soul. He'd practically sworn to Liana that he'd given up music, but here in the moment, something tugged at his spirit. If only there could be a way ... but this time it would have to be God's way.

"Lord, if I'm only supposed to sing for you, I'll accept that. But you've given me a gift. So if there's any chance— and I promise I'd do it right this time—please show me how."

A branch snapped in the woods behind him. Rainey pushed up onto his feet, spun around, and barked. Bryan, unable to forget Rainey's experience with the cougar, twisted his torso, hoping to see a squirrel scurry up a tree.

The creature hiding in the woods wasn't a cougar or a squirrel. Bryan caught a glimpse of the backside of a tall, thin woman with blond hair scampering away. *Camryn.*

&

"Dad, I thought you'd encourage me on this." Liana searched through a stack of binders on her desk. He'd blocked out time to go over a few initial wedding plans with Camyrn, and Liana needed to find the information she'd compiled for her sister.

Her father closed the cottage door, as though someone outside might overhear their conversation. "What makes you think you'd be helping Bryan?"

"I saw a picture of the band in his apartment. Since he kept it, those people and his music are still important to him. He thinks his career is over, but I'm not convinced it has to end this way."

"Didn't you mention earlier that the band has moved on with a new lead singer? They don't need Bryan."

"But the group hasn't seen him since he was in the hospital. Now that time has passed and he's doing better, what's wrong with trying to hook them back up?" She tossed several more binders aside. "Maybe they felt bad about how they treated him. They might welcome a chance to make things right. Maybe they wanted to reunite but didn't know how. Bryan is still hurting about how things ended."

"If you don't let him know why you want him to go to the party, you're deceiving him. And regardless of motives, that's wrong. You know I want to help him too. That's all I've been doing. But not through manipulation."

Liana found the binder with notes for Camryn's wedding and handed it to her father. "Here you go. Where is the blushing bride, anyway?"

"She took a walk down to the river while I finished making a few phone calls, and I decided to pick up the wedding info before she got back." Her dad perused a few pages in the binder. "Sure you can't come up to the house and go through some of this with us?"

Liana waved toward the desk stacked with folders, papers, color samples, and a computer screen opened to an Excel spreadsheet. "Dad, I'm so overwhelmed right now. Between the hospital gala and Ellie Ward's birthday party ..."

"How is the gala coming?"

"Fine. We've had some bumps along the way, but Erik and Maggie have been great, and Dalisay is amazing. I was hoping to find something special for entertainment, but it's probably too late now. The event is in five weeks. Finding someone now feels almost impossible. To answer your question about going over wedding details, I still have a lot of work to finish today, and I'm so tired, I can barely see straight."

"I understand."

"Besides, it's best that you and Camryn go over the budget without me sitting there giving input. She's already making me crazy, and there are eight months to go before their blessed nuptials." Liana grimaced.

"Don't hold back your feelings on my account." He laid the binder down on an end table and reached out his arms.

Liana moved into his embrace. Exhausted, she could have stayed there at length. "Kevin is bad news, Dad, and I don't know how to get through to her," she mumbled into his chest.

"I know, hon." He rubbed her back. "She won't listen to me either. I've tried to convince Camryn to give it more time, but she's determined to marry him. If I push any harder—"

"She'll dig in even more." Liana's mind wandered for a moment, then thoughts returned to Bryan and the band. She sighed.

"What's on your mind, Lee?"

She withdrew from her father's comforting arms. "That you're right. Bryan would never go to the party if he knew Lava was performing." Liana shook her head. "I don't think he'd go even if they weren't. Aside from volunteering at the hospital, he seems to prefer hiding out here with the horses."

"I'm not convinced Bryan is avoiding people because he's scared. I think it's more that he believes he needs to protect them."

"From what?"

"From their own fears. From being uncomfortable. Remember your own reaction?"

"I do. But Bryan is kind, and funny, and loyal ..."

Her father cocked an eyebrow. "You can say that now because the two of you have developed a friendship. You've had a chance to get to know the man behind the face. But don't kid yourself. Before you knew him, if you'd seen him on the street, wouldn't you have found it difficult not to stare?"

Liana's face flamed. That night when she'd first met Bryan in the stable, she'd been shocked, then curious.

"See? I'm right." He gave a fatherly smile. "Those rosy cheeks give you away every time."

"It's a curse." Since she could remember, every time she'd been angry, hurt, or embarrassed, her face flushed.

Her father smiled. "It's endearing."

"Thanks." She drew out the word with a sarcastic tone but smiled back. "So, if Lava isn't the answer, maybe there's another way for Bryan to return to his music."

"Back to that again." His eyes fixed on hers. "Sounds like it's pretty important to you. You have a stronger interest than friendship?"

"No—no." Her pounding heart betrayed her feelings. They went deeper than she was ready to admit.

"Here's the thing, Lee. If Bryan chooses to ever publicly share his musical gift, it's between him and his heavenly Father."

"But don't you think God can sometimes use a little help?"

Her father chuckled. "Maybe that's something you should pray about."

Liana didn't often consider prayer—except in desperate situations—but this problem might call for it.

Twenty-Eight

"This is impossible." Liana massaged her forehead and paced beside the dining table in the cottage while Camryn sat at the table, tapping her pen on the top of her notepad. "You're going to be married in less than nine months. You either make some final decisions now or live with the consequences. June is one of the most popular months to get married. Photographers and caterers—not to mention venues—are booked a year in advance."

Camryn let out a disgusted sigh. "Stop acting so hormonal. It's important that everything be perfect." She crossed her legs and leaned back in her chair. "If you prefer, I can get someone else to help. I understand planning my wedding when you had a thing for the groom—"

"If I ever had a thing for Kevin, I certainly don't now. I don't even like the guy, and I think if you really knew him, you wouldn't either." Her sister needed to face reality. Camryn's fiancé would end up hurting her and probably by doing something far worse than what he'd done to Liana. He'd hit on Liana when they'd announced their engagement, for crying out loud!

Camryn gave a sly smile. "Then who are you into these days? The caretaker?"

"What gave you that idea?" Liana, hoping her cheeks didn't look as flushed as she felt, slipped into the chair opposite her sister. She was falling for Bryan, but she certainly didn't want her sister to know, especially when Bryan didn't treat her any differently than friend.

Camryn shrugged her shoulders and admired her polished fingernails. "I don't know. You invited him to Dad's birthday dinner, so obviously something is going on between you."

"Dad invited him. We're friends, that's all."

"Well, your *friend* sure has a voice."

Liana stared at her. Had Camryn heard Bryan singing somehow? "Meaning?"

"The other day—when I took a walk down to the river—he was sitting there, playing guitar and singing. You never said he was an incredible talent."

Her sister's words stung. Liana longed to hear him sing but had only heard a few odd guitar chords when he didn't know she stood on the other side of the door.

She opened her laptop. With Camryn, the best approach was to never let her know she'd bested Liana. "Get focused. I have the Westin Hotel booked for the ceremony and the reception. We have the grand ballroom, and with the number of people you plan to invite, you're going to need the space. But I need confirmation that you're happy with the venue. You and Kevin did check it out, didn't you? Like I asked weeks ago?"

"Yes."

"And?"

"It's perfect." Camryn twisted strands of her blond hair around her forefinger.

"Colors?" Liana didn't want to discuss Bryan or her growing feelings for him with Camryn. If Liana kept her sister occupied with wedding details, maybe additional questions could be avoided.

"I've chosen pearl pink, white, and black for the main color scheme. Sophisticated and elegant."

"Good choices. Especially in that room. Sounds like you're opting for a soft look. Would you like to use pale pink and white floral arrangements? That same shade of pink can be used as an accent color around the room. The florist should be able to come up with something. I'd also ask about adding some pale green lisianthus flowers to the bouquets."

"I like it," her sister said, nodding.

Liana removed a copy of an empty calendar from a black binder and slid it across the table. "Fill in your schedule as best you can, and I'll work on setting up appointments with the florist and caterer."

Camryn picked up the calendar. "I've already booked an appointment with the florist you recommended for this Saturday morning."

"Why didn't you check with me first?" Liana couldn't keep the frustration out of her voice nor did she care to. "Why ask me to be in charge if you're going to make decisions without talking to me?"

"You keep nagging me to nail some things down, so I thought I was helping. I leave on Sunday for a two-week photo shoot in Mexico. Then I'm only home for a few days before I fly to New York for a week. I thought you'd be happy to get it checked off the list."

"Camryn, I have a huge event for two hundred people on Saturday, and I have to be on Bainbridge Island early that afternoon. You'll have to meet with the florist yourself." Liana couldn't take on one more thing that day.

"C'mon, Lee. I don't want to pick out bouquets and arrangements, then have you tell me later they're not right." Camryn cocked her head. "Please. The appointment is for nine o'clock. It shouldn't take long. We'll be done in plenty of time."

Liana thought a moment. She and the florist had a good working relationship, and if she left Camryn alone with her, Liana might be looking for another favorite floral designer. "Okay. But you better be on time and ready to get down to business."

"I will. I promise." Camryn filled in a few dates on the calendar. "What else do you have for me?"

"The photographer you requested is already booked, but his partner is willing to take the job. I can vouch that he does excellent work. He's one of the best in Seattle."

"You're really on it, aren't you?"

Liana raised an eyebrow at her sister. "Was that a compliment? Or are you surprised?"

"It's just that—"

"Did you think I'd try to ruin this for you?" Liana locked eyes with her sister.

Camryn shrugged. "It's crossed my mind. You've made it clear you don't want me marrying Kevin."

"Not because I'm interested in him, but because I'm worried that he's not the best choice for you." Liana sat down in a chair next to Camryn. "But I would never ruin your wedding. First of all, it's my job to create perfect events. Two—I'm not the kind of person who sabotages another person's plans. Three—you're my sister, and I really do want your wedding to be even more beautiful and wonderful than you've dreamed."

Camryn's eyes glistened. "I didn't know—" A melodic

song played from inside her purse. "It's Kevin." She pulled out a smart phone and cradled the unit to her ear. "Hi, honey." She listened for a moment, then her expression soured. "But that's not what you told me." She stood and sauntered from the table. "Kevin, please ... no, I don't—but you promised." Camryn lowered her voice to a whisper before stepping outside the cottage and closing the door behind her.

Liana poured two glasses of iced tea while she waited. Camyrn had almost cried at Liana's declaration of wanting her sister's wedding day to be perfect. Maybe it was more important to Camyrn than what Liana had imagined.

Almost ten minutes passed before a blotchy-faced Camryn scuffled back in, shoulders drooped, looking as though she carried a weight far greater than what her small frame could bear.

Empathy for her sister won over any frustration Liana had felt earlier. "You okay?"

Camryn's head jerked up, revealing pain-filled eyes. "We—never mind." She shook her head, stiffened, and threw her phone back into her purse. "Everyone has little arguments. It keeps things interesting. You'd know that if you ever had a serious relationship."

Liana bit her lower lip. "I'll let that one go."

"Sorry." Camryn slid onto her chair. "I didn't mean that," she whispered with a voice that sounded repentant.

"Camryn, I'm worried about you. So, I need to ask. How well do you know your fiancé?"

"How well does anyone ever know another person?" Camryn took a sip of her iced tea. "How well do you and I know each other?"

"We don't. And that's pretty sad." Liana caught Camryn's

274 | DAWN KINZER

eye. "Aren't sisters supposed to be best friends?"

Liana wished for that kind of relationship, but after she caught her sister making out with Jason Henderson in high school, Liana's and Camryn's relationship had become strained. Liana had made it clear that her boyfriend was off limits, but Camryn didn't care who she hurt. Only out for herself, she pursued any guy she pleased, whenever she pleased.

"Yeah, well ... obviously that belief is a myth," Camryn said with a bit of sadness in her tone, and she grabbed her purse. "I gotta run. I'll e-mail my schedule."

"Just make sure you get it to me by tomorrow morning." Liana stood and walked to the door with her, feeling an odd sense of disappointment that her sister wasn't staying longer.

"Thanks, Liana. I know this isn't easy, but I do appreciate your help." No cutting remark—no biting tone of voice—just a rare, quiet humbleness.

"You're welcome."

Camryn hesitated at the door. "About Kevin ..."

"Yes?" Maybe Camryn would share something that proved she knew and understood the man she'd agreed to marry.

"Sometimes I wish ..." Camryn closed her eyes and sighed. "I watched Bryan the night of Dad's birthday dinner. I can't help but wish that Kevin would look at me the way Bryan looked at you."

"In what way?" Bryan couldn't have feelings for her—he treated her like a sister.

"You're not stupid, Sis." She flung the purse strap over her shoulder and skipped down the steps. "Figure it out.

Twenty-Nine

If she didn't leave the cottage for the ferry in the next fifteen minutes, Liana would miss the one arriving at Bainbridge Island ahead of the caterer and other venders hired for Ellie Ward's birthday bash.

That morning, Camryn had finally appeared—twenty-five minutes late—for an appointment with her wedding florist. Liana should have insisted Camryn reschedule. The appointment could have easily been delayed until she returned from the New York photo shoot.

The meeting lasted nearly two hours longer than what most brides needed. Camryn questioned every suggested floral arrangement. The poor designer had popped several pain relievers by the time they'd finished.

Organizing everything a day in advance had saved Liana more than once. If only she'd had the foresight to take everything with her to the meeting with the florist, she could have eliminated a trip home before driving back for the ferry. Liana couldn't imagine how last-minute, fly-by-the-seat-of-your-pants people survived in the event business without experiencing stress-related health issues. Regardless, Liana didn't plan to find out.

She surveyed items needed at the party—four boxes of miscellaneous items, a gift she'd chosen for Ellie, her purse with wallet and keys, a black leather bag that contained a notebook, and a binder with set-up information and copies of signed contracts. Liana threw her smart phone into the leather bag. She'd leave her purse in the trunk of her car while at the Wards' home, but she'd want a phone handy. Some people thought it overkill to use both hard copy and electronic devices to keep track of a calendar and notes. But there was still something to be said about having paper in hand.

Liana opened the front door of the cottage, scooped up a box overflowing with decorations, and carried it to the car. Out of the corner of her eye, she glimpsed Bryan sauntering toward her with Rainey trotting beside him. Dropping the box to the side of the Volvo, she offered a smile. "Hey, there."

"Hi." Dressed in jeans and a pale long-sleeved shirt to protect his scarred arms from the sun's rays, and a cowboy hat to shield his face, Bryan looked like a rancher. He'd told her once how important it was to keep his skin covered. He slacked one hip and leaned against the car. "I was heading down to the stable to exercise one of the horses. Since it's such a nice day, I wondered if you'd be interested in taking a short ride."

A fluttering, like butterflies freed from their cocoons, tickled inside her stomach. She probably needed to eat something. Despite the trauma his body had experienced, the work on the estate contributed to Bryan rebuilding a more-than-healthy physique. Funny she'd never noticed before.

"I'd love to, but I'm running late. I need to catch a ferry for Bainbridge Island." She opened the back seat of the car, grabbed the box, and shoved it across the seat. "I'm working a party over there."

"Big deal?"

"Yes, this might be another good break for me. The Wards are a prestigious family in the Seattle area, and if I impress them with my stellar party planning, this job could lead to more opportunities. And besides that, I like the birthday girl. Ellie is down-to-earth and fun. I don't want anything to spoil her eighteenth birthday."

"Gotcha."

"Not to mention that my mother referred my services, and if I don't pull this off with rave reviews, she'll kill me." She grinned at him. "Now instead of standing there and yakking away precious time, you could offer to help load the car."

Bryan saluted. "Sure thing, boss."

Grabbing what looked to be the heaviest box in the cottage, Bryan hefted the container into his arms, hauled it outside, and deposited the cargo in the trunk of the car. He spun around to return for another as Liana struggled with the weight of her load. Striding to her side, he relieved her before she dropped it.

"Thanks."

"Don't you think you should pack a little lighter?" he teased.

Liana sighed. "I know—I know. I'll find someone to help me unload when I get there."

A thought nagged Bryan. "Lee, can I ask you something?"

"Make it quick."

He plunked the box into the trunk next to the other and

slammed the lid. "Is this the gig you almost lost because you drove me and Rainey to the vet hospital?"

Perching hands on both hips, Liana peered straight into his eyes. "Yes. But I didn't lose the job, did I? The Wards are dog lovers, so they understood. No problem. End of story. No guilt trips. The important thing is that Rainey is okay."

"Sure." Bryan didn't know how he'd cope if something happened to the Lab. Since returning home from the hospital, Bryan had counted on having Rainey at his side. The animal's companionship provided both comfort and friendship. Bryan and Rainey were both indebted to Liana for helping save the dog's life. When Bryan later pressed Liana to tell him why she'd been all dressed up that day, he couldn't help feeling guilty that while driving him and Rainey to the vet hospital, she was expected at an important meeting.

Bryan stashed the last box in the car's back seat, and Liana tossed her purse onto the front. "Oh! I promised to leave Dad a note about the meeting with the florist. He wanted to know the final cost. I'll give him a copy of the invoice later. Would you please grab the black leather bag inside for me? If I forget that, I'm doomed. It contains my lifelines."

Bryan ran up the few steps into the cottage and swiped the dark bag lying on the table. He tossed it onto the floor in the back of the car before Liana scurried back from the big house.

Breathless, she panted, "Did you find the bag?"

"Got it."

"Thanks!" Liana slid into the driver's seat.

Bryan leaned down to window level. "Hey, Lee, okay if I'm in the cottage while you're gone? I'm finally getting around to putting in a new disposal. A heavy duty model."

Liana flashed a warm smile. "Are you kidding? You're my hero. Go for it."

With a wave, she peeled out of the driveway and onto the road leading out of the estate.

Timing couldn't have been better for Bryan to get the new disposal installed into Liana's kitchen sink. She'd be gone for hours, and he could take his time without imposing. He opened the tool chest and pulled out a wrench. He should have replaced the old disposal when it first gave her trouble, but it had taken a little time to convince the doc that it wasn't operator error. The time had come to retire the unit.

Hopefully, Liana's event would go well. As hard as she worked, she deserved success.

And from her comments, he'd picked up that Liana had a need to prove herself to her mother. Not that she blatantly ever expressed that, but Bryan had acquired a deeper sense of people—an intuition—that he hadn't known before the accident. He guessed Liana didn't feel the same kind of unconditional love from her mother that she received from her dad. Pulling off this party with accolades was one way for Liana to gain her mom's approval.

Bryan glanced around the comfortable room, and his eyes caught what looked to be a black bag leaning against the couch. His heart rammed his rib cage. Black leather. Picking up the bag, he peered inside, and his gut plummeted. Inside he discovered the binders, notebook, and phone she insisted were vital to pulling off the party. Bryan plopped down on the chair.

He'd sent her off with the wrong leather bag.

Burying his head in his hands, Bryan leaned on the table.

After all she'd done for him and Rainey, he'd let her down. He couldn't even do this one thing right. Liana mentioned the information was important, but he hadn't even bothered to make sure the bag he sent with her contained what she needed.

Her cell was password protected, so he couldn't access any phone numbers there. This was one time he couldn't be concerned about Liana's privacy. Bryan rummaged through the papers and notebook, looking for an address or phone number where she could be reached. Ward was the last name of the family. Under the letter *W*, Bryan found the information he needed. After punching the number into his cell, he paced the kitchen floor, waiting for someone to pick up.

"*Hola.*"

"Hello? I'm trying to reach Liana Tate."

"No Li-ana Tate here."

"Is this the Ward residence?"

"*Sí*. But no Liana Tate."

"She's the lady who's running the party there today."

"Sí, we have party but no Liana."

Bryan shut his eyes and leaned his forehead into the palm of his hand. "Is there anyone else I could please talk to?"

"No. We have party. Everyone busy. Call back later."

"This is important. I can't call back later."

"Please call back later." Click.

"Ahhhhhh!" Bryan wanted to pull out what little hair he had left. No, not a good idea. He was grateful he still had hair—except for the area around his right ear.

It was his responsibility to get the bag to her. After leaving the hospital, the doc planned to have dinner and attend a play at the 5th Avenue Theater with friends. He couldn't bother him with the problem. Bryan had to do this on his own.

It wasn't like he never left the estate. The grocery store had become a comfortable place because he could joke around with the clerks, and if needed, escape. Trips to the gas station, library, and hospital were routine and safe. But he'd be trapped on the ferry alone, and there would be no leaving the boat until it docked. No escaping stares, taunts, or practical jokes. As a precaution, he'd drive onto the vessel and stay in the truck while crossing over to the island.

Bryan needed to focus on the task. He'd done fine at the vet hospital because his only concern was that Rainey would be okay. With the address from Liana's notes, and directions from GPS, he'd deliver the necessary items to her, and then quietly slip away.

Chills played his body, even though his hands sweated profusely. Bryan's stomach churned as though preparing to relieve its contents. He needed to pull himself together and do this. Lee had become a friend, and friends were there to help when needed.

The boxes unloaded, with the help of several young men working for a rental company delivering extra tables and chairs, Liana peered in the back seat of the Volvo for the bag containing her binder with notes and contracts, her additional notebook, and phone.

"Oh, no, no, no!" She slammed her hand on the door

frame when she really wanted to beat her head against the sedan. Bryan had accidently sent the wrong bag. The one she needed was *black* leather. What she held in her hand was dark brown and held information pertaining to the hospital fundraiser.

One of the young men assisting her stopped with a large box in hand. "Something wrong, miss?"

"Nothing you can fix. Thanks." Liana closed the car door and leaned against the body. She'd have to recall all the details for the party as best she could from memory and wing the rest. It wasn't Bryan's fault. He probably grabbed the first thing he saw. If she hadn't been in such a hurry, by habit, she would have double-checked. Liana took a deep breath.

"Liana, you're here. Great timing." Debra Ward, dressed in a yellow sundress, white sweater, and sandals, looked stunning. Her simple gold-chain necklace and earrings gleamed in the sun. "I overheard a conversation our cook had on the house phone with someone asking for Liana. She didn't know who you were, and by the time I asked her to hand over the call to me, she'd hung up."

"Did she get a name or number?"

"No, I'm sorry, and I didn't think to look at the caller ID." Debra pulled the pair of sunglasses from the top of her head and placed them over her eyes. "Do you have any idea of who might be trying to reach you?"

"Possibly. Could I use that phone? I don't have mine on me right at the moment."

"Is everything all right?"

Liana gave the most confident smile she could muster. "Yes. Thank you, though, for asking. Your job is to relax and enjoy the evening."

"This week at the magazine has been rather taxing. I could stand a night without responsibility." Debra sipped from the glass of white wine in her hand. "Let me show you to the phone and then leave you alone." She led Liana through the house to the kitchen. "I can't tell you how excited Ellie is about this party. She's been talking about it non-stop."

Muscles tightened in Liana's shoulders. She needed to rally and make things work.

"The phone is over there on the counter. Help yourself."

"Thank you."

Bryan planned to work in the cottage. She'd try to reach him there first. There wasn't time to return home for the bag, but she could ask him to feed her pieces of information over the phone while she jotted what she needed into a spare notebook.

Liana dialed the number to her cottage. She rarely used the landline, but now she was grateful it was still connected. One ring, two rings, three. "C'mon Bryan, pick up." Her nails tapped the counter as anxiety hatched in her stomach, then slithered toward her throat, threatening to suffocate her. After the sixth ring, the call went to voice mail. Liana hung up.

Either he didn't feel comfortable picking up her phone, or he'd already left. What was his cell number? She'd only called it once, and now nothing came to mind. Liana could only hope that everyone working the party showed up on time and there were no more glitches.

Thirty

Bryan paid his fee to the toll collector in the booth. By wearing a cowboy hat and keeping his left profile toward the raven-haired woman, he seemed to prevent her from noticing anything different about his face. He sighed with relief as he pulled away from the booth. If people were curious and wanted to ask questions, especially kids, he usually didn't mind answering. But he wasn't in the mood for any long interrogations today or misperceptions of what someone like him might be doing to cause trouble.

Following the line of traffic, he drove onto the ferry and parked the truck in the outside lane on the vessel's open-aired port side. As soon as people shut off their vehicles' engines, they hiked to the ferry's upper deck. There they could either walk the perimeters outside or sit comfortably inside while consuming drinks and snacks. Either way, the view of the city from the stern, or the sight of the mountains and the island from the bow, would be spectacular.

Bryan rolled down his window, closed his eyes, and turned his face into the breeze coming off the water. It had been a long time since he'd made this journey, but he hadn't forgotten the salt-water smell, the engine's hum, the waves breaking against the ferry, or the cry of the gulls as they hovered above, waiting for morsels of food tossed their way. For a moment—but only a moment—he forgot why he needed to get to the island.

☙

Her memory served her well, but she sure could have used her notes. Liana stood on the house's top deck and surveyed the progress below. The beaches in the Pacific Northwest tended to be rocky as opposed to covered with soft, beautiful sand. Fortunately, this one had a little of both, and she'd done her best to use the layout for the benefit of the vendors and partygoers.

The rental company had delivered and set up the rock wall and the trampoline. Since Ellie and her friends leaned more toward spending time in the outdoors than in cultural settings, Liana strove to provide a few challenging but fun activities. A sigh escaped her lips.

Unfortunately, her camera lay in the bottom of the bag left behind. There wouldn't be any photos to add to her portfolio unless she could borrow a digital camera from the Wards. Requesting to use their computer didn't feel comfortable, so someone else would have to upload and e-mail the photos. Forget that idea. Not professional. Lesson learned. Don't leave the camera behind.

Ellie appeared on a lower deck wearing jeans, a forest-green sleeveless shirt, and sandals. Glancing toward the upper deck and seeing Liana, she bounded up the stairs. "This is going to be *soooo* awesome! My friends will love it." Her eyes sparkled as she flashed a grin. "Thank you, thank you, thank you!"

"I'm glad you like it."

"My mom wanted to throw a stuffy, boring party, but I'll remember this for the rest of my life." Ellie surveyed the area. "This is totally me. I love my mom, but she doesn't get it. She doesn't get me. You know what I mean?"

Ellie had no idea of how much she and Liana were alike. Although their mothers loved them, entrenched in their high profile careers, they seemed to have their own agendas and ideas of what they thought best for their daughters.

Debra Ward slid open the glass doors to the upper floor of the house and joined them on the deck.

"Mom, this is going to be a great party. Thank you." Ellie stole a sip from her mother's wine glass.

"Ellie," her mother scolded.

"I barely got a taste." Ellie, four inches shorter than Debra, perched on her toes and gave her mother a peck on the check. "Is Dad going to be home soon?"

"He's on his way."

"Oh, I forgot to return Amanda's call." Ellie scrambled down the steps to the lower deck, yelling over her shoulder, "She's going to be so psyched about the rock wall."

Debra smiled and spoke with fondness. "Like her father, my daughter has an uninhibited zest for life." She leaned against the deck's railing. "How are things coming?"

"Great." Liana pointed to the left. "The climbing wall and the trampoline are ready. There's staff to man both to make sure your guests are safe. Kayaks with life preservers are available along the beach over there. The truck is out front with more tables, chairs, and umbrellas. They'll be put over to the right." She pointed in that direction.

"The firepit where the bonfire will be lit later this evening is stocked with plenty of wood. All the lights have been strung, and the rest of the decorations and flowers are ready to be put out an hour before guests arrive." Liana turned her back toward the beach.

"I'm expecting the band to show up any minute, and they'll set up on this deck. We'll show them where they can plug in their gear, and they should have everything else that they need." She'd done her best to cover all details. "I laid down runners so they won't scratch your wood floors while bringing in their equipment."

"And the caterer?"

Liana hoped to avoid the question but couldn't lie. "The crew should have arrived a half hour ago, but I haven't heard from them. I tried reaching the location they work from but no luck." She'd called directory assistance but didn't want to confess to Debra and Ellie that the lead person's cell number was written in her binder, not to mention programmed into her phone. And she didn't have either one. "I gave them your contact information in case they couldn't get ahold of me, so I'm sure they'll get in touch if they've run into any problems."

"Oh dear, I hope the call Maria answered earlier wasn't the caterer."

So did Liana.

"Mrs. Ward, people are here." Maria stood in the doorway to the home's interior. "They say they are the band for the party."

"Excellent. Thank you, Maria. I'll introduce myself, and then Liana will take it from there."

A mixture of nausea and excitement burst inside Liana, like a flood breaking through a dam. The people playing for this party had been an important part of Bryan's life before the fire. Liana didn't know how she should feel or what to expect. An odd desire and curiosity to meet the former band members warred with protectiveness toward Bryan. Whatever their reason, his former friends had walked away from him when he needed them most. It was delusional thinking for even a moment that bringing the band and Bryan together would provide an avenue for his return to music.

She ached for his happiness—for him to gain back what he lost. When had she grown to care so much for the man?

"We were told this is where the band sets up."

Liana twirled around to face an ordinary but pleasant-looking man with sandy-colored hair and hazel eyes, wearing jeans and a black polo shirt. His arms wrapped around a small drum.

"You're in the right place." She extended her hand. "I'm Liana, the event coordinator."

The man lowered the drum to the deck, smiled, and extended his hand in a brief shake. "I'm Ted—drummer for Lava. Nice to meet you." He swept the air with his hands from his shirt to his pants. "I hope this attire is okay. We were told it was a beach party and to dress casual, but we brought dressier stuff, if preferred."

"No, that's perfect. You're fine." This guy seemed to be genuinely friendly. "Before you get all your gear unloaded, I'd like to meet the rest of the band, go over a few details, and then let you set up."

"Sounds like a plan."

"What sounds like a plan?" A man wearing jeans and a black dress shirt rolled up at the sleeves and open nearly to his waist stepped through the open door to the deck. His unshaven face gave the popular scruffy look, and his hair was a rich coffee shade.

Next to him and holding his hand, stood a pretty woman with thick, long hair and dark chocolate-colored eyes, dressed in a short black dress and sandals. The bottom of the dress barely covered her rear end, but slender, tanned legs extended below the hemline. If she didn't have something warmer to change into later, once the sun went down, the woman would be chilled. So be it.

Ted nodded toward the couple. "This is Mack, our bass guitarist, and Jenny is keyboardist. She also sings and has a voice that can belt with the best of them. Guys, this is Liana, the event coordinator for this gig."

"Hi." Guilt nagged Liana's conscience for not telling Bryan that Lava would play at the party. She'd convinced herself that knowing would rip open old wounds, and that she was protecting him. But now, not sharing the information felt more like betrayal. She tried to imagine Bryan hanging out with this group, but the image didn't fit the man he'd become. Not just physically but also in the self-absorbed vibes given off by Mack and Jenny. Bryan presented humility and concern for others.

"Where's Chris?" Ted directed his question to Mack.

"He's on the phone with his girlfriend outside. Our sound guy is pulling speakers out of the van."

Ted hefted his hands in the air. "I'm sorry Liana, if he's on the phone with her, no telling how long it'll take."

"I trust you to make sure that you're all ready to play when it's time. You can pass on any info you think he might need." Liana remembered all three from the photo of Lava that Bryan kept in his apartment. Chris must be the guy who replaced Bryan. "This whole space is yours."

Mack grinned and placed both hands on his hips. "Sweet. This deck is huge. There's plenty of room for us."

"The caterer is going to set up on the deck below. We're

expecting about two hundred guests to arrive between three and six o'clock, so you have about an hour to set up. Is that going to work for you?"

"No problem." Mack glanced around the space. "We've done this so many times we could do it in our sleep."

"What about the schedule?" The dark-eyed beauty's eyes sparkled with enthusiasm.

"You play until 10:00 p.m. I realize that's three hours longer than most gigs."

Ted chuckled. "Hey, as long as we're paid, we'll play until you tell us to quit."

"Be sure to take fifteen-minute breaks on the hour and an hour for dinner. Appetizers and snacks will be set up right away, and dinner will be served at seven. Eat freely and enjoy. I have someone lined up to provide tunes through an MP3 player and sound system during any breathers and after you're finished for the night." Liana mentally went through the list of details she'd written up for them. What else did she need to relay? *Oh, yes!*

She waved toward the beach. "Guests will scatter throughout the area, but once the sun goes down between seven-thirty and eight, they'll primarily hang out around the bonfire and chairs below. You have some fans here, so please feel free to mingle and chat with them."

"Any issues with sound that we need to be concerned about?" Jenny offered a cheerful smile while she twirled her sunglasses in a circle around a feminine hand with fingers that looked like they could reach more than an octave on a keyboard.

"We've cleared noise levels with close neighbors, and with ending live music by ten, we've covered our bases. But still try to be careful about keeping it under control. Being near the water, the sound will carry farther. Oh, and outlets run all along the outside wall here for you to plug in your amps."

Ted clapped his hands together once. "Let's get to it."

Maria poked her head out the door. "Ms. Liana, the man to take pictures is here. He says he needs to talk to you."

Liana hesitated. She felt torn between staying on the deck a few more minutes and leaving to check in with the photographer. But now was not the time to cleverly make subtle inquiries about Bryan's connection with the band. She'd look for an opportunity during one of their breaks to speak to Ted, who seemed to be the most likely candidate to open up and chat with her. In the meantime, she followed the cook back into the house. Hopefully, the caterer would show up soon.

Thirty-One

With one hand resting on Liana's bag, Bryan sat in the parked truck, debating his next move. The activity in front of the Wards' home reminded him of the ant farm he had as a kid. Two men pulled up with a truck filled with kayaks. They slowed down, then drove down a side road, one that possibly gave access to the beach. Another delivery man passing by on his way out gave him a strange look, and Bryan tipped his cowboy hat lower.

No one held a gun to his head. Bryan could turn around and drive back to the ferry. Stepping on the clutch, he turned the key in the ignition. No, Liana said she needed what the bag held, and he wouldn't forgive himself for being a coward. His foot came off the clutch, and he removed the key and stuck it in his pocket.

Bag slung over his shoulder, Bryan stepped from the truck, and glancing to his left and right, strode to the front door. Several cars, including Liana's, and a large van were parked in a gravel area next to the three-car garage. Voices from within the home filtered out through open windows. Faint notes from a guitar carried through the air. It would only take a few minutes to rap on the door, ask for Liana, and hand over the bag. Then he could be on his way.

Several knocks didn't bring any results but ringing the doorbell did. A short Latino woman opened the door with a grin.

Her eyes widened and her smile faded. "May I help you?"

Bryan felt the urge to turn around and leave, but he didn't move. "I'm a friend of Liana Tate's. I need to see her for a moment. Could you find her please?"

Her forehead furrowed, as though she thought hard about his words. "You're a friend of Ms. Liana?"

Perhaps this was the one who'd answered the phone earlier? "Yes. Please tell her Bryan is here." Maybe he should give the bag to the woman and ask her to deliver it. Then he could make a fast getaway and save everyone, especially Liana, embarrassment.

"I'm Maria." Another smile lit her face. "Come in. Ms. Liana is good person. You must be good person. I'll find her for you. *Un momento.*"

Bryan removed his hat and stepped inside but stayed near the door as Maria went to find Liana. Even though September temperatures remained in the low to midseventies, his palms were moist, and his shirt stuck to his skin where sweat dripped down his back. He took a deep breath and anticipated Liana's welcome. At least he hoped she'd offer a smile once she saw the bag and not be too mad at him for messing up.

From where he stood, Bryan listened to the band run through sound checks on guitar and keyboards. Vocal checks followed with the male's voice sounding clean and strong. A female's voice, too familiar, came through the mic as she gave instructions to the person at the sound board. Bryan leaned against the wall for support. His heart raced. Liana would come looking for him, only to find the bag on the floor, but he had to get as far away from here as he could.

He opened the door to escape and had one foot out when

the band played the introduction to a ballad. Only they weren't playing something original, they played *his* song. One he'd written and was asked to record as part of the record deal. He wasn't familiar with the lead singer, but the licks on the guitar were Mack's, and the female voice unmistakably belonged to Jenny.

Lava was here.

They had no right to perform his music. After all he'd done for the band, wasn't it enough that they'd cut him out of their lives and gone on without him, they also had to steal from him? Fury burned in his gut. Without thinking, he stormed through the house in the direction of the music until he found the deck where the band played.

Feelings he thought he'd dealt with—a belief that his future had been destroyed—surfaced and boiled over.

"Stop!" Bryan, with unleashed anger, picked up the lead singer's mic stand. The music stopped—the new guy just stared at him.

"Bryan?" Jenny stepped back and crossed her arms over her chest, as though protecting herself. From what? From him? That cut deep. There was a time when she would have welcomed him with open arms.

"What are you doing, man?" Mack grabbed his arm.

Bryan dropped the stand and shoved Mack hard enough the guy fell back on the deck. "You have no right! That's my song. I wrote it, and it belongs to me."

Mack sat halfway up, leaned on his elbow, and sneered. "It belongs to the band, buddy."

"Enough!" Ted stepped between the two men. "Bryan, what are you doing here?" He sounded genuinely concerned. "Where have you been?"

"Teddy—" He wanted to calm down, and in the past, Ted had kept Bryan grounded, but his heart raced, and his labored breathing kept him tense. When would he stop hurting? How much more betrayal did he need to endure?

"I'm glad to see you." Ted put his hand on Bryan's shoulder and looked him in the eyes. "I've wondered what happened to you."

"Nice to know." Had Ted thought about him? Cared about how he was doing? "It—it felt like you gave up on me." Bryan's head pounded as his breaths slowed and he regained control.

"Dude, I even talked to Beth. She said with all the surgeries, you wanted to be left alone. But you're right. I should have checked in later, and I didn't."

"She mentioned it once. Thanks for that." He did need some solitude during recovery, but he never meant forever. Was it his fault that he didn't hear from Teddy? Or anyone else from the band?

Bryan didn't belong here—he needed to leave—remove himself before he did or said something he'd regret. "I—I should go. Let you guys get back to what you were doing. Go ahead and use any of my songs. Just not that one, Ted. Please. Leave that one alone." Bryan had written the love ballad for Jenny. They all knew that—especially Jenny. Hearing it again was painful. He took several steps toward the door.

"Wait!" Jenny grabbed Bryan's upper arm. Warm eyes pleaded for him to look at her, and he saw the Jenny he once knew. The woman he'd once given his heart to completely. "I'm sorry, Bryan. For everything."

He nodded. Bryan had imagined Jenny becoming coldhearted because that image was easier to live with. But that picture was flawed. There was still kindness within that woman—she just didn't love him anymore—not the way she once had.

Bryan had forgiven her, but he couldn't forget. Maybe that was more than okay. Maybe it was necessary. His band buddies had all moved on—and although he thought he had, seeing her and the guys stirred up unresolved grief. But wasn't death like that? About the time you thought you'd healed, something came along that reminded you of your loss. It was sometimes the same with relationships.

She let go, and a light breeze cooled the area where her hand had connected them. "Goodbye, Bryan."

"Bye, Jenny."

Was this what people meant when they talked about having closure? It certainly felt like *the end.*

Bryan took in a deep breath, and his gaze moved in the direction of the door where he'd escape back into the house. *Liana.* How long had she been standing there?

"It sounded like World War III had started up here, so I came to see what was going on." By Liana's pained expression and serious tone, she probably guessed Bryan's encounter with the band hadn't gone well.

"I brought your stuff. Thought you might need it." Bryan picked up the black leather bag he'd dropped, thrust it at her, and reeled around to leave.

How could he have been so wrong about her? He'd trusted Liana. He'd opened his heart to her. Bryan even hoped she might be capable of loving him—even though he didn't fit in with her high-profile family. But not mentioning that she was working with his old band felt like a knife to his gut.

Liana pursued him all the way to the truck, and with the window fully rolled down, was able to grasp the door.

Bryan stared ahead. He didn't want to see or talk to her. He wanted to get as far away from her as possible.

"Please look at me."

Her voice cut into his heart, but he couldn't expose the pain or anger her betrayal caused.

"Bryan, you have to know that I didn't hire them. That was already settled before I took the job. I figured I would do the party, it would be all over, and then I'd move on. I never meant to hurt you."

"I know. But you did." Bryan placed one hand on the steering wheel and stared straight ahead. "I thought we could trust each other."

"We can! I should have told you. I almost did—several times." He could hear the regret in her voice. "If I'd known ..."

"Yeah, if you'd known ..." Bryan sighed. "Can you understand what it felt like to walk into that house, thinking I was making up for messing up your job, and hearing them play one of my songs?"

"I'm so sorry ..."

"Me too, Lee." Bryan glanced at her, then regretted showing Liana his pain. He stepped on the clutch, started the truck, and put it in gear. Now wasn't a good time to focus on his problems and talk. He needed a little time and space to think, and she had an important event to finish. "You better get back to your party."

Liana released her hold on the truck and, still clutching the black bag, stepped back.

Bryan drove off without another word.

❧

As much as Liana ached to follow him, she still had a job to do.

"Liana, is everything all right?" Debra stepped from the house and approached her. "There was quite a commotion earlier."

She blinked back the pools of liquid blurring her vision. "Everything is fine, Debra. I've got it all under control."

"Okay, then. Let me know if you need anything." Debra went back inside.

Liana gulped back a sob. "Is a miracle too much to ask?" Her head pounded, and her throat felt raw. No time for tears. Guests would arrive. And the caterer still hadn't shown.

She opened her bag, dug out her phone, and called the catering service's contact.

"Hello?" Carol, the lead waitress answered.

"Carol, it's Liana."

"I'm sorry we're so late." Carol's voice sounded tense. "Did you get my messages? One of the vans had engine trouble." Her words tumbled out. "We called for backup—then missed getting on a ferry by a few vehicles. I called your cell, but you didn't pick up."

Liana kept her voice low. "I accidentally left it at home. Someone brought it a few minutes ago. Where are you?"

"We're off the ferry and should be there soon."

"Thank goodness!" One thing at a time. She'd get through the party and then try to fix things with Bryan.

Within fifteen minutes the catering caravan arrived.

Carol hopped out of the first vehicle and shook her head. "I apologize, Liana. We thought we'd left in plenty of time to get here an hour early, but we didn't expect a breakdown."

"That's behind us now. We need to focus on getting your crew ready." Liana was relieved they'd arrived safely, but they'd lost too much time to waste even a minute more.

"Where can we unload and set up?"

"I'll hop in a van with you. There's an access road to the beach. We can drive down and unload right there without carrying everything through the house. The buffet tables are set up on the lower deck. There's a full kitchen and a bathroom on the lower level for your staff to use. Two large grills are available for cooking corn on the cob, garlic shrimp, and that amazing grilled pizza you create—and a third grill is already in the hamburger stand."

The rest of the day flew by in a blur. Liana functioned on autopilot, making sure the party flowed smoothly. She assured the band members and Debra Ward that Bryan had left and wouldn't be causing additional upheaval.

Ellie's spontaneous hug raised Liana's spirits, but still worried about Bryan, she struggled with staying late. However, as a professional, she wouldn't leave until after cleanup.

The band took a break before playing their last set, and Liana leaned against the deck railing, observing the party on the beach below. She heard the water lapping up on the beach, more than she viewed it under the darkened sky. A few stars twinkled above, and a light breeze brushed her loose hair across her cheek.

Earlier that day, she'd arrived on the deck in time to catch Bryan and Jenny talking. Though the other band members were within hearing distance, it was clear by the way the two looked at each other that they'd shared a strong connection. No one intruded—even Mack, her apparent boyfriend, allowed them a moment.

Liana's throat burned as she held back unexpected tears. Were Bryan and Jenny together before the fire that changed Bryan's life? If so, did he still have feelings for her?

Mack and Jenny avoided mingling during breaks. They now lounged in chairs some distance from the remaining partiers, while Ted and Chris sat near one of several firepits on the beach, chatting with guests.

Hoping to talk about Bryan, Liana tried several times to catch Ted alone for a few minutes, but either a guest wanted his attention, or a vendor needed hers. Maybe there was a good reason for bad timing.

She had no intention of asking Ted about the possibility of Bryan rejoining the band. After the fight, it was obvious that wasn't possible, nor was it a good idea. Liana wanted to better understand Bryan, the singer. What kind of person was he while performing? Liana could only imagine that he would joke with his fans, unselfishly give them his attention, and make them feel special.

"Enjoying a breather?" Debra and her husband joined Liana at the railing. "You certainly deserve one."

Roger Ward, youthful in appearance, despite graying hair, wrapped an arm around his wife. "You know, it was a big disappointment for all three of us when we had to cancel the trip to Greece. Ellie looked forward to going since her sixteenth birthday." Roger flashed a grin. "But we couldn't be happier with the party. The guests have had a great time, and her face has been lit up all day."

"Thank you. I'm so glad you're pleased." Liana smiled. The day had been personally rocky, but she'd kept her emotions hidden and performed the best she could. Their praise brought relief that despite several disruptions, she hadn't professionally blown it. Her personal life—not so sure.

"When your mother and I had lunch, she mentioned that you're coordinating the Northwest Medical Center Gala this year." A cool breeze blew across the deck. Debra pulled her sweater closed and leaned into her husband.

"Yes, that's right." Her stomach knotted. Liana wished Debra hadn't brought up the gala. Liana had enough on her mind worrying about Bryan, and she didn't want to start stressing about another event that night before finishing the one in front of her.

"Good for you!" Roger seemed genuinely supportive. "I'm sorry we'll be in LA and will miss it this year."

"How is the planning going?"

She didn't know quite how to answer Debra's question. Tired of worrying about making a good impression, Liana decided to tell the truth. "I think it's going to be a great success. There's only one disappointment for me. We'll have a dance band, but I'd hoped to be able to entice a big-name entertainer to perform as a special treat for the guests. People I've contacted either have other commitments or they require hefty fees."

Debra gazed up at her husband. "Honey, is there anything you can do?"

While making her confession, it had slipped Liana's mind that Roger Ward was an agent for professional musicians. Embarrassed, she hoped they didn't think she was asking for help. "No—no, that's not what—I don't expect you to—"

"Liana, hang on. I'd like to help. Give me a minute to think." Roger seemed lost in thought, then he snapped his fingers. "Casey Marks. He's performing in Frisco the week before, but then taking a week off to visit his family in Houston."

Liana gasped. Was Mr. Ward actually considering—? "Casey is your client?"

"He is, and he tries to perform at several benefits a year, so I can almost guarantee that he'll be willing to swing up here and sing at the gala before taking a vacation."

"That would be amazing! Thank you." Liana suddenly felt a bit lighter. Miracles did happen. *Thank you, God.* Casey Marks! Dalisay would freak out. A few weeks ago, Liana never would have believed that landing this job would lead to a solution for the gala.

Now, if God could help her make things right with Bryan, she'd believe even more in the power of prayer.

Thirty-Two

Sprawled on the couch, Bryan stared at the colorless ceiling in his apartment, drained of any energy or ambition to even climb into bed.

He'd spent time on his knees, praying and asking for clarity. Ted mentioned he'd checked in with Bryan's sister, Beth, while he was recovering from the fire. There were days—months—when he'd been in pain and wanted to be reclusive, but had he shut out possible opportunities to keep in contact with his friends? Was Bryan also at fault for failing relationships?

Seeing the band together—hearing them play his song—had released hidden anger. And then there was Jenny ...

What also hurt? Liana not telling him that Lava was contracted to play at the big shindig. She knew the band's history. He'd opened up to her and shared his loss, but she avoided telling him the truth. He'd wanted to be her hero today, delivering her bag of supplies—her lifeline—but instead he'd walked right into an ambush. Not that Liana had purposely set him up. He knew better. But evil forces understood Bryan's weaknesses and what could bring him down faster than free-falling off the Columbia Center in Seattle.

Bryan closed his eyes.

Lord, I come to you ... I ask ...

❧

Almost one-thirty in the morning, Liana turned the car into her parking spot next to the cottage and turned off the ignition. She sat in the dark, tired, listening to the quiet. Massaging both temples, she attempted to soothe the nagging pain wedged between them.

She swung open the car door and stood, then pulled her black leather bag from the back seat. *Stupid thing.*

Liana trudged to the cottage stairs. The bag slipped from her shoulder and dropped onto the top step, and Liana lowered her weary body next to it. Her wool sweater jacket kept her comfortable, despite the chilly night air.

A dim light shown in Bryan's window, and a shadow moved back and forth, as though pacing the room.

Maybe she wasn't the only one who felt restless. Soft wind blew strands of hair into Liana's eyes, and she tucked them behind her ear. She pushed up from the steps. Should she try checking in on him now? It was late, but would either of them get any sleep if they didn't talk?

Liana crossed the distance between the cottage and the stairs leading to Bryan's apartment. One foot resting on the first step and one hand gripping the railing, she hesitated. Her heart beat against her chest. Maybe this wasn't such a good idea. He felt betrayed, and she couldn't blame him. But what if he never forgave her?

Her foot lowered to rest next to the other one, and her thumb rubbed the wood on the railing, almost in a frenzied motion. She didn't have to do this. Didn't have to go up there and face him. Liana took a deep breath. Yes, she did. She could imagine that his anger and disappointment had only surfaced because of buried pain.

No matter what Bryan said, or how he might act toward

her, she needed to talk to him.

Liana scampered up the stairs, and before she could change her mind, she knocked boldly on the door. Her breathing involuntarily stopped while she waited for an answer. Various noises filtered from the apartment. Rainey pawed on the door from the inside, whimpering to get out. A soft light, filtering from a window, went dark.

"Rainey, come!" Bryan's muffled voice called to the Lab.

Liana closed her eyes and propped her forehead against the door. "Bryan, please. Neither of us will get any sleep if we don't talk, so please open the door." She rapped one more time as a plea to let her in. "I'm not going away until we do, so unless you want me standing here all night ..."

The door swung open, throwing Liana off balance for a moment. Rain clouds had moved in, hiding the moon and stars. With the apartment completely dark, the cottage porch light alone illuminated that side of the house.

Bryan towered over her, an ominous black silhouette.

Liana's breath caught in her throat.

The Lab squeezed between Bryan and the door frame and pawed Liana's leg while nuzzling her hand with a wet nose. In his enthusiasm, his tail thumped against Bryan's leg.

Liana scratched the top of Rainey's head. "At least one of you is glad to see me," she whispered.

"What are you doing here?" His voice contained no animosity, only resignation.

"Bryan, about today ..." Liana said a few silent words, hoping they'd be good enough for a prayer. She was still out of practice. "May I please come in?"

He stepped to the side, which she took as a sign she could enter.

"Can we turn on a light?"

"Sure. Give me a minute." He placed his hands on her shoulders and guided her safely to the couch, where she carefully lowered her body. The clouds shifted in the sky, and the moon's milky beams bathed the room in a soft, wispy glow. Bryan remained in the shadows, but at least she could see his presence, not just sense it.

He turned the lamp sitting on the side table next to her on low. Then he sat as far away as possible on the other side of the couch, propped his elbows on his legs, and dropped his head into his hands.

Liana didn't know if he was praying or if he was waiting for her to speak.

Bryan raised his head, but his chest remained bent toward his knees. "I'm so sorry."

She'd come to apologize to him, and *he* was sorry? She'd kept the truth from him, thinking it best, but now she knew she'd only intensified his ache. "Bryan ..." How could she comfort him? Help him put what happened at the party behind him?

His back straightened, then he swiveled his body and faced her. "Liana, I'm so sorry. I lost my temper at the Wards' this afternoon, and I hope my behavior didn't create any problems for you. I won't ever do anything like that to embarrass you, or cause you distress, again."

"I know you didn't ..." Concern about Bryan's feelings—not her own—had weighed heavy on her mind all day.

"Okay. Good." Bryan stood and seemed to be waiting for Liana to do the same. "Now that's understood, hopefully we can both get some sleep." He spoke like the hurtful interactions that day had been neatly erased, and she was being excused.

Liana sensed feelings—a whole potluck—simmered beneath his calm exterior.

"If you think I came over here to get an apology, you're wrong." Liana slid off the couch, but instead of heading toward the door, she moved closer to him. "I'm not going anywhere yet."

Thirty-Three

Arguing would only widen the crevice she felt between them, so Liana refused to succumb to debate. Instead, she took Bryan's hand, hoping to bridge the gap. His heavy breathing was the only sound breaking the stillness of the dark night.

The physical closeness, the warmth emanating from his body, and the faint scent of his woodsy cologne, gave the moment an unexpected intimacy. She drew him back to the couch, and they both sat. Liana left space between them, not because she didn't want to be near him, but because she believed that was what he wanted—needed.

"Please give me a chance to say what's on my heart." Her voice was barely audible even to her own ears. "When I realized you were shaken by Lava playing at the party today, I felt horrible that you were taken off-guard and hurt. Your trust is important to me, and I let you down. I'm so sorry.

"You were put in a tough spot, and you thought you were protecting me." He didn't sound angry, only weary. "It took a few hours before I realized that." His shoulders sagged. "Sometimes my pride gets in the way of seeing things clearly."

She'd take a risk and say what was on her heart. "Next to my father, you're the most caring and gentle man I've ever met. I want to know you better and understand what you've been through, but I'm only half of this friendship. I can't force you to share your past, but I want you to believe that I'm here for you, and I'm willing to listen—for as long as you want to talk.

ॐ

The room was deafeningly quiet, which made the sadness in Bryan's heart even heavier. After all the nights he'd prayed for Liana to care even a little for him, and all the days he'd wish for time like this to be alone with her, he never envisioned his hopes becoming reality under such painful circumstances. Because now he realized he hadn't completely healed inside, and he was afraid he never would. Seeing Jenny again exposed the hurt and despair he'd felt after the barn fire.

Here he sat with the one person Bryan had dreamed might be God's gift to him—if he could be patient and faithful to God and his word. But he'd been a fool. He should've known that to have someone in his life who could love him—even with all his outward scars—was folly. At one time, Liana's words would have sparked hope that she might one day grow from caring for him to loving him. But what happened at the party reminded Bryan that although he had a place on earth, it would be different from what other people—*normal* people—could experience.

Liana reached over, and her soft thumb caressed his rough hand, sending a signal that she was still there waiting. Then, she removed her hand and sat back.

"I ..."

"It's okay," she whispered.

"You deserve to know why today was—rough." Maybe

then she'd see why he'd kept most of his life private.

"I don't deserve anything, Bryan, but I do want to understand."

"I know, but I'm not sure where to start." Bryan took a second to think. "Ted hasn't changed. He's always been a great guy. But he opened my eyes up to some things about myself that were difficult to face—like the fact that while I've blamed friends for abandoning me, I might have had a part in that." Bryan had been doing a lot of thinking about that since he'd gotten home earlier.

"I didn't get many opportunities to talk to him at the party, but he seemed like a nice guy." Her smile faded. "Mack wasn't as friendly."

"Yeah, my old buddy, Mack." If Bryan and Liana were going to establish renewed trust, he needed to be honest about his life, including past relationships.

Why did his throat feel like it was going to close up? "Jenny and I were close."

"I recognized her from the group photo I found in your apartment." Liana folded her arms in front of her. "And after seeing you two together today, I guessed as much."

Liana had figured that out by watching them for only a few minutes—if that long? What had the other guys picked up on? Or imagined? That Bryan and Jenny still cared for each other?

"She was more than a girlfriend. We lived together for almost two years. Before I got straight with God." Bryan cleared his throat. Why was it a relief to finally get it out in the open? "I thought we'd get married, and when the band was more established, we'd even have a few kids. But the accident was too much for her."

He shifted his weight on the couch. "Three years have passed, so I don't know what she's like now. But when we were together, she was sweet and compassionate. Most people our age don't spend time in nursing homes, but she loved the elderly and felt they were owed special care. She spent every Sunday morning she could singing at the home down the street from our apartment—no matter what time we got in the night before after a gig."

Bryan closed his eyes, trying to block out the memory of the day he found out she'd left him. Maybe if he verbalized it, he'd be able to maneuver past it, without losing too much of himself. "She came to see me only once. Right after I was hospitalized. No one had prepared her. She always did have a weak stomach."

"Oh, Bryan ..."

"Not a pleasant visit." He opened his eyes and sat up straight. "I ... ahhh ... I found out after I got out and went back to our apartment that she'd taken all her things and moved in with Mack."

"The band's guitarist?"

"He always wanted to take the lead—with the group and with Jenny. And he got what he wanted."

"Do you still have feelings for her?" Her voice sounded hesitant but also concerned. "Do you love her?"

How could he answer truthfully? He would never stop caring for Jenny, but did he love her? *No.* Not the way God intended a man to love a woman. Maybe Bryan hadn't gotten over what their relationship could have been if she'd been faithful. If he admitted to that, would Liana feel sorry for him? He didn't want pity. He wanted her respect—and when he believed it possible, her love.

"Today, Jenny and I said said goodbye." Hopefully, that would answer Liana's question. Jenny was no longer a part of his life, nor would she be in the future. "What made me so angry today was being reminded of who I was, what the band stole from me, and what I lost."

"I get that. But what if you had a chance to gain a new version of those things? Maybe even a *better* version?" Her voice hinted frustration. Hopefully she could tap into more patience while he explained. She'd been kind enough to hear him out so far.

Bryan needed to at least try to explain, even if Liana, in her world of perfect appearances and numerous opportunities, couldn't relate. "I'll never have someone in my life who can love me as I am." He stated the fact with little emotion. He'd resigned himself to this fact the first time he'd found a mirror at the hospital. He couldn't ask a woman to overlook all that—even after several surgeries. "And I'll never be able to perform again. That makes me ache inside—not because music defines who I am—but because it's what I had to offer. Something that might have made a difference for people." And letting it go still dug a hole in his heart.

He took a deep breath. "Sometimes the loss is unbearable. And when that happens, I get furious at myself for going into that barn fire—and at God. I know he loves me, and I want to trust that he knows what's best for me, but I get angry because I'm still human."

"Bryan ..." Liana sniffed. She tucked her knees underneath her, and kneeling on the couch, leaned in closer to him. The fresh citrus scent of her perfume reminded him of bright summer sunshine, just as she had been a bright ray of sun in his life.

Liana's soft hands held both sides of his face, half of his jaw sporting the stubble from a day's growth, and the other rough and scarred. Relief flooded Bryan that he'd kept the lights low. That feeling was followed by overwhelming sadness that her touch hadn't come at a different time and place when he could have offered her more. When he was whole and more than a scarred, ugly creature. Her hand on his disfigured face now? Painful, but not physically. He tried to flinch away, but she held fast.

"You are a kind, wonderful man, and friend." She gently kissed his disfigured cheek.

Air rushed from Bryan's lungs as a chill skittered up his back. No one had ever touched him with such tenderness. She'd offered him acceptance that he couldn't even offer himself.

Liana hadn't planned to kiss Bryan, but she was so moved by what he said about wanting to share his talent, she wanted to console him. She should have found another way. He'd said goodbye to Jenny, but he never denied still being in love with her. Liana needed to keep some emotional distance or she'd be the next one with a broken heart.

"Bryan, you're crying." Liana caressed his wet cheek. "It's okay. You're going to be okay." He stiffened next to her, as though she'd hit a nerve, and she moved back on the couch.

He got up. "It's late. You should get some rest."

"Yeah, you're right. We're both beat." Liana pushed off from the couch and headed for the door, then turned around. "Thanks for the talk."

Bryan wanted to play music, and Liana wanted to help him in any way she could—encourage him. "Maybe there are options you haven't considered," she said softly."

"Options?" His laugh sounded forced.

In a desperate move to fix it for him, she offered a suggestion. "What if you practiced on the guitar your sister left here and worked on writing more songs?"

"I appreciate your confidence in me, Lee." He gave her a sad smile. "Maybe I will write again someday. I shouldn't give up hope, eh?" He rubbed his eyes as though they were irritated or tired. "I've been thinking about giving professional photography a try. It would give me something new to explore as a career, but I still have a lot to learn."

"Really? That's a great idea, Bryan. You seem to enjoy having a camera in your hands."

"Always have—and thanks. My sister agrees with you, and I have a feeling she'll keep me accountable."

"Good. I'm glad." Liana opened the door. "Good night, Bryan."

So, he hadn't given up on his future. Liana had wanted to give him a boost, but now his willingness to still dream despite all he'd gone through, gave her hope. That was the feeling—*hope.*

It had come at a good time because now she faced challenging weeks ahead. Most important on her agenda— Camryn's revised wedding plans and the final details for the hospital gala.

Thirty-Four

C amryn was late. Again.

Liana had downed the last drop of her triple Americano fifteen minutes ago. She paced the hall, passing the door to Camryn's condo. No access to a bathroom out here. She quickened her steps to keep her mind off any physical discomfort. Her sister had promised to meet her there at three o'clock so they could finalize contracts for the wedding reception. But of course, her sister was on Camryn-time.

The bride-to-be insisted on a full band that not only incorporated strings, but also a playlist that included ballads, a little bit of country, pop, and of course—jazz. Camryn had also submitted a list of unacceptable songs. Liana didn't blame her sister. She could live with never dancing the "Macarena" again.

She heard the clinking of keys before Camryn rounded the corner and strolled toward her with several bulging shopping bags. The familiar pink one probably held lacy undergarments that Liana never quite felt comfortable wearing. She didn't deny they were beautiful. She just never felt her body did the pieces—or the designers—justice.

"Finally!" Liana picked up the canvas satchel from the floor holding several heavy binders, and instead of focusing on Camryn's purchases, glanced at her sister's profile. Dark circles under her eyes made the usually perky Camryn look like she hadn't slept in days. "Are you coming down with something? You're a little pale."

"I'm fine." Camryn unlocked the door to her home and Liana rushed past her, dropping accumulated wedding info on the floor.

"First things first. I've had the equivalent of three cups of coffee, and you're twenty minutes late!" Liana slammed the bathroom door behind her.

A crystal vase filled with white Dahlias and greenery resembling delicate feathers sat on the black marble countertop. Fresh flowers even in the guest bathroom. On a Wednesday. She'd have to give her sister credit for style even if she couldn't give her a high five on keeping to a schedule. Before she left the bathroom, Liana dried her hands on a small, white guest towel and attempted to leave it folded as neatly as she found it. Impossible.

No sign of her sister in the living room or kitchen.

"Camryn, what are you doing?"

"I'll be out in a minute!" Camryn's muffled voice came from the master bedroom.

"You're not taking time to try on everything you bought again, are you? I'm meeting Dalisay for dinner before we go to a gallery for a friend's showing. Just so you know. Some people do try to make their appointments on time."

"I'm just changing. I promise." A moment of silence. "Liana?"

"What?"

"Nothing ... There's cranberry juice and soda water in the fridge if you want something to drink."

The infrequently used kitchen boasted cherry wood cabinets, granite countertops, and stainless steel appliances. Beautiful, but beyond Liana's own budget. She was still thrilled that the new disposal worked in her own kitchen. She poured a glass of juice, and attempting to be patient, strolled onto the balcony off the living room where she could take in the view of Lake Washington and Seattle just beyond.

October's weather influenced the foliage. Splashes of amber, ginger, crimson, and saffron livened up the hills—also covered with homes—across the lake. Camryn lived on Mercer Island because of the community feel and the short commute. From there, she could take I-90 across the floating bridge and through the short tunnel into Seattle.

Mt. Rainier, to the left, gleamed bright in the fall sunlight, and boats skimmed across the lake waters with billowing white sails. Liana breathed in fresh pine air. It was moments like this when she felt even more grateful to live where she had access to both water and mountains.

She meandered back into the living room and slid the balcony door shut. Even Camryn shouldn't take this long to change. Liana knocked on the bedroom door.

"Camryn, let's get cracking here. We have a lot of stuff to go over."

As always, the only person who counted in Camryn's eyes was herself. Liana had explained she had somewhere else to go. And now her sibling, with her usual selfishness, was going to make her late.

"Camryn, if you don't get out here in one minute, I'm leaving. And you'll have to deal with these contracts yourself."

The response was so muffled she couldn't make out the words.

"Camryn, c'mon."

The bedroom door opened, and Camryn, who usually appeared anywhere—any time—with perfect hair, makeup, and clothes stood in front of Liana wearing gray sweats, a clean-washed face, and sporting a low ponytail. Her eyes were red, puffy, and void of their usual sparkle.

"Wow. Okay. So, why didn't you admit to not feeling well? I can come back another time." Liana did a one-eighty and zeroed in on the satchel holding the contracts. Maybe Dalisay could meet her a little earlier than planned.

"Wait!" Camryn's voice hitched. "I'm not sick."

Liana studied her sister's expression, and her heart filled with compassion. Something was very wrong. She laid the bag on the counter between the living room and kitchen. "What's going on Camryn?"

"I need to talk to someone." She sank into an oversized, stuffed sea-blue chair, the kind that could almost hold two people but was perfect for those rainy days when you just wanted to spend the afternoon with a great book.

"Okay." Liana followed and curled up on the end of the sofa, across from her sister. "I'm listening."

Camryn pulled a tissue from the box sitting on the end table next to her and blew her nose, sounding like a goose.

"Are you pregnant?"

"No! Not even close."

"I don't think there is a close. Either you are, or you aren't," Liana attempted to tease, but as the words escaped, they sounded lame and unkind. Conviction worked her over.

"Lee, this isn't the time for a comedy act." Camryn wiped fresh tears from her cheeks with a new tissue and red blotches appeared on her face.

"I'm sorry." Liana sent a silent prayer heavenward. Bryan and her dad were having an influence on her—praying was getting easier. She wanted to be present for her sister and help, if she could. "I've never seen you this way. Not even when you were grounded from going to the prom with Kenny Jackson after Dad caught you smoking pot down by the river. I even felt bad that you missed it."

The hint of a smile slipped onto Camryn's face. "I made up for it the next year when I was crowned queen at my own prom."

"I guess you did." Liana couldn't help it when the corners of her own mouth fought a grin.

But the lighter moment floated away with the delicate breeze coming through an open nearby window. Camryn's demeanor changed again. What had triggered this sense of defeat in her sister? Camryn always bounced back. Nothing ever kept her down, and Liana had often been envious of her sibling's healthy self-esteem. But now, looking at Camryn, her unbreakable confidence appeared shattered. Was Kevin responsible? Had he finally revealed the ugly man beneath the handsome exterior?

Camryn's eyes shimmered sadness. "I knew what time it was, and that I would be late, and I also knew that you'd be here waiting for me." She drew her lower lip in and chewed on it. "But I just kept shopping. Because that's what I do to avoid anything difficult, or even uncomfortable. I buy things. Anything. And for a moment, I feel better. I needed to reach that point today, even if it didn't last, in order to face you."

"I don't understand." But she wanted to.

As she played with a fresh tissue, she tore it into two pieces. "The wedding is off." Her voice was steeped in pain.

"He broke the engagement?" That would be Kevin. Love 'em and leave 'em. She'd certainly experienced it herself with him, but at least they hadn't gotten as far as planning a wedding.

"I know it would probably be more satisfying to you to see me left at the altar, but he didn't break it off." Camryn sighed. "I did."

Thank goodness! A heavy burden lifted from Liana's shoulders, and she felt twenty pounds lighter. Was Camryn serious? Or were the bride's nerves reacting to stress? Liana would tread lightly until she heard the entire story. "I thought he was everything you wanted—handsome, successful."

"Lee, I need you to be on my side for a change."

"Of course I'm here for you. I'm just a little surprised. You haven't come to me about anything since we were kids." Being able to confide in each other and be close again was something Liana had desired for so long, could she trust it was actually happening?

"You're the *only* person I can go to."

"What about your friends? What about Mom?"

"I'm not you, Liana. I don't have close friends. I'm not even sure I have any real friends. And I can't tell Mom just yet. She was ecstatic that I was marrying Kevin. You know what she's like. She's all about social status and money. He was someone who could take care of her baby girl after the modeling career is over. It's going to be almost impossible to get our mother to understand, unless ..."

"Unless what?" Had Kevin done something so horrible that even their mother wouldn't tolerate the behavior?

"I'm honest with both her and Dad. I thought it might be easier if I told you first." She grabbed a small pillow lying next to her and hugged it close to her chest. "Lee, Kevin isn't who he presents himself to be. He's a controlling, mean, angry man."

Liana straightened. *Finally.* Her sister had seen the truth. Lee had seen red flags herself—like the gutsy female advising her in the jazz club restroom to stay away from Kevin. The lady had dated him and had tried to warn Liana. But she'd convinced herself to dismiss the woman's words and then wished she hadn't. Kevin had tried to manipulate her that night at Salish Lodge, despite knowing in advance how she felt about sleeping with him. But the red flag that included blaring sirens was waved when he hit on her, even though he was engaged to Camryn.

"He got angry when I didn't do things the way he wanted them done, or I didn't feel like going to a business function with him." Camryn blew her nose, then cleared her throat. "If I didn't wear something sexy or entertain his peers with witty conversation, he'd turn on me later."

"Physically hurt you?" Liana's imagination kicked into gear, and she didn't like the destination it ran to.

"Once, he grabbed my arm too hard and it bruised. Another time he got so angry, he slapped me across the face." A tear trickled down Camryn's cheek. "I told him if I showed up with marks on my body, people would ask questions. I couldn't do photo shoots black and blue. He didn't want his model fiancée to give up jobs for magazine covers that he could show his buddies, so the physical stuff stopped. But the verbal attacks got worse."

Liana's stomach knotted, and she clenched her fists. He didn't have any right to hurt her sister—to hurt anyone! She wanted to wrap her arms around her sister, but she held back, afraid that if she did, Camryn would fall apart and stop talking. And Liana was sure there was more to tell. "I'm so sorry he put you through all that."

Camryn sat still for a moment, seeming to contemplate her next words. "It just seemed that no matter how hard I tried, it was never good enough. *I* was never good enough. I kept hearing that I was lazy, and fat ... and stupid. I've heard stories like this on TV talk shows, but I never thought it would happen to me."

"Until it did."

"In living color. And then a few days ago, I snapped. I was staying at his place for the weekend, and when he went to run an errand, I packed my overnight bag, laid my engagement ring on the counter, and left."

"He didn't follow you?"

"Oh, he did. But not because he loves me. He came over here and pounded on the door a few times. Left harassing voice messages." She sighed. "But I figured him out. I called him and told him that he could tell everyone—put a billboard up for all I cared—that he broke it off with me. I knew he was more concerned about being humiliated than he was about losing me. He never loved me. He just wanted to use me to bolster his own pathetic self-worth."

Liana couldn't stay rooted to her spot any longer. She bolted from the sofa and enveloped her sister in her arms. Camryn's self-control also must have weakened, because she sobbed for several minutes, until Liana's blouse lay soaked against her shoulder. Dalisay would understand Liana canceling dinner and the art exhibit. They could go tomorrow night, or the next. For the first time, in a long time, Camryn needed her.

ॐ

Since it was going to be a girls' night in, Liana talked Camryn into ordering pizza—something neither of them indulged in anymore. A large with pepperoni, black olives, onions, mushrooms, and extra cheese. They turned on the gas fireplace and lit several cinnamon and spice candles. Liana took a large bite and savored the salty taste of the pepperoni and tomato sauce. Why had she given up this delicacy? Oh, yes ... the constant fight to be thin and win her mother's approval. No more starving herself to lose weight and no more people pleasing. She was working hard to break free from those patterns.

Camryn seconded her sister's thoughts. "I am in love. This has to be the best tasting pizza I've had in a year. And it doesn't even matter that it's probably the *only* pizza I've had in a year!" She giggled.

It was good to see her sister this way. Liana had missed her sister's friendship. She swallowed the spicy food and quenched her thirst with diet soda. "I'll go with you to tell Mom and Dad. If you want."

Camryn laid her empty plate on the end table. She'd devoured three large slices of the forbidden food. "Thanks. I'd like that."

"How do you think they're going to react?" Liana had her own guess, but it would be good for Camryn to go in prepared.

"Mom will be upset because she thinks she's a good judge of character. She'll make it all about her. Dad will go into protection mode and want to kill him. So it will be up to me—up to us—to stop him from doing bodily harm to the guy and ending up as breaking news on KOMO."

"Mom loves you. Maybe she'll surprise you." Liana knew her voice held bitterness, and her heart clenched. She refrained from mentioning that Camryn was their mother's favorite. No. That was wrong. Liana was never in the running for the title.

Camryn studied her as though trying to analyze Liana's words. "Lee, you may think Mom and I have some kind of special thing going on between us, but she's just as hard on me as she is on you. Actually, more so."

"I have a difficult time believing that." Liana's eyes welled up, and her throat tightened. She took another sip of soda. "You've always been the pretty one. Women want to be you, and men want to be with you. You have an amazing career, wear expensive clothes, travel all over the world, and your face is displayed on high-end magazines across the country."

Liana looked down at her diet drink, her thumb making a line through the condensation that had formed on the outside of the glass. "I'm average looking, I live in a cottage on our parent's estate, and I can't get any man to love me. Yeah, I'm a prize. No matter how much I've tried, I've never been able to win our mother's approval."

"Wow." Camryn started to laugh.

"What's so funny?"

Camryn stifled her chuckles by covering her mouth with a pillow.

"Hey! I just poured my heart out, and you're acting like it's a joke." Frustration bubbled inside.

Her sister lowered the pillow, this time tears flowed from the laughter, not the pain. "It *is* a joke. On both of us."

"I don't get it." Her sister had really lost it this time, and

Liana was beginning to lose patience.

"All this time you've been jealous of my relationship with our mother, and I've been envious of the one you have with Dad."

"Seriously?"

Camryn's smile vanished. "I've tried to get Dad's attention, but every time I seemed to wiggle into some kind of space with him, you turn up, and *show* me up."

"Wow. I never meant to ..." Had she really done that to her sister? Hearing Camryn's perceptive—maybe she had tried to ace Camryn out.

"Lee, you may have thought I had advantages because of my size, my lustrous blonde hair, and my gorgeous, deep blue eyes." She winked but then grew serious again. "But you were always smarter, and that's what got Dad's attention. He'd light up when you brought home your report card with straight As. I barely passed with Cs."

Camryn twisted long strands of hair around her finger. "When we were in high school the two of you would sit up late at night talking about his day and what new advances were being made in medicine. I couldn't compete. Even when I wanted to give some input on the gala for the hospital, I was immediately shut down. Because nobody thinks I'm smart enough to have any good ideas. You even run your own business, for heaven's sake."

Liana's face flushed with the memory of that day in her father's kitchen when Camryn wanted to stay and join in the conversation about the event. Her sister was right. Liana hadn't even considered that Camryn might have something to contribute to the discussion. Shame filled Liana, and her face flushed. "I'm sorry. You're right. I guess I found every way to push you out of my life because you intimidated me. It was wrong of me to do that."

"I'm sorry too." Camryn focused on the invisible drawing her finger was doodling on the pillow. "I've done things on purpose to hurt you. Like when we were in high school. I knew you were hung up on Jason, but I didn't care. I went after him anyway."

"Jason and I had been best friends since kindergarten, but you never gave him a second glance until then. I knew as soon as you'd realized our relationship had become something more that you'd start flirting with him. And you did. I tried to warn him, but he didn't believe me. And after you broke his heart, I just couldn't bear to be the one to pick up the pieces."

"There's no excuse for what I did, and I don't know if you'll ever be able to forgive me. But I hope you can." She tugged on the end of her ponytail. "I have another confession to make."

"Another?" Liana's neck and shoulder muscles tightened.

"I knew you and Kevin were a couple before I showed up that day on the waterfront while you were having lunch together. I'd seen you at Pike Place Market one afternoon. He bought a bouquet of fresh flowers and kissed you. Seeing your face light up like that ... But when Kevin invited me to join you for lunch, I played it cool and pretended to go along with you just being friends."

"But you flirted. I sat there and watched the whole thing. If you knew I cared for him, why?" Her suspicions that Camryn had been playing a game were now confirmed. The reality still stung. Maybe nothing had changed since high school.

"Competition."

"And like all the other times, you got the guy. You won. Because that's what you do. You get men to fall for you."

"But this time, I fell too. Hard. He was so attentive, considerate, and entertaining at first. Kevin played the part well until he got tired of the role and showed his true character. As for men wanting to be with me—we've just seen where that got me." Camryn sniffed. "I'm so sorry, Lee."

"Because he tricked you into believing he was someone else?"

"Yes—but more that I didn't listen to you when you tried to warn me. I should have trusted you, but we haven't had the best relationship, and I selfishly wanted to show you that I knew better." Camryn chewed on her lower lip, then looked Liana in the eyes. "I'm also sorry that my flirting has been hurtful. I promise that I'll never do it again."

"Thank you," Liana whispered. Dalisay would tell her not to trust Camryn yet, but Lee heard sincerity in her sister's voice and saw it in her eyes.

"We can't get away from it though, can we?"

"Away from what?" Camryn had skipped down a mental trail and lost Liana along the way.

"People thinking they have to look or act a certain way to be loved—or even liked. Doesn't seem fair. Why can't people just be appreciated for who they are?"

Liana had never heard her sister talk like this. Like she was ... well, human. With real and deep feelings and perhaps a desire for something outside of herself. "I've learned there is someone who doesn't judge us by our appearance or our accomplishments. Instead, he looks to see what's inside. What's going on in our hearts."

Camryn sat up straight and swiped her cheek with her hand. "Are you talking about Bryan?"

"No—yes—but that's not who I was talking about. Bryan does care about people that way, but God also loves and accepts us just as we are." Was she really going there? Liana's heartstrings tugged. *Lord, please give me the right words.* "Good grief, I don't know a lot about the Bible, but I looked up a verse Bryan mentioned and memorized it. In 1 Samuel 16:7, the Bible says, 'The Lord doesn't see things the way you see them. People judge by outward appearance, but the Lord looks at the heart.'"

"You're going religious on me? Like Dad?" Camryn's eyebrows knitted, and she sounded confused by Liana's confession to reading the Bible.

Liana only wanted to help her sister feel better. But she couldn't blame her for the confusion. Liana herself couldn't swear to always living how God probably wanted her to. "No, I wouldn't call it that. It's just that spending time with Bryan has helped me see God differently. And I understand more of what Dad has been trying to tell me for a long time." She was also beginning to better understand herself.

Camryn cocked her head. "Bryan is important to you, isn't he?"

"He's been a good friend." More than that. The memory of being near him in the dark, kissing him, and the intimacy it created replayed in her mind.

"I think he wants more than friendship. He's in love with you, Lee. You're a lucky girl."

If Camryn knew Bryan hadn't denied feelings for Jenny, she wouldn't be so convinced about his interest. "Since when have you been a fan of Bryan's? He hasn't exactly been on your top-ten list of people you'd want to hang out with."

Camryn frowned. "I know. I thought he was just a charity case for you and Dad to fawn over."

"And now?"

"He—he's not like anyone I've ever met—except maybe Dad." She smiled. "Bryan is a good man. It's easy to see how much he cares by the way he looks at you."

"Well, that may have changed." A sadness stung Liana's heart. "He ran into an old girlfriend. I think that encounter may have stirred up some feelings. I'm not convinced he's over her."

Camryn adopted a determined look. "Do you love him?"

"Yes." She did love him. Liana loved so much about him. His kindness. The way he made her laugh and was protective of her. The way she'd catch him looking at her. And he'd taught her about God's unconditional love.

"Then do something about it."

Thirty-Five

Nervous energy had caused Liana to push herself hard through the woods during her morning run. The refreshing October air cooled her body while her feet pounded the dirt path. Focusing on avoiding tree roots helped keep her mind off the upcoming gala, but an hour after finishing the run, as she stood in front of the massive building that would house the event, her stomach flip-flopped. Two weeks. That's all they had to pull everything together.

"About time you got here!" Dalisay teased, striding toward Liana, dressed in jeans, a black sweater, and short black boots. A plaid scarf wrapped around her neck, and a beret covered the top of her head. Always stylish. Even while swinging a hammer.

Liana glanced at her watch. "It's only ten after eight."

"Yeah, well, I've been here since seven. You better have brought coffee."

"There's a large thermos in the car. If you were hoping for Starbucks, you're out of luck." Liana opened the passenger door, pulled out a stainless steel container, and handed it to her friend.

"Is it strong?"

"Is there any other kind?" She handed Dalisay a plastic bag with cups, paper plates, and napkins, then grabbed a small cooler from the back seat. "I brought lunch for the two of us. Veggie subs on whole grain—plain mustard—and apple slices."

"No cookies? You've seen how crabby I get if I don't have sugar."

"For someone who's getting a free lunch, you're mighty picky." Liana bumped her hip against her friend's. "I threw in some dark chocolate."

"You've saved me. And possibly the crew from seeing me turn into a witch by two o-clock."

"I'm sure they're used to it by now." Liana gave her a wink.

"I guess you'll have to ask them to find out." Dalisay leaned against the car. "Bryan's here."

Liana's heart picked up its pace. "He is?"

"Have you talked to him?"

"Not for several days. Family stuff going on." Liana had spent more time with her sister, and they'd also met with their parents to explain Camryn's decision to break her engagement. Both Mom and Dad had reacted as expected.

Liana reached into the back seat for her canvas bag holding the binders with her notes. "I'm surprised Bryan is here."

"Arrived shortly after I did. Didn't say much. Just asked to be put to work. He's helping the guys put up some basic structures." Dalisay balanced the load in her arms and strolled toward the building.

Liana matched her stride, her own hands full with the cooler and canvas bag. Dalisay opened the front door to the building that would first house the hospital gala, and then Erik and Maggie Jones' restaurant and event space.

The sound of pounding blasted Liana's ears. She perused the area and activity. Workers from the theater community were scattered from the back where several tree houses were being constructed, to the stage that protruded ten feet from a wall, to the entrance where colorful mushrooms loomed over them like canopies.

Dalisay had posted information about the gala on an Internet message board for theater professionals, asking anyone with set construction experience to offer their services for a reasonable hourly fee. Since the construction would remain as permanent fixtures in the event space, Erik was happy to pay for expertise that general carpenters wouldn't have when it came to specialty items.

"This is going to work, isn't it?" Liana grinned, relieved to see the progress made.

Dalisay's eyes crinkled at the edges as her smile showed perfect white teeth. "Well, I don't know about your end of this extravaganza. But as far as I'm concerned, this place is going to become magical. For one night, those stuffy executives are going to feel like they've stepped into a fantasy. If I have to get out my bull whip to make it happen."

Liana dropped the bag and cooler next to the wall and draped her arm around Dalisay's shoulder. "You're my fairy godmother."

"Then bring me a tiara next time." She held up the thermos. "I could use some of this before we get to work."

"I could use some myself." Liana spotted Bryan handing a two-by-four to a guy on scaffolding. She took the cup of coffee Dalisay had poured and took a sip. "Ah!" The liquid burned her tongue.

"Too hot?"

Liana nodded. "Be careful."

Bryan shook his head and laughed at something his partner said before picking up a hammer from a toolbox, and

Liana couldn't help staring. She'd seen Bryan interact with few people like that before—like himself—carefree and not worried about reactions to his scars.

Dalisay stepped in front of her, hands perched on her hips. "I can see your mind isn't on what I'm talking about." She nodded in Bryan's direction. "That's Andy Sinclaire on the scaffolding. He's a carpenter—one of Bryan's friends."

"Bryan's mentioned him a few times. They met at church through a men's group."

"You've never been introduced?"

"No." She missed bantering back and forth with Bryan the way his guy pal seemed to be doing now. The last time they were together, serious conversation had replaced joking around. "Bryan is having a good time."

"You're surprised?"

"A little." Liana was trying to reconcile Bryan's insecurities with what she was witnessing. "But if he can trust that people will see him for the man he is, maybe ..."

"Talk to him. At least for my sake. We're not going to get any work done until you do."

Her friend was right. Liana couldn't work in the same room as Bryan, not even in this enormous space, without saying hello. "Just give me a few minutes."

She inhaled deeply several times and strode across the center of the room. Andy made a wild gesture and said something that must have been humorous, because Bryan responded with a belly laugh. Maybe she should just leave him alone. Let him enjoy this day without her intruding on his fun.

No. She needed to do this. Liana waited until he'd handed Andy a piece of plywood and then tapped him on the shoulder. "Hi."

He swung around to face her. "Liana." Bryan's warm smile melted her fear that he wouldn't welcome her intrusion. He seemed glad to see her.

"Hey, I'm Andy!" Sporting a wide grin, the guy with auburn hair and a trimmed beard waved down at her from the scaffolding. "You must be Liana."

"I am." She attempted a return smile.

"Wondered if you'd be here today. This is quite a deal you're putting together."

"It's for a good cause. Thanks for helping out."

He saluted. "Glad to be a part of it." He nodded toward Bryan. "And it's always fun to hang out with this guy." He dropped his hammer into a loop on his tool belt. "I've gotta take a break, if you know what I mean, so you two chat, and I'll be back in a few." He crawled down the rungs of the scaffolding and sauntered off.

Bryan picked up his toolbox. "I could use a break myself."

"I brought coffee." Liana pointed to the left. "There's plenty if you'd like some."

"I'm on caffeine overload already, but thanks for offering."

Liana felt conspicuous standing in the open where workers could easily observe their interaction. She shifted and rested her weight on her left hip, glancing around to see if people were watching. "Can you give me a few minutes?"

He nodded toward a door. "I brought my camera to take a few shots of progress as it happens. Thought Erik and Maggie like to have them. I'd like to include the garden outside. Wanna come?"

"Sure." Liana welcomed a chance to talk and see how he

was doing after the fiasco at the Wards' party. "I love the idea of putting together a photo documentary of the renovation."

Bryan led her outside to a small garden, overgrown with wildflowers nearing their end, but still lightly fragrant. A dingy, white bird feeder, chipped and covered with spots of moss, stood in the middle of the garden. He motioned for her to sit on a weathered gray bench. "It's old, but safe."

Liana followed his instruction and sank onto the wood, hoping she wouldn't encounter splinters in her bottom later. Her shoulders and neck muscles were tight. Even the strong morning sun didn't melt the tension that had grown as the gala drew closer.

Bryan lifted his camera and focused on the area in the garden with the most blooms. Liana was curious about the view through his lens, but she didn't ask to look. She'd get a chance to see his final work later—or so she assumed.

Her heart clenched. Had Jenny poured over photos with Bryan in the past? Had she been the subject? Liana remembered that night in the stable when he'd taken some shots of Liana with Mitzi. He'd described the images as beautiful, but she'd shied away from viewing any.

Why? Why had she been so insecure? So stubborn?

Somehow, Bryan had helped her grow in confidence and in her weak but now existing faith. What had she done for him? What *could* she do for him?

Were things really over with Jenny? Would telling him that she loved him make a difference?

❧

Bryan grasped the edge of the bench with his hands and stared at the ground. All he wanted was to hold her close enough to feel her heartbeat, inhale the scent of her hair, and kiss those lips. But he couldn't. Not if he wanted the best for her.

After what happened at the party when he blew up at his former band, embarrassed Liana, and potentially caused her major problems, once he cooled down, he was convinced she'd be happier in the long run with someone else. Someone with a future. A man she would be proud to introduce to her family's social circles. What was that saying? You don't marry a spouse—you marry a family. Liana deserved more than what a scarred caretaker could give her.

Besides that, her mother and sister would never accept him, and Bryan didn't want to cause any more division in the family than what already existed. He knew how important it was for Liana to have her mother's approval, and he couldn't live with Liana regretting choosing him.

"How are you doing?"

"Great." As best he could be doing, considering he couldn't tell Liana he loved her. Bryan was grateful for Andy and the other guys who had offered their friendships. They'd become a lifeline, especially when he needed to keep his feelings for Liana in check. It wasn't fair to her to depend on her companionship. Dr. Tate was a wonderful mentor, but he carried numerous responsibilities, and Bryan couldn't monopolize his time either.

Liana brushed her hair away from her face. "I know I haven't been around, but a lot has happened in the past few days."

"Good things, I hope." He'd noticed she hadn't been at

the estate much, and her cottage had been dark when he'd come up from the stable in the evenings, but it wasn't his place to ask where she'd been.

"Yes! And I know she wouldn't mind me telling you." Liana moistened her lips. "Camryn broke off the engagement."

"Wow, that's a relief!" Knowing how Kevin had treated Liana, Bryan worried about Camryn himself.

"We were right. He could only pretend so long. He was emotionally abusive, but it had also gotten physical. She finally saw him for who he really is. Attractive on the outside but mean and coldhearted inside."

"I'm glad things turned out the way we'd hoped." Two Tate women had been spared a life with a man who would have made them miserable. He glanced at his watch. "Andy is probably wondering if I took off." Dark clouds had blown in, covering the sun. "Besides, it looks like it could rain any minute. We should head back inside." He stood and turned in the direction of the building but felt her hand on his upper arm and stopped.

"Bryan, wait." The wind ruffled her hair, and her thumb caressed his lower bicep. He felt the warmth of her body against him. "My timing is probably horrible, but if I don't say it now, I may lose my nerve."

"You can say anything to me, Lee. You know that."

"Okay." She took a breath. "Here goes nothing—or everything." Her gaze, filled with fear, held his. "I—I can't keep pretending that I want to be friends."

His heart tore. It had finally happened—she was letting him know that she'd had enough. The drama he'd created at the Ward party must have created a bigger problem than he thought.

"I get it. You don't owe me anything, Lee." He shouldn't have used her nickname—now that she'd declared their friendship over.

"Apparently, you don't get it at all." Liana's voice was soft, and her hand on his arm was shaking. "This isn't easy for me, but I need to tell you ... I'm in love with you."

His heart ripped further. She loved him. *Him?* If only he could accept that gift.

Bryan removed her hand, then laid both of his on her shoulders and bowed his forehead to hers. Her touch had weakened him, leaving him without enough strength to lie. "I love you, too, Lee," he whispered. "But that doesn't change anything. We can't be anything more than friends. Not if I want the best for you."

He released her, and without looking back, he strode toward the building, leaving Liana alone under the gray sky.

Thirty-Six

Guests wouldn't arrive at the gala for several hours, but Liana couldn't relax at home. Her nerves weren't on edge—they'd already fallen *off* the edge. It was more efficient to pace on site, where at least if a problem arose, she could address it.

Her eyes scanned the venue's main floor, and a sweet sadness stung her heart. If only her grandfather could have seen his words come to life. Erik and Liana had Dalisay to thank for making sure the designs and construction were true to the descriptions of Manalee in the book. Having lighting and other technical designers for friends didn't hurt either.

Liana peered up at the thirty-foot high ceiling and the illusion of deep blue sky with twinkling stars. Surrounded by the gigantic created cedar and alder trees, she felt like a miniature person standing on the floor of an enchanted forest. Fairy homes sat cradled in the wide branches of trees, and pieces of wood protruding from the massive tree trunks served as stairways to the ground. Enormous iridescent flowers and colorful mushrooms, at least seven feet tall, stood along the edge of the forest clearing. Dark green tablecloths covered the dining tables, and in each center, an assortment of fresh cut flowers and foliage filled whimsically-shaped wooden vases.

At the end of the room, the stage gave the illusion of being built in the hollow of a mammoth oak. There was a back entrance to the performance area, but the crew had also laid steps down to the main floor with real tree trunks cut in half and sealed with a varnish to preserve the wood.

Such a romantic setting. If only she could share it—share the entire night with Bryan. The hospital meant a lot to him, and he'd done his part to make sure the gala took place. Not only had he introduced her to Erik and encouraged the man to seriously think about having the fundraiser here, Bryan had helped where he could with the construction. He'd also patiently listened to her go on and on about the event, and then offered his support and encouragement.

She blinked away the prickling sensation in her eyes that threatened to move her sorrow from within to public view. The vast room buzzed with staff completing the setup.

Liana and Bryan hadn't even spoken the past two weeks—not since they'd both confessed their feelings for each other—here, outside in the garden. Not since he'd walked away from her. Would he show up at the gala, knowing that he wouldn't be the only burn survivor there? Former patients from the burn unit, among others, would be sharing their personal stories.

"You're here even earlier than I expected."

She whirled around.

Erik whistled. "You look great." His eyes sparkled as he chuckled.

Liana pushed back her emotions and grinned. "Can't beat gray sweats, can you?" She struck a pose. "I hung my dress behind the stage. Thought it was a bit early to put it on."

Erik gestured toward the room. "This is amazing. It's far more than what I dreamed. My grandfather would have been so proud of what we've accomplished here. It's a beautiful space for dining and entertainment."

"I was thinking the same thing just a few minutes ago. About my own grandfather and how pleased he'd be to see the setting for his book come to life."

"Are we ready for this?"

Liana perched her hands on her hips and glanced around. "I hope so. I mean, we should be. But I came early in case something unexpected came up."

"We've done all we can do to prepare. Now we play it out."

"I guess." She wished the queasiness in her stomach would go away. "Have you talked to Bryan? Is he coming?" Liana felt confident her anxiety level would go up if she knew he was there because of how they'd left things in the garden. She'd exposed her heart, and so had he, but so much was left unresolved. They'd confessed their love—now what? Would Bryan accept that being together was more important than appearances or what anyone else thought? Including her family?

"I don't know, Liana." Erik rubbed his chin. "He showed up a few times this past week to help Andy with last-minute construction but barely spoke a few words. Acted like something's been on his mind, but I don't have a clue what."

Disappointment flowed through her veins, and she realized she'd held on to a bit of hope that Bryan would be there for her and the patients he prayed for and visited every week.

But he wasn't coming.

Liana needed to let go of expectations. Bryan needed to choose what was best for himself without pressure from her.

"Anything I need to know before this party gets started?" Erik pulled a small pad of paper and a pencil from his back jeans pocket.

"The orchestra will set up about an hour before guests arrive so they can tune up and do a sound check. They'll quietly play through dinner but will increase the volume when dessert has been cleared and people are ready to dance."

"We'll keep coffee and wine available at the tables."

"I know that's what the committee requested, but please ask your staff to watch for anyone who may be overindulging with alcohol." Liana shuddered at the frightening thought. "We don't want anyone who shouldn't be driving getting behind the wheel."

"Got it."

Liana massaged her upset stomach, trying to soothe the churning. "After dinner, several committee members will speak briefly about the hospital and ask for donations. Then the emcee will introduce Casey Marks, and he'll give a thirty-minute performance before the music is turned back over to the orchestra."

"I can't believe you got a top recording artist to come here for a benefit."

"I have a hard time believing it too." She was convinced Casey was the reason for the record-breaking number of people planning to attend that evening.

"So, I never heard." Erik scratched behind his ear. "How? You know somebody who knows somebody?"

"After I organized a birthday party for his agent's daughter, the agent offered to talk to Casey about the gala. His presence made a big impact on ticket sales for tonight. I imagine if he makes any kind of plea for donations, they'll increase, as well."

"Maggie has been primping all day. So, don't forget that you promised to introduce her to Casey, or I'll have a mess on my hands for weeks. I think meeting him is a bigger deal for her than even opening up this restaurant and event space."

Liana chuckled. "I've already spoken to him. We'll sneak her backstage before he leaves to catch another plane." She sobered.

"Something bothering you?"

"Nothing can go wrong tonight, Erik. *Nothing*."

Liana didn't want to disappoint her father or mother. But even more importantly, she didn't want to let patients in the hospital down. They deserved the best treatment the medical profession could offer, but unfortunately that cost money. Hopefully, the funds raised that evening would surpass the financial goal set by the gala committee.

She pressed a cool, wet paper towel to her forehead, and worried eyes stared back at her from the bathroom mirror. Spicy food, wine, and emotions running close to the surface always initiated rosiness. Not a desirable delicate pink shade, but crimson, making her appear feverish. Or terribly sunburned. She hated it. Nerves caused the elevated color now, and she hoped to tone it down. People had begun to arrive for the gala, and she didn't want to greet them flushed.

The bathroom door opened. "I've been looking all over for you." Dalisay looked stunning in the strapless sapphire gown with a swirling pattern in blues, greens, and gold sewn on the bodice.

"Wow! That dress is amazing."

"It pays to have costume designers for friends." Dalisay laid a gold handbag on the counter and propped one hand there. "There's no way I could afford this, but Maria insisted she needed practice using her new machine." She put her hands in the air, shrugged, and winked. "So what could I say?"

"I'd say yes, please, and thank you!"

"And you look so—glamorous." Dalisay smiled. "Like a fairy princess."

"Thanks." Camryn had chosen the shimmery strapless emerald gown for her, and Liana had to admit, it did make her feel pretty. The full skirt, overlaid with yards of delicate sheer material, flowed in the slightest breeze of her movement. Camryn had even offered her emerald teardrop necklace and set of earrings for the evening.

Dalisay folded her arms and cocked her head. "Are you doing okay?" Her eyes narrowed. "Your face is the color of a ripe tomato."

"Why do you think I'm in here?"

"You haven't eaten anything spicy, have you?"

"No."

"Hit the wine cellar?"

"No!"

"So, you're either really angry at someone, or you're terrified about this evening."

"The latter."

"Aw, honey." Dalisay reached over and gave Liana a gentle hug.

As if she hadn't had enough to stress over, their main draw was a no-show, so far. "Casey Marks was supposed to be here an hour ago. But he hasn't shown up, or called, and I'm freaking out. He's the special entertainment for the evening. People bought tickets expecting to see him and his band."

"Don't worry. He'll be here. Maybe they just hit some rough traffic coming from the airport."

"Then why hasn't he called? I've checked my cell every two minutes."

"Lee, everything is going to be fine. Holding the event here is fantastic publicity for Erik and Maggie. People who can donate big bucks to a worthy cause will pack the place. The committee will be thrilled, and they'll probably hire you for the next ten years."

Liana felt her lips form a slight smile. "Just ten?"

"You'll only want to commit to ten, because by then you'll be in such demand they won't be able to afford you."

"I'd still do it because even with the stress, it's been an a wonderful journey. We met Erik and Maggie and helped them bring their dream to fruition. We watched Manalee come alive before our eyes. And knowing that the end result of our hard work is going to benefit those who need a little help is so rewarding."

"The evening is going to be a great success, Lee. I promise, it will be worth all the headaches you've endured these past months."

"Thanks." Liana gave her friend a quick hug. "I know I complain about the challenges, but I do love my job. I get to meet great people, be creative, and hopefully, bring joy to people."

Dalisay nodded and picked up her handbag. "You know this is a public women's restroom. You can't hide out in here all night. At some point, and probably very soon, other females are going to find their way here."

Liana checked her makeup one last time. "Okay, let's go." She grabbed her friend's arm before they stepped out of the room. "Wait."

"What?"

"Thanks for being here."

Dalisay grinned. "C'mon."

They stepped into a world created to give adults escape from the stress of their hectic lives. A place where they could dine on Pacific Northwest cuisine, visit with friends, relax, and perhaps even spark a little romance. The orchestra played soothing music as guests arrived and mingled. Both rhythm and decibels would kick up later when the evening moved into dancing. Waiters strolled, serving champagne and hors d'oeuvres. Scanning the room, Liana spotted her father greeting the governor and her spouse. A roaming photographer snapped a photo of the three. Liana smiled. Her father looked dashing in a tux.

"I'm starving, and those shrimp thingies I saw being passed around looked de-lish." Dalisay stretched her neck, apparently searching for a waiter.

"Shrimp thingies? Really?" Liana raised one eyebrow and feigned mortification.

Dalisay scowled. "Oh, don't give me that look. I don't have to know what they're called to eat them."

"When people discover that you designed this space, they'll love you no matter what you say or do. Personally, the way my stomach is rolling, I couldn't eat anything right now.

But it probably wouldn't be too cool for me to stand here next to the lady's room all night either."

"Don't worry. I'll stick to your side all evening. Like a leech."

"Thanks for the lovely visual."

"Just making a point. You're not in this alone. I'm your wingman." Dalisay grinned. "Or *wing-girl*, in this case."

As grateful as she felt to have Dalisay for support, she still wished Bryan were there, celebrating with them.

Bryan and Liana had talked about this night for months. He'd mentioned praying every day for the project. It had given him purpose. A way to contribute in his own way toward a greater good. Her heart sighed. It was one thing for him to hang out with a few guys who accepted him. But maybe it was too difficult to walk through those doors, face seven hundred strangers, and risk having to deal with stares and questions.

Liana laid her hand on Dalisay's arm. "If you're willing to be my wing-girl, I guess I can locate a waiter with those 'shrimp thingies' for you. I should mingle anyway. Besides encouraging people to donate tonight, this is a perfect place to casually network, and I shouldn't blow the opportunity."

"Spoken like a true Tate. Maybe you have a bit of your mother in you, after all."

"You *are* hungry. You're becoming delusional." Liana pointed toward several waiters emerging from the kitchen. "If we just pick a spot where there's a little activity, they'll find us, and we won't have to chase them down."

With Dalisay following, she sauntered as gracefully as she could in her new heels toward the center of the room, welcoming those she knew by name or face. While acknowledging a wave from one of the hospital's board members, she almost bumped into a waiter holding a large silver tray of not only "shrimp thingies," which consisted of garlic shrimp wrapped in crisp bacon, but also stuffed mushrooms with a crab mixture, bacon-wrapped dates, vegetarian delicacies, and an assortment of canapés. Everything looked delicious, but she didn't trust her stomach to even nibble.

However, her friend took one bite of the shrimp appetizer and her face melted into one glorious grin.

"That good, huh?"

Dalisay nodded and finished chewing. "I was so busy working here all day on last-minute details, I didn't even think about eating. The only thing I consumed was vast amounts of coffee. I am now in heaven. If the rest of the food is this yummy, Erik will have reservations booked for this place for months." The smile dissolved as her eyes moved to someone behind Liana.

Liana followed the gaze and twisted around to see who or what had caught Dalisay's attention. "Mom."

Eva's white gown with several folds draped over the shoulder gave her the appearance of Hera, Zeus's wife. Camryn, dressed in a sleeveless salmon chiffon gown with a low-cut V neckline looked like Aphrodite.

"Hello, dear." Liana's mother offered a warm smile, but it quickly cooled. "Good evening, Dalisay."

She swallowed and licked her lower lip. "Good evening, Mrs. Tate."

"This is amazing." Camryn stared at the starlit ceiling and then gestured around the room. "It's just so much more than what I even expected. You should be so proud."

"Thanks, Camyrn." Liana put her hand on Dalisay's

shoulder. "Daysie had a lot to do with it. Not only did she draw up designs, she helped organize set-building crews, and put in many hours herself. She made sure everything got done right and on time." Her friend gave her a grateful smile. They had each other's backs.

Liana's mother nodded and extended a hand to Dalisay. "Then thank you for all you've done."

The words sounded sincere, and Dalisay must have thought so too, because she grinned and accepted the handshake.

Her mother faced Liana. "May I speak to you privately?" She strolled toward an area beneath a giant mushroom that wasn't inhabited by guests.

Liana shrugged and gave Camryn and Dalisay an I-don't-know look, then followed her mother. "What's the problem?"

Her mother's smile collapsed. "Despite Dalisay's superior work, I'm very disappointed in you, Liana."

Her stomach sickened. "Disappointed? How?"

"Didn't you think I'd recognize this place?" Her mother studied their surroundings. "It's Manalee. I used to read that story to you every night until you grew old enough that you wanted to read it yourself."

Liana had forgotten. How could she have buried that memory, now surfacing, of her mother tirelessly reading the bedtime story?

Her mother glared. "How could you?"

Was her mother losing it? She approved of Dalisay's work, but Liana had done something wrong? "Wh—what? I don't understand. You knew we were going with a fantasy theme."

"But you never asked permission to use what your grandfather created as a permanent structure in a—a space like this. You never even mentioned that you were using Manalee in your design. It's disrespectful."

"What is, Mom? Is it disrespectful to share Grandpa's imagination? Or is it disrespectful because you have no control over it? You must have forgotten that I inherited the book and anything associated with it, so I guess that gives me the right to use it however I please. That's what Grandpa wanted, and I think he'd be thrilled with what we've done."

Liana's cell rang, and she was forced to refocus. "Sorry. I had reasons for leaving it on." She pulled the phone from her handbag. "Hello, this is Liana Tate."

"Ms. Tate, this is Casey's manger."

"Who is it?" her mother asked.

Liana held up her hand to quiet her mom while she finished listening.

"Our flight was late, but we're on our way and almost there. Will we have access through a back entrance once we get there?"

"Yes, the door is unlocked. See you in a few minutes. Thanks for the update." She ended the call and tossed the phone into her bag.

"What's wrong now, Liana?"

Liana bit her lip to stop herself from responding with a smart remark. "Nothing is wrong. That was Casey Marks's manager. Their flight was delayed, but they'll be here soon. He just wanted to confirm access to the building."

Liana massaged the aching muscle in the back of her neck. Somehow she would get through the night.

Thirty-Seven

Liana twisted the cap off the bottle of pain relievers, shook two into her hand, and downed them with champagne before tossing the pill bottle back into her handbag.

"That bad?" Dalisay snatched her own glass of champagne as a waiter strolled by. "What could Eva possibly have a problem with tonight?"

Liana briefly pressed her eyes shut. "Her little snit was all about this fantasy we created."

"Snit? She had the appearance of a lioness ready to pounce on a baby goat—after not eating for several days."

"She recognized the setting came from my grandfather's story."

"But that's a good thing. Right? I mean, it should be. It shows that we were true to the book." Dalisay's expression soured, and she shook her head before taking another sip of her drink. "I don't get it. I would think she'd feel honored."

"I believe my mother was insulted because she wasn't consulted."

"Eva wanted you to ask her permission?"

"I don't know what she wants from me. I've tried my whole life to please her, and I've never been able to get it right."

"Maybe you should stop trying."

"Pardon me?"

"May-be-you-should-stop-try-ing."

"I'm working on that." She'd come a long way, and tonight was proof. "Would you believe I actually stood up for myself?"

"You did?"

Liana nodded and managed a small smile. "I hope I wasn't disrespectful—if I was, I didn't mean to be—but she was out of line." Liana shrugged. "I wish it weren't important to me that she approved. I actually hoped she'd be pleased with what we've all created here."

"If it makes you feel any better, my parents thought the place looked amazing. My father said to tell you he liked it very, very much. And that you should be very, very proud." Dalisay strongly enunciated each "very."

"When did they ...?"

"This morning. They felt they could leave the restaurant in other hands for a few hours on such a momentous occasion." Dalisay grinned. "They couldn't afford the $350 per person to attend this thing, but we've talked about the fairytale setting for so long, they had to see it."

The ticket prices were high, but every penny went to help support people getting necessary medical care. Liana's father had paid for Dalisay's admission and insisted she attend. Knowing that her friend couldn't afford the expensive evening on her own, Liana was grateful for his generosity.

Something caught her friend's attention, because the almond-shaped eyes became the size of walnuts.

Dalisay clutched her friend's arm. "You said he wasn't coming."

"Who?" Liana spun around, and her breath lodged in her throat.

Bryan, dressed in a tux, accompanied Liana's father.

"I just assumed since he's uncomfortable in crowds ... and after what happened in the garden ..." But there he stood. "My dad must have invited him as his guest."

A low whistle slipped from between Dalisay's lips. "In that tux, he's ..."

"I know." Liana saw a handsome man whose eyes could warm her soul.

Rarely noticing the disfigurement anymore, Liana had fallen in love with Bryan's heart—his kindness and courage. But for some reason, though he could believe God loved him for who he was underneath the flesh, he couldn't believe he was enough for *Liana*. That she loved him and would continue—no matter what obstacles they'd face.

"I need to talk to him." She moved to approach him, but Dalisay grasped her arm.

"Do you think it's such a good idea right now? Your dad is introducing him to some guy."

"Since Bryan came with my dad, he'll be seated at our table." Her palms dampened just thinking about it. "If I don't get a chance to clear the air with Bryan, dinner will be—"

"Uncomfortable?"

"Unbearable." The thought tugged on her heart. Liana didn't want to sit that near to Bryan and be forced to make small talk like strangers. She missed joking around and laughing with him. She missed being able to talk to him about anything. She missed *him*.

"Liana." Mandy, one of the volunteers for the evening, appeared panic stricken. "Were we supposed to hand out the gift bags as people checked in?"

"No. As they leave for the evening. If guests receive them now, the bags will clutter the tables and surrounding areas."

"Well, that's what I told Ashley, but she didn't believe me. Would you please talk to her? Otherwise, she'll just go ahead and do what she wants."

Liana sighed internally. She'd not only gone over everything verbally, she'd also sent out written instructions for the evening to every volunteer. But Ashley had missed the meeting Liana called prior to guests arriving. One of the other girls commented that Ashley usually did as she pleased, and she was only serving as a volunteer because her father, a well-known surgeon, insisted.

"Okay, I'll talk to her." Liana glanced at Dalisay and shrugged her shoulders. She'd have to approach Bryan after she resolved the gift bag issue. As she followed Mandy, she caught another glimpse of him. Only this time he wasn't making conversation with a gray-haired businessman. Liana's heartbeat halted for a split second, and she almost tripped on her own gown. His attention seemed to be focused on the attractive woman handing him club soda—Camryn.

A trickle of sweat slid between Bryan's shoulder blades and down the center of his back. His armpits were damp, despite the cool night and air conditioning in the room. Even though the enormous room boasted high ceilings, he still felt claustrophobic. Despite the dim lighting, people seemed to stare and whisper. Or was it his imagination? His breathing grew so shallow, he could barely tell if he'd inhaled or exhaled.

Dr. Tate had asked and encouraged him to attend the gala. Bryan had declined, but he gently persisted, hinting that

Bryan could make a difference in guests supporting the burn unit. The doc wasn't a manipulative person. He cared deeply for his patients and would do whatever necessary to raise funding needed to help them. Feeling he owed the man, not to mention the hospital for saving his life, Bryan changed his mind at the last minute.

Dr. Tate's hand rested on Bryan's shoulder and guided him to face a gentleman with graying hair, skin dark enough that he must either spend time in the sun or tanning beds, and blue eyes as clear as an untouched mountain stream.

"Carl, I'd like you to meet Bryan Langley—not only one of my favorite patients but an amazing man and friend."

The gentleman's face broke into an almost too perfect smile when he extended his hand to greet Bryan. "I'm very glad to meet you, son. Jonathan has told me a lot about you."

"Carl Makon is the Senior Editor of *Explore Washington*," Dr. Tate interjected.

Bryan, accepting the man's hand, studied his eyes and perceived only acceptance. He didn't notice any flinching or nervousness connected to the editor in the least. "I'm familiar with the magazine. You cover outdoor life—hiking, camping, and fishing. It's great."

The gentleman nodded. "I'm glad you've read it. We also feature places and activities that our readers can enjoy during winter months, like skiing. Americans work too hard. We need to take more advantage of what's around us and escape for a few hours."

"I totally agree." Bryan's anxiety diminished while talking with Mr. Makon.

"I recently stopped by Dr. Tate's office and saw your work hanging on the wall. I was impressed with the photos you took on Tiger Mountain."

"Thank you, sir." Bryan thought his photographs weren't half bad, but hearing a professional compliment them suddenly made the air around him much easier to breathe. He felt a bit lighter, himself.

"I'd like to see more of your work. The magazine uses freelance photographers for some articles, and I might be interested in using some of yours in the future."

"Any time, Mr. Makon. I'd appreciate that." Maybe the night wasn't going to be so bad after all. Photography had become a way for him to express himself and fill that creative void in his soul. To have his images printed in a widely read magazine would be mind-blowing.

The editor excused himself, and Dr. Tate was drawn into a medical debate on a procedure currently banned in the United States.

Fighting the urge to keep his head down and hide, Bryan's eyes swept the room, searching for Liana. Dr. Tate had informed him that she'd be seated at their table, along with Dalisay and three other couples—friends and peers from the hospital. He missed Lee, but after what happened between them the last time they saw each other, would his presence make her uncomfortable?

The renovated building looked amazing, and his heart swelled with pride as he overheard a group of people discussing the stunning décor. Nearby, an elderly woman with snow-white hair and large rings on her fingers explained to the people around her that she was on the committee for the event. Bryan couldn't help but smile at hearing Liana's name and praise for her work.

He spotted Lee across the room, speaking to a young

woman who appeared to be a little distressed. Camryn swooped in to stand beside Bryan, distracting him.

"Here. You look like you could use this." She handed him a chilled glass of club soda.

"Thanks." He diverted his eyes from her bared cleavage to gaze on Liana, but she followed the upset young woman through the crowd and out of view.

"Look, I don't know what's going on between you and my sister, but the two of you have got to get it together."

"What do you mean?" Camryn showing interest in his and Liana's relationship—whatever you'd call it—was definitely a surprise. Even more so since Camryn seemed to care.

"Oh, please. It's obvious the two of you have a thing for each other. Get over yourselves, and get on with it." Camryn gave a sly grin.

Bryan sighed but allowed a smile. "Get over ourselves, huh?"

Camryn slacked her right hip and raised her eyebrows.

"Fixing what's between me and Lee isn't as easy as you think." The grief Bryan felt over losing his career didn't compare to the pain he'd felt the past two weeks knowing that in order to do what was best for Liana, he had to give up any hope of sharing a life with her. She didn't seem to understand just how different their lives were from each other.

He wanted to protect her. If they were a couple, she'd be stared at and made the subject of brutal jokes behind her back. Liana's life would be completely changed, and he didn't want to hold her back or make her feel uncomfortable or confined in any way.

"From my experience, most relationships aren't easy."

Camryn frowned. "Especially when you don't even try."

With the obstinate volunteer informed that attendees received gift bags as they *left* the event, Liana maneuvered her way around people in search of Bryan. She wanted to welcome him and try to put both of them at ease. There wasn't much time before dinner, and they'd either find themselves sitting next to each other or forced to face each other from across the table. Liana was glad he'd come—she wanted him to enjoy the evening—not feel uncomfortable around her.

If she wasn't successful in relaying that to him, she had a list of responsibilities and plenty of reasons to excuse herself. If she'd known Bryan was going to accompany her father, she'd never have agreed to dine with him.

Liana found a small clearing in the room, and turning a full circle, scanned the area. There, toward the entrance, she recognized the broad shoulders, his dark hair, and his gait. She practically skipped in order to pick up her pace and nearly knocked a glass of wine out of a man's grasp in her effort to catch up to Bryan.

She grabbed his bicep. "Bryan, wait."

He swung around. "Lee ..."

Liana couldn't read his eyes and stepped back as heat rose from her neck and flooded her cheeks. "I—I wanted to talk for a minute. I saw you arrive with my dad." He stood there, not making this any easier for her. "Since we're seated at the same table, I didn't want it to feel—weird."

Bryan's eyes softened. "I don't want to do anything to make you uncomfortable either, Liana. I'm only here because your father said it was important. He wants me to speak to several people on the hospital's behalf."

He was there to please her father. Not her. "I understand." She tried to swallow, despite the knot wedged in her throat. "We haven't spoken to each other since the afternoon in the back garden, so I thought it might be good to talk before dinner." She brushed a lose strand of hair back from her eyes.

"Liana ..." He didn't finish but instead gestured for her to look to her right where a volunteer stood waiting to speak to her.

"Ms. Tate, we need you at check-in. An attendee wants to add another guest to his table." Her name tag said Emily. "No one told us how to handle those requests."

"That's because we shouldn't be receiving them." This was the last thing she wanted to deal with right now, especially when she desperately wanted a few minutes with Bryan. But she was there in a professional capacity, and the job had to come first. "Don't worry, Emily. We'll get this straightened out." Liana wheeled around to explain to Bryan.

"Go do your thing. Dinner will be fine." He gave a slight smile. "And, Lee?"

"Yes?"

"I'm proud of you."

A heart could burst after receiving such a gift, and she thanked him with a smile. Hearing those words from Bryan lifted her spirits. But she couldn't take time now to savor his affirmation. There was another problem to solve.

Thirty-Eight

Bryan admired Liana as she gracefully maneuvered through the crowd on her mission to save the volunteers at the check-in station. As though on cue, people eased into chairs around reserved tables. He searched for a place to land, scanning the numbers on cards near centerpieces. He discovered number twenty-three near the stage and took a seat.

Dalisay slipped into a chair next to him. "Where's Lee?"

"Nice to see you again too." Bryan gulped a portion of the ice water in the glass in front of him in an attempt to stop sweating. No one else seemed bothered in the air-conditioned space, but the room would probably feel even more stifling as the night progressed if his nerves didn't calm down. He should be used to curious stares by now. With time, they were getting easier to ignore, but sometimes the attention made him feel like an exhibit on display.

"Sorry. I didn't mean to sound snippy. It's just that I saw the two of you talking, and then she disappeared. Taking care of a crisis?"

Bryan nodded. "An unexpected guest wants to crash the party. I could offer my spot."

"No way." She pointed a butter knife at him. "This is a big night for her, and you're staying."

Dr. Tate arrived and settled in, leaving the chair next to Bryan vacant, probably for Liana. Boy-girl-boy seating must be assumed. The other couples arrived, and the doc introduced them. Only one of the wives seemed a bit squeamish while acknowledging Bryan. He'd prepared himself for the likelihood, but it still caused his spirit grief. He didn't want to ruin the woman's evening and vowed to keep his scarred profile turned away from her as much as possible.

A familiar middle-aged blonde woman tapped a microphone on stage. "Good evening, everyone. I'm Mary Shepherd. I anchor the nighttime news at KOMO, Channel 4, along with my esteemed colleague here with me tonight, Kenny Matamoto. Welcome to this year's gala supporting Northwest Medical Center." She smiled during the applause. "We're so honored to be your emcees again. Every year the gala becomes more extraordinary!" She gestured toward one of the fairy houses. "Isn't this amazing?" More clapping.

"The funds raised this evening, as you know, are so important to the patients who are served at the hospital. One hundred percent of the net proceeds will benefit Northwest's Mission of Caring, which serves vulnerable populations. Although more than thirty-five percent of the medical center's revenue comes from patients with private insurance, this hospital provides the most charity care in the state. Those who benefit are children, the working poor, and people who used to have some type of government assistance but are no longer eligible. Your generosity plays a big part in what this charity-care program can provide and its success." Applause thundered.

Bryan ignored the impulse to shift his body around and search the room for Liana. Despite not having a chance to clear the air before dinner, he was anxious to have her near. Hopefully, she'd join them soon.

The emcee's red sequined dress flashed in the spotlight. "We're in for a wonderful night. Dinner will be served in a moment. While you're enjoying an assortment of lovely desserts, two of our guests, former Northwest patients, will share their stories and what the hospital has meant to them and their families. The live and silent auctions will take place later in the evening. To top off this celebration, the orchestra will get you on your feet and dancing. And as a special treat, we're honored to have a performance from Casey Marks." Even the older generation clapped loudly at the mention of the singer's name.

He'd never met Casey or heard him play in person, but Bryan respected and enjoyed his music. Several of his albums were included in Bryan's playlist.

Servers strolled around the room, carrying trays laden with food. Bryan could only imagine the chaos happening back in the kitchen, but out here, the staff appeared calm and collected.

A light citrusy fragrance greeted his senses as Liana reached their table. Bryan stood to help with her chair, but her father was a beat faster, and she gracefully slid into the saved spot. A green salad with apples, walnuts, cranberries, and blue cheese was placed in front of him. He wished he had the appetite to eat it. He fidgeted in the chair, trying to get comfortable, and smoothed the napkin lying across his thighs.

Dalisay, seated to the right of him, was engaged in conversation with one of the couples about the show *Hamilton* at the 5th Avenue Theatre in Seattle. And one of the ladies across the table questioned Dr. Tate on the best places to stay while touring Italy.

Bryan had to say something to Liana. He couldn't just play with the salad. "Everything okay?"

Liana gave him a warm smile. "Yes. Thanks for asking. I got it all squared away." She removed the napkin, folded into the shape of a fan, from her plate and draped it across her lap. "Thanks for being here. I know it can't be easy for you."

"I ..." Words evaporated from his brain as he drowned in her gaze.

"I miss you," she whispered, her eyes not wavering from his.

Bryan wanted to stay bathed in those golden-brown eyes forever. "I miss you ..." He mouthed the words more than he spoke them.

"Are you Liana?" A man's voice broke the connection, and they both peered behind them to see who had the audacity to have such poor timing.

"Yes." Liana recognized him. "You're the drummer for Casey Marks."

"I'm Kyle." He squatted next to Liana and whispered, "We've got a problem. Casey ain't feelin' too well. He didn't say anything till we got here, and now he's worse."

Liana's stomach plummeted like a gondola from an amusement park drop tower. "What do you mean by 'not too well'? What's wrong with him?"

"There's a doctor with him, and he thinks it's Casey's appendix. We called for an ambulance, but we asked them to turn off the siren before pulling in so the noise doesn't disrupt the event."

"Of course." Liana stood and tossed her napkin on the table, but she kept her voice low. "Yes, of course he needs a hospital right away."

Bryan grasped her arm, his eyes full of concern. "Can I help?"

"The ambulance is on the way, but I can't just sit here," she whispered back. "I need to make sure Casey is taken care of. He's my responsibility."

"I'll go with you." Bryan rose to his feet and pushed his chair in.

"I'm coming too." Dalisay jumped up.

"Stay here and have fun. Both of you. There's really nothing we can do." Liana didn't need the guests to observe them all running backstage like the Three Musketeers to the rescue.

Dalisay raised one eyebrow in warning. "I'm coming, whether you like it or not. So, don't make me twist your arm."

"I'd rather you didn't." Liana gently bumped Daysie's arm. "You know how wimpy I am about physical pain."

Bryan nodded his head toward the stage. "Come on." The people around the table stared. "Excuse us, please. Small matter to take care of. Looks like they're serving salmon. Enjoy!"

Liana led the charge out a side door and up the stairs to a backstage dressing room. The singer lay curled up in a fetal position on the couch, groaning. One of his backup singers mopped his forehead with a damp cloth, while a gentleman with light brown hair in a black tux stood nearby relaying instructions over his cell phone to whoever was on the receiving end at the hospital.

"Lord ..." Liana breathed an almost silent prayer.

Two EMTs hiked in with a stretcher and spoke briefly with the doctor before carrying Casey outside to the waiting vehicle.

"Jim, what's going on?" Liana's father approached the attending physician. He must have followed Liana and her companions to the room.

The two doctors shook hands. "It looks like acute appendicitis. They're taking him to Overlake since Bellevue is closer than Seattle. I've called ahead and made the arrangements to do surgery as soon as they can get him prepped. Casey's asked me to see this through instead of handing him over to another physician. I'll take my car, and some friends will take my wife home."

"You better get on the road then." Liana's father gave the other doctor a pat on the back. "I'll stop by and check in on the two of you later. Treat you to an early breakfast since you're not going to get any dinner tonight."

"Thanks, Jonathan." Jim pocketed his cell phone and left with the ambulance.

Liana slumped down on a stool and buried her head in her hands. Emotions took up their weapons, ready to fight until one conquered. Liana wanted the best care for the singer and for him to get relief as soon as possible from the physical torture he seemed to be experiencing. But the selfish part of her heart couldn't believe this was happening to her.

Casey's performance was supposed to be her coup. Getting him to sing had been a way to prove that she could be just as successful as her mother and sister. It didn't matter that everything else might be perfect. Casey Marks was going to be the star on the Christmas tree. The chocolate sauce on the ice cream. The flag planted on top of the mountain. But it wasn't Christmas, the ice cream had melted, and the mountain was too formidable to climb.

"Honey, he's going to be okay." Liana's father laid his hand on her shoulder. "I've known Jim for years, and he's a good doctor. Casey will get excellent care."

Liana raised her head and sniffed. "I know, Dad. It's just that ..." Her eyes burned as though something acidic had been sprayed in them, and her vision blurred. This was not cool for her to fall apart now with her father, Dalisay, and Bryan all staring at her, waiting for her to be a grown-up and get on with the evening.

"What in the world is going on back here?" Liana's mother stood with her hands perched on her hips. Camryn, hovering behind, frowned and shrugged her shoulders, as if to indicate that she'd tried to keep their mother from investigating.

"And I thought the night couldn't get any worse." The words slipped out before Liana could hold them in, but her mother didn't seem to hear them.

"I got your back, girl," Dalisay muttered.

"Eva, everything is under control," Liana's father spoke up. "Go back to the party."

"No. Not until you explain why the four of you ran up here like sheep being followed by a pack of wolves. Others may not have noticed, but even though we're not living together, Jonathan Tate, and our daughters are no longer children, I'm still aware of things that pertain to my family." She crossed her arms and leaned on her right hip. "And what about that ambulance I just saw drive away? Who was in there?"

Liana expelled the pent-up air from her lungs. "Casey Marks."

With a few rushed steps, Camryn passed their mother and sat on the edge of the couch. "No! He's supposed to be the hit of the gala. People have been talking about it for weeks."

"Jonathan, is that true?" Her mother's voice was stern yet held a hint of disbelief. "He's not performing tonight?"

"He has acute appendicitis, Eva. The young man has to go in for emergency surgery."

Liana's mother scowled. "I just knew something like this would happen."

"Of course you did. Because why would anything I did work out right?" Liana glared at her mother. "I'm sure you think this is entirely my fault."

Her mother shook her head. "That's not true."

Liana's father lowered himself onto the couch next to Camryn. "We shouldn't be making such a big deal out of this. People might be disappointed, but they'll understand. The poor guy can't help it if he got sick. Maybe Casey's band can jam for thirty minutes. I don't think they've left yet. It would give people a chance to check in one last time on the silent auction or hit the restroom."

Liana sighed. "I know people will still leave with fond memories of the evening. I know that after tonight, Erik will have so many dinner reservations, he won't know what hit him. And more importantly, I know a lot of money will be raised for the hospital."

"But ..."

"It's selfish of me, and I'm ashamed that I'm also thinking of myself right now, but this event was supposed to be a big night for me too." She attempted a smile. "It's okay. I'll just punt like I always do, and it will have to suffice."

Bryan seemed to struggle with clearing his throat, and his face paled. "Or..."

"Or what, Bryan?" Liana needed to solve a problem, so if there was a solution, he needed to share sooner than later so she could implement the save.

"I'm no Casey Marks. But I—I could do it."

Thirty-Nine

L iana's mother gasped and covered her chest as if to protect her heart. "Are you out of your mind?"

"Mom!" Liana stepped between her mother and Bryan. Not believing what she'd heard but wanting to with all her heart, Liana searched his eyes. "Are you sure?"

He nodded.

Liana caught Dalisay's eye. "Check and see where they're at in the program, and then ask the guys from Casey's band to meet us back here ASAP."

"Liana, you can't be serious!" Her mother's nostrils flared, and the veins in her swan-like neck bulged. "There are people out there who could help make big things happen for you. If you let him do this you'll—"

"Eva! Not tonight, please." Liana's father rarely spoke that harshly.

"I'll what, Mom?" Liana tried to remain calm. "I'll tell you what. I'll be grateful. Bryan is a talented professional. And if he's willing to go out there and entertain the guests, then you should be grateful too."

Liana's mother glared back. Her lips pinched together and drew a straight line. "You're making a huge mistake if you let him walk out on that stage."

"I don't want to argue." Liana closed her eyes and sighed. At that moment, she knew the truth. Maybe it was the Holy Spirit speaking to her, like he'd spoken to her father and

Bryan. Sweet peace gently wrapped around her like a shawl made of the finest alpaca wool. "You know what? Whatever happens will be okay. If Bryan is brave enough to go out on stage, then somehow God is going to work things out. And considering what Bryan has gone through, his willingness to perform is the best witness possible for how important the gala is to burn survivors."

Her mother's diamond necklace rose and fell with her heavy breathing. It was obvious she was working hard at keeping her emotions in check, but she remained silent.

"We have to focus on pulling this together, Mom, so why don't you and Camryn go back to your table and try to enjoy yourselves. It will be great. I promise."

Her mother shot daggers at Bryan with her eyes but directed her words at Liana. "I hope you won't regret this." Then she and Camryn vacated the room.

Liana fixed her gaze on the man she not only adored but respected more than any other guy she knew, including her father. "Thank you," she whispered.

Their eyes locked, and Bryan gave her a weak smile. This might be one of the most difficult things he'd ever do, but she was confident that if he got on that stage, he'd discover a part of himself he thought was lost.

Dalisay burst into the room, followed by Casey's band and sound tech. "Dessert has been served, and the first patient testimony is about to start. We have about thirty minutes before they go on. I've already talked to the emcees, so they're aware of what's going down."

"Thanks." Liana ran her tongue over her bottom lip. "Are you guys filled in?" They nodded but seemed to await her direction. "We don't have much time. But you're all professionals and probably used to last-minute changes. Bryan is going to take Casey's place. As a favor to me and tonight's guests, would you be willing to back him up?"

"We're in," the keyboardist said, stepping forward. "If he just gives us a beat and the key he wants to sing in, we can follow."

"Everything is set up, so we're ready to go," the drummer added.

"Perfect! I'll let you talk it over while I check on a few other things." She glanced at her watch. "Be on stage in twenty. And thanks again, guys. All of you." She looked each of them in the eyes but lingered on Bryan's a bit longer than the rest. "We appreciate your generosity and willingness to come through for us."

"No problem. Our pleasure," the drummer said, and the others nodded in agreement.

Liana retrieved her handbag lying next to the stool where she'd perched, then peeked over at Bryan, who appeared as scared as a rabbit trapped by wolves. The bass player and sound tech exchanged a look after introducing themselves to Bryan.

Her heart pounded. Liana didn't want Bryan to be hurt. Was she wrong to agree to this? She'd told herself this would be a chance for him to prove to himself that he could perform in front of people, but what if deep down what she really wanted was for herself not to fail?

Bryan leaned against a wall outside, inhaling the fresh, cool night air. He dug the handkerchief from his pocket and wiped the trickle of sweat dribbling from his hairline down over his right temple. Then he rubbed the cloth over his damp hands. His shirt clung to his back, and he was thankful for his tux jacket.

What was he thinking? He couldn't go out on that stage. Perform in front of all those people. Seeing Liana look so defeated had done him in. He wanted to rescue her—be a hero. But he was no knight in shining armor. He wasn't even a squire.

A man stepped from the entrance to backstage, and his silhouette stopped a few feet from Bryan. "You only have a few minutes," Dr. Tate said in a gentle tone.

"I—I can't do it, Doc." Bryan's legs might as well have been cemented into the ground. His stomach churned, and he tasted bile.

Dr. Tate let out an audible sigh. He shuffled his feet and repositioned himself with his back and hands against the wall. "As much as you may want to, you can't hide in the stable the rest of your life."

Although the words rang true, Bryan didn't want to hear them. "I don't hide."

"You rarely leave the estate, except to visit the hospital and other patients."

"I've got friends." Like Andy Sinclaire from the men's Bible study group. Doc Tate couldn't argue with him there.

"I know. But there was also a time when you hoped to inspire not only people who have suffered like you but also people who need to believe that everyone has worth and something unique to offer. What happened to that man?"

"Reminders of his past life were thrown in front of him. And just like a face, a burned heart can end up pretty damaged. So, even if it survives, some scars don't heal." Bryan gulped back a sob before it escaped. "Sounds like a premise for a country song, doesn't it?" His forced laugh held a hint of bitterness, even though he fought it. "I'll have to think about that one. Burned face, burned heart. Scarred face, scarred heart. Has potential."

"I heard about the party on Bainbridge. You got into an argument with one of the guys from your old band. It's okay to grieve all you've lost. But Bryan, there also comes a time when you have to move on."

"I'm trying."

"I know." The doc shifted his weight against the wall. "Remember that music isn't all of who you are. There's a lot more to Bryan Langley than the voice or the scars."

"Yeah. I've been working on figuring out what that is, but change is hard. For a long time, music was all I ever wanted."

"It can still be a part of your life. Know this—God may have a higher calling than for you to be admired by a bunch of swooning, lovesick girls. Maybe the reason God allowed music to be taken away from you was because that's all you ever wanted. All God ever wanted was *you*."

Bryan stared at the ground, seeing nothing but shadows formed by the dim light hanging over the back door. Since first waking in the hospital after the fire he'd wanted and needed to believe that God loved and wanted the best for him.

His voice now sounding contemplative, Dr. Tate continued with, "In 1 Corinthians 13:12 it says, 'Now we see things imperfectly, like puzzling reflections in a mirror, but then we will see everything with perfect clarity. All that I know now is partial and incomplete, but then I will know everything completely, just as God now knows me completely.'"

"I know that verse well." It was highlighted in his Bible.

"But do you accept it as truth? Do you believe that God will reveal why he allowed you to go through such physical and emotional pain? There will come a day when you'll clearly see purpose in all of this."

"I hope so, Doc." Bryan peered up at the star-studded sky. "I sure hope so."

"For now, we have to trust and do the best we can. And ... you may need to ask yourself, what will happen the next time you're faced with a difficult decision? Are you going to push through, or give up?"

Bryan forced the words past what felt like a golf ball lodged in his throat, "Would you pray for me?"

"Of course I will, son." Dr. Tate waited only a moment before his voice, strong and calm, petitioned the Lord. "Father—God—I know you love Bryan more than he can even fathom. But right now he needs to feel your arms wrapped around him. He needs to feel the peace that only you can give. Release the fear from his body, soul, and mind so that he may do whatever it is that you've called him to do. In your blessed name, amen."

Dr. Tate shoved off from the wall. "Coming?"

Bryan stood in the wings, pleading with God to rescue him from the paralyzing fear that threatened to keep him from walking out on that stage. He hadn't sung in public since the fire. What if he bombed and embarrassed Lee, the doc, and everyone else counting on him? He could barely breathe and leaned against the cool wall, which helped to keep him in an upright position.

There was a time when he would have already been high from the natural adrenaline rush that always came with playing a big concert. He'd be pumped and anxious to bask in the spotlight. Now, he could barely stand, let alone comprehend running out in front of people, expecting and absorbing their adulation. In contrast, instead of being overly exposed by glaring illumination, Liana had assured him the stage lights would be kept soft.

The female news anchor, acting as emcee, approached the mic. "I know you've been looking forward to hearing Casey Marks this evening." Clapping and a few whistles. "First of all, I want to assure you that he's okay, but earlier this evening he was taken from here to the hospital by ambulance because of appendicitis." Groans, murmurs, and sounds of concern spread throughout the room. "However, another singer present tonight has graciously offered ..."

Bryan didn't hear the rest of the introduction. He'd forgotten to breathe and choked when his body finally demanded that he provide it with oxygen.

Someone gave him a pat on the back. Possibly the drummer. "C'mon, dude. She's called us out. It's showtime."

Bryan followed the last guy out onto the stage, picked up a borrowed guitar, and swung the strap around his neck. In his glory days, he'd strutted back and forth on stage, making eye contact with the females. Tonight, he was grateful for the stool that would help prop him up. He positioned the mic in front of him and faced the audience. The welcoming applause died down. A hush moved through the people before him, like a breeze blowing through a wheat field, causing the grain to wave.

In the amount of time it took him to make his way out there, his throat had become dry and scratchy. A bottle of water sat at his feet. "Excuse me," he barely croaked out. With the guitar swung to the side, and keenly aware of the silence and eyes focused on him, Bryan leaned down and grasped the bottle between two fingers. He took several swallows and recapped the bottle. When had plain water tasted so good?

It might have been his last drink. He was going to die a slow death in front of a massive group of people. Bryan surveyed the audience. What he could see of them. Inquisitive faces stared up at him, waiting for him to do something.

Then he spotted her. Liana. She smiled. Nodded. Signaling her belief in him. For thirty seconds, he became unaware of the sounds, smells, and sights around him. He only saw her. And a reflection of love.

She'd found a home in his heart the night they first met in the stable. He was risking humiliation for the good of those in need at the hospital, especially Kylee. But he was also doing it for Liana, and he couldn't let her down.

Bryan inhaled a deep breath and blew it out. And then another. He swiped away the flow of sweat trailing from his forehead past his right eye. The crowd fidgeted—his delay seeming to make them uncomfortable and restless.

Then words came. "Good evening. You may be wondering why a guy like me would be up here performing for such an esteemed group as yourselves. Up until just a moment ago, I was asking myself the same question. But the truth is, like someone reminded me earlier, maybe I'm the right person to be here. Similar to previous speakers, I was also treated at Northwest after being burned in a barn fire."

The room fell silent. From what he could tell in the darkened room, even the servers in the back stood still.

"A large part of why I survived is due to the care I received in the burn unit. I didn't have health insurance at the time. When you're playing full time in a band, it doesn't come with the job. But I had a modest inheritance, which helped. Other people aren't so fortunate. Like my little friend, Kylee. One night, while her father was high on meth, he poured gasoline over the child and set her on fire. Her mom got the fire out and called for an ambulance, but not before a large part of the girl's body was badly burned."

Bryan glimpsed more than several people wiping their eyes. "Kylee's dad is in jail. Her mom makes very little and has no insurance. Without the kind of help that money raised at this event provides for people in need, Kylee might not have received the care that saved her life."

He strummed the guitar. "We're going to perform songs you're familiar with tonight, but I'd also like to share several new tunes I've written the past few months. So tonight, please accept my music as a thank-you for any help you've given and hopefully will continue to give." The room clapped, and Bryan breathed easier.

He continued strumming. The familiar chord sequence he played helped his neck muscles relax. He played the intro again. *Lord, help me.* He signaled the band to come in. Once the guys picked up the feel of the song, he could back off and focus on the vocals.

Eyes closed, he sang the first line. The notes were shaky, but the second line sounded stronger. *Focus on the meaning of the words.* If he could connect emotionally with the people listening, they might forgive his flawed technique and appearance.

The piece was haunting and romantic. As he laid his heart out, open and vulnerable, he opened his eyes and found Liana, sitting near the front in the soft glow of the stage lights. A tear had left a trail down her cheek. His heart drummed, and he ached to enfold the woman he loved in his arms. Take her far from here. Be alone. Just the two of them.

The song came to a close, and the crowd's reaction jerked him back to reality.

Stunned by the approval, Bryan glanced back at the musicians supporting him. Large grins broke out on their faces. The keyboardist motioned for Bryan to continue. For thirty minutes, the group moved through the playlist they'd scribbled out. Since all but two songs were familiar covers, the band moved through them with ease.

They picked up the tempo with a few tunes, but he saved an original ballad for last. He'd written out the chord progressions for the musicians to follow and had run through it with them prior to going on stage. The message, which encouraged listeners to maintain hope when following a dream, was for Kylee.

The last chord died out. Silence. The blood pumping in his ears sounded like rapid beating on timpani inside his brain. Then in an explosive movement, the crowd rose to their feet with thunderous applause, and even a few whistles.

Bryan's eyes burned. They liked his music. They liked *him*! His mouth opened to speak, but the words jumbled in his brain, and he made no sound. Shaking, he removed the strap across his shoulder, laid the guitar in its stand, and walked off stage. With blurred vision he stumbled down the back stairs into the night.

Liana, surrounded by people giving the standing ovation, did her best to maneuver through them. She desperately wanted a few minutes with Bryan away from public view. The music—so moving—had touched her soul, as well as so many other people. Liana had never been so proud of anyone.

Just before she reached the door, a familiar hand grasped her arm.

"Liana."

She twisted to see her mother posed next to a gentleman who appeared to be in his forties, with gray eyes and light brown hair long enough to touch the top of his jacket collar.

"Mom, I need to get backstage." This was not the time to make chit-chat with one of her mother's friends. "Maybe we can talk later."

"You're going to talk to Bryan."

"Yes, so if you'll please excuse me." Her mother wasn't taking the more than obvious hint, and if she thought for one nanosecond that she was going to set Liana up with this guy, she was mistaken.

"This is actually about Bryan." She gestured. "Liana, please meet William Kendall. William, this is my daughter, Liana."

The gentleman smiled and offered his hand for Liana to shake. "Nice to meet the woman who almost single-handedly put this extraordinary event together."

Heat crawled up the back of Liana's neck and flooded her

cheeks. Who had given him that idea? "Thank you for the compliment, but I had a lot of help."

His eyes twinkled. "Well, according to your mother, any success is owed to your skills."

Liana glanced at her mother, who gave a small smile. She'd never outwardly expressed approval of anything Liana had done—at least nothing she could remember. What was the catch?

"But I can see for myself the result of your work, or should I say labor of love. From what I hear, people are expressing quite a bit of praise for tonight's gala." William reached into his pocket and handed her a business card.

Liana scanned the content. "You're a composer?"

"I'm currently working on a musical score for a movie produced by Leonard Marshall. Bryan has talent, and I'd like to work with him. Your mother mentioned you might have some influence with the young man. I was wondering if you'd be willing to introduce me."

"Yes, of course. I'll go find him now." Working with this professional would be an amazing opportunity for Bryan. Liana wanted to scream with excitement, and it took all her willpower to remain calm. *Thank you, God! Thank you, for this amazing gift!*

"Please excuse me, William." Liana's mother took her aside. "Before you see Bryan, I just want—I need—to apologize."

"Apologize?" Liana couldn't remember any time when her mother had told anyone she was sorry for anything. This was a moment to mark on a calendar—write in a journal—capture on film.

"I was wrong." The words sounded choked out.

"About what?"

"Bryan is a gifted and exceptional man." The corners of her mother's perfect lips turned up slightly. "He's a much better person than I am, Liana. You're lucky to have him in your life." She tucked a lose tendril of hair back from Liana's face. "Go tell him the good news about William's offer."

God was sure full of surprises. Liana would never have imagined her mother supporting a relationship with Bryan. And on top of that, God was answering prayers and opening doors for Bryan to use his musical gifts.

Backstage, Liana searched everywhere—the rehearsal room, the storage room, even the small bathrooms, but she finally accepted the disappointing truth.

Bryan was gone.

Forty

The gala was over, and Liana could breathe again. The knots in her shoulders could finally loosen. She could get back to living, back to focusing on other things. Like Bryan. She climbed the stairs to his apartment. Her watch showed almost two thirty in the morning, but she couldn't imagine he'd be able to relax any more than she could after the night's events. There certainly would be no rest for her until she shared the good news about William Kendall wanting to collaborate with him.

Liana knocked on Bryan's door several times. No answer. There. A light in the stable.

Shivering from the night air, Liana wrapped the shawl around her bare shoulders as she descended the stairs and followed the path to the structure. Picking up her long skirt, she waltzed into the dimly lit building.

Bryan stood with the Arabian, Lexus—just as he had the first night they met. How things had changed. At first the caretaker had frightened her, and then she'd felt sorry for him. But Bryan had offered friendship, made her laugh, and taught her to laugh at herself. He supported her dreams and encouraged her to follow them. By all appearances, this caring man liked and accepted her for who she was, and in return, she'd grown to love him.

"Couldn't sleep?" she asked softly.

He stopped brushing the Arabian's neck. "No." He spoke

with a husky voice. "Doesn't Cinderella change out of her ball gown at midnight?"

Rainey woke from sleep and slowly padded across the wooden floor to her, as though he were recuperating from his own party that evening. Horses nickered quietly.

Anxious to see Bryan—talk to him—she hadn't given a thought to switching her attire for something more casual and appropriate for venturing into animal domain. She stepped close enough to stroke the horse's neck. "We raised millions of dollars tonight. Funds that will enable the hospital to take care of a lot of people."

He smiled, and his eyes peered deep into hers, searching. "I knew you'd be a success."

Attempting to keep her emotions in control, she broke away from the intense gaze. He'd once told her he loved her, and he'd confessed to missing her earlier that night, but she wanted—needed—him to welcome her into his arms. She wouldn't push herself on him.

Liana's fingers grasped the edges of her shawl, drawing the fabric tighter around her upper body. "Erik will probably be flooded with dinner reservations. People loved the food and ambiance."

"That's great news." He turned back to the animal and resumed brushing. "I'm happy for Erik. He's a good guy. He and Maggie deserve it after all they put into the place."

"You were amazing, Bryan. I was so proud of you. And I can't thank you enough for rescuing me. I know it wasn't easy for you to step out on that stage."

"What you should label as amazing was Casey's band. He's lucky to have a group of musicians like them."

"What happened afterwards?" Mystified, Liana wanted to

understand. "The crowd loved your music, but when I went backstage, you were gone. You left without saying a word."

"It's hard to explain."

She placed a hand on his arm. "I wanted to celebrate—together." Liana's throat ached, and the back of her eyes burned.

"Not sure I'm ready to. Everything about singing tonight is still kind of a shock—people's reaction—even me actually getting through the set. It's like I was in a dream. I couldn't have done it without God holding me up." Bryan focused on the ceiling for a second and shook his head, as if in disbelief. "I was scared to death, Lee. But I did it. And now I'm terrified that I'll be asked to sing again—and I'm petrified that I won't. I'm worried that tonight was a one-shot deal that God offered as a gift."

"God doesn't give that kind of talent to have it wasted." She grinned. "And I can prove it." Liana pulled Kendall's business card from her handbag and held it out. "I met a composer at the gala who's writing music for a movie soundtrack, and he's interested in working with you."

Bryan took the card and held it up to the light. "William Kendall? You gotta be kidding."

"No, he's really interested. He wants to meet you." Maybe if Bryan could see that his music had a future, he might believe their relationship did too.

"The guy has won Academy Awards for his musical scores." Bryan stared at the information again.

"So, you'll call him?"

"Sure. Tomorrow." Was he standing taller than before, or was that only her imagination?

"Good." Liana yawned. "I suppose we should both try to

get some sleep."

Forgetting Rainey stood near, she stepped back and bumped against the pup, throwing her off balance. Before she toppled over him, Bryan's arm reached around her waist and drew her to him.

Bryan held her against his chest, laid his head against her soft hair and inhaled the delicate citrus scent. His other arm wrapped around her other side, cuddling the woman he cherished close. "Please don't go," he whispered.

She reached for his hands, led him to a wooden bench sitting next to the wall, and eased down onto the seat. He settled next to her.

"I'm sorry, Lee. I wish I could have stayed at your side the entire night." He took her hand in his and caressed it with his fingertips. He imagined those hands, as soft as a butterfly's wings, on his body. Embracing him. Loving him. He saw the hint of a sad smile on her face. "I had to get out of there. To think. The whole thing was overwhelming."

"You went to the gala with my father. How did you get home?"

"I drove the truck. He knew I needed a way to leave if I couldn't handle being there. When I realized what I'd done—walking out on you during your big night—I felt ashamed. The last thing I wanted to do was let you down. But since getting home, I've been doing a lot of thinking and praying."

"Did it help? To pray?" Her voice sounded hopeful.

A sweet sadness stung his heart. "Yeah, it helped." He smiled. "God spoke to me in a big way tonight, and he used you to do it."

"Me?" Even in the dim light, he witnessed the color darkening her cheeks.

"I would never have pushed myself to perform if it hadn't been for you and the gala. I tried to convince myself that because of my scars, music could no longer be a part of my life—at least on a professional level. But that was a lie. The real reason? My huge ego was in the way. My pride. I was used to standing in front of people who looked up to me. *Who wanted to be me.* I couldn't stand the thought of being rejected and booed off the stage."

"But that didn't happen tonight."

"No." Bryan traced the curve of her cheekbone with his thumb. "God and I had a long talk after I got back here. I realized that I've been angry with him ever since the fire. I may never know why he allowed me to go through that agony until I'm with him in eternity. But I do know that if I hadn't experienced the fire, I wouldn't have met you, your father, Andy, or a lot of other good people. Instead of leaning on my faith, I'd be counting on getting my next gig or record contract to give me happiness. But that kind of fulfillment is temporary."

"What about your music now?"

"If God can still use my talent, this time he's my manager, and he gets final say."

Tears nipped at Liana's eyes, but she blinked them back. This was what she'd hoped for. Prayed for. That Bryan would believe in what he had to offer.

He leaned over and wrapped his arms around her. She nestled in, and laying her head on his chest, heard the thumping of his heart as hers raced to meet his and beat in unison. He released the hairpins, and her mane tumbled down onto her shoulders. As his fingers combed through the tangles with care, Liana heard him sigh. She clung to him, wanting to never leave.

"Lee?"

"Mmm?"

"You told me once that you loved me." His voice was soft and thick with emotion. "Do you still?"

Liana drew back from him, just far enough so she could see his eyes. Those beautiful, tender eyes that now held such longing. "I love you, Bryan."

"Are you sure? What about appearances? You were raised ..."

"It doesn't matter. That's not me. At least, it's not who I am now. And if you're concerned about my family and what they'll think or how they'll treat us, there's no need to worry. Dad and Camryn adore you, and you've even won over my mother. She introduced me to William Kendall—and she admitted that she was wrong about you. I have a feeling you'll be getting an apology in person."

"Wow! I missed out on more than I thought by leaving early." He snuggled her close.

Liana ran her palm over his chest. "I've been angry at God too, because life hasn't always gone the way I wanted. I thought he chose favorites, and I wasn't picked. But I was wrong."

"He's been working on both of us, huh?"

"He sure has ..." Liana gazed up into his eyes. "You once

said you loved me ..."

"I knew I was in love with you the day I convinced you to watch baseball and eat chili dogs. Remember?"

"How could I forget?"

"I just couldn't believe that you could ever love someone like me. Someone who didn't fit into your world—your *family's* world. What could I offer someone like you?"

"Your kindness. Your understanding, humor, and companionship. Your heart."

Bryan's lips teased hers softly like a gentle, summer breeze, creating hunger for more of him. His mouth met hers with all the tenderness she'd ever hoped for. Her skin tingled and her pulse raised as their kisses grew stronger until Bryan, breathing heavy, pulled away. He held her tucked in the crook of his arm.

"I don't know what the future holds, but God's written our story and he knows the end." He kissed the top of her head. "Could you trust us both?"

Liana pointed to Rainey, lying on the floor in front of them with Mitzi, the three-legged cat, curled up next to him. "If those two can trust each other, don't you think we can?" She brushed her fingertips across Bryan's lips and then smiled up at him.

A slow, teasing smile grew on his face, and then his warm lips possessed hers.

Acknowledgements

Readers ... You motivate me to continue writing.

Annette M. Irby & Ocieanna Fleiss ... Your encouragement and enthusiasm for this story confirmed what I felt in my own heart—it was time to share it with others. Thank you for sticking by me, being sounding boards, and serving as my ongoing cheerleaders. I'm so grateful that we've been on this writing journey together for more than a decade.

Robert Morrison ... Years ago, when I began researching the effects of burns on young men physically, emotionally, mentally, and spiritually, you were willing to share your personal journey with me. Thank you for opening up that world to this writer who had nothing to give in return but a desire to write this story. I'm beyond thrilled to see what God has done in your life since then through your work with the homeless in Los Angeles.

Karla Cruz ... Thank you for giving your input on scenes in the book regarding Filipino culture. It was important that I portray Dalisay's family with sensitivity.

Tina Boyd & Leann St. Germain ... Best friends forever! Thanks for always being there through days that are joyful and others that are challenging.

Sandra Byrd ... I appreciate your wisdom and knowledge about the publishing world and life.

Ana Safavi ... I've watched you over the years create amazing celebrations and fundraisers. Although you're no longer professionally planning special events, you continue to host beautiful, welcoming gatherings. Daughter, your warm hospitality continues to inspire me.

Brooke & Doug Hills ... I've gleaned much from you about the theater community and the music industry. It was all helpful in writing this story. I'm proud of you both!

My Family ... Sonny, you encourage and help me keep balance in my life when it would be so easy to let work consume me. I'm grateful for your unconditional love and support. Brooke, Doug, Ana, Shawn, and Katrina—you're the best!

God, my Father ... You love and accept me as I am, and I'm beautiful to you. I'm humbled beyond words.

Meet the Author

Dawn Kinzer, a mom and grandmother, lives with her husband in the beautiful Pacific Northwest. Favorite things include dark chocolate, cinnamon, popcorn, strong coffee, good wine, the mountains, family time, and *Masterpiece Theatre*.

You can find out more about Dawn and her books by visiting www.dawnkinzer.com.

She loves to hear from her readers. You may contact her at dawn@dawnkinzer.com.

Other places to connect: Facebook, Goodreads, Pinterest, BookBub, Amazon Author Page, and Instagram

FREEBIE! Download *Maggie's Miracle*—a short story—as a gift when you visit www.dawnkinzer.com and sign up to receive Dawn's author newsletter sharing interesting tidbits about her books, photos, and other fun stuff about her writing world.

Sarah's Smile

The Daughters of Riverton (Book 1)

A would-be missionary longs
to leave heartbreak behind.
A widowed pastor yearns
for the way things were.
They shared a past,
but can they share a future?

Available in e-book and paperback on Amazon.
Available in paperback on Barnes & Noble.com
and Books a Million.com

Hope's Design

The Daughters of Riverton (Book 2)

*An independent city girl aspiring to
be a fashion designer falls for a
stubborn artist from the country.
One desires to be known,
the other to work in secret.*

Available in e-book and paperback on Amazon.
Available in paperback on Barnes & Noble.com
and Books a Million.com

Rebecca's Song

The Daughters of Riverton (Book 3)

*A small-town school teacher
who lost hope of having her own family.
A big-city railroad detective driven
to capture his sister's killer.
And three young orphans who need them both.*

Available in e-book and paperback on Amazon.
Available in paperback on Barnes & Noble.com
and Books A Million.com

Made in the USA
Lexington, KY
24 November 2019

57614564R00223